ACROSS A DEEP CHASM OF DARK SUSPICION . . . A DAWNING ADMIRATION.

"I have no lover . . . would it matter if I did?"

"Yesterday I would have said no. Today maybe I'm not so sure."

"What is that supposed to mean?"

"That if you were a man, I'd admire your courage."

"But I'm a woman, so instead of being brave, I'm just a fool."

Morgan didn't answer.

"Tell me, did you play the gentleman last night—or breach my somewhat tattered modesty?"

"I prefer my women awake, Miss Jones." Morgan's mouth curved up in amusement. "Though there's hardly an inch of you that hasn't been soothed by my hand." He indicated the basin of water and the damp cloth on the table beside the bed.

Silver felt the fire in her face burn through her limbs.

Morgan's voice turned gentle. "You've nothing to be ashamed of, Silver. And neither have I."

With that he walked out the door.

Kat Martin

Savannah Heat

A DELL BOOK

SAVANNAH HEAT
A Dell Book

PUBLISHING HISTORY
Dell mass market edition published February 1993
Dell reissue edition / September 2004

Published by
Bantam Dell
A Division of Random House, Inc.
New York, New York

ISBN 0-440-20804-1

Manufactured in the United States of America
Published simultaneously in Canada

OPM   13   12   11   10   9   8   7   6   5   4

To Damaris Roland, for her faith in me

Chapter 1

Savannah, Georgia
1841

Escape! It was all she could think of, all she could dream. The word possessed her, crowding her thoughts and blotting her senses until it formed a prison all its own.

Silver Jones sank down on the low wooden cot in the corner of the rat-infested storeroom. Her blood still pumped from her latest unsuccessful effort: stacking heavy wooden crates and boxes one atop the other, then climbing the unstable pyramid to the small dirty window a dozen feet above her head.

This morning she had finally succeeded in prying open a side door, and though she hadn't found an avenue of escape and only succeeded in tearing her nails and bloodying her fingers, she did find enough boxes in the adjoining room to build her shaky ladder.

Damn it to hell! Silver slammed her slender fist against the cot, then cursed again for her self-inflicted pain. She'd been so sure that once she reached the window she'd be able to squeeze through the opening and make her escape. Instead she'd discovered, even as slenderly built as she was, the opening was just too small. Hours of shouting for help had only made her hoarse.

Silver released a weary sigh and glanced at her dismal surroundings. Along with the heavy boxes and her narrow wooden cot, a chipped pink porcelain water pitcher sat in a basin on an upturned crate next to a partly burned candle. The place smelled moldy and abandoned. Flies buzzed above a tray laden with a half-eaten crust of bread and an empty bowl of mutton stew.

From the corner of her eye, Silver spotted the gray-brown fur of a rat as it skittered behind a hogshead barrel in the corner, and clenched her teeth to stifle a scream. God, she hated the dirty little creatures. Bugs and spiders she could stand; there were lots of them where she came from. And lots of them here in the hot and humid climate of Savannah.

But rats—even tiny little field mice—were another matter altogether.

Silver shivered as the rat raced by just a few feet away and eventually disappeared. Ignoring thoughts of when it might return, she ran her fingers through her hair, tugging at a snarl here and there, and worked to comb out some of the tangles. The long, usually glistening silver strands that had inspired her nickname hung in grayish ropes around her face. Her low-cut white cotton peasant blouse and simple brown skirt, the uniform of the tavern maid at the White Horse Inn, where she had been working, were stained from the grime that covered the walls and floors and torn in several places.

At least they hadn't mistreated her. Just spotted her in the tavern, then waited in the alley until she finished her duties and left for her small attic bed-chamber above the carriage house in the rear.

"It's her all right," the tallest man had whispered, just before his hand clamped over her mouth. Using the heavy weight of his body, he had forced her up against the building. "Hair as pale as spun silver, eyes like soft brown velvet, skin so fair and smooth makes a man itch to touch it."

"Don't get any ideas," Ferdinand Pinkard warned. "You know the deal—the girl goes back in good condition. There'll be no reward if she's been harmed."

"Bloody hell!" Silver cursed behind the man's foul-smelling fingers. Struggling wildly, she lashed out with her slender hands and feet. One solid blow connected with a heavy calf, eliciting a yelp of pain and a string of oaths, and her free hand clawed the side of the tall man's face. With vicious determination, she sank her teeth into his palm.

"You damned hellion!" He shook her so hard she feared her neck might break.

"You'd better behave yourself, Miss Jones," Pinkard warned. The chill in his voice sent a tremor of fear down her spine. "It's a long way back—plenty of time for a few minor bruises to heal."

Wiping at the blood on his cheek, the tall man tightened his hold. "You damnable she-devil." Lacing his hand through her hair, he jerked her head back until tears stung her eyes.

"Careful, Julian." Pinkard's voice rang with a note of sarcasm. "We wouldn't want His Lordship to be displeased." There were four of them: two burly sailors, the tall, spidery man with the rancid breath who held her, and Ferdinand Pinkard.

"How did you find me?" Silver asked through clenched teeth, fighting the pain in her arm that the

man called Julian twisted up behind her back. "How
—how did you know where to look?"

One of the sailors, a big, red-haired, mustached
man, chuckled softly. "Pinkard could find the last rat
on a sinkin' ship. That pale hair o' yours—and a face
just as perty—you weren't hardly no trouble a'tall."

Silver felt a wave of despair. She had come so far,
been so sure this time she would succeed. She wasn't
really afraid; she knew exactly what these men
wanted. Though she'd done her best to throw them
off her trail, she should have known someone would
find her.

She should have known he would never let her go.

Arms bound behind her, an oily rag stuffed into
her mouth and tied so tight she could barely breathe,
Silver had little choice but to let Pinkard and his
henchman drag her into the darkness of a waiting
carriage. *Stay calm*, she told herself over and over.
*Keep your wits about you. You've come too far to fail
now.*

Working to control her pounding heart, she leaned
against the padded wall of the sleek black carriage,
listening to the clatter of the wheels against the cob-
blestone streets, then to the whir of wooden spokes
as the road became a dusty lane. She should have
kept running, should have gone inland.

She thought of the misery she had left behind and
could almost taste the blood in her mouth, feel the
heavy blows of his fists. How many times had she
suffered his abuse? How many times had she quietly
submitted, believing she somehow deserved it, sure
each time would be the last? How many times had
she rebelled and fought him and in the end endured
far worse?

Silver watched the passing blur of darkness outside the carriage window. *God in heaven, would this nightmare never end?*

It hadn't taken long to reach their destination—an old abandoned warehouse somewhere distant from the docks. Pinkard had locked her in, leaving her bound and gagged all night just to make his authority clear. Her arms and mouth felt numb by morning, her tongue dry and swollen. She wished she could cry, but she didn't dare. There wasn't room for weakness, wasn't room for tears.

In the early hours of the morning, Pinkard returned with one of his men, bringing water and something to eat, and releasing her from her bonds. They had come each day since, always careful, never sending a man alone, never allowing her to get too near them. They'd been schooled well—the man who would pay for her return had told them in no uncertain terms exactly how desperate she was.

Major Morgan Trask strode the long wooden dock toward the ship *Savannah*, just arrived from Charleston. As always, he admired her low, sleek lines, her graceful bowsprit arching out over the water, the two tall masts of stout spruce that soared upward into the dark night sky. Above them, clouds covered the moon, and a heavy drizzle hinted at a mild spring storm.

Morgan had owned the 145-foot topsail schooner for the past six months, but he rarely captained her. He'd given up that wandering existence last year since the profits he'd long saved and invested had made him a wealthy man.

As he strode the dock, Morgan caught his reflection on the surface of the water, his tall, broad-shouldered image rippling with the incoming tide, his dark blond hair mussed by the wind. Over the years he'd grown used to the jagged scar that marked his cheek, but he found the military uniform he now wore, with its garish gold bars and shiny brass buttons, far too pretentious. He much preferred the dark brown breeches he usually wore at sea, often without even a shirt.

But the Texians—as the newspapers sometimes called them and they often called themselves—had insisted on the formality of his rank. "It just wouldn't do," Stephen Pearson, President Lamar's representative, had said during his most persuasive visit, "for a civilian—a man not even a citizen of the republic—to be involved in a weapons negotiation with the British."

They'd decided on the temporary commission of major in the Texas Marines. A man with enough rank to command respect, but not so much that the British liaison might feel intimidated.

The offer the Texians made had intrigued him from the start. It was a chance to sail the seas again, a chance for a little more adventure. But the real motivation for Morgan's acceptance of the Texians' proposal was his worry for his brother.

Always brash and impetuous, Brendan Trask had been intrigued by the vast landscape and the limitless possibilities the young Republic of Texas had to offer. He had left Georgia two years ago and promptly enlisted in the Texas Marines. Now he was on assignment in Mexico, where his countrymen had gone to assist the Federalist rebels in an attempt to overthrow the Mexican government, a constant source of harassment for the fledgling Texas Republic. Brendan was bound to be in the thick of it. This trip would give Morgan a chance to check on him, assure himself that Brendan was safe.

Morgan climbed over the port taffrail onto the

deck of the *Savannah*, nearly empty of crew since most had gone ashore. He had bought the vessel on a whim—not that it wasn't a damned good investment. Owning the schooner had been a way of keeping in touch with the sea that had so long been his home. Now he was glad he had.

Morgan strode the deck toward the wheelhouse, looking for Solomon Speight, the man who usually captained the ship on her trading voyages along the coast. Morgan spoke to Sol only briefly, while the lanky gray-haired man collected his gear and left to go ashore.

"It'll be good to have a little time off," Sol said with a smile. He shook Morgan's hand and walked toward the rail with a rolling seaman's stride. "A man needs some time to himself once in a while."

Morgan didn't believe a word of it. The sea was in Sol's blood; he was the kind of man whose bones would wind up in Davy Jones's locker. Morgan trusted him implicitly, but the Texians had insisted Morgan command the ship himself. Besides, it would be good to leave the comforts of his Abercorn Street mansion, leave the demanding schedule of his cotton business behind and take the helm of a ship again.

"Good evening, Major," came a voice from the ladder leading down to the main salon, an elegantly appointed room where the captain and first mate and any passengers who might be aboard took their meals. Paneled in oak with carved built-in hutches in each corner, the room centered on a heavy oak table and chairs. Behind it lay the plush captain's cabin and another small room that adjoined for the steward or cabin boy. "I'm Lieutenant Hamilton Riley. I'll be your attaché for this leg of the journey."

Riley climbed down the ladder, and Morgan shook

his hand, noticing the slim but confident grip. "Nice to meet you, Lieutenant. Anything new I should know?"

"Nothing important. Trip appears to be pretty routine. We meet the Brits in Barbados, trade the cotton for sugar, the sugar for guns, then take the arms on down to the Yucatán. The Texas troops are holding their own, but these additional weapons will certainly be useful."

Riley looked no more than twenty, though Morgan knew from his file that he was twenty-three. With his sandy hair and light blue eyes, Ham had the look of an innocent—which, even after his years at West Point, in many ways he was.

"We should be ready to leave in two more days," Morgan told him.

"That's fine. We've plenty of time before our scheduled rendezvous. In fact, we'll probably arrive well before the Brits do."

"Any other Texians coming aboard?" Morgan asked.

"There'll be five of us in all, counting myself. I understand you'll be sailing with a crew of fifteen."

"That's right. She'll carry as many as fifty, but I don't expect a difficult voyage, and the fewer people involved, the better."

The young lieutenant grinned, exposing a dimple in his cheek that made him look even younger. "Quite right, sir."

"If you need me for anything else, you can find me in my cabin."

"Yes, sir," the lieutenant said with a smart salute.

"And you can cut all that military cock and bull right now. A simple 'yes, sir' from you and your men will do just fine."

"Yes, sir," he repeated, snapping another salute. Then his ears turned red with embarrassment.

"That's all, Lieutenant." Morgan fought a smile of amusement as Hamilton Riley turned and hurried up the ladder.

After crossing the salon to his quarters, Morgan sat down at his desk and began going over his orders and any last-minute details he might need to know before their departure. As soon as the rum in the hold had been off-loaded and replaced with cotton, they'd be on their way. Morgan almost smiled. After the hectic pace he'd been leading, he looked forward to a few restful weeks at sea. He could almost hear the sound of canvas snapping in the cool dawn breeze, see the clear blue waters of the Caribbean rushing beneath the hull. Morgan could hardly wait.

"Better wrap that blanket around ya," the red-haired sailor warned. "It's startin' to rain pretty hard."

Though the scratchy wool itched something fierce, Silver did as she was told. Maybe they would leave her hands free to hold on to it, and she could find the opening she'd been seeking, catch them off guard, and make her escape.

"Not a chance, girlie," the one named Julian said, yanking her arms out in front of her and lashing her wrists together. He stuffed his dirty handkerchief into her mouth and tied another around her head, securing the first one in place.

They tossed the blanket over her shoulders but left her head exposed to the wind and rain as they tugged her out the door. Dodging the rapidly growing puddles on the muddy, water-soaked street, they made their way to the carriage some distance away. By the time the men had Silver settled across from a dry Ferdinand Pinkard, her blanket had fallen in the mud and been left behind, and her clothes and hair were plastered wetly to her body.

Though the other men's eyes homed in on the soft mounds of her breasts, the way her skirts clung to her hips and thighs, Pinkard just smiled.

"You're looking a bit bedraggled, my dear. Let's hope the good major can provide a change of clothing."

Damn you to hell! Silver silently raged. If there were ever a man on this earth who deserved the wrath of the Lord, it was this one. Dark-complected beneath his pencil-thin mustache, the Spaniard was as heartless a pursuer as ever she could have encountered. Back home she'd heard his name often. He was a man who hired himself out for a price, and no job was too demeaning, no task too distasteful.

The carriage pulled up at the docks, the door swung open, and the three men who rode outside lifted her onto the street. Pinkard pulled his narrow-brimmed hat down low, his long black cloak more firmly around him, and followed along behind.

"Watch your step," Julian warned, jerking her roughly over the rail of the ship and onto the deck.

"We've something to discuss with the major," Pinkard told a sandy-haired man in a dark blue uniform.

"He's in his cabin," the young man said. "Whom shall I say is calling?"

"Ferdinand Pinkard. Tell him I've a treasure of some worth that belongs to a friend of his."

The soldier eyed her curiously, taking in her wet clothes, bound hands, and the gag in her mouth. With a sympathetic glance, he went below, only to return a few minutes later. "He says you can go on down."

"Thank you." Pinkard turned to the others—"You two wait here"—then to Julian, who gripped her arm in a deathlock. "Let's go."

Down the ladder, across the salon, a quick knock on the low wooden door, and a deep voice told them to come in. Julian thrust her through the opening, making her stumble; Pinkard stepped in behind her; then Julian walked back outside.

"What the hell's going on?"

Silver's brown eyes swung to the tall dark blond man with the scar on his cheek who surged to his feet at their dramatic entrance.

"Salena," Pinkard said to her, using her given name, "this is Major Morgan Trask, recently of the Texas Marines." He arched a thin black brow in amusement and looked at her as if expecting her to give a formal greeting in return. "I'm afraid Salena can't answer," he said to the major, "but I'm sure she's pleased to meet a man who was once her father's friend."

Silver cursed behind her gag and tried to kick the Spaniard in the shins. She got a ringing slap across the face for her effort. The tall major's brutal grip on Pinkard's arm and his hard warning glance stilled the blow that would have followed.

"I asked you what's going on," the major said. "Now either you tell me, or I untie the girl and she tells me."

"I wouldn't advise that if I were you. Salena has a terrible temper."

"So it would seem."

"The friend I'm speaking of is the earl of Kent."

The major seemed annoyed by Pinkard's game. He was a tall man, well built, without an ounce of excess flesh. The scar on his cheek gave him a hard look but didn't detract from the strong line of his jaw or his straight patrician nose.

"What's she got to do with William?" he asked.

Pinkard chuckled softly, and his thin mustache tilted up in a crooked half-smile. "That dark-eyed, vile-tempered bundle you see before you is none other than his daughter." He untied the gag and pulled it from her mouth. Silver cursed him roundly and tried to kick him again. "Major Morgan Trask meet Lady Salena Hardwick-Jones."

Morgan's practiced eye moved over her. She stood no taller than the average female, but the way she lifted her chin and squared her shoulders made her seem so. Her stringy gray-blond hair clung to a pair of smooth pale breasts that rose and fell above the low-cut bodice of her blouse.

"My name is Silver Jones," she said. "I work at the White Horse Inn on Bay Street. This man is out of his mind."

Morgan's mouth twitched in what, under different circumstances, might have had the makings of a smile. Even with her dirty face and soggy garments, he couldn't miss William's defiant stance with its healthy dose of arrogance or Mary's big brown eyes and thick-fringed lashes. The slim, straight nose and delicate cheekbones were all Silver Jones.

"Silver, is it? Not Lady Salena?" The last time he'd seen William, Morgan had been a youth of fifteen. The earl of Kent had been a friend of his late father's, friend and mentor to him. Salena had been a toddler, smiling and climbing up on her father's knee.

Then William had broken with family tradition and set off on his own. He bought a tiny island in the West Indies named Katonga that he had never seen and sailed away to run a plantation. Time and again

Morgan had wondered about him but had never taken the time to visit.

It was beginning to look as though he'd finally get the chance.

"I told you my name is Silver. I work at the White Horse Inn. These *gentlemen* are mistaken."

Morgan ignored her, turning his attention instead to Pinkard. "What exactly is it you want me to do with her?"

"Take her home," the Spaniard said simply, "which, you may rest assured, will be no easy task."

Morgan fastened his eyes on Salena. Wet clear through, the bodice of her blouse revealed a pair of pert pink nipples that had hardened against the cold and a waist so narrow he could span it with his hands.

"Why did you run away?" He forced his eyes back up to her face and noticed the dirt that smudged her chin, covering a dainty cleft in the center. A tinge of pink crept into her cheeks, as if she knew where his eyes had been.

"She's bent on marrying a man her father deems unfit," Pinkard answered for her. "Some ruffian who passed through on his way to the States. Her father forbade the marriage, so she's run after the scurvy fellow."

"You're a liar, Pinkard," she spat.

"And you're not Lady Salena," Morgan said mockingly. "You're just Silver Jones, a hardworking tavern wench who's here only by mistake."

Silver didn't answer. If Morgan Trask was a friend of her father's, there was nothing left to say.

"Why come to me?" the major asked Pinkard.

"Believe it or not, beneath all that mud, Silver is a beautiful young woman. There are few men I'd trust to see her safely returned."

"You mean there are few men you'd trust to get her there unharmed so you can get paid."

"Precisely."

Morgan had known Pinkard and his sell-his-soul-for-a-dollar business dealings for years. He wasn't surprised to find him returning a runaway girl to her grieving parents for money—but he was surprised to find the wayward young lady was Salena Hardwick-Jones.

"My sources tell me you're headed for Barbados," Pinkard added. "Katonga isn't far out of the way. You can return the girl and pick up my money. And William will see you're taken care of as well—unless, of course, you want me to go along."

"Not a chance, Pinkard. An hour with you is just about all I can stand."

Pinkard let the words pass. "Then you'll take the girl home?"

"I seem to have no other choice. I'm not about to leave her with you and your thugs. She may not whet your appetite"—he glanced once more in the girl's direction, at her nipped-in waist and the alluring curves of her breasts and thighs—"but I don't doubt the others would find her a tasty morsel. I'm surprised you've been able to keep them in line this long—assuming you have."

"I assure you the lady's virtue remains intact. William was quite adamant about that." He arched a black brow. "Speaking of which, I hope I can count on your loyalty to William to overrule the sexual prowess women seem to find so attractive in you."

Silver glanced at Morgan, who shot her a look that told her exactly the appeal she held for him. She was dirty and ragged and rain-soaked. And she hadn't bathed in a week.

"Don't say it," she warned, watching his eyes

move over her soggy clothes and matted hair. Handsome or not, he was just a man. What he thought of her meant nothing.

Morgan just smiled.

"Take care, Major," Pinkard cautioned as he turned to leave. "She'll do anything to keep from going back to Katonga. I'd watch my back if I were you."

"I'll keep that in mind." The major's look said Pinkard's warning concerned him not in the least.

Good, Silver thought. *A man who underestimates his opponent is the easiest to defeat.*

"You know where to find me," Morgan finished. "I'll have your blood money ready and waiting when I get back."

"You do that, Major. Both William and I are more than grateful for your assistance—even if it has been given with some reluctance." With a last glance at Silver, Pinkard walked out the door, closing it firmly behind him.

Morgan turned his attention to Salena Hardwick-Jones. Though she held her head high, there were smudges beneath her eyes that betrayed her fatigue, and her wrists were chapped and raw from the too-tight bindings. His brows drew together as he assessed the red mark across her cheek left by Pinkard's hand. The bastard hadn't the conscience God gave a snake.

Pulling open the door, he leaned into the passageway and caught the attention of Hamilton Riley, who sat waiting in the salon. Morgan explained to him about their newest traveling companion, then asked him to have Cookie, the ship's cook, heat water for a bath.

"She'll need something dry to wear," Morgan added. "Jordy's about her size. Get something from him." Jordan Little was his cabin boy, a youth of just thirteen.

Once the tasks had been set in motion, Morgan stepped back inside and closed the door. "We need to talk, Salena."

"My name is Silver."

He watched her for a moment, noting the rise and fall of her high, round breasts, the color that tinted her cheeks. Even tired and bedraggled, and wet clear to her bones, she had an air about her. Morgan scoffed at the idea of aristocratic bloodlines that William held so dear, and yet . . .

"If that's the name you prefer—"

"It's the only name I'll answer to."

Morgan ignored a pinprick of anger. If he just took it slowly, made her understand that her father had only her best interests in mind, the girl would soon settle down and accept the inevitable.

"If you promise to behave, I'll cut your bindings."

Silver nodded. Morgan slid a small stag-handled knife from the sheath at his waist and slit the leather thongs that bound her wrists. She glanced toward the door.

"Don't even think about it," he warned.

"I was just hoping the bath would hurry." It was a lie, and they both knew it.

"Your father was a friend of mine," he told her, hoping to ease the moment. "We knew each other in London." But at his words, she grew only more tense. She glanced away for an instant; then her brown eyes fixed on a point on the wall above his head.

"What are you planning to do with me?"

"I'm going to take you home."

You're going to try, Silver thought. "I don't suppose there's anything I could say to change your mind."

"I owe your father. It's a debt I've never repaid. Seeing his daughter returned to him safely is the least I can do."

A shiver raced up Silver's spine.

"You're cold." Morgan stepped toward her, but Silver instinctively stepped away. "I was just going to get you a blanket."

"The bath will warm me enough."

A soft knock sounded at the door. The major opened it, and two young seamen walked in, one with a heavy copper bathing tub, the other carrying dry clothes tucked beneath his arm and two steaming tin pails. The cabin boy, a youth with auburn hair, freckles, and wide hazel eyes, arrived with a pot of tea, cold chicken, and cheese.

Silver had to admit the bath and food looked good. As soon as she was clean and dry and had eaten her fill, she would plan her next move.

"I'll be just outside if you need anything," Morgan told her when the men had left. He stepped out into the passageway.

"Thank you, Major." It was all she could do not to smile. The man underestimated her sorely. She'd be bathed, dressed, and away before he knew what had hit him.

And hit him she would. One solid blow to the top of his dark blond head, and he would be out for the night. She would do her best not to hurt him, but he had left her no choice.

She shivered inside her wet clothing and glanced at the steaming hot water. In the meantime, she looked forward with relish to the moments she would spend in the tub.

Chapter 2

Nothing in recent memory had felt as good as the warm, sudsy water that caressed her naked body. Silver ducked her head beneath the surface, used the cake of soap to scrub her hair, then rinsed and leaned back in the tub.

Soon she would be leaving, but for now, sitting before the tiny fire in the corner, being warmed by the water, and sipping a cup of jasmine tea seemed like heaven. Outside this cozy room, she would be faced with the storm and the task of getting safely away. Once that happened, she would dye her hair brown, head north, and lose herself in some big city. Philadelphia—or maybe even New York. The colder climate wouldn't quite suit her, but that was the least of her worries.

Silver sighed with resignation and forced herself to climb from the warmth of the tub. She dried herself on a white linen towel and pulled on the canvas breeches the sailor had brought, finding them such a snug fit she nearly blushed. A white cotton shirt came next. Then, using the comb she found on the bureau, she worked the tangles from her hair and dried the unruly silver mass in front of the fire.

God, she felt like a brand-new woman, one ready to meet the challenge that lay ahead.

A search of the room turned up a pistol, which she shoved into the waistband of her breeches, and a heavy wooden belaying pin that would make a perfect weapon. Now all she had to do was lure the major back in and hit him over the head.

Silver grimaced at the thought but pushed her reluctance away. *You'll just have to do it*, she told herself firmly, and bent to the task ahead.

After tying her shirttail up around her waist and out of the way and securing her hair at the nape of her neck with the leather thong the major had cut from her wrists, Silver dragged a chair behind the door and positioned it to give her the access she needed. Then she stuck her head out into the passageway.

Morgan Trask leaned against the back of a small tapestry-covered settee, his booted feet crossed in front of him, reading the newspaper in the yellow glow of the brass reflecting lamp that hung on the wall behind him. He was definitely a handsome man, she thought, in a tough, no-nonsense sort of way. He had the greenest eyes she had ever seen, and his skin, tanned dark by the sun, looked smooth except for the jagged scar that marked his cheek.

She wondered fleetingly what kind of man he was, then, remembering his friendship with her father, figured she already knew.

"Excuse me, Major," Silver said sweetly, "could I see you for just a moment?"

Trask set the paper aside and stood up, his tall frame nearly touching the low ceiling in the elegantly furnished salon. Silver slipped back inside the cabin and eased the door closed. Picking up the belaying pin, she took her position on the chair and waited till the door swung wide.

Morgan glanced up just as Silver swung her heavy blow. Cursing, he tried to duck out of the way, but Silver anticipated the move. The blow glanced off the side of his head and onto his shoulder, sending him crashing to the floor.

Damn! Silver swore, wishing the blow had done more damage, but she couldn't bear to hit him again. Morgan sat there groaning, trying to recover. Silver ignored him and raced through the door and into the salon. After stopping to check for the others, she climbed the ladder to the deck, ran to the rail, and climbed over.

Nothing to it, she thought with a surge of satisfaction and a last glance over her shoulder to the deck she had left behind. Silver sucked in a breath at the sight of Morgan Trask, racing determinedly along behind her, his face a dark mask of rage.

Damn her conscience! It was always getting her in trouble. She should have made sure she'd knocked him out cold.

Silver ran faster, dodging sailors who strolled the dock, flea-bitten mutts that sniffed through rotting garbage, and a doxy or two who busily plied their wares. When she bowled into a woman she hadn't seen, the whore cursed her soundly, but Silver just kept running. She had to find someplace to hide, some dark alley where the major couldn't find her.

Rounding a corner, Silver fought the stitch in her side, the pounding of her heart, and every burning breath she had to take. Her legs were beginning to ache with the powerful effort, and still she drove on. A glance over her shoulder told her she had left the major behind, but she dared not slow.

Not until an arm snaked out of nowhere, circled her waist, and slammed her up against a rough brick wall.

Morgan Trask towered above her, his hard body pinning her, his green eyes glinting with rage. Silver struggled against the corded muscles of his chest, tried to duck beneath his arm, tried to pull her pistol, fought to kick and bite him—all to no avail.

"Enjoy your bath, milady?" his deep voice mocked, but there wasn't a trace of amusement in the unforgiving lines of his face.

Silver lifted her chin. "I found it quite delightful."

"Good," he said, jerking the pistol from her waist and stuffing it into the back of his breeches, "because you're just about to have another." With one quick move, he scooped her into his arms, carried her the few feet to the edge of the dock, and dumped her in.

Bastard! Silver swore as the icy water swept over her, knocking the air from her lungs and chilling her far worse than the rain. She broke the surface, sputtering, cursing, fighting the hair that covered her nose and mouth, and threatened to drown her. Morgan Trask stood on the dock, grinning, enjoying her torment, and stirring her anger to heights she had rarely known.

Why, that arrogant, blackhearted—Grabbing a quick breath of air, Silver went under again.

Morgan watched with satisfaction as she came up twice more, thrashing the surface and fighting to catch her breath. He'd let her get good and tired, then throw her a line. He'd been a bloody fool not to heed Pinkard's warning. But she'd looked so damned pitiful—and far too exhausted to cause him any trouble.

Now he had a pounding head and a bruise on his

shoulder to remind him not to make the same mistake again.

Morgan glanced at the water. Only a few tiny bubbles arose where Silver had gone under the last time. She should have come up by now, he realized, and cursed himself again for a fool.

Bloody hell! Calling her every vile name he could think of, Morgan pulled off his boots, shed his heavy blue uniform jacket and the pistol she had stolen, and dived into the water. When he found no trace of her, he began to worry in earnest. Just his luck the wench couldn't stay afloat long enough to learn her lesson. Then a niggling suspicion crept into his mind. Morgan broke the surface just in time to see Silver grinning, climbing up on the pier some distance away.

Damn her! Hauling himself up a rickety wooden ladder, he raced after her, catching up to her a block away, barreling into her, and knocking them both to the ground.

"Lady, you are really pushing your luck," he said through clenched teeth. His body pressed her hard against the rough wooden boards of the dock, making it difficult for her to breathe, but Morgan didn't care. Dragging her to her feet, he forced one of her arms up behind her, brushing his palm across a taut wet nipple in the process. Her slender derriere pressed seductively against his lower body. Morgan felt a tightening in his loins and cursed the bitter fortune that had placed her in his care.

"You're going back to the ship one way or another," he said, determined not to spend the next few weeks putting up with the hateful little wench. She'd learn to do as she was told or damn well regret it. "You might as well resign yourself."

Silver ignored him, struggling and squirming and trying to jerk free.

"Stop it, Silver," he warned, his voice so hard she finally quit fighting. Morgan pulled his soggy kerchief from around his neck and tied her arms behind her back. Shaking his head at the task he had set for himself, he made his way back to the ship, stopping only long enough to pick up his jacket, boots, and pistol.

Jordy, Cookie, and Hamilton Riley stood at the rail when they arrived. Only Cookie had the courage to admire openly the curvaceous bit of baggage Morgan tugged along.

"My, my," the old cook said with a grin that split his weathered face from ear to ear. A short, stout gray-haired seaman, at sixty Grandison Aimes was still as tough as shoe leather.

"I guess Mr. Pinkard had her tied up for good reason," Hamilton Riley said, as if a light had just dawned.

Morgan swept past without a word, hauling Silver down the ladder and across the salon. She looked worse than she had before, except now her face was clean and he could see her smooth complexion, the delicate line of her jaw. Too bad the wench hadn't inherited her father's common sense or her mother's sensitivity, instead of her grandfather's temper.

"Take off your clothes," Morgan commanded when they reached his cabin.

"What?"

"I said take off your clothes."

"Pinkard isn't the only one who's out of his mind."

"Do it," he warned, taking a step in her direction, "or I'll do it for you." For the first time since she'd stumbled into his life, Morgan spotted a glimmer of fear. It was just the tiniest flick of an eye, no more than a heartbeat. Most men wouldn't have noticed, but Morgan did. It was enough to take the edge off his words.

"Your clothes need time to dry, and I'm tired of chasing after you. You can have them back in the morning."

She eyed him suspiciously but apparently didn't doubt the threat he had made. "I'll toss them out as soon as I'm undressed."

Morgan nodded. "You can wrap yourself in a blanket before I come back in."

Silver's head snapped up. "What? Why are you coming back in?"

"Because this is where I sleep. You can sleep in the berth next door." His mouth curved up in bitter amusement. "I'd planned to give you my berth, but after our little . . . adventure . . . I've decided against it. When you start behaving, we'll talk about it again."

Silver shrugged as if she couldn't care less, and Morgan gathered dry clothes for himself and stepped outside. She was an odd one. As hard to figure as any female he'd ever met. She certainly had more spirit. He had never seen such fire in a woman, so much determination.

One thing was certain: Salena Hardwick-Jones was a beauty. The face of an angel and a body ripe for sin. Thank God his taste ran to the soft-spoken, do-as-you're-told type of woman, the kind who knew exactly the way things were, or who pleasured a man for the gold in his purse.

They were easier to deal with and a lot less trouble.

Morgan smiled to himself. Whatever man she'd run after owed him a debt of gratitude. The poor son of a bitch would never know how close he had come to a life of misery with Silver Jones.

"All right, all right," Silver called out at the pounding on the cabin door. Checking to be sure the blanket fitted her snugly from bosom to foot, she waited for the door to open, then tossed out her clothes.

"Good evening, milady." Dressed in a pair of snug brown breeches and a clean white shirt, Morgan Trask stepped into the room and gave her a mocking bow. Behind him, the freckle-faced cabin boy picked up her soggy clothes and walked away.

Wordlessly the major indicated a tiny door on one side of the cabin. Silver opened it to find a narrow berth along the wall, a sea chest, and a chamber pot.

"Your quarters, milady," Morgan said with heavy sarcasm.

"Don't let me put you out," she snapped. Trask didn't answer, just let her walk past him into the tiny room, then locked the door behind her.

Silver sank down on the bed. Her spirits were low, but not dead. Tomorrow brought another day and with it new opportunities. As long as they were in port, there was always a chance for escape. Once she gained her freedom, this time she would make it. With that thought in mind, Silver curled up on the bunk and fell into an exhausted sleep.

Bright yellow rays, peeping through the six-inch porthole, warmed her face and finally awakened her. She stretched and yawned, wrapped the blanket around her, and tried the door. She was surprised to find it unlocked.

In the major's cabin she found a tray of food: porridge, a thick slab of ham, a steaming mug of coffee, and several warm buttered biscuits. Beside the tray sat a second set of clothes, these more frayed than the last, and a pitcher and basin of water. Silver dressed quickly in case the major returned, then combed her hair.

After washing her face, and pinching her cheeks to give them a bit of color, she looked in the mirror and was surprised to see how good she looked. Even her saltwater swim hadn't dimmed the sheen of her hair, and the night's sleep had freshened her complexion.

A key turning in the lock drew her attention. Morgan Trask walked in just as she turned toward the door. He stopped short, his eyes sliding along the curve of her hips, and down her long slim legs, more than evident in the snug-fitting breeches.

Silver felt a rush of warmth to her cheeks. "I assure you, Major, if there were something more modest for me to wear, I'd be happy to do so."

"As soon as your other clothes have been cleaned and dried, they'll be returned, though when it comes to modesty, they aren't much better."

"Those were my working clothes."

"From the White Horse Inn, I believe."

"Yes."

"And you would rather stay here in Savannah and work in a den of thieves like that than return to your home"—his mouth curved up in a mirthless smile—"but then it isn't our tropical climate that keeps you here, is it? It's your lover who holds such appeal."

"I told you Pinkard is a liar. I have no lover. I only wished to live my life on my own."

"What's his name?" Morgan asked, as if she hadn't spoken. "Maybe I know him."

Silver clenched her fists. "If believing a man like Pinkard suits you, go right ahead. What I say means nothing to you anyway."

Morgan fell silent. His eyes, so unbelievably green,

centered on her face. "You'll stay in this cabin until we set sail. That's tomorrow morning with the tide."

"Pinkard said you were going to Barbados."

"Katonga and then Barbados," Morgan pointedly corrected, and Silver set her jaw. "Do you read?" he asked, changing the subject.

"Of course I read."

"There are books on the shelves above my bed."

"I know," she said, but at Morgan's hard look she wished she could call back the words.

"I'd appreciate it if you didn't rummage through my things. There are no weapons left in here. You've already found the pistol and I removed my saber this morning. You'll find little else of interest."

Silver didn't answer. In an hour's time she'd know more about Morgan Trask than he knew about himself. *Know thine enemy.* It was a motto she had come to live by.

"If there's anything you need, don't ask," Morgan finished coldly. "You'll get no better treatment than the rest of the crew—aristocratic blood or not."

"I've asked for nothing, Major Trask. I don't intend to."

A dark blond brow arched upward in surprise. He studied her a moment, appraising her, it seemed. "Tomorrow, after we leave, you may join us for supper."

He's doing it again, she thought. *He actually believes I'll sit in here and do nothing.* "I look forward to meeting the others," she couldn't resist putting in. But at Trask's sudden wariness, knew she shouldn't have.

"Behave yourself, Salena. I'm older and wiser— and a whole lot tougher. Do as I say, and you and I will get along fine."

"My name is Silver."

Morgan worked a muscle in his jaw. "I stand corrected." But his green eyes said as soon as they set sail, he'd call her what he damned well pleased.

Silver refrained from her retort by biting the tip of her tongue. She had more important matters to attend. As soon as the major locked her in, she set to work.

Going through his shelves and cupboards, she discovered Trask was neater than most of the men she knew. Neat and well organized, but nothing like her father, who would discipline a servant for a book left out of place or a piece of lint overlooked on the mantel. On more than one occasion she had seen him take a clean white glove and run it across the surface of a table, just to be sure the servants were doing their job.

Trask dressed well, she decided as she sifted through a closet. She liked the tailored lines of his clothes, not foppish but masculine. Several pairs of boots, crafted of fine Spanish leather, had been polished to a glossy sheen. Expensive clothes, she noticed; nothing cheap or shoddy in Morgan Trask's wardrobe. Nothing shoddy about the way he looked in them either.

His taste in books was impressive, if he really read them. He had everything from poetry to the latest in medical journals. One drawer held a beautiful conch shell, and there was a belt of heavy Spanish silver. In his trunk at the foot of the bed, she found a lovely string of pearls, obviously meant as a gift, and wondered which of his women he had bought them for.

Silver felt a twinge of irritation though she wasn't quite sure why. Pinkard had spoken of the major's prowess in bed. It was a subject she usually thought of with some distaste, yet in Morgan's case she found the topic intriguing.

Instinctively she believed Pinkard was right. She knew some women enjoyed such things, and Morgan Trask was certainly an attractive man. She could still recall the hard muscles of his chest as he had pressed against her on the dock, the corded strength in his arms. It had stirred an odd sensation, one that would bear reflection once she was safely away.

Searching further, Silver still found nothing that would help her. Instead she found maps of Mexico, several of the Yucatán Peninsula rolled and stored in the bin beside his desk. One envelope held his orders. Silver read them carefully.

Cotton for sugar, sugar for guns. The major was aiding the Texians. Probably for money, since it appeared he lived not in Texas but in Georgia. Just another bloodsucker. Probably not much different from Ferdinand Pinkard—only a lot better looking.

Silver thought of how handsome he'd looked standing in the doorway. His clothes fit perfectly, not too tight, yet they left no doubt about the virility of the man who wore them.

She shook her head, surprised by the train of her thoughts. She'd rarely been attracted to a man. Most reminded her of her father: overbearing and cruel, self-indulgent and dictatorial. The fact was she hadn't known many, mostly her father and his friends and a few of the servants.

Of course, Quako was nothing like that. Black as he was, poor and illiterate, Quako was a man among men. Knowing him had given her some small hope that not all members of the male gender were worthless philanderers.

Silver closed the lid of the trunk and sank down on Trask's wide bed. She'd been through almost everything and still found nothing that could help her. Then an idea struck, and she slid her arm between

the mattress and the head of the berth. As her fingers
closed over the handle of a pistol, Silver smiled with
satisfaction. A man like Trask was bound to have
more than one weapon. He'd just hidden it so long
ago he'd forgotten it was there.

Silver's smile broadened to a grin, her heartbeat
quickening as a new plan formed in her mind. With a
flick of her hand, she tossed her heavy pale hair back
over her shoulder. Morgan Trask be damned. This
time she would get away!

"Think she'll settle down now, Major?" Hamilton
Riley sat across from him in the salon, sipping a cup
of strong black coffee. Most of the crew had returned
to help with the onloading and the final preparations
to make way. The rest would be back by nightfall.

"She'd damned well better, if she knows what's
good for her."

"I've never seen the likes of it." Riley shook his
sandy-haired head. "Most of the women I've known
would have fainted dead away just at the sight of the
three who brought her here."

"She's got guts—I'll give her that—even if she
hasn't got the sense God gave a wren."

"She looks like a woman, but she acts like a man."

"It's hard to believe she's Mary's daughter. Mary
Hardwick-Jones was as gentle and kind a woman as
I've ever met." Morgan scowled. "I don't think
there's a gentle bone in Salena's body."

"Maybe not," Ham said softly, "but in that depart-
ment she certainly isn't lacking."

Morgan's gaze fixed on the young lieutenant. "I
expect you and your men to act with restraint when
it comes to Miss Jones. She's a lady, even if she
doesn't behave like one."

Hamilton Riley grew serious. "You've nothing to

worry about from us, Major, but what about the crew?"

"I'll deal with them." Morgan came to his feet. "I've got a few last-minute details to attend. I'll be back before dark. Whatever you do, don't let Silver out of my cabin."

"No, sir. You can count on that, sir." Riley started to salute, but Morgan's hard look stopped his hand in midair.

"I'll be back as soon as I can."

Silver waited until dusk began to fall before setting her plan in motion. But all day long she had fanned the low flames in her tiny corner fireplace, carefully adding a chunk of coal now and then to keep it going. No one had brought her food or answered the pounding on her door when she'd demanded it, as she'd been sure someone would.

Trask was being more careful this time.

But very shortly now Trask and his men would have no choice.

Silver watched darkness fall outside the small windows above Morgan's wide bed, the fading sun lighting the horizon to a soft orange glow that slowly disappeared. Dressed in the cabin boy's frayed breeches and shirt, she knelt before the fire, added the last of the coal from the tin bucket beside it, and blew until hot red flames licked the grate.

Taking bits of a rag she had found and torn up, she dipped them in water and dropped them carefully atop the fire. Smoke began to curl and billow, then roll across the floor as the cloth began to burn but couldn't quite catch flame. She added more damp cloth and fanned the fire until the room filled with thick white smoke and she began to cough.

"Fire!" she yelled, covering her nose with a hand-

kerchief and banging on the cabin door. "Somebody
help me!" Fanning the smoke beneath the bottom of
the door, Silver banged more loudly. Footsteps
sounded on the ladder, a key grated in the lock, and
the door swung wide.

"Good Lord!" The slender young lieutenant she
had seen the night before stepped into the room,
tried to see her through the heavy smoke, but
couldn't. "Miss Jones, where are you?" Then he felt
the cold steel muzzle of the pistol she stuck beneath
his chin.

"Don't move," Silver warned. "Not a single, soli-
tary muscle."

Riley coughed several times, but the smoke had
already begun to dissipate through the open doorway. "Please, Miss Jones. The major's going to be
furious if you're not here when he gets back."

"To hell with the major. The man's an arrogant
pain in the neck. I hope he's so mad he chokes on his
fancy gold epaulets." Silver moved closer, careful to
keep the gun steady against the young man's neck.
"Start walking, Lieutenant, and don't do anything
foolish. You may rest assured that I will not hesitate
to pull this trigger."

Hamilton Riley swallowed so hard the muzzle
moved up and down against his throat. "What about
the fire? Surely you don't want the ship to go up in
flames?"

"There is no fire. Now very carefully, Lieutenant,
move through the doorway. If anyone tries to stop
us, order them to stand aside."

Riley nodded, and they walked into the passageway. Several crewmen who had answered her alarm
backed up the ladder to the deck while she and the
lieutenant moved along the hall. They'd gone
through the main salon and gotten as far as the lad-

der when Morgan Trask's steel-edged voice stopped them cold.

"Going for a stroll, milady?" He stepped from behind a door that led into a storage space.

Silver tensed. "You might say that," she answered coolly, though she was far from feeling cool.

"We thought the cabin was afire, Major," the lieutenant tried to explain. "There was smoke everywhere and—"

"It's all right, Lieutenant. It appears Lady Salena has a little more intelligence than we believed."

Silver ignored the barb, though it pricked her sorely to do so. "Tell your men to get out of the way, Major, if you want this man to stay alive."

"You're willing to commit murder? Shoot a man down in cold blood to keep from going home?"

Silver's hand shook. She wet her suddenly dry lips and eased the young man forward. "If I have to. But you'll be the one pulling the trigger." Even in the dim glow of the lamp, Silver could see the fury in Trask's handsome face. A muscle ticked in his cheek, and his hands balled into fists at his sides.

Dear God, let him believe I'll do it. Let him believe I'm the ruthless bitch he thinks I am.

Morgan smiled, but the smile didn't reach those hard green eyes. "If you want to go that badly"—he made a sweeping bow—"be my guest."

He let her move past him. Inch by inch they climbed up the ladder, the young lieutenant in front, Silver behind, the barrel of the gun still taut beneath his chin.

She had just reached the top rung when Morgan's booted foot shot out, knocking her legs from beneath her and slamming her hard to the floor. The pistol discharged with a deafening roar, and in an instant Morgan was sprawled on top of her. He jerked her to her feet and dragged her back toward his cabin. Silver clenched her fist and swung at him. Morgan blocked the blow, the scar on his face tightening in surprise and rage.

No! her mind screamed. She swung at him again, aiming for his jaw, but Morgan caught her wrist and forced her arm behind her back. "Let me go!" she shrieked, her control slipping farther away. "What does it matter to you if I get away? What does it matter?"

Morgan hauled her into his cabin, slammed the door, and hurled her toward his bed, where she landed in a sprawling heap. Across the room, now clear of smoke, his bright green eyes flashed his fury, but it couldn't top Silver's own.

"This is none of your business!" she raged. "Why can't you just let me go?"

"You're wrong, Silver. This *is* my business. You made it my business when you threatened one of my men."

Silver grabbed a leather-bound book from the ledge above Morgan's bed and hurled it at him. Morgan ducked, and it crashed against the wall. "I'm not your prisoner! I'm a grown woman! I just want to be left alone!"

"A grown woman?" he mocked as she tossed a second book in his direction. It landed against the mirror, which crashed to the floor and shattered into a thousand pieces. "A woman doesn't behave like you do. A woman doesn't rant and rave and destroy things. A woman doesn't curse and fight and try to act like a man." Morgan started toward her; Silver slid to the side of the bed near the bureau, picked up the empty porcelain water pitcher, and threw it at Morgan's head. The sound of shattering glass rang with the angry din of their voices.

"You're going home, Silver. After the trouble you've caused, there is no amount of money that could keep me from getting you there. I just hope to God William will listen to my advice and take you in hand, because you most sorely need it."

At the mention of her father Silver's last thread of control snapped. "I won't go back there! Not you or anyone else is going to make me!" She charged into Morgan, dragging her nails down his cheek until he bled, slamming her slender fists against his chest. Morgan tried to still her flailing arms, but she jerked one free and slapped him hard across the face.

"Damn you!" He stared at her in disbelief. "What kind of woman are you?"

In answer, Silver kicked him in the shins and tried once more to jerk free. Her hair, loose from its bindings, tumbled wildly around her shoulders. Morgan laced his fingers in it and dragged her head back. While she kicked and screamed and cursed him, Morgan hauled her toward the bed.

"You little vixen," he growled through clenched teeth, pulling her across his lap. "You're going to learn to behave if it's the last thing you ever do!" With that his palm came down hard across her bottom, searing her flesh through the taut canvas breeches. Silver shrieked in rage, her fury so great she could barely feel the heavy blows.

Again and again Morgan's calloused palm descended, the noise drowned out by the sound of Silver's violent oaths. Just about the time he was sure she'd had enough, her teeth sank into his leg. Morgan swore loudly and brought his hand down painfully again.

"I can do this longer than you can," he warned, but in truth he was beginning to wonder. As if in answer to his thoughts, Silver renewed her struggles, twisting and thrashing until Morgan jerked her off his lap and pinned her beneath him on the bed.

"Stop it, Silver!" he warned, his voice so hard she stilled. "I don't regret the thrashing I gave you—no one ever deserved it more—but you seem bound and determined to make me hurt you, and that I will not do!"

Dark and defiant, Silver's eyes glared up at him. "Why not, Major Trask? I should think you'd like nothing better!"

Morgan swore an oath beneath his breath. "Because I'm twice your size. Because I'm a man and you're a woman. Because a man is supposed to protect a woman, not hurt her."

Silver stopped straining against him. Her eyes, now a softer shade of brown, filled with tears, and her lush bottom lip began to tremble. "Not the men I've known." Her thick dark lashes swept down, and the wetness gently slipped along her cheeks.

Morgan stared down at her, feeling a sudden stab of remorse, which he knew was a mistake, and some other emotion he couldn't quite name. For an instant the vixen had disappeared and he'd glimpsed the woman beneath—or had it been just an illusion?

Morgan let go of her wrists. "You're going back, Silver. Resign yourself to it. There are twenty-one men aboard this vessel. After tonight they'll all be wary of you and your tricks."

"You're a hard man, Major Trask." She wiped the tears from her eyes with the back of her hand. "You may be certain my father will be pleased."

Morgan watched her a moment more. "Get some rest," he finally said, wondering why her words made him somehow feel unclean. "We set sail in the morning." She glanced away, and Morgan moved to the door. Once outside the cabin, he just stood there, listening to the water that lapped against the hull.

The sound he heard next was so soft he thought for an instant he'd imagined it. Then he recognized it for what it was—the anguish of a woman's tears.

Morgan raked a hand through his dark blond hair and headed up on deck. He needed some air, needed some time to sort things out.

You were better off before, his mind said. Better off before this nagging suspicion had begun to eat away at him. Better off before he'd begun to wonder if, beneath her tough facade, Silver Jones was a woman after all.

Chapter 3

How long had it been since she'd let herself cry? She had forgotten how good it felt, how much it helped ease the pain. She hadn't meant to, especially not in front of *him*.

What kind of woman are you? he had said. What kind indeed? Not nearly the tough, unfeeling person he believed. Not nearly so hard, not nearly so fearless.

She shouldn't give a damn what he thought of her, but she did. If only he hadn't interfered. If he hadn't returned, she'd be free by now. If only she hadn't lost her temper so completely. Damn him, it was all *his* fault. Morgan Trask had a way of driving her over the edge.

It happened that way sometimes. More often than she cared to admit. Being hot-tempered was a flaw she wasn't much proud of. She worked constantly to overcome her unruly nature, and for the most part she could.

Quako had shown her the folly of losing control. He was a master of it. He had to be. For beneath his humble exterior, Quako was a man who bowed to no other, only to his god. He had been born a Masai warrior, and though he'd been captured as a child, enslaved, and sold on Jamaica, no master had ever subdued his spirit. When Silver thought of Quako and his woman, Delia, it gave her courage—they had suffered far more than she at her father's hands.

Silver washed the last of the tears from her cheeks and dried her face on a damp linen towel. A knock at the door drew her attention, and she opened it to find Jordy, the freckle-faced cabin boy, standing in the passageway.

"Cap'n's on deck and he's watchin', case you try to make any trouble." Standing tentatively just outside the door, he looked as if he might bolt at any second.

"Captain? I thought he was a major?"

"He'll always be Cap'n to me and Cookie—that's what you call the cook aboard a ship."

"I see."

"Me and Cookie been sailin' with the cap'n for the past five years. He give up—gave up," he corrected, "the sea last fall. . . . He's just back for this one trip." Closing the door behind him, Jordy edged farther into the room. "Don't you try nothin'."

"I'm afraid I've just about run out of things to try." She flashed him a weak attempt at a smile.

Jordy looked at her strangely. Standing about her height, Jordy was small for his age, his auburn hair a little too long, but his hazel eyes looked intelligent, and there was a pleasing quality to the gentle shape of his mouth. "Ain't never—haven't ever seen a woman could fistfight like a man."

The way he looked at her, as if she weren't really human, made Silver feel like crying again. "I'm not usually that way. I just need to get off this ship."

Skirting her carefully, Jordy placed a man's long white cotton night rail on the end of the bunk, then turned to pick up the pieces of broken glass left from her clash with the major. Fleetingly it occurred to her that she should have hidden one of the sharp broken edges to use as a weapon.

Tomorrow, she thought. *Tomorrow you'll have the strength of will to start all over again.* Kneeling down, she began to help him pick up the shards of splintered glass, but as soon as she touched the first piece, Jordy leaped away.

"You get back there," he warned, pointing toward the opposite side of the room. It was obvious Jordy and the rest of the crew had seen and heard enough of her battle with Trask to know exactly what had occurred in the major's quarters. "I'll take care of it," Jordy finished, and Silver's temper fired again.

"How do you know I don't already have a piece? That I'm not just waiting for a chance to cut your throat?"

Jordy swallowed hard and eyed her warily. "Cap'n says you wouldn't really kill anybody. Says you're probably not as bad as you put on."

Silver wasn't sure if that was a compliment or an insult. "And just how, exactly, would he know?"

"Cap'n knows ever'thing about ever'thing. He kin —can—size a man up in the flick of an eye."

What kind of woman are you? "And you think that goes for a woman, too?"

"Cap'n's got a real reputation with the ladies." Jordy grinned. "Not your kind, o' course. Cap'n likes his women to mind their manners."

Silver bristled but didn't speak.

"Leastwise most women like him," Jordy continued. "Course, some is—are—afraid o' him. With that mean-lookin' scar and all."

"Well, I'm not," she said with a toss of her head.

"You should be. If he whupped you as hard as he whupped me . . . I sure don't want no more o' it."

"He beat you?" she gasped.

Jordy grinned again, his expression jaunty and boyish. "Gimme a lickin' for callin' some old man names. Old man didn't deserve what he got. I did."

Silver smiled at that. She glanced around the cabin, at the glass and books and general havoc she had created. "I guess I did, too."

Jordy finished picking up the broken shards of the porcelain pitcher and the now-shattered mirror and hung what was left of it back on the wall. He went out, careful to lock the door, then returned a few minutes later with a cornhusk broom to sweep up the pieces of glass too small to gather. Silver picked up the leather-bound volumes she had thrown and returned them to the shelves above the bed.

Jordy watched her from the corner of his eye, surprised, it seemed, that she should be willing to help. "Ain't never—haven't ever met no—any—real bluestockin' lady neither," he said.

Silver didn't miss the way he was working to improve his speaking. She thought it bode well for his future and wondered who had been helping him in his task. "It's only a title. To me it means nothing."

She glanced toward the window. Tomorrow they'd be leaving, returning her to that other existence, where she played the proper, genteel daughter of an aristocrat, a rich plantation lord. Tonight was her last chance for escape, yet there seemed no way. Outside, the stars twinkled brightly, flaunting their freedom. If only the narrow windows were big enough for her to slip through. If only she were a little bit smaller . . .

If only she weren't afraid to go home.

"Cap'n'll be here pretty soon," Jordy reminded her. "You'd best get changed and into your berth."

Silver nodded. "Thank you, Jordy."

"How'd you know my name?"

"I'm wearing your clothes, am I not?"

Jordy grinned, his youthful gaze traveling along the curves of her body with something close to awe. "You surely do look some better in 'em than I do, ma'am."

Silver laughed. Laughing again felt even better than crying. "As soon as I get my own clothes back, I'll return yours."

"You'll be needin' a change now and again. You kin—can—keep 'em till you get back home."

Silver's smile faded. "Good night, Jordy."

"Good night, ma'am."

"She don't—doesn't—seem so bad to me," Jordy said.

Seated at the carved oak table in the salon, Morgan just grunted.

"She said she deserved the lickin'."

Morgan's head came up. "She said that?"

"Said she just had to get off'n the ship."

"Off the ship," Morgan corrected, setting aside the paperwork he'd been scanning.

"Off the ship," Jordy repeated. "Why's she want off so bad, Cap'n?"

"I'm not sure." Morgan fixed his gaze on Jordy, who flushed guiltily and shuffled the toe of his flat-heeled boot. "Don't you have some sail to mend?"

"Aye, Cap'n." A little disgruntled, Jordy climbed the ladder to the deck, leaving Morgan alone. Morgan sighed. He felt tired yet restless. He needed some sleep but knew he'd be hard pressed to get it. Not with Silver Jones sleeping just a few feet away. He'd given her the nightshirt just so he wouldn't have to think of her lying there naked.

Damn, the woman was a worse pain in the neck

than any dozen men. Morgan had known Silver only two days, and she'd already turned his life upside down. Two weeks would seem an eternity.

Morgan sighed at the thought. With a grumble of resignation, he headed for his cabin. He'd go over the charts one more time, though he practically knew them by heart; then maybe he could get some sleep.

Tomorrow he'd talk to Silver, try to make her understand that it was in her best interest to go back to Katonga. If William was being unreasonable, maybe he could intercede. In fact, he'd offer her his help.

Morgan felt better already. Once they were at sea, things would return to normal. Silver would realize she had no place to run, accept his offer of assistance, and start behaving herself. Morgan yawned. Maybe he'd get some sleep after all.

It was the screaming that awoke him, echoing through his cabin and cutting through the fog of his dreams in an instant. Morgan hit the deck running, racing toward the narrow steward's quarters before he realized he wore not a stitch of his clothes. Cursing, he pulled on his breeches, buttoned up the front, and unlocked the door.

The screaming had ceased, but Silver sat on the end of the bunk, her legs drawn up beneath her chin. Moonlight lit the cabin and gleamed off the sleep-rumpled pale blond hair that spilled around her shoulders.

"What is it?" Morgan strode into the room and stood in front of her, his legs splayed against the steady roll of the ship. "Tell me what's wrong."

"R-Rats." Silver pointed toward the corner where a furry gray-brown rodent squeaked beside the chamber pot.

"What?" he asked, incredulous.

"Over there in the corner."

"You're afraid of mice?"

Silver lifted her chin, working to summon her dignity. "It isn't a mouse; it's a rat. I hate rats." But she wouldn't look him in the eye.

"You hate rats," Morgan repeated. He lifted a dark blond brow, and his mouth curved up in amusement. Then he started to laugh. At first just a chuckle, then a full-blown roar.

"Stop it, damn you! It isn't funny!"

Morgan laughed until his insides began to hurt and tears had gathered in his eyes. "You take on a twenty-man crew, kidnap a lieutenant in the Texas Marines, go fist to fist with me—and you're afraid of a mouse?"

He started laughing again, and Silver edged away from him, furious and determined to leave.

"Where do you think you're going?" Morgan's tone turned sharp.

"I'm not staying in here with you or that—that creature."

Morgan laughed again. "You won't have to. Come on." Taking her hand, he led her into his cabin. "I'll be right back."

He hadn't been gone long when he returned with an orange-striped cat whose patchy fur had surely seen better days.

"You're not afraid of cats, too, are you?"

"I love cats," she said indignantly.

Morgan touched the scratch she'd left beside the scar on his cheek. "Figures." He carried the cat across the room to where she stood outside her tiny cabin. "This is Sogger. He'll take care of things for you."

With that Morgan stepped through the opening,

dropped the cat on her berth, and closed the door, leaving the animal inside. In minutes the sound of screeching, scrambling, and fighting filled the room; then there was nothing but silence.

Morgan opened the door, and Sogger ran out with a lump of gray-brown fur in his mouth, the rat's skinny, hairless tail dragging the floor.

"Oh, God," Silver moaned, jumping backward.

Morgan grinned. "You know, Silver, I'm beginning to believe you're not as tough as you'd have us believe."

She pinned him with a hard brown glare. "Don't bet on it." With that she stormed past him into her room and slammed the door. Morgan's hearty laughter rumbled through the walls.

Surprisingly she was able to go back to sleep. It was the pitch and roll of the ship, the creak and moan of the timbers as the boat sailed from the harbor that awoke her. Rubbing the sleep from her eyes, Silver peeked out her tiny porthole. Damn! Dawn had arrived, and the tide was right. They'd already raised anchor and had nearly reached the mouth of the harbor.

Silver raced from her small cabin into Morgan's bigger one but, as she expected, found the door that led outside securely locked. Heart pounding, she flew to the windows above his bed to watch her last chance for freedom slipping away.

If only the windows were bigger. Frustrated, she slammed her fist against the narrow teakwood sill, then cursed at the sharp jolt of pain.

Silver sucked in a breath as an idea struck with another sharp jolt. Individually each small square window in the row above the berth was too small, but if she could break the wooden bars between them, she might be able to slide through.

A quick glance around the room showed there was little she could use to accomplish her task. The three-legged stool would have to do. With the shoreline slipping farther away with each passing moment, Silver grabbed up the stool, returned to the window, and, kneeling atop the berth, crashed the stool through the panes.

Though the sound was loud, the noise of the wind and the sea, the shout of men's voices calling cadence as the sails unfurled, covered her movements. Silver brought the stool down again and again, finally splintering the wood and providing an opening just big enough for her to slide through. There wasn't time to change out of her nightclothes; she just rolled up Jordy's breeches and shirt, tucked them under her arm, and slid through.

Even as slender as she was, the fit was so snug that for one terrible, heart-stopping moment she was certain she would get stuck and Morgan Trask would arrive to find her top wedged outside and her bottom left to his mercy inside the room.

Gratefully she squeezed the last few inches and dropped quietly into the water. It was a long way to shore—farther than she realized—and certainly farther than she'd ever swam before. Still, she knew she could make it—if she left Jordy's clothes behind. Reluctantly she let them sink below the surface and with long, graceful strokes started swimming toward the distant shoreline.

"Good God, Major!" Hamilton Riley gaped wide-eyed toward the shoreline. "Tell me I'm not seeing what I'm seeing."

"Lower a shore boat!" Morgan shouted. "Every man jack of you make haste!" Around him, men scrambled to do his bidding, hauling away with steady, determined hands. In the distance Morgan watched Silver's small pale figure cutting sleekly through the water, leaving hardly a ripple in her wake. Damn her! At every turn she'd tried to outfox him. Well, this time she had outfoxed herself.

Bloody hell! He should have known she'd make one last try—just as he knew without doubt she'd never make it. He might, if the tide wasn't too strong, but she'd be lucky to get halfway. Morgan's stomach tightened. There wasn't a second to spare, and still, he might not get to her in time.

The boat hit the water with a heavy splash. "Ready, Cap'n!"

"Willis, Gordon, Flagg, and Benson—you men, get ready to man the oars." The four men descended the rope ladder and took their places while Morgan climbed down and stepped aboard. "Cast off the lines!" he ordered. As soon as the boat was free, the men rowed for all they were worth. None of them needed to be told they were running a life-and-death race against time.

Ahead of them Silver swam hard toward shore, and Morgan was amazed she'd gotten so far. It would do no good to call out to her, plead with her to swim toward them instead of away.

He knew as surely as he knew death awaited that she would try to escape with her very last breath.

"We're given ye our best, Cap'n," one of the men called out to him.

"You're the only chance she's got, boys," Morgan told them. They began to row in cadence, putting their backs into it, pulling as they'd never pulled before. None wanted to see the young woman die.

None of them—and least of all me. Morgan stood barefoot in the bow of the boat, stripped to the waist, ready to dive for her the moment she went under.

She's still too damned far, he thought, calling her one vile name after another, swearing he'd beat her within an inch of her life this time, and knowing if she survived, he'd be so damned grateful he'd probably kiss her instead.

"She's starting to falter, Cap'n."

"Keep pulling. Get me as close as you can."

Silver took another burning breath and forced her arms through the water one more time. She hadn't counted on the seas being so cold, hadn't really believed the shore was that far away. *I don't want to die*, she thought, forcing one more stroke, one more breath. *I want to live.*

But her leg cramped at the chill she wasn't used to, the terrible exertion she required of her body. The pain came again, harder this time, shooting upward through her stomach. Still, she drove on. *I won't give up, I won't*, she thought, but the ache in her thigh drew the muscles up short, and her arms couldn't seem to hold her head above the water. She caught one last breath and went under, broke the surface to catch another, then went under again.

For a single fleeting instant, she thought someone had called her name but scoffed at the foolish notion. Then again, maybe it was the Lord, for surely this final searing breath would be her last. Silver tried to reach the surface one more time, saw the opaque light above her, but couldn't quite seem to get there. Her lungs felt near to bursting; she could hold her breath no more.

Morgan pushed through the water, using every ounce of muscle, every ounce of strength he could bring to bear. *Come up again, Silver*, he silently pleaded, but no pale head broke the surface. *Don't you dare die, damn you!*

The thought of her slender curves lifeless and floating in the water drove him on, giving him a strength he hadn't known he possessed. *Where the hell are you?* Hoping he had found the spot where he'd seen her go down, Morgan dived deep. Twice he came up empty. On the third try his fingers slid into the long, silky strands of her hair, and Morgan hauled her to the surface, cursing her limp figure even as he thanked God he'd found her.

The shore boat sat there waiting; the men rushed to help him lift her unconscious body aboard. They placed her facedown on one of the gunwales, and Morgan set to work pumping the salt water from her lungs.

"Breathe, damn you!"

For a moment nothing happened, and Morgan cursed her roundly. Then, for the first time since he'd met her, Silver did what she was told. Coughing and sputtering, retching into the bottom of the boat, she took in great gulps of air, and Morgan took a breath of relief.

"Hand me that blanket," he ordered the lanky brown-haired sailor named Flagg, second mate aboard the *Savannah*. From where she now sat on the gunwale, Silver's eyes followed Morgan, who wrapped the warm gray wool around her trembling body.

"It was you, wasn't it?" she said softly.

"If you mean was I the man fool enough to save you, yes. Though God alone knows why I bothered."

Silver stared out across the water. "The water's much colder here."

While the men pulled on the oars, Morgan propped a foot on the seat beside her, his hands splayed at his waist as he bent over her with a glare. "That's all you have to say for yourself, the water's colder here?"

"My leg cramped."

"Bloody hell!" Morgan moved away from her toward the bow of the boat. If she said one more word, he was liable to throttle her. They reached the ship, and the men climbed up the rope ladder and over the rail. Pulling the blanket around her in an effort to cover her nearly transparent nightshirt, Silver started to follow but missed the first rung and stumbled into Morgan.

Cursing, he slung her over his shoulder and climbed the ladder as if she weren't there. He didn't stop until they reached his cabin.

"I believe, Mistress Jones," he said tightly, "you and I have spent quite enough time in the water." He set her on her feet, trying to ignore the curve of her hips and thighs beneath the soggy night rail. "Take those wet clothes off, and put on my robe." He moved away from her toward the door. "You can sleep in here tonight. We'll find something to cover the broken window."

Silver nodded. She'd never felt more weary in her life. "I'm afraid I've lost Jordy's clothes."

Morgan's temper snapped. He stormed across the room, grabbed her arm, and hauled her against him. "You little vixen, you damned near lost your life! When are you going to get it through your head you're going back?"

"Not as long as I've the slightest chance of getting away!"

Clamping his jaw, Morgan dragged her over to the broken window. "If you want to kill yourself, go ahead. This time I won't stop you."

Silver jerked free. "I almost made it. If it hadn't

been so cold . . ." She tried to focus on his face, but the image grew suddenly fuzzy. Swaying on her feet, she rested a hand on his chest for support. *Odd, the way a man's chest feels,* she thought. So hard, yet each stiff strand of his curly dark blond hair seemed to tease the ends of her fingers. The room felt hotter than it should have, and the major's voice seemed somewhere far away.

"Morgan," she whispered, and her knees gave out just as he scooped her into his arms.

Morgan cursed roundly. He should have known this would happen. Sooner or later her recklessness was bound to take its toll.

Crossing the room, he laid her gently on the bed and, with swift, sure movements, stripped away the soggy nightshirt. His hand trembled at the touch of her skin beneath the heavy mass of her hair. He lifted the water-slick strands and spread them across his pillow.

God, she was lovely. Every pale inch sweetly curved and tempting to the strongest-willed man. He had never seen such beautiful breasts, such an incredibly tiny waist. Even though she lay unconscious, Morgan felt his building desire for her, burning hotter than it had for any woman since Charlotte Middleton.

Charlotte. Sweet, sweet Charlotte. Beautiful and innocent, all softness and feminine delight. Gentle and kind—and a liar.

Morgan tugged the sheet over Silver's naked body, his passion for her already beginning to wane. She was just a woman—for all her toughness, for all her bravado. Even now her forehead burned with fever. Already she coughed and thrashed; soon the pneumonia would start to set in. It wasn't uncommon in a near drowning such as this. Yet Silver seemed so

strong, so invincible he hadn't even considered it
could happen to her.

Morgan strode to the door, crossed the salon, and
climbed the ladder to the deck. He'd have Cookie
look after her. He was captain of this vessel and a
major in the Texas Marines. It wasn't his place to
care for some stubborn, headstrong woman—no
matter how young and tender she might be.

But when he reached the galley and crossed the
room to where the tough-skinned gray-haired cook
bent over his steaming pots, Morgan couldn't say the
words. Cookie was older, yes, but he was far from
old. As caring as his friend could be, Grandison
Aimes was a man. The thought of him staring at Silver's naked flesh, of running a damp cloth over her
lovely bare breasts was more than Morgan could
handle.

"She's going to get the pneumonia. Bring me the
things I'll need to tend her—and something to fix the
broken ports above my bed."

The barrel-chested cook looked up from his steaming pots. "You sure you don't want me to do it?"

"She's my responsibility, not yours. I'll take care
of her."

"Aye, Cap'n." Cookie added nothing further, but
Morgan didn't miss the knowing look in his hard old
eyes. There wasn't a sailor aboard who hadn't recognized by now exactly what Silver Jones had to offer a
man—any man strong enough to take it, that is. It
didn't surprise them one little bit that Morgan Trask
would be that man.

Chapter 4

It wasn't the pneumonia after all. Just a case of exhaustion and a lung full of salt water. Her fever had eased before daybreak, to Morgan's vast relief.

He had bathed her hot, dry skin throughout the afternoon and evening, fighting to keep her cool. After her hair had dried, he'd combed out the tangles, admiring the silky texture, so pale against his dark-tanned hand. Even in the dim glow of the lantern beside the bed it gleamed seductively.

Just like her soft ivory skin and her high, round breasts with their dusky rose nipples.

He had weakened his growing desire for her by reminding himself of Charlotte, imagining Silver in bed with her lover, her legs spread wide, her mouth ripe and bruised from another man's kisses. He imagined her lying and cheating as Charlotte had done.

Morgan had found his beloved in a Savannah hotel room, merely by chance, just a few days after their wedding date had been set. Charlotte had come into town to shop for her trousseau. But the merchant's son had proved more entertaining.

That was the day Morgan met Jordy, just a skinny little orphan looking for a handout. Morgan had seen him behind the hotel where he spotted Charlotte's carriage and asked him where the pretty blond lady who rode in it had gone. Jordy innocently told him of the room she and Tom Hadley had rented upstairs.

Certain there was some other explanation, Morgan climbed the stairs and knocked on the door. Tom's voice, husky with passion, ordered him to leave them alone just before Morgan kicked in the door.

It was a wonder he hadn't killed them. He'd wanted to. God, how he'd wanted to. Instead he'd turned and walked away. If he'd thrown one punch, he wouldn't have been able to stop until Tom Hadley lay dead. Charlotte was smart enough not to go after him. He just walked down River Street, sick to his stomach, climbed aboard his ship, and stayed drunk until she set sail six days later. Three days after that Jordy had been discovered hiding in the hold.

Silver stirred on the bed, drawing Morgan's attention. Was she really like Charlotte? It seemed unlikely. Silver Jones wasn't like any woman he'd ever known. What was her secret? he wondered, for surely she had one.

Was Pinkard telling the truth about her lover—or was there something else?

Morgan reached over and brushed wispy silver strands from her cheek. Silver's eyes fluttered open. Her brows and lashes, much darker than her pale blond hair, accented the velvet brown eyes that looked up at him with uncertainty.

"You had a fever," he explained, remembering how she had called him by name just before she fainted. He'd liked the sound of it more than he should have. "We feared it was the pneumonia, but it wasn't."

Silver started to sit up, realized she was naked beneath the thin white cotton sheet, and blushed crimson. It was the first real blush he'd seen, and Morgan found it enchanting.

"Did you—are you the one who took care of me?"

"Was there someone else you would have preferred?"

"No," she said, shaking her head in emphasis, and slid farther beneath the covers.

Morgan chuckled softly. "I'll take that as a compliment."

Silver glanced away, willing the color to drain from her cheeks. It wasn't like her to be thrown so off guard, but then she'd never been in quite this position. "I suppose I should thank you . . . yet knowing I'm once more your prisoner, I find the task most difficult."

"I prefer to consider you a guest," he said, "but under the circumstances I suppose I understand your somewhat reluctant gratitude."

They sat in silence for a while, Morgan trying not to notice the peaks of her breasts, which pushed against the sheet, Silver trying not to remember the feel of her fingers in the tight dark blond curls on his chest.

"Do you love him that much?" Morgan finally asked, breaking the silence.

I hate him that much. "I told you before, I have no lover . . . would it matter if I did?"

"Yesterday I would have said no. Today . . . maybe I'm not so sure."

"What is that supposed to mean?"

"It means if you were a man, I'd admire your courage."

"But I'm a woman, so instead of being brave, I'm just a fool."

Morgan didn't answer.

"Since there's no place left for me to run, would it be all right if I went up on deck a little later? The fresh air would surely do me good."

"Cookie washed and dried the clothes you had on when you came." He pointed toward the chair where they sat neatly folded. "Rest awhile longer; then call me when you're ready, and I'll show you around."

"All right," she said. When Morgan walked to the door and pulled it open, Silver sat up in the bed, the covers drawn up to her chin. "Are you a man of your word, Major Trask?"

Morgan turned to face her. "Yes." The simple word was spoken without arrogance, and Silver believed him.

"Then tell me, did you play the gentleman last night—or breach my somewhat tattered modesty?"

"I prefer my women awake, Miss Jones." Morgan's mouth curved up in amusement. "Though there's hardly an inch of you that hasn't been soothed by my hand." He indicated the basin of water and the damp cloth on the table beside the bed.

The fire returned to her cheeks, then burned down her throat and over her shoulders. "I think I shall see the ship a little later," she said, "when I'm feeling a bit stronger."

Morgan's voice turned gentle. "You've nothing to be ashamed of, Silver. And neither have I. Call me whenever you're ready." With that he walked out the door.

Sitting on the edge of the bed, Silver hugged her arms around her. It wasn't cold in the room, but she felt a bit of a chill. Morgan Trask had seen her naked, had touched her—all over. Yet she believed his words. He had not taken advantage.

Unconsciously her palm skimmed over a breast and down her body. She thought of Morgan's wide hand touching that same flesh, and the heat curled softly in her stomach. How could that be when the thought of a man's touch sickened her?

She recalled her days in the tavern, the way the men had looked at her. Too often one would soundly pat her bottom or try to cup her breast. She'd given them a ringing slap, and a tongue-lashing to boot.

What was it about Morgan Trask that beckoned her to trust him? He was a man, wasn't he? That in itself should make her wary. On top of that, he was a friend of her father's. She knew the kind of people William Hardwick-Jones chose as friends: people he could dominate—or people he could use.

Morgan didn't seem to fit either of those categories, but then she didn't really know him. And there was always the possibility that Trask had something her father wanted. He could be quite charming when he had something to gain.

Dressed once more in her simple brown skirt and clean white peasant blouse, Silver pulled open the cabin door, grateful to find it unlocked. She'd gone only a few feet into the salon when it occurred to her that she'd forgotten to tie back her hair. Forgotten because it was tangle-free, carefully combed, and left to fall loose around her shoulders.

Would Morgan Trask do that? Surely a man as hard and unbending as the major wouldn't play lady's maid to an unconscious woman. Or would he? He was a difficult man to figure, but figure him she must. She had only one chance of escaping Katonga, and Major Trask was it.

Somehow she had to convince him to take her on
to Barbados, to forget his promise to return her, and
instead to set her free. What price was she willing to
pay for it? Was she willing to forfeit the very part of
herself she had worked so hard to protect?

No, she vowed. Her virtue was hers alone to give.
She would fight to keep it just as hard as she fought
to be free of her father. It was the most precious gift
she owned, and she would guard it until she wished
to give it freely.

But she might walk that delicate, teasing line that
made a man think what he would. She hadn't had
much practice, but the instinct was there. If she
played the game carefully, she just might win.

Against her will, the image of Morgan Trask's half-
naked body as he carried her over his shoulder, the
feel of his sinewy muscles moving and flexing beneath her came to mind.

It was a dangerous game she played. Dangerous
and seductive. She prayed to God she would win.

Silver climbed the ladder to the deck. The stiff
wind felt brisk and clean and reviving. The wooden
planks beneath her mud-spattered slippers, now dry
and made as presentable as possible, felt solid and
weathered and somehow encouraging.

The seas were still dark and a bit frothy, but the
last of the storm had passed. It took a moment for
her legs to adjust to the pitch and roll; she steadied
herself against a deck box that held wet-weather
gear. Around her, sailors in duck pants and homespun shirts mended line, or scrubbed the deck, or
hauled away on the great white sails that snapped in
the wind above her head. They glanced at her only
briefly; obviously the major had warned them
against stepping out of line.

Morgan Trask stood near the bow, looking out to sea. He seemed even taller out here among the crew, his shoulders far broader, his legs long and lean. The sun gleamed brightly on his wavy dark blond hair, a pleasant accompaniment to the golden brown color of his skin. When he turned in her direction, she caught his look of concentration and then the flash of a smile.

It took her breath away.

Morgan strode the deck toward her, reaching her side almost too soon. She needed time to steel herself, to calm her rapid heartbeat and restore her mask of control.

"Good morning, Miss Jones."

"Good morning, Major."

"Feeling better?"

The wind whipped strands of her hair. She caught them and shoved them behind an ear. "I'd forgotten what it's like to be at sea."

"Then you like to sail."

"Not in steerage, the way I left Katonga, but on a ship like this one, yes."

Morgan's green eyes turned dark. "You traveled to Georgia belowdecks?"

Silver shrugged her shoulders in a gesture of nonchalance. "I had no choice."

But Morgan's look said he knew exactly what she had suffered traveling that way. Passengers were jammed four or five to a two-berth room; what little food existed was almost inedible; and modesty, even for the most intimate functions, was nearly impossible. Steerage passengers weren't allowed on deck. When the seas grew rough, the smell of vomit had stifled the air until she could barely breathe.

Unconsciously Silver shivered.

"Are you cold?" Morgan stepped closer. "I can get you a coat from below."

"I'm fine. It's really very nice out here." Besides, she'd found a warm black knit shawl on the table in the salon that someone had set out for her. She pulled it closer around her shoulders. "Thank you for the shawl."

"One of the men had purchased it as a gift. He brought it to me this morning for you to use instead."

"Thank him for me, will you?"

"Of course." They walked the deck in silence. When the ship pitched harder than she expected, Silver stumbled against Morgan and his arm went around her protectively.

"I guess I haven't got my sea legs yet."

"You will. You're probably still a little bit weak."

Morgan led her to the wheelhouse, where the young lieutenant she had threatened at gunpoint stood beside a brawny dark-haired sailor Trask called Gordon, who gripped the huge teak wheel with beefy, calloused hands. The lieutenant moved away from the man and walked toward them.

"This is Lieutenant Hamilton Riley," Morgan said by way of introduction, as if they had never set eyes on each other before. A smile of amusement played on finely carved lips she knew could look cruel but now appeared sensuous. "I believe you remember Miss Jones," he said to Riley, whose boyish face turned crimson.

He knew her all right, and he obviously hadn't forgotten what a fool she had made of him.

Silver's chin came up, and she straightened her spine. "How do you do," she greeted him as if this were truly the proper introduction Morgan's words implied.

"Miss Jones." Riley's finger touched his forehead, where his hat might have been if the wind had permitted. He was dressed in the same dark blue uniform he had worn the day before, while Morgan looked casual, and far more attractive, in his snug brown breeches and snowy linen shirt.

Morgan spoke briefly to Riley, then escorted Silver down the ladder in the forecastle that led down to the galley, where Jordy worked beside a short, stout sailor with thick gray hair.

"This is Grandison Aimes," Morgan said. "We call him Cookie. And you know Jordan Little."

"Yes."

"Mornin', ma'am," Cookie said a little gruffly, barely nodding in her direction.

"He's just as tough as he looks," Morgan said, then went on to tell her he had met the weathered little seaman at a noisy cantina in Spain. It seemed he was quite a scrapper, siding with Morgan when the odds were against him.

"We made a good team then," Cookie said a bit wistfully.

"We still do," Morgan agreed, and the older man seemed pleased.

Whistling a sea shantie all three men seemed to find amusing, Cookie turned back to the wooden counter where he worked, picked up a heavy steel meat cleaver, and brought it down on a leg of mutton with a ringing blow. On the big iron stove nearby, a huge black kettle boiled, and steam rolled upward, filling the room with the delicious smell of the small white beans that simmered away.

Jordy's attention swung from Cookie to Silver. "You kin—can—sure swim, Miss Jones," Jordy said, and this time it was Silver who flushed. "I thought for a while there you was—were—gonna make it."

Silver smiled forlornly. "For a while I thought so, too." She felt Morgan's hand on her arm, his grip a little tighter than necessary.

"That'll do, Jordy," he warned. "Let's go back up on deck," he said to Silver, turning her firmly toward the ladder and leaving her no other choice. Silver climbed the stairs, and Morgan followed.

"Jordy's young and easily influenced," he said when they reached the deck. "I hope to hell your behavior doesn't give him any ideas."

Silver bristled. "My behavior, Major, is neither his business nor yours."

"As long as you're aboard this ship, everything you do is my business."

Silver's mouth tightened, but she didn't argue. She had to win the major over, and arguing with him hadn't worked so far. When Morgan released her arm, she moved closer to the rail, using the moments before he joined her to bring her temper under control.

Overhead, the sun came out from behind a cloud, and both sky and sea appeared an azure shade of blue. Sea gulls winged and screeched, and the mast creaked pleasingly, soothing her a little. Silver forced a smile. "Jordy says he's known you five years."

"More or less."

"He thinks a lot of you."

Morgan's stiff posture relaxed a little. He leaned indolently against the rail, looking down at her through eyes as bright as her mother's emerald necklace she had worn once back home.

"Five years ago he stowed away aboard my ship *Sea Gypsy*. He was an eight-year-old orphan with no place to go and nobody who gave a damn one way or the other."

"So you helped raise him?"

"Life aboard ship is hard. Jordy pretty much raised himself."

"He seems like a good boy."

"Jordy's had his problems," Morgan told her, "but I think he's finally growing up."

"Meaning?"

"Meaning that for a while I was worried about him. He got involved with a couple of unsavory characters off the docks in New Orleans. Men in the crew who were setting him some pretty bad examples. He started fighting whenever we were in port, started thieving, picking on people who couldn't defend themselves."

"What happened?"

"We . . . came to an understanding."

This time Silver's smile was genuine. "I believe he may have mentioned that."

Morgan smiled, too. "Sometimes being a captain takes a lot more than sailing a ship."

She liked it when his mouth curved up that way. It softened his features though he would never have the too-handsome face some women found attractive. Her eyes fixed on the dark blond chest hair that curled above the open front of his white linen shirt, and her fingers tingled at the memory of how the stiff strands had felt against her skin.

"Are you the one who is helping him improve his speech?"

Morgan nodded. "About a year ago he came to see me—wanted to talk 'man to man,' he said. He told me he wanted to command his own ship one day. Asked me what he would have to do, and I told him. He's been studying hard, working on his reading and ciphering. He's got a long way to go, but I think he just might make it."

"I hope so."

Morgan looked at her with eyes that missed nothing. Was it so hard to believe she might care about a young boy's future? Morgan cared, for Jordy and the rest of the people around him. Silver envied that caring, she realized, then worked to force the notion away.

Morgan's eyes held hers, and beneath that penetrating gaze, Silver's heart began to pound. "I'm beginning to feel a little tired," she lied. "I'd better go back down to the cabin."

Morgan followed her across the deck and helped her descend the ladder to the salon. "Supper's at seven," he said. "We'll dine with Lieutenant Riley and Wilson Demming, my acting first mate."

"Acting? That means temporary, doesn't it?"

He nodded. "Once we reach Barbados, a big, burly Frenchman named Hypolyte Jacques Bouillard will take over. He's sailed with me for years."

Silver thought of the detour from Katonga she hoped Trask would make and tried to look disappointed. "I'm sorry I won't be able to meet him."

Morgan caught Silver's expression, and his easy manner fled, replaced by a shot of anger he welcomed. He hadn't missed her less than subtle attempt at manipulation. If arguing didn't work, she was set to try sweetness and honey. He thought of her soft, alluring curves, those velvet brown eyes. Sweetness from Silver was the last thing he wanted.

"Maybe I should change course," he said sarcastically, "head for Barbados instead. Then you could meet Jacques, maybe convince him to help you. How would that suit you?"

Silver stiffened, but her smile remained in place. "I was only being polite."

"Polite is not in your vocabulary, Miss Jones."

Go to hell, she thought. "You might be surprised, Major Trask."

"Nothing you could do would surprise me."

Damn him! Could he read her so easily? "Thank you for the tour, Major. I look forward to this evening."

Trask left her alone, and Silver headed for his cabin. Once she closed the door, she slammed her fist against the bulkhead and silently seethed. Damn him to hell! The man was an arrogant, insolent bastard! Handsome, yes, masculine, yes, at times he could even be charming, but he was also dominating and utterly infuriating. She thought of his earlier words, and her temper burned brighter. He hoped she wasn't a bad influence. A bad influence! She had wanted to choke him. Still, she had guarded her temper well, and she hoped Morgan hadn't noticed how close she had come to losing control.

At least now she wouldn't feel guilty. Tonight her plan would go forward, though she couldn't move too fast. Morgan was far too smart to believe she had changed overnight, and she didn't want to rouse his suspicions. Yet there was no time to lose either.

She wished she knew just exactly how to proceed in this game of seduction. Though she'd had the best tutors money could buy, been schooled on everything a proper lady should know, she had rarely had a chance to test her feminine wiles. Her father invited few visitors to Heritage and only occasionally traveled himself.

Once he had taken her to a ball at a friend's plantation on nearby St. Vincent. The young men had seemed interested, and she had actually gotten to dance. She discovered she liked it and was enjoying herself immensely, until she and Michael Browning walked out onto the terrace for a breath of fresh air.

"You are more lovely than all the stars in the heavens, Lady Salena," Michael had said. It was trite, and no doubt well used, but still, they were the first courtly words from a handsome young man that Silver had ever heard.

"Thank you, Michael." A little self-conscious, she tugged at the bodice of her dark green satin ball gown, exactly the color of the emeralds her father had insisted she wear. Though the dress was hardly daring, with Michael's eyes fixed on the portion of her bosom swelling above the neckline, somehow it seemed so.

"Only one thing could make this night more perfect," he whispered.

With that he leaned down to kiss her, and Silver decided to let him. She wanted to know what the mystery was, wanted to know what a man's lips felt like. Michael's arms went around her, pulling her against him. His mouth felt soft and warm; she could smell his musky cologne. Then her father's voice, heavy with outrage, sliced through the damp summer air.

"I should have known better than to trust you. The first time I take you somewhere, and you embarrass me in front of my friends."

In his fury he called her every vile name he could think of, ranting and raving until a terrified Michael Browning was nearly forced to call him out. Thank God he hadn't. William Hardwick-Jones would have killed him.

Instead her father dragged her home in disgrace, setting tongues wagging all over the island and all the way back to Katonga. She had never ventured into society again.

Nor tried her feminine wiles on another man.

Silver sank down on Morgan's wide berth. All of a

sudden she really did feel tired. Tired and uncertain. She thought of the time she had spent at the tavern. At the White Horse Inn she had seen a far different approach to attracting a man. The lusty tavern wenches she had worked with were blatant and bold and shameless, urging their customers to take liberties Silver would never have dreamed of. More than once she'd come upon one of them in a darkened corner of the tavern, skirts hiked up, some man rutting drunkenly between the woman's legs.

If that was what it took to convince Morgan Trask to help her, he could go straight to hell!

Still, there must be something she could do without degrading herself that way. If only she had one of the lovely silk gowns that hung in her carved rosewood armoire back home. At home she had hated to wear them. Here they would heighten her appearance and lull Morgan Trask into seeing her as a woman alone who desperately needed his help—which, in fact, she was.

The evening went smoothly, though far from the way Silver had planned. Both Wilson Demming and Hamilton Riley were pleasant, but Morgan remained reserved. When the meal ended and she asked if one of the gentlemen might escort her up on deck, the major declined, saying he had some work to finish. He asked—no, ordered—Lieutenant Riley to go in his stead, which Riley seemed loath to do.

Silver believed he was worried she might throw him overboard—or at least give it a try.

Instead she smiled at him warmly, asked after his military career, asked after his family, and left him with a far different impression of her from the one he'd had before. Surprisingly she had gained a different impression of him as well. Riley was a dedicated officer and very much a gentleman. He was

kind and considerate—nothing at all like Morgan.
But Riley couldn't help her. Only Trask could do
that.

The next night went no better. Trask assigned the
job of watching over her to Wilson Demming, whose
conversation was as dull as dishwater. He was a
short, nondescript man with thinning brown hair
whose looks matched his personality. Still, she
smiled and feigned interest in his conservative political views, most of which she silently refuted. Eventually they hit on the subject of his travels, and Wilson
surprised her with rousing tales of faraway lands. In
the end they wound up friends, and she was sure
he'd sing her praises to the major.

It wasn't what she had planned, but at least Trask
could see she wasn't quite the hoyden she appeared.

And the days went somewhat better. Whenever she
saw the major on deck, she started a conversation.
As a gentlemen—no matter how questionable that
might be—he was duty-bound to reply with at least
some measure of civility. Once he asked about her
mother. Apparently he had heard rumors of her
death years after it had happened. Silver only confirmed the news, unwilling to discuss her family
more than she had to.

She worked hard to be open and friendly, smiled a
lot—although that wasn't something that came easy
for her—and watched him through her thick dark
lashes in a manner that she hoped might at the very
least stir his interest.

"Did you order this beautiful weather just for me,
Major?" She walked up to where he stood at the rail,
a booted foot propped on a ratline, his shirtsleeves
billowing in the wind. Wavy dark blond hair curled
loosely above his collar.

Morgan clenched his jaw. Where the hell had she

come from? It seemed every time he looked up, Silver Jones was standing there beside him, smiling and looking at him with a pair of warm brown eyes that looked decidedly doelike, her hair hanging loosely around her shoulders and so pale it did indeed look like silver. "If we're lucky," he replied with a sour note, "we'll get fair weather all the way to Katonga."

That wiped her smile away—and good riddance, Morgan thought. If she'd been beautiful before, sullen and angry, shouting and throwing things, she looked incredible when she smiled like that or gazed at him so sweetly.

"Katonga," she repeated, her tone a little flatter than before. "Have you ever been there, Major?"

"No. But I can hardly wait to get there." He was being surly, and he knew it, but he was tired of her not so subtle attempts to manipulate him and even more tired of fighting his attraction to her. Silver Jones was no more docile than she'd ever been, no meeker, no milder, no sweeter. She was just more desperate.

"Well, you haven't much longer to wait," she said.

"Sometime next week, if we don't hit the doldrums, which isn't likely this time of year." When Morgan turned to face her, she was standing so close he could feel the heat of her body through the fabric of her flimsy cotton blouse. He started to speak and had to clear his throat. "When we get there, I'll speak to William, if you like. Maybe he's changed his mind about the man you want to marry. If not, and you're still that determined, I might be able to convince him."

"There is no man, Major. I've tried to tell you that, but you refuse to listen."

"Then why have you run away?"

Silver glanced off in the distance. Her fingers tightened on the tarred hemp stay she held to steady herself. Her breathing seemed a bit more shallow than before. "My father is a very strong man," she said. "He wants to run my life. I, on the other hand, wish to be independent, to live life as I see fit."

She was lying, and he knew it. Silver was good at hiding her emotions—but her eyes gave her away.

"As I said before, I'll speak to him. Maybe it will do some good. Now, if you'll excuse me, I think I'll take a turn at the wheel."

Silver laid a hand on his arm, forcing him to stop. "It was kind of you to offer, Major."

Morgan didn't answer, just turned and walked away. Damnable vixen! The touch of her slim fingers still burned like a poker on his arm. The sun had pinkened her nose and her cheeks, making her look radiant and oh so tempting. If she knew what was good for her, she'd damned well keep her distance. Morgan shook his head. As a seductress she'd obviously had little experience. Still, it was those exact amateurish efforts, her obvious inexperience that made her all the more attractive.

"As God is my witness, William," he muttered beneath his breath, "this bloody well cancels my debt." But he couldn't resist a last glance over his shoulder to where Silver still stood by the rail.

She stared down at the frothy blue water, Morgan's words still ringing in her ears. *Then why have you run away?* He had every right to ask, but she couldn't tell him—not Trask or anyone else. Not now, not ever. *Seduction,* she thought for the hundredth time, *it's the only chance you've got.* But even that effort seemed doomed to fail.

What in the name of Hades am I doing wrong? Silver bit her lip in vexation. She'd been polite when it galled her to do so, been sweet when she wanted to call the wrath of God down on Morgan's head. She thought she'd been at least a trifle seductive. Trask was buying none of it. Still, she knew she had captured his interest. She had worked in a tavern long enough to recognize the heated look in Morgan's eyes whenever she stood too near or "accidentally" bumped against him.

The major was definitely not immune. Unfortunately neither was she.

The more time she spent with him, the more she noticed how handsome he was. She had never seen a finer specimen of a man. Though she was no smaller than most other women, when she stood in Morgan's tall shadow, within inches of his wide, muscular shoulders, she felt tiny. And those eyes! So green they seemed bottomless. And there were tiny crinkles in the corners whenever he smiled, which he hadn't done much lately.

Silver sighed, wondering who was seducing whom. To make matters worse, time was running out. They'd be in Katonga by the end of the week. She had to try harder.

Determined to make her plan succeed, Silver doubled her efforts, spending more and more time on deck, more and more time in his company. She always stood as close to him as she dared, touching him now and again just to heighten his awareness of her. Still, he never made advances and rarely spent more than a few short minutes at her side.

In fact as the days progressed, he seemed to grow more and more distant. She admired his determined role as gentleman, though it heartily pricked her vanity, and it certainly played havoc with her plans. She had to do something, she knew, and she had to do it fast.

By the tenth night out, Silver's frustration had reached its peak. Major Morgan Trask would succumb to her dubious charms—one way or another.

"The meal was delicious," she said that night after supper, gently shoving her heavy white china plate away. "You must tell Cookie how much I've enjoyed the food." She flashed the major a smile. "What I'd like now is—"

"I'd be happy to escort you, Miss Jones." Hamilton Riley shot to his feet, a look of adoration on his face.

"I believe it's my turn." Wilson Demming reached for her hand.

"If the rest of you will excuse me," Morgan said, "I have some work to do." Though his dark look held censure, he said nothing more. Just shoved back his chair and started for his cabin.

"Major Trask?" Silver said sweetly. "I've a matter of some importance I'd like to discuss. Might you spare me a moment?"

Morgan turned, his expression even darker than before. His green eyes settled on the swell of her breast above the low-cut bodice of her blouse, pulled purposely lower than she'd ever dared.

"Of course."

"I'm sorry, Wilson." Silver flashed him a soft, warm smile. "I'll see you tomorrow." She turned to the lieutenant. "Get a good night's sleep, Hamilton."

"Good night, Miss Jones."

"Shall we go?" Morgan said tightly, grabbing her arm a bit more firmly than she would have liked. He helped her climb the ladder to the deck, then pulled her straight to the rail near the bow. None of the men were around. It was silent and dark, except for the moon overhead, lighting a gleaming trail across the water, the creak of the forward mast, and the clatter and clank of the rigging.

"All right, what is it?"

Silver looked up at him. Why was he making this so difficult? "I just wanted you to know how sorry I am for all the trouble I've caused." She stepped a little closer. "I know you're still angry with me, and now that I've had time to think things over, I don't blame you." She linked her arm through his and felt the muscles beneath his shirtsleeve bunch.

"Now you see the error of your ways," he mocked, and Silver wanted to hit him.

Instead she let go of his arm and rested her hands on the rail. She wished she could make them tremble. "Oh, I still hate the thought of going back—in fact, it's imperative I don't return to Katonga—but I understand now that you have your duty to my father to consider. You're doing only what you feel you must."

A muscle twitched in Morgan's cheek. "It's amazing the change of heart you've had of late. No longer the willful vixen, just sweet Salena Jones, hoping to make amends."

"Something like that," Silver said.

Morgan glanced down at the soft round globes of her breasts, exposed above the bodice of her blouse. The fabric was frayed from being washed so often, but it was clean and white—and far too revealing. Worst of all, it was pulled low on purpose. God, he ought to strangle her.

Watching her, Morgan inwardly groaned. One more night of her untutored seductions, and he just might go crazy. Moonlight lit her hair, and her skin looked almost translucent. It was all he could do not to pull her down on the deck and take her right there.

Thank God neither Demming nor Riley had the power to alter the course of the ship—at least not without committing mutiny. He hoped to God she wouldn't go that far.

Then again, he wasn't really so sure.

Chapter 5

"It's getting chilly," Morgan said. "I think it's time we went below."

Silver silently cursed him. The man was as hard to breach as a fortress wall. She smiled up at him softly. "I'm not cold at all," she said. "In fact, I'm feeling a little bit . . . warm." Moving closer, she slid her arms around his neck, tilted her head back, and closed her eyes. This was the way she had been with Michael Browning, just before he kissed her. If her father hadn't interrupted, it would have been a pleasant experience. What harm could there be in giving Morgan one little kiss? Maybe it would cut through his defenses.

Silver waited a moment, enjoying the silky texture of his hair against her fingers and hoping to feel Morgan's mouth over hers. When nothing happened, she opened her eyes.

She almost wished she hadn't.

The major glared down at her, green eyes glittering with something she couldn't quite fathom. He reached behind his neck, grasped her wrists, and pulled her hands away. "Come with me," he said, his jaw tight.

Hesitant but determined to see this through, Silver let him lead her below. What in God's name had she done? Surely he didn't find her that repulsive? Silver stumbled across the deck, trying to keep pace with Morgan's long-legged strides. He tugged her down the ladder and into the salon.

"Excuse us, gentlemen," he said to Riley and Demming, who sat at the polished oak table playing checkers. Flashing them a meaningful glance, he dragged Silver toward his cabin. "We don't want to be disturbed—not unless the ship is going down." With that he opened the door, pulled her inside, and closed it soundly behind him.

"What—what are you doing?"

Morgan tugged his shirt free of the waistband of his breeches and began unfastening the buttons down the fly. "Giving you what you've been asking for all week."

Silver swallowed hard. "I think you must have misunderstood."

Morgan shrugged out of his shirt and tossed it over a carved wooden chair. As he strode to her side, the muscles in his wide chest rippling in the soft yellow glow of the brass reflecting lamps, Silver had trouble dragging her eyes up to his face.

"So I've misunderstood, have I? It seemed when we were on deck that you wanted me to kiss you." Morgan ran a finger along her cheek, quickening the pulse in the hollow of Silver's throat. Sliding an arm around her waist, he drew her closer, until his thighs pressed against her and gooseflesh shivered along her spine. Her heart, already pounding, began to hammer wildly.

"You're an attractive man. . . . I might have considered letting you—"

Morgan's mouth came down over hers, cutting off

her words. Silver gasped at the fiery sensation, the jolt of heat that slid into her stomach. His lips felt warm and full; his skin felt hot beneath the fingers she pressed against his chest.

Morgan's tongue teased the corners of her mouth, and a wave of dizziness washed over her. She could feel his fingers splayed across her back, the movement of muscle in his powerful arms and shoulders. She tasted the brandy he'd been drinking and opened her mouth to his sensual urgings. When Morgan's tongue swept her lips then plunged inside, melting heat unfurled through her body and her knees felt so weak she wasn't sure they would hold her up. God in heaven, it wasn't supposed to be like this!

Silver started to tremble. She was playing a game of fire, and she knew it. But the stakes were too high to run scared now. As long as she didn't let things go too far . . .

Morgan deepened the kiss, and Silver slid her arms around his neck.

This was nothing like Michael Browning—nothing at all!

Morgan broke away from her, and she tried to read his expression. His chest rose and fell, his breathing was nearly as ragged as her own. "Is that what you had in mind, Silver?"

Unconsciously her fingers touched her lips, still warm and tingling from the heat of Morgan's mouth. "I'm—I'm not sure." She was rarely at a loss for words, rarely felt uncertain, but she felt uncertain now.

Morgan's eyes seemed to glitter. She didn't exactly know why.

"On the other hand," he said, "maybe you'd prefer something a little more passionate." He tightened his hold on her waist, crushing her against his solid length. Then he kissed her hard, bruising her mouth, battering her soft pink lips. When she tried to protest, he roughly thrust his tongue between her teeth, and Silver's eyes went wide

She tried to break free, but Morgan's arms constricted, holding her like twin steel bands One hand pressed against her back, while the other slid lower, to cup the cheeks of her bottom and force her even closer. She felt something hard and throbbing, something hot and rigid that left no doubt about what it was

Silver tensed, uncertainty turning to fear. When she tried again to twist free, Morgan shifted his weight, lifted her up, and in an instant she found herself sprawled beneath him on the bed

"Let me go!"

"Is this what you wanted, Silver?" One big hand cupped her breast and he kneaded it mercilessly Using a long sinewy leg to pin both her own, Morgan forced her wrists above her head. One hand hiked up her skirt and petticoats, and his fingers found the waistband of her thin cotton drawers. He released the tie and yanked them down, exposing the soft white skin of her belly.

"Shall I go farther?" he taunted, his palm teasing the smooth flat surface below her navel, threatening to stray lower, to the triangle of downy blond curls that lay just a fraction of an inch below his hand. "Did your father raise a whore as well as a vixen?"

At the hateful taunt in his words, something snapped in Silver's head. An instinct to protect herself born of the life she had led, something so wild, so primitive she felt she might explode with the fury of it.

"Let go of me!" she shrieked. "Get your hands off

me, you bloody bastard. If you don't, I swear I'll kill you!"

Morgan's mouth, little more than a thin, grim line, turned up in a contemptuous half-smile. "Now that's more like it. Sweet Salena replaced by that heartless bitch Silver Jones."

Beneath him Silver writhed and twisted and struggled to break free, but Morgan held her fast. He chuckled mirthlessly. "What's the matter, sweeting? My kisses didn't please you after all?"

"Touch me again and I'll kill you."

"So you have said. Still . . ." His finger moved lazily from her belly button to the edge of her drawers, skimming along her flesh and making it tingle. "It might be worth it."

Silver twisted and arched her back but couldn't break free of his hold. "I hate you!"

Morgan laughed aloud, the sound harsh and grating in the confines of the room. "You know, Silver, I think I like you better this way. At least we both know where we stand."

"You knew, didn't you? You knew what I was doing all along."

"I suppose I might have hoped once or twice I was wrong."

What did he mean by that?

"I'm returning you to Katonga, Silver. Nothing you can do is going to change things." Morgan tugged her drawers back up over her hips and flipped her skirts back down.

Her face flushed scarlet, but she forced herself to look at him. "If I'm a heartless bitch, Morgan Trask, you're a cruelhearted bastard."

Morgan merely grunted. "Some would say we make a perfect pair."

Releasing her wrists, Morgan stood up leisurely.

He didn't bother to hide the thick hard bulge at the front of his breeches, just picked up his shirt and drew it on. He left without a backward glance, slamming the door behind him. It occured to Silver then that Hamilton Riley and Wilson Demming had seen them come into Trask's cabin After the way he'd behaved, they were sure to believe the worst

Damn him to hell! She hated him for what he had done and hated herself even more.

Tears stung her eyes, but she quickly blinked them away. Trask was a man, nothing more It didn't matter what he did; she wouldn't let him defeat her In truth the anger she felt was directed more at herself than at him Trask had merely bested her at the dangerous game she had played Another man might not have stopped when he did. Another man might have done the terrible things . .

Silver shuddered at the painful memory and swung her feet to the side of Trask's wide bed. She felt drained and humiliated yet strangely keyed up Maybe she should be grateful to the major instead of angry, she mused with a trace of bitterness For in truth, in those few brief moments before his kiss had turned cruel, Trask had aroused something in her she hadn't really believed existed

Trask had made her feel passion

After what had happened on Katonga, she wasn't sure she'd be able to feel that kind of emotion Michael Browning had conjured little more than a pleasant stirring. One brush of Morgan's lips had turned her to flame.

Damn him! Why did it have to be a mean-tempered, arrogant rogue like Morgan? A man she clearly loathed The way he treated her was inexcusable. He was a cad of the very worst sort. Then again, what should she have expected? He was a friend of her father's. Obviously they were very much the same.

Dismissing Jeremy Flagg, the lanky, crooked-toothed second mate, Morgan took the wheel. The smooth, weather-worn wood felt good beneath his hands, steady and solid and reliable. A ship was something a man could count on. Something to depend on, even when the seas got rough. Not like a woman. Not at all like that vixen Silver Jones.

He shouldn't have kissed her. At least not the way he had at first. He hadn't meant to when he hauled her down the ladder to his cabin. He'd meant to punish her, teach her a lesson about playing games with a man like him.

Then she'd looked up at him, and he'd seen a spark of something in those big brown eyes. No matter what deceitful games she played, those twin dark pools always spoke the truth. He had read desire in those eyes—not an act, not a game—desire, pure and simple.

And Morgan had to taste it. He just couldn't help himself. Worst of all, the feel of her in his arms, his mouth against hers had been so heady he would never forget it. Lips as delicate as rose petals, skin as soft and smooth as silk. He could still smell her feminine scent where it clung tenaciously to his clothes.

Morgan felt little remorse about the way he had treated her. She was lucky she'd picked on him and not somebody else Any other man would have done more than ruffle her skirts! In truth it had taken a will of iron for Morgan to keep from taking more liberties than he had. If it hadn't been for William, he probably wouldn't have stopped until he'd bedded her.

He couldn't help wondering, if he'd let her continue her game, would she have let him?

Morgan cursed roundly, furious that a willful bit of baggage like Salena could draw him into her net. What would William say if he knew what Morgan was thinking?

Fifteen years ago it had been William Hardwick-Jones's swift intervention that had saved him from Newgate Prison—or worse. Morgan's father, once an adviser to the king, had died when Morgan was twelve, and his mother'd lived only a short while longer. Morton Paxton, his mother's brother, had been forced to take Morgan and Brendan in.

Morgan's teeth clenched at the memory though his rage should have long been spent. Paxton was a meanspirited, tightfisted man who goaded Morgan endlessly. No matter how hard he studied, it wasn't enough. No matter how long he worked, the hours were too few.

Not used to that kind of treatment, Morgan had grown surly and begun to rebel, getting into one scrape after another. The youths he ran with drank too much and brawled at the slightest opportunity. Then one night, while he and his friends were raising hell at the Draught and Garter, the heir to the marquess of Devon insulted the tavern wench Morgan was wooing, and Morgan called him out.

In a saber duel the following morning, fifteen-year-old Morgan Trask killed the Viscount Halsey.

The only man Morgan could think to turn to was William Hardwick-Jones, an old friend of his father's Morgan had always admired and respected. A man he prayed would help him. William didn't hesitate. He made arrangements for Morgan and Brendan to leave England on the next ship out of Liverpool and gave them money enough to start a new life in America.

Morgan Trask owed the earl of Kent and was duty-bound to repay him.

One way or another Salena was going home.

The quiet routine Silver had been used to changed dramatically after her encounter with Morgan. Both Lieutenant Riley and Wilson Demming avoided her; they were congenial and polite—and sure she was the major's woman. Silver found the notion infuriating, but she wasn't about to admit it. Let them think what they would. Once they reached Katonga, she would never see any of them again.

Morgan avoided her even more—and that was fine with Silver. Oh, he was polite enough, almost too polite. Every time he opened his mouth with a cordial hello, Silver wanted to slap him. Because every time she looked at those beautifully carved, oh so sensuous lips, she remembered the feel of them moving over hers. She could still recall the silky warmth of his tongue, the masculine, brandy-tinged flavor of his breath.

The memory seemed burned into her brain. Yet she was sure that to Morgan their encounter had been only another means of proving his authority. From what Jordy said, he had women in every port. A kiss to him meant nothing.

Unconsciously Silver clenched her fists. Sitting on a deck box, the noon sun bright overhead, she glanced out across the water, almost too lost in thought to notice the buzz of flying fish that leaped in the air beside the ship. A school of them must be running nearby, she thought, just as one of them landed with a dull thud upon the deck.

The poor scaled creature looked so helpless lying

there at her feet, gasping for air. She didn't relish the idea of picking the slippery thing up, but she couldn't stand to see it suffer.

It was a feline growl, not far away, that moved her to action. Silver scooped the poor fish up by its sheer, wiry fin, raced to the rail, and tossed it over just as Sogger bolted up the aft ladder at a dead run.

"Sorry, my friend," she said with a sympathetic smile, "you'll have to stick to rats a bit longer." She almost felt guilty. Everyone enjoyed a tasty fish dinner once in a while; why shouldn't Sogger? She reached out to pet his mangy orange-striped fur and scratched behind a mashed and torn ear, probably the result of some battle he had fought. Sogger purred contentedly.

"At least *you* haven't abandoned me," she said, then noticed the shiny brown boots that appeared in her line of vision. Her eyes followed them up to a pair of long lean legs. She lifted her gaze to his face.

"And you think I have?"

Silver's face flushed crimson though she tried to will it not to. "Actually, I'm grateful, Major. The less I see of you, the better I like it."

Trask didn't answer. Backlit by the bright Caribbean sun, he looked taller than ever. She had never seen a man with shoulders so wide or a waist so narrow. With his feet splayed against the roll of the ship, the muscles in his thighs strained against his tight-fitting breeches. So did the hefty weight of his sex.

"Then you should be happy to know," he said, "that day after tomorrow we reach Katonga. You'll be rid of me for good."

"There's always something to be thankful for."

"Yes . . ." Trask started to leave, then turned back. "There is one thing I'd like to know."

Silver eyed him warily. "What's that?"

"What happened in my cabin . . . I've been wondering about that kiss . . ."

Silver tensed. She should have known the rogue would never play the gentleman and let the incident pass. Then another thought occurred: At least the major had been thinking about it, too. "What about it?"

"In the beginning . . . were you pretending, or is it possible you enjoyed it, maybe just a little?"

Damn him! And damn his boundless arrogance! "As you so clearly pointed out, Major Trask, I'm a heartless bitch. Of course, I was pretending."

"Of course," he said coldly. "Enjoy what little you have left of the voyage." He turned and walked away.

Silver watched his retreating tall figure and wondered why the thought of never seeing him again cast a dim haze over her day. She didn't care about him; why should she? He certainly didn't care about her. *It's just because you're going back*, she assured herself, the awful knowledge that she had only two more days of freedom—such as it was.

"Afternoon, Miss Jones." Jordy sauntered up beside her, his eyes shyly cast down.

"Hello, Jordy."

"Pretty day, ain't it?"

"Isn't it," she corrected.

"Isn't it."

Silver released a weary sigh and glanced out to sea. "I suppose so."

"You're feeling bad 'cause you gotta go back home, ain't—aren't you?"

"Yes, Jordy, I am."

For a moment he looked uncertain. "Seems to me you oughta be glad you got one—a home, I mean.

Cap'n Trask says your daddy's an earl. That means you're rich. You probably live in some fancy mansion, like the cap'n."

So Trask had money. No wonder her father called him friend. "A house doesn't make a home, Jordy, no matter how fancy it is. You've got more people on board this ship who care about you than I've ever had."

Jordy chewed on that for a while. "Your father's payin' a heap of gold to get you back. That must mean he cares."

Silver felt an unwelcome burning behind her eyes. *If only that were so.* "You wouldn't understand, Jordy. Cookie and the major, they watch out for you because they want to see you happy."

"I'm almost grown up," Jordy said, setting his jaw in a way she hadn't seen. "They won't be around to look out for me much longer. I gotta find a way to take care a myself."

Silver reached for his hand. "I know exactly what you mean." She felt the calluses in his palm. Then he drew away.

"A woman shouldn't have to take care of herself," he said, looking suddenly older. "Maybe if you had someone to watch after you, you wouldn't have to go 'round acting like a man."

"Belay that, sailor," Jeremy Flagg said, interrupting them, for which Silver was grateful. "Cookie needs your help in the galley."

"Aye, Mr. Flagg." With a last glance at Silver, he turned and walked away.

"Sorry about that, ma'am. Jordy don't mean no harm; he's just young, is all."

Silver just nodded. "Thank you, Mr. Flagg." She forced a smile she didn't feel. "I believe I'll go below."

She did for a while, spent some time reading, trying in vain to occupy her thoughts. When all her efforts failed and the cabin grew warm with the afternoon sun, she returned to the deck.

She hadn't been there long when the lookout spotted a ship off the starboard bow. She was a sleek white schooner about the same size as the *Savannah*. The winds had died down, and the seas were calm, barely moving the two ships through the water. Apparently it was someone Trask knew because when the *Rival* drew near, both ships lowered their sails and hove to alongside each other.

Silver watched the sailors aboard each ship swing long metal grappling hooks over the rails, drop woven hemp bumpers, then begin to pull the two boats side by side. It seemed the major intended to board the *Rival*.

Silver enjoyed the ship's sleek lines, watched the men aboard her scurrying to do their captain's bidding. She was a neat, well-kept ship much like the *Savannah*. Only she was headed in the opposite direction.

Silver's heart leaped hard inside her chest. The *Rival* was sailing west, back toward America. If she could find some way to board her, stow away without anyone knowing, she might be saved yet.

"You even think about trying to go aboard," Trask warned, walking up beside her, "and I'll lock you in my cabin until she's gone."

Silver subdued a guilty flush "I'm not a fool, Major Trask. It's obvious you would spot me the moment I stepped over the rail."

"There's always the water," he said sarcastically.

"Maybe if it were dark, but I doubt I could make it in broad daylight."

Trask eyed her warily. "You'll do well to remember that. I'm not in the mood for a swim."

He strode away, and Silver released a sigh of resignation. Even if she got around to the opposite side without being spotted, she probably couldn't find a way to climb aboard. As Silver stood watching, Morgan stepped over the starboard rail and briskly climbed the last few steps of the stiff rope ladder that hung from the side of the *Rival*. Apparently carrying less cargo than the heavily laden *Savannah*, the other ship rode higher in the water.

Damn, if there were only some way to sneak aboard! Silver glanced to the rail. Both Demming and Riley stood beside it, standing guard, it seemed. A pelican screeched overhead, and Silver looked up. The tall twin masts of the *Savannah* swayed gently back and forth. A few feet away, the *Rival*'s masts also dipped and swayed, occasionally brushing near those of the other ship.

Silver's eyes went wide with a sudden shot of hope. Maybe there was a way! With only a moment's hesitation she turned and raced below. In her tiny steward's cabin she found Jordy's threadbare breeches and shirt—the first ones he had lent her—washed, dried, and ready to wear again, and she quickly put them on. In Trask's quarters she rummaged through a trunk and found a small-billed seaman's cap and stuffed her long hair up under it and out of the way. She belted her shirt around the waist with a piece of line, then glanced at herself in the broken mirror. She could barely see her face beneath the brim of the cap, and though she couldn't view the rest of her clothing, she figured as busy as the crewmen were she could probably pass among them without being noticed.

Once on deck, Silver skirted the starboard rail,

where Demming and Riley stood watch, and headed larboard instead. The horizontal rope rungs of the tarred hemp ratline would carry her aloft to the forward yardarm, the huge crossbeam that projected out past the sides of the ship. Other sailors worked below and elsewhere in the rigging, so as she started climbing, no one paid her any notice.

Thank God the breeze was light, she thought as she climbed farther and farther aloft. She hated high places almost as much as she hated rats. In a stiff wind the dip and sway, more pronounced with each nervous step upward, would be enough to terrify even the stoutest heart.

Though Silver took her time and moved cautiously, one bare foot slipped out of the rungs, and only her death grip on the stays kept her from falling. The stiff tarred hemp bit into her tender skin, and the roll of the ship made her dizzy.

Don't look down, she told herself firmly, forcing one slender foot in front of the other, ignoring the vessel below, which had begun to look more like a toy ship in a bottle than the 145-foot schooner it was. On board the *Rival* nothing seemed amiss. Sailors worked picking oakum, scrubbing the decks, or mending sail. Then she saw Morgan Trask emerging from belowdecks, a stout man's arm across his shoulders.

Keep him talking, she silently prayed, finally reaching the massive spruce foremast just below the topsail. Above her, the widely protruding yardarm swayed with the roll of the ship, and the rigging clanked in the freshening breeze. Silver wrapped both legs around the heavy beam, locked her arms as well, and began to shimmy carefully toward the end that yawned over the water. It seemed hours before she reached the midway point, though in truth it took only minutes.

With no time to spare, she took a deep, steadying breath and continued, inch by inch, to move along. Near the end of the yardarm she waited. The *Rival*'s foremast reached into the sky almost parallel with the *Savannah*'s, though it rose just a wee bit higher. The yardarm angled a foot or so off to her right. When the sea rolled beneath them, the yardarm dipped and leaned and came within inches of Silver's grasp.

She didn't reach for it.

Her hands were slick with perspiration, and her body had begun to tremble. If she missed, certain death awaited sixty feet below. Silver wiped her hands on Jordy's canvas breeches, closed her eyes, and took a last deep breath. She opened them to see Morgan Trask climbing back aboard the *Savannah*, the grappling lines being cast off It was now or never.

"Where's Silver?" Morgan asked Riley the moment he reached the deck of the *Savannah*.

"She went below," Riley said

"Cap'n Trask!" Jordy raced toward him, his hazel eyes wide with fear. "It's Miss Jones!" When he reached Morgan's side, he shaded his vision from the sun and pointed up into the rigging. "I think she's up there, trying to cross over to the other ship."

As he looked up at the tiny figure clinging tenaciously to the yardarm, Morgan's stomach clenched so hard he felt as though someone had kicked him. There wasn't a doubt in his mind it was Silver.

"I saw this fella up in the rigging," Jordy was saying. "There was somethin' funny about the way he moved."

"Good God," Hamilton Riley said, following their upward glance, "what should we do?"

"You gotta get her down, Cap'n," Jordy pleaded.

"There isn't time," Morgan said. And there wasn't. Calling out to her would only distract her, adding to her peril. There was nothing Morgan could do but stand by helplessly and watch. His chest felt leaden, and his stomach balled even tighter. The next few seconds would determine whether Silver Jones lived or died.

Now or never, she repeated. When the yardarm swayed again, tilting just within her reach, Silver set her jaw and reached for it, praying her grip would hold. She felt the sturdy wooden bar beneath her fingers, tightened her grip, and pulled herself over, letting the roll of the ship carry her across the gap between the two vessels.

Heart pounding so hard she could hear it, she locked her legs around the yardarm and held on for all she was worth. The ship rolled to starboard, and Silver's grasp held. *I made it! God in heaven, I made it!*

Fighting to slow her heartbeat, shaking all over, Silver inched along the yardarm. There were only seconds to spare before the crew of the *Rival* would be climbing into the rigging to unfurl the sails and speed their departure. She needed to descend the ratline and blend in unnoticed. Then she'd find someplace to hide.

She could hardly believe she'd made it this far. *Please God*, she prayed, *you've got to set me free.*

Chapter 6

Morgan didn't realize he'd been holding his breath until he released a sigh of relief. Silver was still in danger, but the crucial moment had passed. Besides, he silently swore, if she didn't fall and break her neck, he was going to strangle her himself!

"Signal the *Rival* to come about and heave to," Morgan commanded. "Then lower a shore boat."

"Aye, Cap'n." Wilson Demming turned to one of the crew, gave the order, and waited as colored flags were unfurled and the signal flashed across the water.

By now every man on the ship had his eyes fastened on the tiny figure descending the ratline of the rapidly departing *Rival*. There wasn't a sailor aboard who hadn't heard by now who it was and exactly how she got there. And there wasn't one who didn't admire her courage, even if he figured she must be at least half crazy.

"Get Benson and Gordon on the oars," Morgan said to Jeremy Flagg, striding toward the starboard rail as the shore boat descended and splashed into the sea. He climbed the rail along with the others, descended the rope ladder, and they set off in the shore boat to bridge the distance between the two ships. By the time Morgan reached the *Rival*, he was in such a blinding rage he could barely speak.

"What's the problem?" Call McWhorter asked as Morgan climbed over the rail. The big sea captain stood a little shorter than Trask, with a stocky build and curly brown hair. He was keen-eyed and jovial, a man well liked among his men. Morgan had known him for years. There wasn't a finer man to sail the seas.

"You've got something of mine," Morgan said, though he could barely grind out the words with his jaw clamped tight.

"How's that?"

"She climbed across the yardarm."

"She?" he repeated, incredulous.

Morgan just grunted.

"Where is she?" Call pressed.

"Got to be here someplace, probably down in the hold." *And I hope the damned thing's full of rats!* he added to himself.

"I'll have my men comb the ship."

In minutes a surprisingly docile Salena was escorted up on deck by three brawny sailors. Morgan recognized her bitter expression as one of resignation. She stopped dead in her tracks when she spotted him standing next to the captain.

"How did you—what have I done to make you hate me so much?"

"What have you done?" he repeated. "What haven't you done?"

Silver turned to McWhorter, her big brown eyes huge and pleading. "Captain, I beg of you. This man has kidnapped me. He is holding me against my will. I beseech you to help me."

McWhorter chuckled, a heavy rumble in his chest. His eyes roamed over Silver's snug-fitting breeches, moved to the piece of frayed line that marked her tiny waist, then upward to the swell of her breast, barely concealed by the looseness of the tattered homespun shirt.

"I might believe you, gal, if it were any man but this one. He likes his ladies sweet and gentle. You're hardly his cup o' tea." He chuckled again. "Course, that ripe little body o' yours'd suit just about any man well enough."

"I'm returning her to her father," Morgan explained. "As soon as we reach Katonga, I'll be rid of the willful little baggage once and for all." He grabbed Silver's arm and jerked her so hard her hat flew off. Wild pale blond hair tumbled loose around her shoulders, and the captain's brow shot up.

"Don't say it," Morgan warned, knowing his friend was about to suggest he broaden his appetites in this young woman's case. "Besides, you don't know her like I do. It wouldn't be worth the trouble."

This time the captain laughed heartily. "Don't know as I'd agree with you on that, my friend. But I wish you the best o' luck."

Morgan tugged Silver toward the shore boat, helped her descend the rope ladder and settle herself aboard. All the way back to the ship, his fury mounted. One problem after another, all because of a stubborn young woman bent on self-destruction. No ploy was too deceitful, no means of escape too dangerous. She had little regard for the trouble she caused and even less regard for herself.

By the time he dragged her down to his cabin,

trying to ignore the whispered remarks of the sailors who looked at her with awe along the way, he was so angry he felt he might explode.

Silver said nothing. Just crossed the room and sank down on the edge of his bed. She didn't even look at him.

Morgan's temper grew hotter. "How many times do I have to say this before you understand? You, Salena, are going home."

Silver just stared straight ahead as if he hadn't spoken.

"There is nothing you can do to avoid it, nothing you can say, no one you can dupe into helping you."

She didn't even blink.

"You are without a doubt the most stubborn, the most willful, the most hotheaded, craziest damned female I have ever had the misfortune to meet." When Silver seemed unmoved, Morgan grabbed her shoulders and hauled her to her feet. "You little idiot! Don't you understand, you could have been killed?"

Silver's face flushed crimson. If she'd been wallowing in the depths of despair, now she erupted in white-hot fury. "I understand exactly the risk I took, Major. I know very well I could have been killed. What you don't understand is that I'd rather be dead than go back there!"

"Of all the bloody—"

"You don't know what it's like there. You couldn't even imagine." Tears of anger and frustration stung her eyes. "You don't know what it's like to be treated that way. You don't know—and you'll never have to find out!" She slammed her fists against his chest, first one and then the other. "I hate you for what you're doing. I hate you!" Morgan caught her wrists,

but she tore herself free and started hitting him
again.

"I hate you!" she shouted. "I hate you!" She was
crying now in earnest, hot salty tears that soaked her
cheeks and dripped onto the front of her borrowed
shirt. Again and again she hit him, though her blows
were ineffective, little more than a measure of her
despair.

Morgan didn't try to stop her. There was something so sad in her expression, something so defeated he just let her vent her fury until she sagged,
spent and exhausted, into his arms.

"Please don't make me go back there," she
pleaded. Her fingers clutched the front of his shirt;
her face pressed into his chest. "Please." Her body
shook with the force of her tears, huge, deep sobs
that tore at Morgan's heart. He slipped an arm beneath her knees and carried her over to the bed, setting her in his lap and cradling her against him like a
child.

She cried until his shirt was soaked clear through,
and still she didn't stop. What had brought her to
this? Morgan wondered. What had caused her so
much pain?

Finally her tears began to slow, and she started to
hiccup softly. Morgan pulled a handkerchief from
the pocket of his breeches. "Here. Blow your nose."

For once she didn't argue.

"Why don't you tell me the truth?" he gently prodded. "Maybe I could help you."

If only I could, she thought. It was her only hope
now, and still she couldn't say the words, she
couldn't stand the thought of facing him, once he
knew the truth. She felt so tired all of a sudden, so
bone-achingly weary. Morgan seemed to sense it.

Lifting her off his lap, he settled her onto his berth, then pulled the quilt up under her chin.

"Whenever you're ready to talk, I'm ready to listen," he said.

When he turned to leave, she found herself clinging to his hand. Reluctantly she let it go. Morgan watched her for a moment from the doorway, an uncertain expression on his face. Then he stepped outside and closed the door, leaving her alone.

Alone and in turmoil.

How could she have lost control so completely? It was the tension, she knew, the fear, the life-and-death moment when she had clung to the yardarm suspended above the deck. It was the hope of being set free and then seeing those last hopes dashed.

It was Morgan Trask himself.

Just being near him seemed to stir her to frenzy. She had fought with him again, though they both knew her heart wasn't in it. Still, he could have lashed out at her, could have beaten her if he had wanted, and no one would have said a word. Instead he had held her and comforted her as no one had since her mother died. It had only made her feel worse.

For the first time in years, Silver thought about her mother. Mary Hardwick-Jones had died giving birth to Silver's sister, Elizabeth. Silver had only been five years old, and now she could barely remember her. Bethy's memory had stayed with her always. She was the sweetest, kindest, gentlest little girl Silver had ever known.

Nothing like herself. Not willful, not stubborn, not headstrong. They didn't even look alike, Bethy with her light brown hair and big blue eyes. She was even fairer than Silver, fair to the point of being frail.

How her father had loved Bethy. And so had Silver. Bethy was so sweet and pure and trusting. Silver had done her best to protect her. But in the end she had failed. Silver had been ten, Bethy only five when yellow fever struck the island.

The death toll rose highest in the slave quarters, where the conditions were overcrowded and medical attention was spare. Bethy and Silver both came down with it. But Silver had survived, and Bethy hadn't. Her father never forgave her for being the one to live.

It seemed he meant to punish her forever.

Morgan stood alone at the wheel, surrounded by the darkness, the water, and his still-turbulent emotions. Above him the sky blazed with stars, brighter since there was little moon to dim them. Salena had avoided him since their confrontation in his cabin, and tomorrow they would reach Katonga. He'd be rid of her once and for all. His life could return to normal; the peaceful voyage he'd imagined would be a reality at last.

Something sleek and shiny broke the surface of the water. Whatever it was, it was big. Probably a dolphin or a shark. Morgan watched it till it disappeared from sight.

"Good evening, Major." The sound of her voice, so soft and clear, stirred him from his reverie.

"Hello, Silver."

"I came to thank you . . . for what you did the other day."

"Bringing you back from the *Rival*?" He was teasing, but Silver seemed unwilling to take the bait.

"You were kind. It's been a long time since anyone has shown me kindness."

Morgan tried to see her eyes, but they were shadowed in the darkness. "Am I to believe that William has treated you badly?"

Silver glanced out across the water. "How long has it been since you've seen him?"

"Fifteen years."

"A man can change a great deal in fifteen years."

"Some men."

"But not my father," she said flatly, reading his unspoken words.

Morgan didn't answer. There was always that possibility, though he found it difficult to believe. A man like the earl was a man you could rely on, a man you could trust with your life. The years rarely changed a man like that.

"What is it you're running from?" Morgan finally asked when Silver didn't go on.

Say it, she thought. *This is your chance.* What did it matter what Morgan Trask thought of her? Protecting herself was more important. She opened her mouth to speak, but the words would not come forth.

"Tell me," Morgan gently urged.

Silver cleared her throat, determined to try again. *Say it,* she commanded, but found that she could not. "My father is . . . a hard man," she said instead, knowing it was not enough. "He can be cruel, even sadistic. If I go back there, he'll never let me leave again."

"That's ridiculous. Every man wants to see his daughter happy. William just wants what's best for you. Someday you'll meet some nice young man, marry, and have children. If that means leaving—"

"You're wrong, Major. You don't know him anymore. His punishments are often . . . severe. My father intends to keep me with him. If things were different, maybe that wouldn't be so bad, but as it is . . ." Silver felt a tightness in her throat. Her father's face rose before her. His hateful expression, the burning sting of his palm against her cheek, once, twice, the taste of blood in her mouth, the ache in her ribs as she sprawled in defeat on the floor. She thought of the welts on her flesh he had left with his razor strop—

"Excuse me," she whispered, "I'm feeling a little bit chilly. I shouldn't have come out without my shawl."

"Silver—"

"Good evening, Major."

She left before he could stop her. As he had never been able to do anyway. Could he be that wrong about William? He doubted it. More than likely Salena was up to her same old tricks. She wanted her way, and she'd do or say anything to get it. With Silver back home, William would certainly have his hands full.

At least Morgan's debt would be paid—and high time at that.

Morgan searched the rise and fall of the sea, scanning the water for the huge gray fish he'd been watching before Silver arrived. She'd looked beautiful tonight, as always, even in her tattered tavern clothes. He could still see her face in the moonlight, the big brown eyes and clear complexion, the tiny cleft that dimpled her chin.

He had hoped that tonight would be different, that she would finally open up to him. But she had said little more than she had before. He fought down the memory of her haunted expression, the pallor of her skin when she'd spoken of her father, and ignored the unwelcome doubt that kept creeping into his mind.

It would all work out, he assured himself. He

would speak to William on the morrow, satisfy himself once and for all.

Tomorrow he'd make sure that the lie he'd seen in Silver's eyes wasn't a glimpse of the truth.

Chapter 7

"Beautiful, isn't it?" Silver stood at the rail, the wind whipping strands of her wild pale hair. Off to her right, Katonga lay like a bright green jewel atop the turquoise Caribbean Sea.

"It's lovely." Morgan stood beside her, tall and a little forbidding. She could feel his powerful presence almost as if he touched her, though he stood a few feet away. Today he wore his uniform, carefully pressed, gold epaulets marking the broad width of his shoulders.

"Looks can be deceiving," she said, and Morgan arched a dark blond brow. He looked as handsome as always; the scar on his cheek now seemed such a part of him she hardly noticed. "For instance, see that water to the right of the channel?" She pointed a little right of starboard. "There's a reef there on a rocky ledge that surrounds the southeast side of the island. On a day like today, when the sea is flat, it doesn't even break the water. Most know of it, but it's said that a pirate who once owned the island used to hang lanterns on the point to lure the unwary. Their ships breached on the reef. The pirate killed the survivors and stole their cargo."

"Yes," Morgan said, "the practice is not unheard of."

She smiled but it didn't reach her eyes. "Then you can see, Major, a place that seems beautiful can sometimes be deadly."

Morgan didn't answer, just looked at her as if he were trying to read her thoughts.

The ship moved farther along the channel, well marked by buoys. Other reefs, easier to spot, could be seen near the opposite end of the island. Black sand beaches, remnants of Katonga's volcanic beginnings, marked the shore, though today the island was relatively level and no more than four hundred feet at its peak. Palm trees swayed invitingly in the gentle afternoon breeze.

"Arrowroot and bananas are the island's major source of income," Silver said. "Heritage also grows coffee and tobacco."

"William was always industrious, but I was surprised when I learned he intended to join the planter society."

"Apparently he had some sort of rift with my grandfather. He never returned to England, even after Mother was gone and my grandfather died. I don't think his estates there were worth much anyway."

"Katonga certainly seems to be." Morgan's bright green eyes were fixed on the shore. On a gently sloping hill, the great plantation house watched the harbor like a sentinel, its stately white columns and wide, windswept galleries in contrast with the lush green landscape. Numerous outbuildings surrounded the main house, and tiny workers' cabins dotted the open area behind.

"My father has been very successful, which should come as no surprise to you, Major. He's the kind of man who lets nothing stand in his way."

Morgan flicked her a glance and changed the subject. "We're approaching our anchorage. If you'll excuse me . . ." Turning, he headed toward the wheelhouse, where Wilson Demming stood ready to convey his orders to the crew.

Since the mainsail, the staysail, and the inner and outer jibs had already been furled, Morgan ordered the foresail lowered. The men hurried to do his bidding, pulling in the great white sheets of canvas in rhythm to a seaman's ditty.

"Away the aft hook," he commanded as they neared their final resting place in the quiet waters of the harbor. "Furl the tops'l. Make fast the aft rode."

The ship creaked with the sound of the aft anchor growing taut, men and equipment working together in an age-old partnership that had served them well through countless voyages.

"Drop the fore anchor, and haul away on the aft rode until she's fast." In seconds the ship reached a shuddering halt, the gentle lap of sea against hull the only sound. The men relaxed a bit at the feeling of calm and the knowledge that for now they had reached their destination.

With a building feeling of dread, Silver watched from the quarterdeck as Morgan ordered the shore boat lowered and his second mate and another sailor descended the rope ladder to man the oars.

Both Hamilton Riley and Wilson Demming made their way to her side, each clasping her hand in a farewell reminiscent of their earlier friendly attitude toward her. Apparently Major Trask had set them straight about the nature of his relationship with her, for which she was grateful.

If only one of them would help her.

She knew they would not.

Watching from a distance, Jordy hung back, waiting until she walked the few steps between them and extended her hand. "I'm glad to have met you, Jordy. I know if you keep trying as hard as you have been, you'll captain your own ship one day, just as you wish."

Jordy accepted her handshake. "You'll be all right, won't you? I mean no one's gonna hurt you or nothin'?"

"Anything," she corrected, and Jordy grinned. "I'll be all right." She wished she believed it.

"You're not so bad, Miss Jones. Don't let 'em tell you no—any—different neither."

Impulsively Silver hugged him. "Thank you, Jordy." With a last wan smile, she turned and walked away. She'd gone only a few feet when Sogger bounded up the ladder from below with an ear-splitting yowl. His orange-striped fur looked as patchy as ever, but his belly bulged pleasantly. He purred his contentment the moment Silver knelt to pet him.

"I'm going to miss you." She scratched his mashed right ear. "I used to have a cat who looked a little like you on Katonga, but Father said he brought fleas into the house."

Sogger rubbed himself between her legs. Silver ran her hand along his furry back one last time.

"Ready?" Morgan gently prodded. He'd been watching her in silence from the rail.

Silver only nodded. Her face looked as pale as it had the night before. He tried not to notice the rise and fall of her breast above the neckline of her tattered white blouse, the span of her tiny waist. He tried not to remember the softness of her lips when he had kissed her, the slender curves that lay beneath her skirt. Her eyes, always so dark and fathomless, were fixed on the huge white house on the hill. When he took her hand to help her over the rail, he noticed that it trembled.

"William may be difficult, Salena, but I'm sure he'll see reason. I—"

"My name is Silver," she said with a haughty little lift of her chin. "And you needn't be concerned. I'll look after myself, as I always have."

Morgan set his jaw. If that was the way she wanted it, so be it. He was just damned glad to be rid of her.

The small boat sliced through the water in a silence that wasn't interrupted until they reached the shore. Clusters of black people gathered at the edge of the banana groves to watch them. The women wore plain striped linsey shifts, mostly faded into some drab color, and the men wore loose black trousers of osnaburg cloth beneath loose-fitting homespun shirts. Several pointed at Silver, whose pale hair glistened in the sunlight, leaving no doubt about who she was.

"You men stay here," Morgan instructed Flagg and Gordon, the men who had manned the oars. "I'll be back within the hour."

He wished he had more time, but there was the matter of cotton for guns, concern for his brother, and the British who awaited his arrival in Barbados. Maybe he could stop on his return trip. It would be days out of his way, but damn it, he and William had once been friends. And he could make certain that Silver was all right. In the distance a wagon rolled toward them, stirring up dust on the crushed lava road that led down from the big white plantation house.

"Looks like someone saw us coming," Morgan

said. Silver just walked along the path with her head held high, looking neither right nor left.

Finally one of the women broke away from the others in the field where she'd been doling water from a big pottery jug and walked up to her. "We t'ought you was gone fo' good, Miz Silver," she said in that deep, resonant tone of the Caribbean.

Silver turned toward the short, flat-featured woman who looked no more than twenty. A small curly-headed black boy with gentle brown eyes clung to her leg, and a baby nestled at her plump milk-ripe breast.

"So did I, Tomora."

"Miz Delia, she miss you from de moment you gone, but Quako say he know you be hoppy."

"Are they all right?"

"Dey fine . . . dis your mon?"

Silver flushed and shook her head. "He's a friend of Father's."

Tomora's warm look faded. "I go now. I tell Miz Delia and Quako you bock home." Taking the small boy's hand, she tugged him toward the banana grove waving broad flat leaves in the distance. Workers toiled with rakes and hoes, and two-wheeled carts followed along the narrow dirt paths between the fields.

"A friend of yours?" Morgan asked.

"One of my father's slaves," she answered with a hint of bitterness.

"Surely, as a British subject, he freed them in '33 with the abolition?"

"Katonga is not a British possession. My father is ruler here." With that she swept up her tattered brown skirt and moved off toward the wagon rolling to a halt just a few feet away."

"Dey seen de ship come into de harbor," said the

slender black youth atop the driver seat. "Massa Knowles send me down. He be surprised to see you, Miz Silver."

"I don't know why he should be. My father offered money to every scoundrel from here to Jamaica to bring me back." Her pointed look at Morgan said he was just such a man.

Morgan felt a rush of anger but firmly tamped it down. With a firm grip on her arm he helped Silver up onto the wagon seat and climbed up himself. He could feel the warmth of her body through the light cotton barrier of her clothes. His fingers seemed to burn from the warmth of her skin where he had touched her. He wanted her, he knew, more every day. And his conscience was wearing thin. Thank God he would soon be rid of her.

"This is Major Trask, Thadeus," she said to the slender black boy. "He's come to claim the reward."

"It's Pinkard's reward, not mine," Morgan corrected, feeling his anger build. Bringing Silver back was in her best interest, damn it, whether she realized it or not. "I'm just escorting *Her Ladyship* home."

Silver silently seethed. She was glad for the temper Morgan stirred. She needed it to get through these next few hours. Trask would soon be leaving. She'd be left to face her father's wrath, the cuts and bruises he would leave on her body, the hotness in his eyes. She should be used to it by now, but somehow this time it would be worse.

From beneath her lashes, she watched Trask sitting there beside her, ramrod straight, his jaw clamped tight in an expression she had come to know well these past few weeks. For the first time it occurred to her how much she would miss him, angry or not, venting his fury or showing her kindness.

In some strange way she had come to care for him, maybe even depend on him a little.

Soon there would be no one.

Pulled by a sturdy team of mules, the heavy wagon rolled up the dusty lava drive past oleander and frangipani, colorful jessamine, and pink bougainvillaea. Their sweet smells wafted through the air, but to Silver they were the cloying smells of her silk-lined prison.

Morgan climbed down from the wagon seat and lifted her to the ground. On the wide veranda the massive carved mahogany door swung wide, but it wasn't her father who stepped out to greet them. Resignedly Silver crossed the drive and climbed the stairs, Morgan walking behind her.

"Salena, thank God you're safe."

"Major Morgan Trask, this is Sheridan Knowles, my father's manager." Knowles clasped her hand between both of his in a gesture of welcome. Silver withdrew it.

He turned to the major and extended his hand. "Major Trask." Morgan returned the man's grip. "We can't thank you enough. William has been worried sick."

A tall, spare man in his middle forties, Sheridan Knowles had coffee brown hair, refined features, and a fair complexion. His clothes were well tailored: black broadcloth trousers, a silver brocade waistcoat, and a dark gray frock coat. His wide white stock was perfectly tied.

Knowles seemed friendly enough, yet there was something about him Morgan found offensive. Something in his smile that seemed a little insincere, something that didn't quite wash. Then again, Morgan was edgy and eager to be away. Maybe it was just his imagination.

"You'll have to thank Ferdinand Pinkard. He's the man expecting to claim the reward. I merely escorted the lady home."

"I'm sure William would want you compensated as well," Knowles said as he ushered them into the expansive foyer.

Above their heads, a huge cut-crystal chandelier clinked pleasantly in the afternoon breeze. The house was Georgian in design, with great tall ceilings and beautiful carved moldings that framed the doorways and surrounded the brass and crystal sconces that lined the walls. Thick Aubusson carpets warmed the inlaid parquet floors, and gold silk draperies clothed the windows. Magnificent slatted wooden shutters could be closed in time of storm.

"I want nothing from William except a little of his time. Where is he?"

"William has left, I'm afraid," Knowles said. "When no word came of Salena, he sailed to Barbados, hoping to find her himself. He discovered she had left aboard the *Lawrence*, an immigrant ship that stopped here to make repairs. From Barbados William was bound for America, where he knew the *Lawrence* had gone."

"I'm sorry to hear that," Morgan said. "I'd been looking forward to seeing him." *And settling some of these damnable doubts that are driving me crazy.* "William and I have known each other for some years."

"I'm surprised we've never met," Knowles said.

"It's been fifteen years since last I saw him. I've never been to Katonga."

"Then you must accept our hospitality and let my wife and me show you around." He glanced pointedly at Silver. "I'm sure Salena is tired. She'll want to bathe and be properly clothed again." Morgan didn't miss his disdain at Silver's shabby dress—or lack of it. But then Morgan didn't much approve of it either.

"I'm afraid I don't have time," he said, declining Knowles's effusive invitation. "Tell William I plan to stop by on my return. There are some things we need to discuss."

"I expect he'll contact Pinkard as soon as he reaches the States. Once he learns of Salena's return, he'll be back. In the meantime, my wife Rebecca and I will look after her."

"You may rest assured, Major," Silver put in, "that Sheridan will see I come to no harm. He is my father's most valued employee. He's well paid to act in his stead."

Morgan didn't miss the bitterness in her words.

"I think it's time you went upstairs, Salena," Knowles said, and to Morgan's surprise, Silver didn't argue, just looked at the brown-haired man with an expression of resignation and turned to leave. Morgan stopped her with a gentle hold on her arm.

"Give us a moment, will you?" he said to Knowles.

"I'll get the reward money for Mr. Pinkard."

Morgan nodded. Taking Silver's hand, which he found noticeably cold for such a warm day, he led her to the open front door. A thin-faced short black butler dressed in an immaculate black suit saw them coming and walked a discreet distance away.

"I'll be back, Silver," Morgan promised. "William will be home by then, and we'll all three sit down and talk things over."

Silver smiled but it wasn't sincere. When she glanced up at him, she seemed surprised by his look of concern. What kind of ogre did she think he was?

She watched him a moment from beneath her

thick dark lashes, saying nothing, her eyes fixed on his face. Then her hand came up to the scar on his cheek. Her touch was gentle, almost reverent, tracing the thin white line with a delicate finger. At his stunned expression, she realized what she was doing and snatched the offending hand away, burying it deeply within the folds of her skirt.

"I wish it were that easy," she said softly.

"Damn it, Silver, if there's something you want to tell me, say it." He could still feel the warmth of her hand against his cheek. Why had she done that?

She forced a second smile, this one strangely forlorn. "I'll be fine. Really I will."

"You'll be fine," he repeated, beginning to get angry again. Why was she looking at him that way? Making him feel like he was tossing her into some hellish prison, instead of leaving her in a beautiful mansion on one of the loveliest islands he had ever seen. "I told you I'll be back and I will."

"One thing I've never doubted, Major Trask, is your word."

Morgan's mouth thinned. "What is that supposed to mean?"

"It means that my father will be pleased. Your debt to him will be paid in full and then some."

Morgan cursed roundly. "Damned if you aren't a handful, Salena."

"Silver," she corrected, beginning to get angry herself. Why didn't he just get the hell out of there? Every moment he stayed only made things harder. Any second she was liable to disgrace herself, throw her arms around his neck, and beg him not to leave her.

"You'll never change, will you?" He smiled grimly. "I suppose I should feel sorry for you, but in truth I feel sorry for William."

Before she could stop herself, Silver's palm connected with his cheek, the crack resounding in the high-ceilinged foyer.

Morgan's jaw tightened, clamped so hard a muscle bunched in his cheek. He rubbed the spot she had earlier caressed, now bright with the imprint of her fingers.

"Good-bye, Salena." He gave her a slightly mocking bow, his green eyes glinting.

"Good-bye, Major Trask." Silver met his hard look squarely, her expression equally dark. Then her delicate features softened. Deep brown eyes moved over his face, searching past his anger, seeing something more, yet he knew not what it was.

For a moment she just stood there. Then she turned and walked away. Head held high, she crossed the foyer, lifted her faded brown skirt up out of the way, and climbed the spiral staircase. At the top of the landing, she opened the door to her room, stepped inside, and closed it soundlessly behind her.

Morgan cursed again as Sheridan Knowles approached, walking in his direction with a smile. He handed Morgan a fat leather pouch, heavy with shiny gold coins.

"It's all there, Major. Two thousand dollars. You're sure you won't accept some sort of reimbursement yourself?"

Morgan tucked the pouch away. "I owe William a great deal. Returning his daughter is the least I can do."

Knowles extended a fine-boned hand, and Morgan shook it. "It's been a pleasure meeting you, Major." He nodded toward the butler who had returned to open the door. "I wish you godspeed on your voyage."

"Thank you." Morgan stepped out on the porch.

"Thadeus will drive you down to the harbor."

Morgan nodded. With a last glance back at the house, he turned and walked away.

Silver moved to the window facing the rear of the mansion and stared through the heavy iron scrollwork that barred much of the view—as well as any plans she might have of leaving. In the yard below, workers toiled in the bright afternoon sunshine, and farther off, the banana groves waved in the gentle spring breeze. Beyond the island in the distance, turquoise water beckoned, marking the path the *Savannah* would be sailing on its journey to Barbados, the path that might have carried her to freedom.

An ache rose in Silver's throat. The major would return, all right—of that she had no doubt—but what difference would it make? His arrival would be months from now. Months of living with her father, who would surely soon be home. Months of enforced closeness, months of avoiding his advances, the evil she saw in his eyes every time he looked at her.

Every night for years she had fallen asleep listening for his footfalls, praying this would not be the night he chose to come to her room. That had happened only once, but she would never forget it.

She could still remember the smell of rum on his breath, the heat of his sweaty hands on her body, the way he held her down and tore away her soft cotton nightgown. She was only thirteen, but her innocence had not stopped him. He wanted her, would have taken her if one of the servants hadn't heard her terrified screams and come running into the room.

The beautiful black woman, Delia, her father's reluctant mistress, ignored the danger to herself and interceded, shaming William into leaving Silver alone. The next day, beaten and bruised, Delia was returned to the fields, and the others knew better than to interfere.

Since then William had continued to take his pleasure with the dark-skinned women he owned, but it was Salena he wanted, Salena he would one day violate, no matter how hard she fought him.

He had come close several times since then, had stalked her the very night she had finally run away. Only the knife she had stolen from the kitchen had deterred him. And then only for a while. He would have beaten her in the morning, for whatever crimes he might invent.

Instead she had escaped to the ship anchored just outside the harbor, repaired at last and ready to sail. Thank God for the *Lawrence*'s near disaster, the broken rudder that had forced her to their shores. If the ship hadn't come, Silver would have been at her father's mercy.

She felt the sting of tears. She was back where she had started, worse maybe, for this time his anger would know no bounds. That he would beat her she had no doubt. But a beating she could stand. It was the other that she was afraid of. The other unspeakable crime that she feared.

The wetness blurred her vision, and Silver stifled a cry in her throat. She knew without doubt that the next time William came for her, he would succeed.

Or she would have to kill him.

Silver felt the wetness on her cheeks and didn't bother to wipe it away. *What kind of woman are you?* Morgan had said. What kind indeed? What kind of woman aroused lust in her own father? What kind would murder the man whose very loins had brought her into this world?

Silver stood staring out at the water, watching,

waiting, looking for the sails of the *Savannah* and a
last glimpse of the ship that had been her only hope.

What would Morgan think of her if he knew? What
would he think of her father? Why in God's name did
it matter so much?

Morgan rode in silence all the way to the harbor.
Just ahead, he could see the shore boat beached on
the smooth black sand, Flagg and Gordon standing
nearby. Sea gulls circled overhead, and the *Savannah* bobbed at the end of her anchor in the brilliant
turquoise water. The journey he'd looked forward to
at last could begin.

The wagon rumbled along, the mules moving
faster downhill, but the slim black driver didn't
speak. In the fields Morgan spotted the flat-faced
woman who had spoken to Silver.

Silver. Salena. The name conjured memories of a
fiery-tempered woman he longed to forget. He was
finished with her. He had returned her safe and
sound. When his voyage was complete, he would
come back and talk to William, make sure she was
all right. It was no more than he'd do for Jordy or
Cookie or Jacques.

In the meantime, he had his mission to think of,
his brother, the weapons the Texians would be needing in the Yucatán. He was a major in the Texas Marines. He had duties, responsibilities. The last thing
he needed to worry about was an untutored, unsophisticated, willful bit of baggage like Silver Jones.

He was glad she'd made him angry, glad she'd
slapped his face. He didn't want to feel sorry for her.
Wouldn't, he assured himself. Silver hardly deserved
his pity. Wouldn't accept it if he offered.

He fingered the mark on his cheek, still tingling
where she had hit him. Damn her, she would dare

anything. No wonder William couldn't handle her.
What man could? On top of that she was a liar. The
things she said about her father couldn't possibly be
true. William was an honorable man. Silver was wild
and reckless and spoiled. She was willful; she was
stubborn—

Morgan's jaw clamped as a voice from inside
spoke the words he fought to ignore: Silver was
beautiful and intelligent and courageous. She was
alone and afraid, and she just might need his help.

"Christ," he swore, clenching his fist almost as
hard as he ground his teeth. "Turn this damned
thing around. We're going back."

"But I t'ought you—"

"I said, turn it around. And be quick about it before I change my mind."

For the first time since he'd met the black youth,
Thadeus grinned. "Yes, *suh*, Massa Trask." He pulled
on the reins, clucked, and sawed until the animals
complied and they were heading back up the hill.

"Wait here," Morgan commanded when they
reached the circular drive in front of the house. "I'll
be right back." Morgan jumped down, stalked across
the grounds and up the veranda steps. The door
swung wide even before he reached it.

"She still upstairs?" he asked the butler.

"Yes, suh."

Morgan stalked past the little man into the house.
Sheridan Knowles heard his boots ringing on the
hardwood floors and came running.

"What's going on, Major?" he asked with a worried scowl.

"I've changed my mind." He started up the stairs,
but Knowles's hand on his arm stopped him on the
first rung.

"I'm afraid you can't go up there, Major. I don't think William would approve."

"He can tell me that in person when I get back." He jerked his arm free and continued up the sweeping staircase, past the astonished upstairs maid, who stared at him with wide black eyes, and on down the hall.

"I must insist you stop this at once," Knowles shouted up at him.

Morgan ignored him, just strode down the corridor and jerked open Silver's door without even bothering to knock. At his unorthodox entrance she spun to face him, the expression on her face one of sheer astonishment.

"Get your things," he commanded. "You're coming with me."

"What?"

Beyond her he spotted the bars that encased her window, realized she had been looking through them for a final glimpse of the ship. It was a last good-bye, he saw, and something moved inside his chest. Silver's face was wet with tears, her expression desolate, and her cheeks so pale they appeared translucent.

"I said get your things." Emotion roughened his voice. He strode to the huge rosewood armoire that dominated the frilly, white lace bedroom, and threw open the door. The chest was crammed with beautiful silk gowns, velvet slippers, and expensive satin-lined cloaks. There was muslin for morning, lace for tea, organdy for evening, ornate bonnets, embroidered parasols, and hand-painted fans.

"Take some of this stuff with you. I'm tired of seeing you in rags. I'll send someone up to fetch your trunk."

"All right," she said softly, and her heart felt near

bursting. Morgan had come back for her. He had come back! The ache in her throat grew so painful Silver had to turn away.

"I'll be waiting downstairs." With that he strode from the room.

If she hadn't been afraid he might change his mind, she would have sagged down on the bed just to collect herself. She could hardly believe this was happening. Instead she dashed around the room, pulling out her trunk, filling it to overflowing with the gowns she had, until now, dreaded to wear.

But it wouldn't be her father's eyes on her bare shoulders, the rounded curve of her breasts. It would be Morgan's. At last he would see her as a proper lady. She would show him she could be as genteel as the women he found so attractive.

Well, *almost* as genteel.

Hurriedly she laid away her crinolines, embroidered nightgowns, and lacy underthings. How long had it been since she'd worn anything so feminine? She put in her silver-backed hairbrush, comb, and mirror and tossed in a crystal vial of perfume. Downstairs she could hear Morgan's deep voice laced with anger, raised against that of Sheridan Knowles.

A tiny smile crossed her lips. She had no doubt who would win.

Finished at last, she raced to the door and swung it open, then hurried to the top of the stairs. "I'm ready, Major."

Thadeus stood beside him. Together with Ned, the butler, they climbed the stairs to fetch her trunk. Silver descended almost shyly.

"I forbid this, Salena. Your father will be furious. It wasn't bad enough you traveled unchaperoned with this man halfway across the ocean, now you're leaving with him."

"Tell William I'll take good care of her. She'll be back on my return."

"You're asking for trouble, Major. The earl is a man of some authority. He won't sit back and take this lightly."

"William trusted me once. He'll have to do it again."

With that he grabbed her arm and dragged her out the door. The hands that hoisted her into the wagon were hardly gentle, but Silver didn't care. She was leaving the island, escaping at last. Better than that, the man who had rescued her was Morgan Trask.

Morgan joined her on the hard wooden seat while Ned and Thadeus loaded her trunk. Morgan turned her face with a stout grip on her chin.

"I want your word, Silver. I want you to swear on your mother's grave that you will not try to escape. It's the only way you're going with me."

"You would accept my word?"

"Can't you understand—I'm trying to help you?"

She looked at him, and against her will fresh tears gathered in her eyes. It wasn't like her, all these tears, yet she could not stop them. "You won't be sorry," she said. "I'll do whatever you say, and I won't try to run."

He brushed the tears from her cheeks with his fingers. "I'm going a damned long ways out of my way for you. Don't make me regret it."

She shook her head, moving the heavy mass of her silver hair. She felt safe as she never had before. Safe and protected—and something else she could not name.

Morgan turned away from her and raked a hand through his wavy dark blond hair. God, he must be crazy. Then he recalled the way she had looked at him when he'd burst into her room. As if he were some kind of knight in shining armor. It made his heart turn over. He had wanted to pull her into his arms and comfort her, take away the awful pain he had seen in her eyes.

What was her secret? he thought, and wondered if he would ever know. One thing was sure. He had set himself up for more sleepless nights, more tossing and turning, and visions of her luscious body.

I must be mad, he thought. But in truth Morgan knew that no matter the misery ahead, he wouldn't send her back there alone for all the peace and quiet in the world.

Chapter 8

"I know this isn't the time to ask a favor," Silver said as the wagon rumbled along, "but I was wondering if we might make one quick stop before we leave."

Morgan's look said she had some kind of nerve. "What for?"

"It's been so long since I've been home . . . I was wondering if I might have a word with my friends?"

He glanced around the island, looking for other houses, but saw only the tiny workers' cabins, the lush green fields, and the sea. "Where are they?"

"Quako usually works the tobacco. Delia won't be far away."

His brow quirked, telling her he remembered the woman's name from the slave they had passed on the road. "This had better not take long."

"Thank you." Silver flashed him a bright warm smile. Thadeus took a turn in the road, and the wagon rolled off toward a field of waist-high dark green-leafed tobacco. Workers bent over hoes, weeding the troughs between the rows, but one man stood out from the rest, his body so huge it dwarfed the others.

"Quako!" Silver shouted to the massive black man, and he grinned. Not far away, balancing a jug of water on her head, Delia smiled and waved and started in Silver's direction, her graceful movements keeping the water jug perfectly balanced. She was a beautiful cocoa-skinned woman with fine features, very short hair, and intelligent dark eyes, and even her faded smock could not disguise the willowy curves of her slender body.

While Thadeus set the brake, Morgan jumped to the ground and helped Silver alight. He was looking at her oddly, surprised, it seemed, that her best friends should be slaves.

"Yo' all right, Silver?" the black man asked with obvious worry, reaching her in long powerful strides. He eyed Morgan warily. "I mean . . . Miz Silver."

"It's all right, Quako. This is Major Trask. He's taking me away with him."

Quako smiled and then grinned. He was several inches taller than Morgan and at least thirty pounds heavier, though their bodies had the same masculine V shape. Both had broad powerful shoulders, but Quako's arms were massive, his thighs the size of tree trunks. As big as he was, when he grinned like that, Silver thought he looked more like a little boy.

"I tol' Delia you would find the kind o' mon you deserve."

"She's only going with me until her father returns," Morgan corrected. "I'll be bringing her back, and once things are straightened out, she'll be staying."

Silver heard the words but didn't care. Morgan had come back for her. Sooner or later she would find a way to make him understand.

Quako looked him up and down, looked at Silver,

whose cheeks grew pink, and then back again. His grin only broadened, splitting his face with the slash of his large white teeth. "She good wooman," he said, and Silver fought not to smile—though Morgan didn't look amused.

Delia interrupted whatever brusque retort he might have made. "We heard about da reward, Silver. We was so worried for you."

"I'm all right, Delia. What about you two?"

"The work is still hard, but we be all right."

Quako flashed another smile. Reaching out, he patted Delia's stomach, which was no longer flat but now gently rounded. "Soon we have new baby."

Silver shrieked with joy and hugged them both. "That's wonderful!" They had tried before, but Delia had lost the baby three months before it was born. Silver felt an uneasy twinge at the bitter memory.

"You've worked this young woman too hard," the doctor had said to Silver's father. "Her female parts have somehow been damaged. She'll have to get a great deal of rest the next time she conceives." Silver believed her father's harsh treatment was responsible for Delia's fragile condition, but she didn't say so.

The time before, she had interfered on her friend's behalf and both of them wound up with a beating.

"Congratulations," Morgan said, and Quako assessed him once more.

"Silver good woman," he repeated, glancing down at her, "but she need strong mon." He smiled at Delia, and it was easy to see the love in his eyes. "Silver t'ink all mon bad. Once my Delia feel same. Now Delia know better. Right mon, Silver know, too."

Silver flushed. "I think we'd better be going."

"Yes, it is getting late."

"Take care of yourself," she said to Delia, who knew the words for the warning they were. Silver hugged them both again. "I wish you could go with me."

"Take goot care of her," Quako said to Trask.

Morgan only nodded. He was seeing a side of Silver he hadn't suspected. The love she felt for her friends was obvious, and he hadn't missed the fact that they spoke to her as if they were her equal. Apparently that was the way she wanted it, and Morgan admired her for it.

Though he lived in Georgia and made his money off the cotton trade, he owned no slaves himself and hoped one day to see the institution abolished. Most of the West Indies had been freed, and the island economies had survived. It would take some doing, but altering the system in the South did not seem impossible.

After a last farewell, Morgan helped Silver climb back aboard the wagon and they rode the rest of the way in silence. Both Flagg and Gordon openly gaped when they saw him help Silver alight and walk toward them.

"Miss Jones has decided to accompany us to Barbados," Morgan said simply. "Why don't you help Thadeus with her trunk?"

Both Flagg and Gordon grinned. "Aye, Cap'n," they said in unison. For the first time, Morgan realized the enormity of what he had done. The men were already busting their breeches every time they saw her walking on deck. The new clothes might help some, but it wouldn't erase the memories they carried of seeing her in her water-soaked, nearly translucent nightshirt or the snug-fitting breeches that had outlined her pert little derriere when she had climbed into the sails.

Morgan cursed roundly. He must have been crazy.
Stark raving, salt water-drinking crazy. Because the
men in his crew weren't the only ones who thought
of her that way.

The balance of the afternoon passed swiftly, Silver
greeted warmly by Demming and Riley and especially by Jordy, who seemed on the verge of adopting
her as a member of his somewhat ragtag family.
Only the major seemed displeased to have her back
aboard.

To Silver it didn't matter. All that counted was
leaving Katonga, reaching Barbados and safety, at
least for the time being.

As evening approached and the ship creaked its
welcome, Silver dressed for supper, using far more
care than she had before. Tonight she would wear
her dark blue watered silk gown, one of her favor-
ites. It rode low on her shoulders and dipped to a
deep V in front. Before putting it on, she had bathed
in freshwater, since the stores had been resupplied,
and fashioned her hair in elegant silver swirls beside
each ear. Tiny sapphire earbobs, a cherished me-
mento of her mother's, sparkled in the lamplight.

With a last glance in the broken mirror above Morgan's oak bureau, she picked up her painted fan and
headed for the door. A fresh breeze blew in off the
water, and a mantle of stars shone overhead. Walking into the salon, Silver was surprised to find the
table set with expensive porcelain and crystal.

"The seas are calm." Morgan stepped from the
shadows. "I thought you might enjoy a bit of formality for a change." His eyes swept over her, taking in
the full silk skirts of the lovely blue gown that em-
phasized her narrow waist and the high, lush curves
of her bosom. With her hair swept back, the sculp-

tured planes and valleys of her face were revealed, the delicate cleft in her chin.

Bloody hell! He never would have dreamed she could look so refined—or so breathtakingly beautiful.

"That was very considerate, Major. Thank you." She seemed different since her return, softer, almost shy.

Morgan felt a tightness in his chest and a stirring in his body a little lower down. God, he wanted her —badly. Instead they sat on the carved oak settee and made pleasant conversation while he fought to control his growing interest and wished like hell the others would arrive.

Eventually Demming and Riley wandered in, Demming in his seaman's uniform, Riley in one belonging to the Texas Marines. Lamplight reflected off Morgan's own spotless brass buttons.

"You look lovely, Miss Jones." Ham's youthful face flushed a little with his words.

"Thank you." Silver rose from the settee and moved gracefully toward them.

"You're a vision, Miss Jones," Wilson Demming put in, kissing her hand. "More lovely than I would have dreamed."

Morgan scowled, already sorry they were there. "Then why doesn't one of you two gentlemen offer Miss Jones a seat?" Both men leaped to the task, pulling out a high-backed oak chair and helping her alight.

Silver smiled at them warmly. The evening progressed as if the four of them were sharing their first meal. As though the beautiful woman who sat across from them couldn't possibly be the scruffy, ragtag hoyden who had threatened the lieutenant at gunpoint, gone fist to fist with Morgan, and climbed the yardarm in an effort to escape.

Morgan watched Silver play the role of lady and silently saluted her finesse. He wouldn't have believed her capable of the task, but then he'd done nothing but underestimate her since the first time they'd met.

"We should reach Barbados just about dawn," Morgan said as Jordy served them thick dark coffee, along with a slice of warm apple pie topped with cheese. "I'm to meet with Owen Moore, the man who's made most of the trading arrangements, as soon as it can be arranged."

"How long will we be there, Major?" Silver asked.

"Just until the Brits arrive, if they haven't already." He wasn't about to tell her she'd be staying there until his return from Mexico. He'd save that piece of news until he was just about to leave—and pray to God for once she'd keep her word. Of course, the governor was a personal friend who owed him a favor or two. He'd be happy to provide a watchdog, and Morgan intended to be certain he did.

"Wilson, you can leave the ship as soon as Jacques comes aboard. I want you to know I appreciate the job you've done, and if you ever need a berth, I'll be glad to help you find one."

"Thank you, sir," Demming said.

"What about me, Major?" Riley asked.

"You may as well enjoy yourself. Nothing for you to do until we sail."

Hamilton grinned, and Morgan knew exactly what he was thinking. As a matter of fact, he intended a little of the same. Lydia Chambers, Lady Grayson, the beautiful black-haired widow of the earl of Grayson, a prominent assemblyman, was awaiting his arrival. They had been lovers off and on for years, neither demanding much from the other, their relationship little more than a satisfying of physical needs.

Lydia had a tranquil disposition, even if it was a bit contrived, and was forever amenable to doing Morgan's bidding. She epitomized the woman of breeding who always knew her place.

In contrast he glanced across at Salena, engrossed in lively conversation with Hamilton Riley. Though tonight she looked the part, Silver was as far from a gently reared lady as any woman could get. She was nothing like Lydia, nothing like any of the women he sought to warm his bed.

So why in blazes was he so damned attracted to her?

Surely it was just her physical beauty and the close proximity in which they'd been forced to live.

Silver laughed, a soft, tinkling sound, at something Ham said, and Morgan felt an unexpected ripple of anger. When she bent down to retrieve her napkin, which had fallen on the floor, her full white breasts threatened to burst from the top of the gown. Though it was cut in the latest fashion, acceptable in any social circle, Morgan wanted to drag her from the table and insist she put on something else.

Bloody hell, the woman was enough to make a man turn to drink.

Shoving back his chair a little harder than he meant to, Morgan crossed to the sideboard and poured himself a brandy. He took a long, steadying sip before pouring for anyone else. Both Demming and Riley joined him in a glass, and Silver accepted a sherry.

In the glow of the lamplight, Morgan watched her tongue slide over her bottom lip to catch a drop of the amber liquid, noticed that her skin seemed to

shimmer with the same bright sheen as her hair. Her
neck arched gracefully above her slender shoulders,
and her fingers curled delicately around the crystal
stem of her glass. Morgan remembered how gentle
they had felt against the scar on his cheek, the way,
when he had kissed her, she had laced them through
his hair.

Bloody hell! Desire knifed through him like a
white-hot bolt of lightning. Morgan shifted in his
chair. Damn her to hell! He clenched his fist against
the bittersweet ache that made his loins feel taut and
heavy, hating the power she unknowingly wielded
against him.

Silently he thanked God for Lydia. Tomorrow he
would see her, put an end to his days of torment.

They approached Barbados from the southwest,
careful to skirt the barrier reef off South Point. Even
from a distance, Silver could see the bold, rocky
cliffs looming sixty feet above the water.

They passed along the coast and headed for Carlisle Bay just south of Bridgetown, the best
anchorage on the island. Silver had never been to
Barbados, but her father had been there once or
twice. Through him and his few friends, she'd heard
stories of the wealthy society of sugar planters, knew
of their lavish homes and gala parties. She thought
of the expensive dresses Morgan had urged—no
commanded—her to bring and suddenly felt grateful. At least she wouldn't be embarrassed by her
shabby, faded clothes.

The day, mild and sunny, beckoned pleasantly.
Only a few gauzy clouds dotted the horizon, and a
gentle breeze puffed out the sails.

"Barbados is a coral island, not volcanic, like
Katonga." Morgan approached her at the rail. She

stood beside one of the ship's two big five-pound cannon. There was a swivel two-pound carronade aft. "That's why the beaches are pink and white."

"How big is it?"

"A little over twenty miles long and fourteen miles wide. It's the most heavily populated island in the West Indies. . . . I gather you've never been here before."

"I've never been anywhere, Major. Except Katonga—and Georgia."

Morgan eyed her speculatively, apparently wondering, since Barbados was only a day's sail away, why William had never taken her. "Then we'll have to make certain you get a chance to see it."

As Bridgetown drew near, Morgan excused himself, returned to the wheel, and began to call the orders to shorten sail. They passed through the bay, entered the inner harbor called the Careenage, and gently eased up to the wharf. Normally there was a quarantine period for incoming ships, but since his business benefited the British, the authorities were ignoring procedure, baldly looking the other way.

Though the hour was still early, the harbor teemed with activity. Dozens of ships lined the dock, and sailors wearing everything from duck pants and homespun shirts to striped British seamen's uniforms scurried along the wooden planks in a determined attempt to reach their destinations, whatever they might be.

Probably one of the shutter-fronted taverns that lined the quay. Beneath wide wooden porches, drunken men sang sea shanties, and doxies plied their trade, many dark-skinned, others who looked to be British with their fair hair and freckled skin, and even some Orientals. That they were scantily clad, with their legs exposed and most of their bosoms, was to say the least.

"Let's go," said Morgan, once more wearing his uniform as he strode up to Silver. When he eyed the taverns and glanced down at her, his expression told her he well recalled that she had worked in just such a place. With a look of disdain, he grasped her arm and hauled her off toward the gangway.

"Where are we going?" Ignoring his change of mood, Silver let him guide her along. Today she didn't give a damn what Morgan Trask thought of her. She was free of her father, safe at last, and excited just to be in such an exotic, bustling place.

"You'll be staying at the home of a friend, the widow of the late Lord Grayson."

Silver arched a brow. "You were a friend of her husband's?"

"I never knew the gentleman." Morgan's sure grip steadied her as they crossed to the dock. Following in their wake, Jordy trailed behind them, carrying the satchels she had packed for their brief stay.

Today she wore her best rose silk day dress, the belled skirt open in front to reveal an underskirt of darker rose silk heavily embroidered.

Silver glanced at Morgan, trying to read the look on his face. His expression had changed from scornful to guarded, as if there were something more he wasn't saying. She wanted to ask about the woman he had mentioned but didn't, sure she would find out soon enough.

Across the street from the dock, Morgan hired a carriage and settled her inside while Jordy loaded her luggage into the boot.

"Bye, Miss Jones," he said with such finality Silver blanched.

"It'll only be for a few days, Jordy. You take care of yourself."

"You, too, Miss Jones." He turned and walked away.

Morgan climbed into the seat beside her, stretching his long legs out in front of him, and the carriage rolled away. She could feel the heat of his body where his shoulder pressed against hers, and try as she might to ignore it, her heart began to pound. Morgan cleared his throat and shifted on the narrow seat, trying to put some distance between them. His movements rippled the muscles in his arms, Silver felt them bunch, and suddenly the carriage felt overly warm.

"How much farther?" she asked.

"Not far." His voice sounded strangely husky.

Outside the window, the Bridgetown streets swelled with the tide of people. Elegant ladies strolled beneath fringed silk parasols while the men wore high hats, frock coats, and dark-striped trousers. Barbadian women carried baskets on their heads, and higglers hawked their wares—everything from yams to sugarcane meat.

"Get your maubey, sweet, sweet maubey," a wizened old crone called out. It was a bittersweet brew made from dried bark imported from the neighboring islands. The bark was boiled and the liquid flavored with sweeteners and spices.

They passed Trafalgar Square, where a statue of Lord Nelson had been erected almost thirty years before. Huge evergreens towered above the statue, and casuarina trees could be seen.

They passed an open-air barbershop where a long-legged gray-haired man was receiving a shave, his face nearly hidden by the thick white shaving lather. A few minutes later, Morgan pointed out the carriage window toward a house on Chelsea Road near Bay Street.

"That's where we're headed."

The house appeared to be a mixture of Federal and Georgian designs that had been added onto again and again. It was white and shuttered and architecturally rambling, but attractive with its pointed roof, wrought-iron fence, and yard full of brightly colored flowers. There were neat little hedgerows, as well as heliconia, yellow hibiscus, and pink begonia.

"It's very pretty," Silver said, and Morgan's glance swung pointedly in her direction.

For the first time that day he smiled. "So are you. I meant to tell you that last night, but with Riley and Demming doing such a thorough job of flattery, I didn't think it mattered."

Silver smiled in return. She loved it when he looked at her that way. His eyes were warm on her face, their bright green hue bringing a rush of color to her cheeks. "It matters," she said. "Thank you."

The carriage rolled to a stop, and Morgan opened the door. He stepped to the ground, circled her waist with his hands, and swung her down beside him. The driver unloaded her bags, which Morgan picked up, and they walked on the flower-lined path to the house. Morgan knocked on the door, and a short black servant, white-gloved and dressed in black, pulled it open. He grinned when he saw Morgan, crinkling the skin at the corners of his big round eyes.

"Cap'n Trask. It's good to see you."

"How are you, Euphrates?"

"Fine, Cap'n. I be right back." The servant glanced at Silver but made no comment, just ushered them inside and left to get his mistress.

"Morgan—" Lady Grayson arrived in a swirl of

ruby silk skirts. The elegant dress, piped in black with matching corded frogs up the front and brandenburgs about the hem, appeared the height of good taste and fashion—the woman even more so. Small, but well proportioned, she had a clear complexion and lovely cornflower blue eyes. Smiling brightly, she kissed Morgan's cheek. "It's good to see you. Knowing you as I do, I presumed you would arrive very close to the schedule you mentioned in your letter."

"It's good to see you, too." Morgan still held the small woman's hands. "There's someone I want you to meet." He turned to Silver, who until now seemed to have gone unnoticed. "Lady Grayson, this is Salena. Her father is the earl of Kent." His bright green eyes dared her to contradict him.

"How do you do, Lady Grayson." She made a slight inclination of her head.

"How do you do, my dear."

"My friends call me Silver. I would take it as an honor if you would, too." A corner of Morgan's mouth twitched in amusement while a dark blond brow arched upward in silent salute.

"Then you must call me Lydia, for any friend of Morgan's is surely a friend of mine."

Silver wasn't so certain. The way the woman was looking at Morgan made it plain they were more than mere acquaintances. Surely this genteel woman could not be one of his lovers. But catching the intimate look that passed between them, Silver began to have her doubts.

"I need a favor, Lydia," Morgan said. "I'm looking after Silver until her father returns to Katonga. In the meantime, she needs a place to stay."

"Of course. There's plenty of room here and I'm

sure we'll enjoy each other's company." Her eyes, however, said something different.

"Why don't you have someone show Silver to her room?" Morgan suggested, making it clear he needed a moment alone with the woman. Lady Grayson looked smugly relieved.

"Of course." With a much warmer smile, she had the housekeeper lead Silver upstairs while one of the other servants delivered her bags.

At the top of the stairs, Silver took a last glance at Morgan. His expression remained unreadable while Lady Grayson was purely beaming. She whispered something in his ear, laughed softly, and Morgan laughed, too.

Damn him! Silver's fingers tightened on the banister. She might be a little naïve, but she wasn't a fool. Morgan was planning a rendezvous with the woman —while Silver slept under the very same roof!

Hoisting her skirts in the first unladylike gesture she had made since she'd put on her elegant clothes, Silver lifted her chin, cast Morgan a haughty, disdainful glance, and followed the servant down the hall to her chamber. By the time she had reached it, a lace-trimmed ice blue suite done in Barbadian mahogany and very good taste, she was seething.

Bloody bastard! Obviously she had been right about Morgan Trask all along. He was a man, wasn't he? To men women meant nothing. To Trask, who liked his women *genteel*, Silver Jones meant less than nothing. He had helped her leave Katonga out of pity, seen her as a poor, bedraggled creature left alone on an island with only the slaves to call friends. Even her elegant clothing hadn't made him see her as a lady. It galled her, infuriated her!

You have no right to feel this anger, she told herself

firmly. *Morgan owes you nothing.* Yet she could not control the building rage inside.

Nor end her rising determination to stop him.

Why it was so important, Silver refused to ask. She only knew she wouldn't stand by and allow Morgan Trask to bed another woman in her presence. She'd do almost anything to keep that from happening.

Damn him! she railed, pacing back and forth on the thick tartan carpet. *Damn him to hell!* She paced, and stormed, and cursed him—and every other male from Trinidad to Jamaica. But before the hour had passed, Silver had a plan.

Chapter 9

The idea began when the tiny, narrow-faced upstairs maid came in to help her unpack. She was as black as Quako, her smile just as warm. Silver had been walking around the notion for the past half hour, but the presence of the girl, who said her name was Marnie, filled in the missing gap in the plan.

"Marnie," Silver cautiously asked, "is it possible you might know where to find a woman who makes . . . potions?"

Marnie hung Silver's yellow muslin dress in the carved mahogany armoire and turned to look at her, a wary expression on her face. "I not understand."

"I need to find a voodoo mama." She wished she could remember what Delia had called the slave woman who dabbled in black magic back home. "Can you help me?"

"No voodoo Barbados. Haiti have voodoo."

"I need to buy something, Marnie. I promise I won't tell anyone it was you who helped me get it."

"No voodoo," Marnie said, vigorously shaking her head.

Silver glanced at the crystal vial of perfume she

had brought from Katonga. Where there were Africans, there was voodoo. "You like this?" She held up the beautiful cut-crystal vial. Sunlight streaming in through the window turned it into a prism, and rainbow colors danced on the walls of the room.

"Very beautiful," the girl breathed, reaching out to touch it.

"It's yours, Marnie, if you'll take me to a voodoo woman."

For a moment the girl seemed unsure. Then she touched the shimmering glass, grabbed the bottle, and grinned. "Mama Kimbo. She not live far. We go now, must be back before da lady know we gone."

Silver grinned, too, liking the small, too-thin black girl already. "Just give me a minute to change."

With Marnie's help, Silver stripped off the lovely rose day dress and put on the simple yellow muslin gown. They headed down the servants' stairs at the rear of the house and out through the backyard, passing the garden and the two-story outdoor kitchen, constructed away from the main building to prevent any chance of fire. Several black women who worked at the big iron cookstove eyed them curiously as they passed, but Marnie seemed unconcerned.

"They will say nothing."

What seemed a short ways to Marnie turned out to be a brisk midday walk. Silver didn't care. She loved the bustling streets of Barbados, loved the color and the sounds, loved the friendliness of its people. Bajans, she decided, were people who never met a stranger. Nothing like the guarded, hostile men and women who toiled for her father on Katonga. Delia and Quako could be happy here, she thought wistfully, and wished with all her heart the gift of their freedom was something she could give.

Hurrying along, they continued past tiny shuttered houses, through verdant fields, and those of waving cane, finally reaching Mama Kimbo's. Marnie pulled open the door to the thatched-roofed, tin-walled shack.

"Lady need potion, Mama," Marnie said without preamble, and surprisingly the broad-hipped woman merely grinned.

"Not a potion," Silver corrected, "a rubefacient— a nettle or something that will make my skin turn red. I want someone to think I'm sick, but I don't really want to *be* sick. Do you understand?"

Mama Kimbo's huge girth shook, jiggling a set of enormous breasts. "You pretty girl. Play lover's games, I t'ink."

Silver glanced guiltily away. "Actually I hope to stop a lover's game."

Mama Kimbo laughed harder. She struggled out of her rocking chair and moved around the tiny room. Lining the walls behind her were row upon row of bottles and jars filled with liquids and powders, clusters of dried flowers and weeds, and shriveled-up, ugly things Silver didn't even want to think about.

"Urticaceae," Mama said, handing her a long-stemmed, green, barbed-leafed plant. "Stinging nettle. Where it touches will burn like the sting of a bee, but the pain will soon be gone. We dry and use for what you call rheumatism. The seeds good for coughs."

"I have no money. I was hoping you would accept these." Silver handed the obese woman several long satin ribbons of blue, pink, and green.

"Very pretty." Mama accepted the ribbons with a chubby hand. "Use nettles with care," she warned, "and good luck with your mon."

Silver smiled. "Thank you."

They left the shack, carrying the nettles in a small handwoven straw bag that Marnie promised to return, and started back toward the house on Chelsea Road. But the tiny black girl stopped when she spotted a number of unsavory-looking black men gathered in the lane not far ahead.

"We go dis way." Marnie led her down a wellworn path through the heavy vegetation back toward the quay.

The harbor blocked one avenue of travel, forcing them to wind their way through the narrow streets that in this part of Bridgetown were lined with taverns. They hadn't gone far when one of the swinging double doors burst open and a man flew backward into the street. Blood flowed from his nose, down his face, and onto his chest, soaking the front of his redchecked shirt.

For a moment he lay there groaning, and Silver fought the urge to go to him, to see if he was all right. She was just about to weaken when he staggered to his feet. With an unsteady glance toward the tavern, he spotted the big, bearded man who had followed him outside. Huge and muscular, the blackhaired victor stood grinning beneath his thick mustache, his feet splayed and his hands riding low on his waist. He wore dark blue canvas breeches just about the color of his eyes, a wide-striped shirt, and the swaggering look of a seaman.

"Next time you try to cheat, *anglais*, pick on someone closer to your size." His French accent heavy, the big man slapped a beefy thigh and laughed uproariously. The man in the street dusted himself off and worked his jaw back and forth to be sure it wasn't broken. When the Frenchman took an ominous step in his direction, the Englishman turned tail and ran.

With the disruption over, Silver was just about to continue on her way when the swinging doors opened again and Jordy stepped out on the porch, a wide, approving grin on his youthful freckled face. They spotted each other at exactly the same instant, and Jordy's hazel eyes flew wide.

"Miss Jones! What the devil are you doin' here?"

"I—I—" Silver glanced down guiltily, working madly to concoct a believable story. "Marnie was showing me a little of the city." She indicated the tiny black woman beside her, who held Mama Kimbo's straw bag in the folds of her bright cotton skirt. Marnie nodded and smiled.

"Hello." Jordy doffed his floppy-brimmed hat politely, exposing a thatch of thick auburn hair.

"Jordy," the Frenchman broke in, turning toward them, his accent heavy, "you must introduce me to *la belle femme*—your beautiful lady friend."

"Sorry." Jordy twirled the hat in his hands. "Miss Jones, this is Hypolyte Jacques Bouillard. First mate aboard the *Savannah* and the finest who ever sailed the seas."

"M'sieur Bouillard! I feel as if I already know you." Meaning it, Silver extended her hand. From the bits and pieces she had picked up from Jordy, and the hearty praise Morgan had heaped on, she was certain Hypolyte Jacques Bouillard was quite a man.

"Miss Jones is the daughter of an—"

Silver's elbow found Jordy's ribs. "My father is a planter on Katonga." She cast him a warning glance.

"It is a pleasure, Miss Jones." He lifted her hand and gently brushed the back of it with his lips. The tickle of his heavy black beard made the corners of her mouth tilt up in a smile.

"The pleasure is mine, m'sieur." She said the word in perfect French, finally glad she'd had occasion to learn it.

"You must call me Jacques."

"Then you must call me Silver."

"Silver," he repeated. "The color of your 'air. It is an honor, *chérie*."

"She's the girl I told you about," Jordy said. "The one who climbed the yardarm."

Silver grimaced and subdued an urge to kick him.

"No!" Jacques's mouth gaped open. "But that cannot be."

"She sure did. She kin—can—swim like a fish, too. You shoulda seen her."

"Jordy," Silver said sweetly, but couldn't keep the edge from her voice, "I'm sure M'sieur Bouillard isn't interested."

"*Oui*, but I am. Surely you cannot be the woman Jordy speaks of."

"Please, Jacques, I would rather not discuss it."

"The same woman who went toe to toe with Morgan Trask?" It seemed incomprehensible.

"I was trying to escape," Silver said, beginning to get angry. What damned business was it of his? She lifted her chin and cast him a disparaging glance.

Jacques Bouillard ran his eyes up and down her body, taking in her slender build and average height, apparently incredulous that she could possibly be the woman who had wreaked such havoc on the crew of the *Savannah*.

Then he began to laugh. At first it was a chuckle, then a rumble that turned into a deep-bellied roar, and finally a guffaw that seemed unending. "You"—

he pointed at her between fits of hysteria—"*une pe-tite* no bigger than a minute."

"I'm not that small, and if you don't stop laughing, I may just show you how I did it."

That stopped the laughter. At least for a moment or two. "I am sorry. I meant no disrespect." He tried to hold a chuckle back but several more escaped. "It is just that Capitaine Trask . . . 'e is a man few men can best. For a pretty little thing like you to 'ave done it—'e will never live it down." Bouillard chuckled again.

Silver wished she could join him, but the memory of her battles with the major were far too fresh. "I didn't exactly best him. I'm here because he was kind enough to bring me." She glanced at Jacques beseechingly. "I don't suppose I could convince you not to mention it."

"Sorry, there is no way." He laughed a little longer; then his expression changed. "Where are you going, *chérie*? You should not be walking in this part of town."

"I'm staying with Lady Grayson. And it's time we were heading back."

"I will walk with you."

"That really isn't necessary."

Jacques chuckled again. "I am sure it is not, Silver Jones, but I will walk you anyway."

And he did, leaving them only after they had reached the rear yard. He didn't ask why she wasn't using the front door, as any proper lady would. Bouillard seemed a man who respected one's privacy, accepting a person's friendship on merit alone. Apparently hers was enough to satisfy him, and Silver was glad.

Already she found herself liking the big bearded Frenchman Hypolyte Jacques Bouillard.

* * *

Morgan left the *Savannah,* wearing a freshly laundered uniform and a pair of shiny black boots. A tropical breeze ruffled his neatly groomed hair, and he could still smell the spicy cologne he had put on. Behind his back, the sun formed a glowing half dome against the horizon, then slipped lower into the sea.

Morgan crossed the gangway leading to the dock, walked to the corner, and climbed into the carriage Lydia had sent for him, a handsome black calèche with the top down, pulled by a pair of matched gray horses. Morgan leaned his tall frame against the tufted leather seat, thinking about the night ahead. He'd been looking forward to his evening with Lydia for the past three weeks. More so, since his rousing encounters with Silver.

As Jacques, having met her that afternoon, had so clearly pointed out—to Morgan's chagrin—the girl was quite a temptation. Jacques's good-natured ribbing about her had gone on until the big Frenchman had pushed Morgan farther than he'd meant to. Morgan knew his outburst of temper had been unusual as well as unexpected, and the knowledge that it was gave Jacques some idea of the turmoil Morgan was in.

"It appears, *mon ami,* this is no laughing matter," Jacques had said, turning serious. "The silver-'aired woman, she means more to you than you will admit."

"You're wrong, Jacques. The woman is a handful. More than a handful. I feel responsible, nothing more."

"She is beautiful, *n'est-ce pas?*"

"She's also willful, stubborn, and headstrong."

"Then maybe it is I who should woo 'er. Those are the very traits I find attractive in a woman."

Morgan pinned him with a glare. "Fine," he snapped, but they both knew in some way Morgan had laid claim to the girl. Jacques would not interfere.

He chuckled softly. "I think maybe Major Trask has met 'is match."

"I told you, she isn't my type."

"Think of the fine sons she could give you—the sons you 'ave always wanted."

"Having children means a lot to me, I don't deny that. But it also means marriage—and that I'm just not ready for."

"Not all women are like your Charlotte. I was most fortunate in the women who loved me." Jacques had two fine sons, from two different wives. The first had died in childbirth, the second of a fever that swept across France. Since he had married at sixteen, Jacques's sons were nearly grown and already seamen themselves.

"Maybe they aren't," Morgan said, "but that isn't the point. When I'm ready for marriage, I want a woman who knows her place." He folded his arms across his chest. "My wife will do exactly what I tell her—I intend to set her straight on that score right from the start."

Jacques shook his head. "She sounds very dull to me. I like my women fiery, like your Silver."

"She isn't *my* Silver."

Jacques just grinned. "A pity, *mon capitaine*, to waste such a beautiful woman."

Having thought something close to the same, Morgan hadn't answered.

To the whir of the wheels, the carriage rolled along the darkening streets past merchants lowering their shutters to close up their shops and young boys hurriedly climbing ladders to light gas streetlamps. The house on Chelsea Road lay up ahead.

Morgan shifted on the seat of the carriage. He'd been looking forward to his time with Lydia. Now that it had arrived, he suddenly found himself dreading it.

They were going out for the evening; he was taking her to a quiet restaurant on the road that led to Christ Church. Lydia had invited Silver, offering to provide her with a suitable escort, but Silver had refused.

Morgan was relieved.

What he and Lydia had planned for later in her upstairs chamber was something he'd rather Silver didn't know about. Not that it was any of her business—and not that she didn't already have an inkling. He hadn't missed the scornful look she'd cast his way when he had left her. He owed her no explanations. Far from it. Still, it bothered his conscience, and he refused to question why.

"You look lovely, Lydia," Morgan said to her, greeting her at the foot of the wide white-railed staircase.

Tonight she wore a pin-striped black-and-silver gown trimmed with black Belgian lace. Tiny black-and-silver slippers peeped from beneath the hem of the voluminous skirts. Her shoulders were bare, her breasts rising softly with each gentle breath.

"And you, my darling Morgan, look more dashing than ever."

Unconsciously Morgan glanced to the top of the stairs, almost expecting to see Silver glaring down at him with feminine contempt.

"She's fine, Morgan," Lydia said flatly, reading his

thoughts. "After her weeks at sea, she probably needed a little rest."

That was hard to fathom. Silver had more energy than any three people he knew. "We'd better be going." Ushering her out to the carriage, he helped her climb in.

The evening passed far more slowly than Morgan had imagined. Why hadn't he remembered Lydia's conversation consisted mainly of planters' gossip and the latest Paris fashions? In the past they had dined at home during his brief visits and spent most of their time in bed. Lydia was reserved on the surface, but underneath, she was a passionate lover. He hoped to hell she'd be able to arouse more interest in that subject than she had in the others.

When their elegant supper had ended, the carriage returned them to the house, and Morgan walked her to the door. Once she stepped inside, he waited a discreet amount of time then made his way around back and up the staircase that led to the veranda outside her chamber. Lydia hastily opened the door and drew him in, her arms going around his neck as she pulled his head down for a kiss.

"I've been wanting to do this for hours," she whispered into his mouth, her lips soft and moist beneath his, her fingers working the shiny brass buttons that closed up the front of his uniform. Lydia wore a diaphanous white organdy nightgown trimmed with lace, her heavy breasts clearly outlined by the sheer gauzy fabric.

Morgan said nothing, just thrust his tongue between her teeth and tried not to notice how different her cool lips felt from Silver's warm ones. His hands stroked her breasts, and he thought how full and heavy they were, not high and lush and curved to fill a man's eager hands. *Little witch*, he thought, more determined than ever not to let her image intrude on his passion. He pulled Lydia closer against him and filled his hands with her heavy breasts.

Damn him! Silver stormed away from the window. Morgan had done exactly as she'd suspected. She had seen him in the garden, watched him make his way upstairs. Now he was up in Lydia's room, getting ready to make love to her.

Damn him! Working to control her temper, Silver carefully tapped the barbed-leafed plant another time against her cheek, hissing through clenched teeth at the sting. *This almost isn't worth it*, she thought, adding a couple more stinging red spots to her neck and chest. But the burning didn't last long, and the red spots remained, looking angry and painful.

Wearing a white cotton nightshirt, her hair plaited into a single long thick braid, Silver hurriedly pulled on her wrapper, shoved her feet into her slippers, opened the door, and stepped into the darkened hall. Marnie had pointed out Lydia's room, seemingly miles down the corridor in the opposite direction. Taking a determined breath, Silver headed that way. Once outside the door, she could hear noises from inside the room and softly whispered words, but little else.

Silver set her jaw. Her resolve growing stronger, she lightly knocked on the door. No answer. She knocked again. Still no answer. Another series of raps, these a little louder, and she called out Lydia's name. In seconds the door swung wide, and a very perturbed and slightly flushed Lady Grayson stood in the opening.

"What is it, Silver?" There was a decided edge to her voice.

"I'm sorry to bother you. I know it's late. . . ." From beneath the hand Silver brought to her brow, she tried to spot Morgan, but he was nowhere to be seen. Lydia gasped at the sight of the ugly red splotches, and Silver swayed against the doorjamb. "I'm afraid I'm not feeling too well."

Naked to the waist, Morgan strode into the room from the small dressing area off to one side. Lydia's eyes rolled skyward at the sight of him.

"What is it?" he asked, ignoring her displeasure at the scandal he'd just created.

"Morgan—" Silver sagged against him. "What—what are you doing here?" With that she swooned, and Morgan scooped her into his arms. Wearing only his boots and breeches, he carried her the length of the hall and placed her on the deep feather bed in her chamber.

"Get a doctor," he commanded, and Lydia hurried to do his bidding.

Silver's dark eyes fluttered open. "It's—it's probably nothing."

Morgan felt her forehead for fever, then eased open the front of her nightshirt to look for more of the ugly red splotches that reddened her face. Several dotted the delicate skin on her neck and shoulders.

"Could you have eaten something that might have caused this?"

Silver wet her lips as if they felt dry. "Not that I know of."

"Just lie still." Worry etched lines at the corners of his bright green eyes, and a little of Silver's anger slipped away.

Lydia returned a few moments later. "Euphrates has gone for the doctor. He lives close by so it shouldn't take long."

Lydia frowned at Morgan's bare chest, which Silver was fighting a determined battle not to notice. Morgan followed the direction of Lydia's gaze, noticed the grim set to her lips, and excused himself, muttering an oath beneath his breath. He returned a few moments later, dressed once more in his uniform, his hair neatly combed.

"I'd appreciate your discretion," he said to Silver, who looked up at him with eyes full of innocence.

"But of course, Major Trask."

By the time the doctor arrived, Lydia was also fully clothed. They left Silver alone with the doctor, who appeared in the hallway a few minutes later.

"I can't seem to figure it out," he said, scratching his balding head. He slipped the pince-nez spectacles he'd been wearing into the pocket of his frock coat and stuffed his stethoscope back into his black leather bag. "She isn't running a fever. The rash hasn't spread below her shoulders. . . ." He shook his head. "I can't imagine what it could be."

Morgan's jaw tightened as a hint of suspicion crossed his mind. "Then you think she's in no danger?"

"I suspect she'll be fine by morning."

"Thank you, Doctor." He turned to Lydia, whose usual calm had returned. "Give me a moment alone with her."

"Of course," Lydia said sweetly. "Why don't we go down to the parlor and have a cup of tea?" she suggested to the doctor.

As they walked away, Morgan pulled open the chamber door and went in to find Silver lying against the pillows, her single thick braid resting on her shoulder. Now that his worry had passed, he noticed she looked decidedly healthy—except for the small red blotches.

"How are you feeling?" Morgan pulled a chair up to the bed and sat down beside her.

"A little weak, I'm afraid."

"The doctor says you'll be fine by tomorrow."

"I'm sure he's right," she agreed.

"But he thinks you should have a big dose of castor oil, just to be on the safe side."

Silver bolted upright. "Castor oil! But—but that's for stomach ailments, not a rash like this!"

"You never know, it might have been something you ate. Lydia's gone to get it."

"But I—" She knew him well enough by now—he would hold her down if he had to. "Morgan, please . . . I hate that vile stuff. I'll be fine in the morning, I promise you."

Morgan's hard eyes bored into her. "You'll be fine," he repeated.

"Yes."

"How can you be so sure?"

"I, ah, I've had something like this before. It didn't last long, just a few hours."

Morgan came out of his chair and bent over her, his look cold as ice. "Why didn't you say so?"

"Well, I, ah, I forgot all about it. It was a long time ago, you see, and I—"

Morgan grasped her wrists and jerked her up from the pillow. "You little fraud. There isn't a damned thing wrong with you, is there?"

"How can you say that? Look at these horrible splotches."

"No fever, no nausea. There's nothing wrong, yet you stirred up the entire household, embarrassed Lady Grayson, dragged the poor doctor out in the middle of the night— Why did you do it, Silver? Why were you so hell-bent on keeping me out of Lydia's bed?"

"I wasn't. I was sick and I—I needed her help."

"What you need is another good thrashing."

Silver stiffened in his grip, silently daring him to try it.

"Why, Silver?" Morgan pressed. "Why did you go to all this trouble?"

The game was over. "I don't know," she whispered with utter desolation.

Morgan eyed her a moment more. "Well, I do." He hauled her to her feet, and his mouth came down hard over hers. It wasn't a gentle kiss; neither was it brutal. It was a man's kiss, hot and demanding, a kiss that seared right to her bones. Silver felt the pressure of his lips, opened to the thrust of his tongue, then trembled at the feel of it stroking the walls of her mouth. His breath tasted hot and masculine; she caught the hint of his spicy cologne. When he released her wrists, her fingers clutched the lapels of his coat, then slid around his neck to pull him closer.

Silver swayed against him, and Morgan deepened the kiss, his hands moving down her body until one wide palm cupped her bottom to settle her more firmly against him. Rock-hard thighs pressed into her, and the solid thickness of his shaft.

Oh, God, she silently whispered as white-hot fire swept through her body. When one of Morgan's hands moved upward to fondle her breast, Silver thought her heart might stop. What in God's name was happening? She should be disgusted, repulsed. Instead she arched against him, wanting more. As if in answer, his fingers brushed her nipple through the thin cotton nightgown. It throbbed where he caressed, puckered, and tightened. He hefted the weight of it, measuring it, caressing it. . . .

Morgan groaned. Silver trembled harder. *Dear*

God in heaven. She felt breathless and achy, warm and melting all over. Morgan eased up her night-gown; then the warmth of his palm returned its fiery contact as it moved up her thigh and settled once more on the curve of her bottom. When Morgan began to knead the soft round flesh, Silver felt a rush of fire so hot she thought her blood might turn to flame. *Morgan,* her mind screamed. *Morgan, Morgan, Morgan.*

She molded her lips to his, ran her fingers through his hair, and softly called his name. It wasn't she but he who pulled away.

"This . . . is . . . not . . . the place," he said, his voice more ragged than husky.

Silver touched her lips and stared at him in disbelief at what had happened. Her breast still tingled, and there was a burning dampness in the place between her legs.

"I'm sorry," she whispered without the foggiest notion why. "I didn't know this would happen."

Morgan set her away from him. "Neither did I." Taking a calming breath, he raked a hand through his hair. "We'll talk about this later."

Silver sank down on the bed, still more bewildered than embarrassed. "Couldn't we just pretend it didn't happen?"

For the first time Morgan smiled. God, she looked so damned appealing with those crazy red marks on her cheeks and that high-necked prim and proper nightgown. He never would have believed he'd be thinking such things about a woman like Silver Jones. But he never would have guessed she could affect him so profoundly.

"I for one will be hard pressed to forget it, but you may try if you like. It's certainly the wiser course of action."

"You won't tell Lydia." Her big brown eyes looked beseeching.

"Hardly." He adjusted the front of his breeches, cursed the situation he found himself in, then glanced back at Silver. This time she looked embarrassed and for once a little uncertain.

Morgan felt a sudden shot of guilt for the liberties he had taken. Bloody hell! He'd be damned if he'd apologize! She had started this game; he had merely finished it. She was just lucky that Lydia and the doctor weren't that far away. "Get some rest, Silver."

"You won't be . . . staying . . . will you?"

Morgan shook his head. "No." Why did her damnable interference please him so much? In truth he was glad he was leaving, though he couldn't quite say why. He'd be facing another night of torment, his body strung tighter than an anchor line. But the fact was he didn't want Lydia, hadn't since the moment he had stepped through her front door.

Maybe he should take his ease on one of the dusky-skinned women who worked the quay. Morgan sighed. Maybe he should face the truth and stop kidding himself. Silver was the woman he wanted.

At least he knew one thing for sure: When he'd kissed Silver Jones in his cabin, she hadn't been pretending after all.

Chapter 10

Silver didn't sleep well. She spent the night tossing and turning, wondering about what had happened between her and Morgan Trask, and alternating between appall at what she had done and elation at the way he had made her feel.

Delia had told her it could be this way—with the right man. Silver hadn't really believed it could happen to her, but she had been wrong. Drastically, inconceivably wrong. There were no words to describe the way Morgan had made her feel. And even though she shouldn't have acted the way she did, she wasn't sorry.

Determined to get some rest, she punched her pillow and tried again to get comfortable. In the wee hours before dawn she finally fell asleep. It wasn't until late the following morning she awakened to a pounding on her door.

"It's me, Missy Jones," came the thin, high voice through the door. "It's Marnie."

"Come in, Marnie." Silver stretched and yawned, feeling far more refreshed than she should have.

"Dat boy Jordy—he downstairs, missy. He say da cap'n ask him to show you aroun'."

Morgan had done that? "Thank you, Marnie. Tell him to wait for me in the parlor. I'll be right there."

A short time later, wearing a delicate ice blue dimity day dress with tiny clusters of flowers appliquéd near the hem, Silver descended the stairs to find Jordan Little sitting stiffly on the brocade settee in the parlor, floppy-brimmed hat in hand. He smiled when she walked in, jumped up, and slicked back his hair.

"Cap'n says you ain't—haven't—ever been to Barbados. He thought you might like to take a ride around."

"That would be lovely, Jordy. Are you sure you don't mind?"

"I'd love to take you, Miss Jones." Dressed in clean canvas breeches and a fresh white linen shirt, his auburn hair neatly combed, Jordy looked as though he meant it, and Silver smiled.

"We'll start by you calling me Silver." She reached for his arm, linked hers through it, and led him toward the door.

"Oh, no, ma'am, I couldn't do that, you bein' an aristo—aristo—"

"Aristocrat?" she put in.

"Yeah."

The butler opened the door, and they stepped outside into the warm tropic air.

"But I want you to. I never had a brother. If you call me Silver, it will almost seem like we're related."

Jordy looked at her in amazement; then his gaze swung away. What was it she had seen in his eyes?

"I've never had a family," he said, "'cepting the cap'n, Cookie, and Jacques."

"Well, now you have me, too."

Jordy smiled, spreading the freckles across his slim straight nose. For a moment he just looked at her. Then his smile dissolved, and his expression turned serious. "I wish I was old enough to look after you, Mis—I mean Silver."

"Well, you're going to—at least for today."

Jordy seemed pleased. He pointed her toward a rented carriage and driver that Morgan had provided and helped her climb in. They took in the Bridgetown sights, then rode out toward the sugarcane fields in the distance.

She and Jordy stopped in an inland village called Bannatyne and luncheoned on the veranda of a tiny Bajan restaurant. The place served sea urchin, flying fish—which Silver pointedly did not order—and langouste, Barbadian lobster, which she did. With it came yams and eddoes, and papaya for dessert. Jordy tasted pineapple for the very first time and proclaimed it the best fruit he had ever eaten.

"Just like George Washington," Silver said with a laugh.

"What do you mean?"

"I read once that's exactly what Washington said when he first came here and tasted the fruit."

"Must mean we're a lot alike," Jordy said teasingly.

"Decidedly—though you're far more handsome." The meal and the day they shared brought a closeness between them Silver treasured. She had meant what she'd said about thinking of him as her brother.

Apparently feeling that same closeness, when they left the restaurant, Jordy seemed more relaxed than she had ever seen him. As they rode along in the carriage, Silver discovered that he had been orphaned so young he didn't remember his parents at all. He worshiped Morgan Trask and Jacques Bouillard, and he spoke repeatedly of Cookie, of the way the tough old sailor had watched after him since he was a little boy.

"Guess things'll be a whole lot different from now on," he finished, beginning to grow pensive. "Cap'n's quit the sea, Cookie's got a woman he's been courtin', and Jacques is takin' a berth on a brigantine, soon as we git—get—back home. I gotta start lookin' after myself."

"Surely Major Trask won't abandon you."

"Course not. But a man's gotta grow up sometime."

"I suppose that's true." But thirteen was awfully young to start facing life alone. Silver knew more about that subject than she should have. Maybe she could talk to the major. Silver thought of the tall handsome man, and soft heat curled in her stomach. "I've been taking care of myself for quite a while," she said, pulling her mind from its dangerous path. "It isn't really so bad."

"Didn't you get lonely?"

"Yes, Jordy, I did." The carriage whirred along the lane, the sound interrupted only by the clip-clop of the horses' hooves. "Sometimes I still do."

They returned to Bridgetown late that afternoon. "I suppose the major has plans for the evening." Silver worked to keep her tone nonchalant.

"He and Owen Moore got a meetin' out near Gun Hill. There's a big cockfight tonight, back o' one of the old plantations. Cap'n and Moore is—are— s'posed to discuss the mission."

"A cockfight." Silver had heard about such things, but she had never seen one. "Are you going, too?"

Jordy grinned. "Yup. Me and Jacques."

"Can I go with you?"

Jordy looked uncertain. "I don't think the cap'n would like it."

"Come on, Jordy. If I went with you and Jacques, surely there wouldn't a problem. Besides, the major might not even find out."

"I don't know, Silver."

"Where's Jacques? Why don't we ask him?"

That idea seemed to set a little better. "All right. He's either down on the *Savannah* or over at the Bull and Crow."

"Let's try the tavern first." They'd be less likely to run into Morgan. Silver instructed the driver, who seemed a bit surprised, and a little while later they pulled up in front of the same shuttered building Jacques had been drinking in before. Jordy ran inside to look for him. Both men came back outside a few minutes later.

"So, *chérie*, you want to see the fighting chickens?" Though the Frenchman smelled pleasantly of ale, he wasn't the least bit drunk.

"It sounds like fun."

"I am not so sure you will think so." He reached into the pocket of his breeches and pulled out a crumpled piece of paper with some sort of sketch and some printing on it. "There is another problem as well."

Silver gasped as she recognized her own image on the reward poster her father had distributed throughout the islands. "Damn him. He always finds a way to make my life hell."

"You are much prettier than this drawing," Jacques said, "but two thousand in gold is a lot of money."

"Pinkard has already claimed the reward. Isn't there something we can do?"

"I can put the word out, try to let them know. But

it will take time for the truth to spread." He glanced down at Silver, one pawlike hand coming up to her cheek. "Maybe you *should* go with us tonight. At least with Jacques Bouillard you will be safe."

Silver grinned with excitement. "I knew we were going to be friends."

"There will be other women there. Not many, but a few. You will not feel out of place. Jordy and I will call for you at six."

"I'll be ready," Silver said. She would tell Lady Grayson that Morgan had arranged the evening. The way the woman jumped at his every command, Silver was sure she'd have no trouble leaving the house.

"Do not go out alone," he warned.

"I won't."

Jacques lifted her hand to his lips. "Until tonight, *chérie.*"

Several hours later, their rented buggy pulled up in front of a huge thatched-roof shed that sat some distance from the main plantation house. The grounds teemed with horses, buggies, carriages, gigs, and phaetons—any and every conveyance that might carry passengers to the evening's big event.

"This is so exciting," Silver said.

"There will be much gambling," Jacques told her. "The stakes will be high."

Silver frowned. She hated not having her own money.

"Don't worry, Silver," Jordy said, reading her expression. "Jacques will wager for you."

"That wouldn't be right, Jordy. What if I lost?"

"You will bring *bonne chance, ma chère*—good luck. We will all be winners."

Silver smiled at that, liking Jacques Bouillard

more all the time. She took his beefy arm and let him guide her through the throngs of people making their way into the interior. Silver had worn a turquoise silk faille gown trimmed with darker turquoise piping. It was a lovely dress, more beautiful for its simplicity. As Jacques had said, there were other women of quality there, not many, but a few, each dressed elegantly and clinging to her escort's arm.

Of course there were just as many disreputables—sailors, gamblers, rogues of every shape and color. Men from the docks, workers from the cane fields, merchants, peasants, doxies. All were mixed up in a potpourri of sights and sounds and colors that made Silver's head spin.

"Thank you for bringing me," she said to Jacques as they made their way inside.

"Do not thank me yet," he warned, but said nothing more.

Inside the open-air shed, the more elegantly dressed patrons clustered in one area while the less wealthy sat across from them. Dressed simply, in dark blue breeches and a clean white shirt, Jacques escorted her to a place somewhere in the middle. She scanned the crowd for Morgan but didn't see him.

In front of them, taking up the center portion of the shed, sat a low-fenced arena called the cockpit. On one side, crates filled with roosters squawked and crowed as their handlers removed one or another from the cages. The shed itself was noisy and crowded; the smell of fresh-cut straw and sawdust filled the air. Dark-skinned men tipped up pottery jugs filled with kill-devil, a harsh Barbadian rum, while others drank sugarcane brandy.

Silver noticed that tonight Jacques didn't drink.

"What's that man doing up there?" She pointed to
a beetle-browed man suspended in a basket above
the center of the ring.

Jacques chuckled softly. "That blackleg is a
sharper who could not pay 'is bet. 'E must remain
there for the rest of the evening."

Silver laughed. It seemed a harmless enough punishment until someone lofted an ale mug and nearly
beaned the man on the head.

"Well, *ma belle*, which one shall be the winner?"
Jacques pointed to the two birds being lifted into the
ring. One was a white chicken speckled with black,
and the other a huge red rooster called a ginger,
whose light and dark feathers fairly glistened in the
glow of the overhanging lanterns.

"The big red one, surely."

"The black and white rooster is the favorite,"
Jacques warned. "'E has won many times."

"But he looks so bedraggled."

Jacques chuckled, and smiled beneath his thick
black mustache. "An old warrior, I think, is often the
toughest. But we will bet on the red." With that
Jacques left her, eager to wager, it seemed. The instant the gamecocks were set on the ground their
neck feathers puffed out, and they took up their
fighting stances, each warily circling the other. For
the first time Silver noticed the huge metal knives
they wore strapped to their thin black legs.

"What are those metal things they're wearing,
Jordy?"

"They're called rippons or spurs. The owners put
'em on so the cocks can fight better."

Silver looked back into the ring. The speckled cock
chose that moment to leap in the air and plant his
metal knives into the feathered breast of the big red
rooster. Silver gasped at the sight of the blood that

gushed from the deep ugly gouges left by the slashing blades. The big red cock flapped his wings and spun away, only to dart back several moments later. His own gleaming weapons sliced viciously into the underbelly of the white speckled bird, and more blood dripped onto the sawdust in the arena floor. Silver's stomach rolled.

Though each had been wounded, the birds cackled and shrieked their vengeance, neither willing to stop or run away. Again and again they flew into each other, sinking in their metal claws, ripping the other's flesh, tearing, and knifing, determined to become the victor.

Silver clutched the wooden bench and looked away. Why hadn't somebody told her?

Across the arena, Morgan glanced up from his conversation with Owen Moore. They'd finished most of their discussion outside the shed, but Moore had insisted on going in, and Morgan had reluctantly agreed. Cockfighting wasn't a sport that sat well with him. It was bloody and, by all good measure, unnecessarily cruel.

He watched the two birds tearing into each other's flesh, feathers flying, blood oozing from cuts and slashes that gouged their small bodies. The red cock had a wing broken and dragging on the ground. The speckled bird hobbled on an injured leg. It was too soon to tell who would win, but Morgan had had enough.

He was just about to go outside when a woman in a turquoise gown caught the corner of his eye. She lifted her head, and the lamplight reflected off her shiny blond hair. Silver. He'd never known a woman with hair that pale and eyes so dark.

What the hell was she doing here? Then he saw Jordy sitting beside her, and his blood began to boil.

He'd trusted the boy with her care; he sure as hell hadn't expected him to bring her to a place like this! Rising from his hard wooden bench, Morgan began to make his way toward Silver, determined to set both his charges straight. He'd give Jordy more than a good what for, and then he'd deal with Silver.

He'd gotten only halfway there when he saw her get up and begin to pick her way toward the far side of the shed. Where the hell did she think she was going? If the place wasn't safe for a woman escorted by a boy, it was a nightmare for a beautiful woman alone.

Morgan cursed her soundly and shoved his way through the throng of people that barred his way. Once outside, he scanned the darkness but still couldn't see her. Then he spotted her turquoise silk skirt peeping from behind the wide rough girth of an ancient palm tree.

Setting his jaw, Morgan made his way toward her. When he reached her side, he grabbed her arm and heard her gasp as he spun her to face him.

"What the devil are you doing here?" His brows drew together in a frown.

Silver looked up at him, her pretty face ashen. "Excuse me, Major." She tried to jerk free. "I'm afraid I'm not feeling well."

"I've heard *that* before."

Silver just looked at him. "I—I didn't know it would be so . . . bloody." Clamping a hand over her mouth, Silver turned away, bent over, and retched into the bushes behind the palm tree.

"Christ." Morgan pulled her skirts back out of the way, held her head while she threw up several more times, then instructed her to stay where she was. In minutes he returned with a damp rag and a pottery jug filled with water.

Silver rinsed her mouth and accepted Morgan's help in washing her face and the beads of perspiration from her brow.

"Damn it, Silver, what in the world possessed you to come to a place like this alone?"

"I'm not alone." She pressed the cool, damp rag against her cheek. "Jacques and Jordy are with me."

"Jacques brought you here?"

"I asked him to. I thought it would be fun."

"Obviously it wasn't."

"No, it wasn't." She let him guide her over to a wooden bench and sank down wearily. "Those poor, beautiful birds."

Morgan sighed. "I know you find it hard to believe, Silver, but there are some things a woman just shouldn't do."

"Surely *you* don't enjoy this."

"As a matter of fact, I don't. But—"

"Good," she said with a lift of her dimpled chin.

Morgan fought a smile. "Why don't I take you home?"

Silver looked at him with relief. "I should be forever grateful."

"I'll go tell Jacques."

When he returned, he carried the crumpled-up poster Jacques had shown her that afternoon. "Jacques sends his apologies." He didn't tell her that this was probably Jacques's idea of a test and that Silver, with her untimely display of compassion, had passed with flying colors.

Morgan unfolded the poster and scanned the big letters that offered two thousand in gold for her return. "I don't like this, Silver. Not one little bit. If one of these men were to recognize you—which isn't too tough—he might try to force your return to Katonga."

"It really doesn't matter. In a few days we'll be gone." *Wrong*, he thought, feeling a mixture of worry and guilt. "As long as I'm careful, surely nothing will happen."

"With you anything could happen," Morgan grumbled, and Silver squared her shoulders. God, she looked incredible standing there in the moonlight. Her dress, cut low in front, showed the tops of her high round breasts. He could remember the smoothness of her skin, the delicate contours of her body. "We'd better go," he said, forcing his mind in a safer direction.

Morgan had ridden a saddle horse to the cockfight. He left it with Jacques and Jordy, who would ride back with Owen Moore and return the horse to the livery, leaving Morgan the buggy.

He was silent much of the time, until he surprised Silver by stopping at a small roadside inn not far from the ocean. "Do you feel well enough to eat something . . . at least have some toast and tea?"

"That sounds wonderful." They drank several cups of tea and ate hot buttered scones, licking pineapple jam off their fingers. The conversation moved easily, both of them feeling relaxed.

"Tell me about your mother," Morgan said when they had finished and sat quietly beside the window. "I always thought a lot of Mary."

"There's nothing much to tell really. I hardly knew her. She died when I was five, birthing my sister."

Morgan's eyes honed in on her face. "I didn't know you had a sister."

"I don't anymore." Silver glanced down at the dainty embroidered flowers on the white linen tablecloth and traced the pattern with her finger. "Her name was Bethy. She was the sweetest little girl. She died when yellow fever swept the island."

Morgan lifted her chin with his hand, forcing her to look at him. "You've lost your mother, your sister. . . . I'm sorry you've known so much sadness."

There was concern in his bright green eyes and warmth in his fingers. That same strong hand had touched her differently last night, she thought, and then wished she hadn't. After what had happened between them, she should be embarrassed just to be sitting there. Instead she found herself wishing he would make her feel those wondrous sensations again.

"What about you?" she asked. "Jordy said you raised your brother alone. You had no family either."

"You have family, Silver. You have a father."

Silver said nothing.

"My brother means a lot to me," Morgan continued smoothly. "Everything. Brendan's wild and reckless, a little too hot-tempered at times, but eventually he'll grow out of it." He chuckled softly. "As a boy he was full of mischief. He got in a few close scrapes, but mostly he was just full of fun." Morgan smiled. "He isn't nearly as serious as his older brother."

"Sounds like I'd like him."

Morgan nodded. "Brendan's intelligent, hard-working, and trustworthy. He's really a very fine man."

Just like you, she found herself thinking. "Jordy says he's a lieutenant. That he's stationed in Mexico. Isn't that where we're headed?"

Morgan's brows drew together, and his eyes turned dark. "How do you know about that? Jordy doesn't know where we're going—surely Riley didn't tell you."

Silver flushed crimson. She could lie, but he'd probably know it. "I read your orders." She saw his murderous expression and reached for his arm. "Please don't be angry. I didn't know you then. I was just trying to survive. I've never said a word about it, and I never will."

Morgan watched her a moment; then the muscles in his arm relaxed. "I should have known." He looked a bit disgruntled, but his anger had fled. "At this point I don't suppose it matters. Besides, they'd probably have an easier time breaking Riley." Silver wasn't quite sure how to take that. "Come on," Morgan said.

They drove the buggy down to a white sand beach where the waves lapped softly against the shore. Moonlight traced a path across the water, and a breeze whipped loose strands of Silver's hair. After taking off her slippers, she turned her back to Morgan, unfastened her garters, and rolled down her stockings. The sand felt warm as it sifted between her toes. The air smelled fresh and clean and salty. Morgan's hand held hers as he guided her along.

"About last night," he said, stopping her beneath a towering palm tree and turning her to face him.

Silver held a finger to his lips, silencing him. "I'm not a woman of easy virtue, Major. What happened between us was . . . unexpected, to say the least. But I'm not sorry."

"I wish I could tell you I was, but if I did, I'd be lying. I want you, Silver. I know I shouldn't, but I do."

Silver slid her arms around his neck and rose on tiptoe to kiss him, tenderly at first, then with building passion. Morgan's arms went around her, pulling her close. He tasted so very male, felt so incredibly solid and masculine. Heat slid through her at the slick, moist warmth of his tongue, the demanding pressure of his lips. Muscles bunched across his shoulders as he bent his head to deepen the kiss, and Silver caught the faint aroma of tobacco that had swirled around them at the inn. She laced her fingers through his wavy dark blond hair, leaned into the heat of his body, felt his hands sliding down her back to cup her bottom and hold her against him.

Morgan groaned and pulled away.

"What—what's the matter?" she asked breathlessly.

"We shouldn't be doing this." He captured her fingers against his chest and she could feel his rapidly beating heart. "I'll be leaving soon, Silver. The Brits have been sighted. They'll arrive sometime in the morning. We'll transact our business, and the day after that I'll be gone. I won't be back until my mission is complete."

"But I'm going with you."

"You're staying here. Owen Moore has agreed to look out for you. There's a war going on in Mexico— it's certainly no place for a woman."

"But you said—"

"I said I'd take you back to Katonga on my return, and that's exactly what I intend to do. In the meantime, you'll stay with Lydia. I'll expect you to keep your word and be here when I get back."

"But—" Morgan leaned down and kissed her, silencing her protests.

The contact ended far too soon for Silver.

He raked a hand through his hair and looked at her hard. "I'm not about to steal your virtue and abandon you—though right now that's exactly what I'd like to do."

"If you were trying to *steal* my virtue, Major, you wouldn't have a chance."

"I'm not a marriage-minded man, Silver."

"Good."

"Good! What the hell does that mean?"

"Marriage is the last thing I want. Trading one master for another, constantly bending to some man's will. I want no part of it."

Surprisingly Morgan looked disgruntled. "Well, what the devil *do* you want?"

"Right now I just want you to kiss me."

Morgan's eyes bored into her. He seemed to be waging some inner battle of wills. "You are without a doubt the damnedest—" Grabbing her arm, he tugged her across the sand toward the buggy. "It's time you went home," he said through clenched teeth.

Silver didn't argue. If Morgan didn't want to kiss her, that was his problem. She had other things to worry about—like finding a way to stow aboard his ship.

Chapter 11

Silver discarded the idea almost as quickly as she thought it. The outrageous things she had done before were done out of necessity, a driving need to survive. She'd had to escape from Katonga, and she had done everything in her power to succeed.

But stowing away aboard the *Savannah*, leaving the comfort of the house on Chelsea Road to set off with Morgan Trask for Mexico—that was an idea not worth the time it took to think it.

Dressed in her soft white cotton night rail, Silver sat in front of the mirror above the carved mahogany dresser and began to brush her hair. Morgan had returned her home several hours earlier, and an extremely cool Lady Grayson had greeted them at the door.

"So . . . the two of you . . . found each other after all," she had said.

"Jacques wasn't ready to end his evening, so I brought Silver home." Morgan smiled pleasantly.

"Would you like to come in for a brandy?" The way Lydia's eyes moved over his body said that wasn't all he would get.

"I'm afraid I haven't the time. The cargo we've been expecting arrives in the morning. I've some work to do yet tonight."

"I see" was all the small woman said.

Silver remembered the gentle farewell she had received from Morgan, the bitter look from Lydia, and shuddered. With Morgan gone, Silver would be forced to spend weeks with Lady Grayson, whose regard for her rested somewhere between hostility and outright disdain. Since Silver's interference in Lydia's affair with Morgan, the woman had barely spoken to her.

Aside from that, there was the matter of her father. Those reward posters had been distributed not only on Barbados but throughout the West Indies. Any sailor passing through might have seen one. Silver wasn't sure her protector, whoever he might be, would be able to watch out for her every minute, and the idea of going back to Katonga was enough to make her insides churn.

That brought to mind another point. Sooner or later Morgan intended to return her to her father. That left two alternatives: She could break her word and run away—which she found herself loath to do, or she could tell him the truth and pray to God he would understand.

At that notion her stomach rolled harder. She couldn't imagine what Morgan would say to the truth about William Hardwick-Jones. He probably wouldn't believe it, and even if he did, what would he think? The thought of him looking at her with the repulsion he was sure to feel made Silver's churning stomach squeeze into a hard, tight ball.

There had to be a way to convince him without revealing her terrible secret. Whatever it was, it was sure to take time.

More than the day's sail it took to reach Katonga.

Silver finished brushing her hair and plaited it in a long single braid. If stowing aboard the *Savannah* had sounded crazy at first, it was beginning to sound far less so. And there was one more factor in her decision, something she had only begun to suspect but had confirmed tonight on the beach beneath the towering palm tree: Silver was falling in love with Morgan Trask.

He certainly wasn't in love with her—at least not yet. But she was sure he cared for her. Maybe more than he knew. She didn't know where such an attraction might lead, but she damned sure wanted time to find out.

By the time Silver settled herself beneath the mosquito netting in her huge four-poster bed and pulled up the covers, her mind had, in its usual way, sorted through the whys and why nots several dozen times, and she had reached a decision.

One way or another, when the *Savannah* left Barbados and set sail for Mexico, Silver Jones would be aboard.

As Morgan had predicted, the British ship *Horatio* pulled into Carlisle Bay the following morning. Morgan met with Captain Bartholomew and Owen Moore, his liaison, and preparations were made to complete the exchange of the *Savannah*'s load of cotton for Barbadian sugar, which in turn would be traded for the *Horatio*'s supply of guns.

The off and onloading progressed without a hitch until a second ship, the small American brigantine *Adversity*, sailed into the bay midafternoon. Morgan was working in his cabin, going over the bills of lading, making final checks on cargo invoices and congratulating himself on his admirable behavior with Silver the night before.

Of course only part of him was proud of the way he'd behaved—the other part called himself ten kinds of fool.

"Excuse me, Major," came a resonant voice from outside his open cabin door, interrupting his thoughts, for which he was grateful.

Seeing a tall dark-haired man wearing the same blue uniform Morgan wore—and the bright gold braid of a colonel—Morgan shoved his chair back, came to his feet, and met him at the door.

"Constantine Buckland." The colonel extended a hand, which Morgan accepted. "Just arrived from Texas aboard the brig *Adversity*."

"Major Morgan Trask. It's a pleasure to meet you."

"Under normal circumstances, I'd quite agree. However, I'm afraid I've brought some very disturbing news." Buckland's speech, unaffected by the usual soft southern burr, sounded refined. He was obviously well educated.

"I think you had better come in, Colonel."

Buckland unconsciously squared his shoulders and stepped into the cabin. He was a big man, not as tall as Morgan, but heavier, a little less well conditioned. He looked to be ten years older, was beginning to gray, but was still a handsome man. He took a chair, and Morgan sat back down at his small oak desk.

"There's no easy way to say this," the colonel began. "I'm afraid our troops on the Yucatán have run into trouble. Superior Mexican forces have cut our men down to nothing. Over half of our soldiers have been captured. I regret to inform you that your brother is among them."

The air seemed to hiss from Morgan's lungs. "Where are the Mexicans holding them?"

"Somewhere outside Campeche. Both our troop-ships are anchored nearby, awaiting orders. Your mission is no longer just to carry weapons—somehow we've got to find a way to free our men."

Morgan assimilated the news for a moment. "How many soldiers have you brought?"

Buckland looked uncomfortable. "The *Adversity* is not a troopship, Major, merely a courier. I have ten men in my command and the authority to hire another ten mercenaries, if I can find them."

Morgan's jaw clamped, and he surged to his feet, his hands unconsciously balling into fists. "What the hell are you talking about? Are you telling me that the five Texian soldiers who sailed with me and the few men you have are all they've sent to break half the Texas forces out of prison?"

"What I'm telling you, Major, is that the rebellion in Mexico is failing. Our troops have suddenly become an embarrassment to the sovereign Republic of Texas. We cannot afford to escalate the size of this incident."

A muscle bunched in Morgan's jaw. "This is hogwash, Colonel. Those men acted in good faith; now you're abandoning them."

"It isn't as bad as it seems. We still have half our troops. With the weapons you're carrying, we've got a very good chance of mounting a successful opposition."

Morgan raked a hand through his hair, knowing further disagreement would do no good and beginning to resign himself. His breath came out on a sigh. "Jacques Bouillard can help find the mercenaries we need. We'll be loaded and ready to sail on the morning tide."

"How long do you anticipate before we reach Campeche?"

"Three weeks. If we're lucky, maybe a little less."

For the first time Buckland seemed unsure. "I just hope to God the men can hold out until we get there."

Morgan sank back down in his chair. *You hear that, little brother? You damned well better hold out.*

Morgan thought of the long months after his breakup with Charlotte, of the two deplorable weeks he and Cookie had spent in a Barcelona prison for brawling in Santiago's Cantina. The place had been a hellhole. From what Buckland said, allowing time for the news to arrive, Morgan figured Brendan might have already spent months in the same sort of prison. Brendan was tough, Morgan knew, but a place like that had a way of breaking a man.

Morgan cursed beneath his breath. He would push his men and his ship as hard as he dared, get there as fast as wind and God allowed. Then he'd find a way to get in there and get those men out—one way or another.

He just prayed Brendan would still be alive when he did.

"Good-bye, Major." Silver smiled into his handsome face.

"Good-bye, Silver.. Take care of yourself and remember your promise."

"I know you'll get him out." Morgan had told her of Brendan's capture and the urgency of their mission, figuring she already knew most of it anyway. Silver rose on tiptoe to kiss his cheek.

They were standing on the dock beside the ship amid the hustle and bustle around them. Ship's rigging clattered and clanked, and sea gulls swooped

and screeched and sailed high on the wind. Morgan
had said his good-byes to Lydia back at the house,
though her response had been less than cordial. Silver had insisted on returning with him to the wharf.
Morgan agreed, but only because one of Owen
Moore's men was waiting in the carriage to return
her home.

"How soon before you sail?" Silver asked.

"Less than an hour. We're just about ready."

"Then I guess I'd better be going."

"Yes," he said, but neither of them moved.

"I'm going to miss you, Morgan Trask." His eyes
looked as green as the gem-bright Caribbean Sea.

Morgan cupped her cheek with his hand, his
thumb brushing lightly across her jaw. She felt the
feather-soft caress like the brush of wings, and liquid
heat curled in her stomach. Then he did the unthink-
able. In front of God and the dozens of people who
lined the quay, he hauled her into his arms and
kissed her, his mouth moving over her so hot and
hard Silver's knees went weak. When he finally let
her go, she had to steady herself against him to keep
from falling.

Morgan smiled roguishly. "We'll·talk some more
when I get back."

Silver only nodded and watched him walk away,
shoulders squared as he strode the wooden dock.
Turning, she started toward the man who waited discreetly in the open carriage.

"I'm ready," she said when she got there, climbing
in without waiting for his help.

It took only minutes to reach the house on Chelsea
Road, but every second was precious. Silver said a
quick good-bye to her protector, assured him she
wouldn't be leaving the house again that day, and
hurried up to her room. Once there, grateful some

insane instinct had convinced her to bring them along, she changed into Jordy's shirt and breeches.

In preparation for her extended stay, the rest of her clothes had been sent to the house. Silver took as much of her things as she could carry, though the satchels weighed her down, but she didn't intend to lug them that far. Jacques would be waiting at the corner.

How she'd been able to convince him to help her remained a mystery. Mostly she had dwelled on his concern for her safety, convincing him that no one but he or the major could possibly be man enough to protect her from the scurvy fellows who had surely seen the reward posters.

Whether he had his own reasons for helping her she couldn't be sure, but there had been an unaccountable twinkling in his eyes.

Just as he'd promised, Jacques waited patiently at the end of the block, looking as tall and solid as an oak tree. Eyeing Jordy's form-fitting clothes, he handed her a dark blue sailor's cap, beneath which she quickly stuffed her hair. Even as he hefted her heavy leather bags and strode toward the quay, he seemed to be smiling in a way that was far too smug for Silver's taste, but she certainly didn't say so.

"I will keep him distracted while you come aboard," Jacques promised. "You must stay out of sight in the hold at least for the next few days. I do not think Morgan would return you, but it is better to be safe. I will bring you blankets and food."

"Thank you, Jacques. I'll feel a whole lot safer being there with the two of you."

"That, *chérie*, is what the sheep said to the wolf."

True to his word, Jacques boarded first, hid her satchels, and went to find Morgan, signaling her to board while he was gone. Silver kept her head down and climbed the rail. There was more activity aboard ship this time, more men in uniform, as well as the scurvy-looking lot who were the soldiers of fortune Jacques had hired.

With more men to feed, a pigsty sat on deck alongside several crates of chickens. All and all, it was a chaotic scene that made her movements on deck easier. Silver hurried across the holystoned pine, going straight to the ladder that led down into the hold. It was dark and dank in the low-ceilinged room and smelled of bilge water. Silver heard a shuffling sound in the corner and shivered, knowing it had to be rats.

Finding a likely place to hide beside a stack of well-secured gun crates, Silver made herself as comfortable as she could on the cold wooden planks of the hull between the ship's ribs. It wasn't long before she felt the deck heel, heard the creak and moan of timbers as the ship sailed from the harbor.

How long should she stay hidden? she wondered, hoping against hope that it wouldn't be too long. What would Morgan do when she appeared on deck?

Morgan was just as stubborn as she was, just as willful, just as determined. But for reasons she couldn't completely explain, she trusted him. Though he'd often had reason, Morgan had never hurt her. She didn't believe he ever would.

She amended that. When he found her aboard this ship, he was bound to go a little bit crazy. She wasn't about to tell him Jacques had helped her. After all that Jacques had done, it would hardly be fair. Silver cringed just to think of her encounter with the major. God, he'd be madder than one of those mean-tempered fighting gamecocks.

Early in the evening, Jacques brought Silver the

blankets and food he had promised, as well as a small whale-oil lamp. He didn't stay long; he had his own work to do, and he didn't want anyone coming down to look for him. With little to occupy her time, Silver napped for a while, but mostly she fidgeted, certain one of the furry creatures that squeaked nearby would sneak up on her if she weren't looking.

God, she hated them.

Silver shifted on the blanket she had spread beneath her, a bit of insulation from the dankness of the hull. The place smelled of wet timber, tar, and mold, but she'd already grown used to it. Besides, if things worked out, the inconvenience would be worth it. The thought renewing her spirits, she finally fell asleep just before morning, though in the darkness of the hold, night never turned into day.

Jacques returned again some hours later, carrying more food and the latest copy of the *Barbados Advocate*, since she'd told him she desperately needed something to read. Once he was gone, the newspaper occupied her for a while, but the lamplight was so dim it was difficult to see the small black newsprint. Silver fidgeted, paced the confining space of the hull, and grudgingly endured her dank, close quarters. It was dark outside, she was sure, but out of boredom she had slept again during the day, and now she wasn't sleepy.

Silver rubbed the ache in her neck and changed her position on the floor of the hold, propping her back up against a stack of wooden crates. In the distance she heard footfalls ringing on the ladder; then a lantern lit the far end of the cavernous room. Sure it was Jacques, Silver wasn't worried.

She should have been.

The footfalls grew louder, and a man's tall shadow loomed on the hull of the ship, gigantic in the glow of the approaching yellow light. Silver watched the shadow draw near, watched it take shape and form, and knew in an instant the perfect V-shaped figure wasn't Jacques.

"What the—" Rounding the crates, Morgan held the lantern high and stared down at Silver in stunned disbelief. His jaw clamped tight as he set the brass lamp on top of the wooden boxes and glared at her, his green eyes glittering with rage.

Silver swallowed hard. "Good . . . evening, Major."

Morgan's hand snaked out and grabbed her arm, jerking her roughly to her feet. "What the bloody hell are you doing here? How did you get aboard?" His fingers gripped the tops of her arms until she winced.

"I sneaked aboard when you were busy."

"Why?"

Silver stiffened in his grip. "If you think I was going to sit around holding lengthy conversations with your mistress for the next two months, you've got another think coming."

"Is that so? Well, if you think I'm taking you with me, *you've* got another think coming!"

"What are you going to do, turn the ship around and take me back?"

"Exactly." Picking up the lantern, he dragged her toward the stairs, her stumbling footfalls echoing in the confines of the hold. "And when I find out who helped you, he's going to find himself dumped back on that island with you."

"What about your brother?" Silver prodded. "Every day you spend sailing back increases the risk to his life."

Morgan stopped short at those words and turned to face her, his expression thunderous. "You planned this from the moment I told you I was leaving, didn't you?"

"Yes—I mean, no. It occurred to me then, but I wasn't sure until I had time to think things over. Under the circumstances, this seemed the only logical thing to do."

"Logical? What in God's name is logical about a young woman stowing aboard a ship full of soldiers on a dangerous mission to Mexico? This isn't some kind of game, Silver. There's a war going on down there."

I'm fighting a war of my own, she thought. *I always have been.* "I won't be in your way, I promise. When we dock, I'll stay with the ship. Maybe I can even find a way to help out."

"Damn you, Silver."

"Morgan, please. This won't be as bad as you think."

His green eyes raked her, assessing every curve of her body in Jordy's faded clothes. Though he looked furious, the tension in his face had begun to ease. "I hope to hell you brought something else to wear."

Silver grinned, unable to believe she was getting off so easy. "I did."

"I must be crazy," he muttered, beginning to believe he really was. For in truth he was damned glad to see her. On top of his fears for his brother, Morgan had been worried about Silver since the minute he had left her at the dock.

He was worried about that damnable reward money William had offered. Afraid some dockside thug would recognize her and take it into his head to abduct her, just as Pinkard had done. Worried that once the man got her alone, her tender charms would outweigh any thoughts of reward.

He was also afraid she might run away, put herself

in even graver peril. She'd given him her word, but he wasn't sure she would keep it. If she tried to escape, Moore's men would be hard pressed to stop her; he knew that first hand. He still didn't trust her —he wasn't even completely convinced she hadn't fled Katonga to meet her lover, as Pinkard had said.

Morgan glanced down and found her smiling up at him, her pale hair glistening in the lamplight. She looked so appealing in her damnable boy's clothes— outrageous and desirable, as only Silver could. At least this way he could watch out for her. Of course the ship was more crowded now, and there were nearly a dozen mercenaries sleeping on the deck. Morgan shuddered to think of them eyeing Silver's luscious behind.

"Where are your clothes?"

"Over in the corner."

"Do us both a favor and put on something a little less revealing." He thought of Colonel Buckland. What would Buckland say to a woman coming along? Morgan cursed roundly. "I'm warning you, Silver, you had better behave. And if I find out Jordy's behind this, you can bet he's going to get far worse than he got from me the last time."

"Jordy doesn't know anything about this."

Morgan sighed. "Sometimes I think you are bound and determined to make my life a living hell."

Silver just smiled. "You're wrong, Major." In fact, if she had her way, she hoped things might turn out just the opposite.

Refusing to accept Morgan's cabin, Silver settled herself once more in Jordy's. She shook out her dresses and hung them up, and by morning the dampness had eased away the wrinkles. With Morgan on the opposite side of the door just a few feet away, Silver slept soundly. She felt safe and pro-

tected, and now she had the time she would need.
Things would work out, she told herself firmly. Everything would happen in its proper time.

Then she met Colonel Buckland, and as the poet
Burns once said, "The best laid schemes o' mice and
men. . . ."

From the moment of their first encounter, Buckland was enthralled with Silver. Morgan explained
her presence by telling him about the reward posters
and the threat of danger Silver faced.

"She made a mistake by running away from
home," Morgan told him, casting Silver a hard green
glance that warned her she had better play along.
"But she knows that now. Unfortunately, with those
posters around, she was afraid for her safety." Silver's mouth twitched. "She felt she needed our protection, so she stowed aboard. I'm sure she'll be no
trouble," he finished with a last pointed glance.

Seated beside Buckland at the round oak table in
the salon, Silver smiled sweetly. "I really meant no
harm, Colonel. Major Trask promised my safe return
to Katonga. I merely thought coming with him
would be the best way to ensure that. Now that I've
met you, I feel even safer. I hope you don't mind."

"It was a foolish thing to do, Miss Jones," he said
with gruff authority, "but I can certainly understand
your fears . . . a woman alone and unprotected.
You may rest assured that you will be safe on board
the *Savannah*."

"Thank you, Colonel." Silver glanced at Morgan,
who looked torn between amusement and exasperation. When Buckland reached over and patted her
hand, Morgan's expression changed once more.

"Why don't we take a turn about the deck, my
dear?" Buckland suggested.

"Well, I'm not sure—"

His chair scraped back, and he urged her to her feet. "You have no need to worry. I'll be right beside you. The men will know better than to give offense."

"That isn't exactly what I meant." Over her protests, Buckland escorted her up on deck. She didn't see Morgan for several hours, and when she did, he seemed guarded and strangely silent.

That night at supper, Silver wore a fashionable rust silk gown and the men wore their uniforms, in deference to the colonel, she was sure. Throughout the meal of chipped beef, hardtack, and molasses— far simpler fare than they'd shared before—Morgan remained cordial but not overly friendly. Hamilton Riley was also present, bestowing upon her his usual warm greeting, for which he got a stern look from Buckland. Jacques took his meal with the crew.

When supper ended, the men enjoyed brandy and cigars, Silver insisting she liked the aromatic smell. The conversation mellowed, and Silver turned to Morgan, hoping he might walk with her up on deck. It was Buckland who offered.

"A walk after supper is often just the thing," he said.

"I'd love to, Colonel, really I would, but—" Silver glanced at Morgan, hoping he would intercede, but he only excused himself and walked away.

Buckland took her arm and helped her climb the ladder to the deck. The night was warm and tropical, the seas rolling with a light swell. Moonlight bathed the water, and a cool breeze freshened the air. Buckland smiled at her warmly and settled a hand at her waist to guide her along. As the ranking officer he seemed to feel she was his responsibility, assuming the role of escort and protector whenever she was near.

"Shall we, my dear?" Buckland inclined his head toward the bow of the ship.

Silver wanted to say no, that it was Morgan's company she wanted, but Buckland was Morgan's superior. She wasn't sure what power he might wield.

As they strolled along, the men the ship transported moved discreetly out of their way. All except the mercenaries, who eyed her boldly, though Buckland cast them each a glare of warning. He was handsome, she decided, but a bit too mature for her tastes. Still, he was intelligent and an interesting conversationalist. She discovered they both enjoyed playing chess and agreed to a match the following day.

"You're very good, my dear," the colonel said that afternoon, though he had beaten her two games out of three.

Silver laughed softly. "You've thrashed me soundly. I hardly think I deserve the compliment."

Buckland covered her hand with his and leaned over to whisper something in her ear.

That was the moment Morgan chose to emerge from his cabin. He stood in the doorway, his feet braced apart, and Silver recognized the hard glint of his anger. Though what had transpired with Buckland had been perfectly innocent, Silver flushed.

"Enjoying the voyage, Colonel?" Morgan said to Buckland, propping one wide shoulder against the cabin wall.

"Lady Salena has made it memorable already."

"Please, Colonel," she said without thinking, "I had hoped you would call me Silver." When Morgan's dark expression turned even darker, Silver cursed her wayward tongue.

"Oblige the lady, Colonel. You never know what other requests she might have in store."

The mocking tone of Morgan's voice said he was recalling the last request she had made: *Right now I just want you to kiss me.*

Silver's cheeks grew warmer still.

The colonel smiled in her direction. "I'd be delighted to call you Silver, my dear, if you would agree to call me Connie."

Silver could have kicked herself. "Of course . . . Connie."

Morgan turned and stalked from the room.

For several more days Connie Buckland paid homage, filling her hours and keeping her occupied. Wherever they went, Morgan seemed to appear. When they went up on deck, he stood at the rail; while they played cards in the salon, Morgan worked in his cabin. Yet whenever he glanced in her direction, it was as if she weren't there.

Damn, if only she could think of a way to dodge the colonel's attentions, but short of telling him that it was Morgan who held her interest, she couldn't think of a way. She thanked God the man was sleeping in the mate's cabin, up in the foc's'le with the crew.

At least she got to see Morgan for a moment or two each night before bed. He was always polite—exceedingly so—but otherwise cold and distant. She wished she could think of a way to break through the shell he had erected.

Chapter 12

"It's awfully late, Colonel. Shouldn't we be going below?" Most of the soldiers were already asleep, some on deck, some in hammocks strung belowdecks. Only the larboard watch, who had the night's duty, remained up and about, and the helmsman in the aft wheelhouse, who worked the huge teak wheel.

"It's such a lovely night," Buckland said. "It seems a shame for it to end so soon."

"But—"

Dressed as always in his immaculate blue uniform, Buckland took her arm and started toward the bow. There was usually no one sleeping at that end of the ship, so there were several dark places she needed to avoid.

Silver pulled him to a halt. "I really must be going, Connie. I appreciate your company, really I do, but—"

"Nonsense, my dear. You can sleep a little later in the morning."

Silver didn't miss the way his eyes slid down to the curve of her breast. Though the gown she wore was a simple light green batiste, the bodice dipped low, emphasizing the high, round swells, and the matching wide green sash made her waist look incredibly narrow. Buckland's hand moved possessively in that direction, and he firmly urged her forward. Silver hedged. So far the colonel's advances had been subtle, but he was getting bolder every day.

Her mind was working feverishly to find another objection when Jacques Bouillard, wearing duck pants and a wide-striped shirt, appeared from belowdecks. Silver could have kissed him.

"Ah, Colonel Buckland," he said, pronouncing the middle *l* in the colonel's title, "finally I have found you. The men 'ave made a wager about whether or not your Republic of Texas will be admitted to the United States. They are in need of your expert judgment to settle the matter."

Buckland smiled. Silver decided he succumbed to flattery more easily than any man she had ever met.

"You go ahead," Jacques told him. "I will see Mademoiselle Jones safely below."

Buckland released his hold on her waist. "I'm afraid duty calls, my dear." Lifting her slender hand to his lips, his mouth a little too moist, he kissed her fingers. When he was gone, Silver sighed with relief.

"I don't know what I'm going to do about that man."

"You had better figure it out and soon," Jacques warned, "before the *capitaine* figures it out for you."

"What do you mean?"

"If you cannot see it, *chérie*, how am I to explain?"

"But I—"

"Come. It is time you went to bed."

Silver let Jacques lead her down to the salon. While he stood near the ladder, she knocked quietly on the door to the captain's cabin and waited while Morgan pulled it open.

"I'm sorry to be so late, but the colonel—" Before she could finish, Morgan dragged her into the room and closed the door. That he was angry, she had no doubt.

"You and Buckland out for another midnight stroll?" He made it sound so lewd Silver bristled.

"What do you care? You haven't given me the time of day since I arrived."

"How could I? You've spent every waking hour with Buckland!"

Silver's eyes fixed on Morgan's body. He stood naked to the waist, his breeches slung low on his hardmuscled hips. She tried not to notice the lamplight glistening on his curly blond chest hair, the way it arrowed across his flat stomach, then disappeared into the waistband of his pants.

"He thinks he's protecting me."

"Protecting you? That's a laugh. Connie Buckland's no different from any other man on board this ship. He's squiring you around because he thinks there's a chance you'll warm his bed."

"You're crazy."

"Am I? How many times have you kissed him?" He stood with his feet braced apart, glaring down at her, the scar on his cheek white and drawn. Surely he couldn't be jealous.

"I've never kissed him—if it's any of your business —and I don't intend to. I told you once before, Major, I'm not a woman of easy virtue. I don't give my affections lightly."

"No?" he mocked, surprising her. "Why don't we find out?" Morgan moved closer, his arm snaking out, circling her waist, then hauling her into his arms. Before she could protest, his mouth came down hard over hers. Morgan pressed her back against the wall, used his body to pin her, ground his hips into hers. But even as his tongue thrust violently between her teeth, Silver felt the stirring, the longing she had known before.

Morgan's hand slid down her body, gripped her bottom, and forced her against him. She could feel his arousal, hot and heavy, feel the buttons closing up his fly, and soft heat slid through her body. He tasted faintly of brandy, a lock of hair fell over his forehead, and hard muscle rippled across his chest. Unconsciously Silver's fingers pressed into his hot, damp skin, the roughness of his curly blond chest hair. Feeling the slick, moist warmth of his tongue, the demanding pressure of his lips, Silver moaned, and Morgan's movements stilled.

He pulled away to look at her. She should have been angry, she realized; it was anger he expected. Instead her eyes were filled with longing; the blush of passion stained her lips. She should have been fighting, scratching and clawing, demanding that he stop. Instead she looked up at him, let him see exactly what she was thinking. Let him know his fiery thoughts mirrored her own.

With a groan of defeat, Morgan cupped her face with his hands and kissed her eyes, her nose, her mouth. Silver slid her arms around his neck. Morgan kissed her gently, his tongue teasing now, coaxing, almost begging her to give him what he wanted. One hand pulled the pins from her hair, and the heavy silver mass cascaded past her shoulders.

He laced his fingers through it, tilted her head back, and deepened the kiss. His hand moved over her breast, stroking the rounded flesh through the barrier of her clothes, then sliding inside her bodice, cupping the fullness, his fingers stroking the rosy peak to hardness. Each of his touches inflamed her.

Silver's nipples puckered and tightened, and waves of heat washed over her.

"Morgan," she whispered, the word almost a plea.

He kissed the curve of her neck, nibbled her ear, trailed a path of fire to the hollow of her throat. Sliding her gown off one shoulder, he lowered his head to the soft white flesh that filled his hand. Silver's knees felt weak, her body aflame. Morgan suckled at her breast, and the sensuous little tugs sent a bolt of white-hot lightning careening through her body. When she trembled and arched against him, Morgan pulled away.

"Please," Silver pleaded, knowing this was what she wanted—the ultimate reason she had hidden on board his ship.

Morgan seemed uncertain. "You spoke of affection, Silver. It's more than affection that I'm asking from you now. Are you certain you're ready to give it?"

Silver looked up at him. The passion that blazed in his eyes left no doubt about what he meant. "Yes," she whispered softly.

With a groan low in his throat, Morgan bent his head and kissed her. One hand slid beneath her knees, and he lifted her into his arms. Silver wrapped her arms around his neck and leaned against him. He carried her over to the bed, set her down gently, and began to strip off her clothes. She was trembling now, but with anticipation, not fear. She wanted Morgan Trask, wanted to feel his hard frame next to her, wanted to explore the strange and wondrous sensations he stirred in her body.

Morgan worked the buttons down her back, pulled her gown away, and kissed her shoulders. His lips felt hot against her skin, his touch almost reverent.

He cupped her breasts, his strong hands kneading, stroking, sending shivers of heat through her limbs.

In minutes he had removed her petticoats and corset, leaving her in pantalets, garters, and chemise. Propping each leg on his thigh, Morgan rolled down her stockings. He kissed her calf, the dimple in her knee, then moved higher, until she squirmed.

"Hurry," Silver whispered, but Morgan only smiled.

"I've waited too long for this, vixen. I don't intend to hurry now." With a thoroughness she didn't expect, Morgan kissed her, then covered her with his long, hard body and pressed her back on the bed. While his mouth and tongue worked their magic, his hand stroked her nipple, and a fresh surge of heat rolled over her.

Morgan slid up her chemise and fastened his mouth on her breast. At first he suckled gently; then he nipped and tugged, licked, and circled the peak until Silver could barely breathe. Fire seemed to race through her body. Her fingers dug into his hair; she raked his back with her nails and arched against him.

"Morgan," she whispered, the place between her legs beginning to burn.

With hands a little less steady, Morgan pulled the chemise off over her head, worked the tie that held up her drawers, then slid them down her hips to the nest above her sex. His hand skimmed over her flesh, molding her breasts, stroking the flat spot just below her navel.

It wasn't until his long, skilled fingers moved lower, slid inside her pantalets to caress her thigh, that Silver felt the first small twinge of something other than passion.

"I want you," Morgan whispered, his hard body

pressing her down on the bed, his heavy weight holding her immobile. His hand slipped purposely along her skin, into the downy blond triangle of hair at her core, and Silver tensed.

"Easy," he soothed, but the words seemed to come from far away. Morgan kissed her again, long and hard; then his finger slid inside the soft, damp folds of her flesh.

Silver felt the heat of it, felt his probing touch . . . and something snapped inside her head. Suddenly, in the eye of her mind, it wasn't Morgan's lips she felt, wasn't his gentle fingers between her legs. It was something dark and sinister, something evil and repulsive. Something she had to fight no matter the cost. She started to struggle, tried to cry out, but Morgan's hard kiss silenced her.

Silver battled the image that rose before her, fought to recall the handsome face of the man who held her, but all she saw was the ugly face of the devil himself. *Stop!* she tried to cry out, her body growing rigid and beginning to thrash beneath the heavy weight that pinned her down. *Let me go!*

But the words were lost, and the fingers delved deeper inside. Silver felt the bile rise in her throat. She no longer knew where she was or why she was there; she knew only she couldn't stand another moment, knew that she had to escape. Tensing and squirming, beginning to scratch and claw, Silver struggled in earnest. With a whimper of fear, she finally tore free of the hands that held her, only to discover a stunned Morgan Trask looming above her.

Tears flooded her eyes, and a soft sob caught in her throat. Oh God, how could she have let this happen? Morgan's words came back with a vengeance. *What kind of woman are you?* What would he think of her now?

Terrified of what she might see in his face, Silver wouldn't look at him. Instead she felt his heavy weight as he shifted on the bed and swung his long legs to the floor, taking a place beside her. Then he eased her into his arms.

"It's all right, sweeting, I'm not going to hurt you." Morgan hadn't missed the touch of her maidenhead, which he'd only half expected to find. He should have been more careful, but tender young virgins were hardly his style. "I'm sorry I scared you. I didn't mean to go so fast."

Silver shook her head. "It isn't you." She looked up at him through her tears. "I was afraid this might happen." The anguish in her soft brown eyes was unlike anything he had seen. "No matter how much I want this, now I know I can't."

"You're just frightened." Morgan brushed strands of hair from her tear-damp cheeks. "There's nothing to be afraid of."

Silver only shook her head. "You don't understand."

For the first time Morgan saw it—there in her eyes. The unnatural glaze that wasn't fear of him, but something else, some dark emotion that fought to get out yet remained locked away. "Tell me," he said. "Tell me what has happened to you."

She only glanced off in the distance, her gaze fixed on some unknown point on the opposite wall.

Morgan cupped her chin with his hand and turned her to face him. "Tell me."

For a moment Silver said nothing. Then resolve settled into the lines of her face, and something that looked like resignation.

She swallowed back her tears and glanced away.

"I was only thirteen," she whispered, staring once more straight ahead. "There was a man. . . ."

Morgan felt his stomach clench.

"He came into my room. He—" She broke off with a bitter sob.

"It's all right, sweeting. Just take your time."

"I don't want to talk about it. I'm afraid of what you'll say."

Morgan stiffened. "You were only thirteen, for God's sake. Whatever happened, you're hardly to blame."

Silver said nothing.

"I want you to tell me, Silver."

Silver's eyes slid closed against a wave of pain. When she opened them, her lashes were spiked with tears. "He tore off my nightgown." Her tongue ran over her trembling lips. "He was so heavy . . . pressing me down on the bed. I can still remember how hot and moist his hands were, the way they quivered when he held me down and slid them over my body. He touched me . . . where you did. . . . Oh, God, I felt so dirty . . . so terribly, horribly dirty."

Morgan pulled her tighter against him, wrapping his arms around her and wishing he could take away the pain.

"Delia stopped him," she continued. "She risked her life for me."

"It's all right," Morgan soothed. "No one's going to hurt you now." He wanted to ask who the man was, wanted to know if she had told William. But she looked so upset he didn't want to press her.

Silver leaned her cheek against his chest, her trembling fingers resting over his heart. "I wanted you so badly. I was sure with you I wouldn't be reminded. Now I'll never know what it's like to be with

a man." Warm tears wet his skin and glistened on
the thatch of hair across his chest.

"You're wrong, Silver. All it takes is the right man,
a little patience . . . and a little trust." Morgan recognized his words as the truth and made a decision.
With the abrupt end to their lovemaking, he had
been given one last chance to end this madness with
Silver before it was too late.

Morgan wouldn't take it. Silver had responded to
him with a passion as fiery as any he had known.
Even now it was there, simmering just beneath the
surface. Morgan had enough experience with
women to know exactly how to make that passion
erupt.

She brushed the tears from her cheeks and looked
up at him, hope and something more in her eyes.
"Do you really think so?"

Morgan bent his head and kissed her, a soft, gentle
kiss meant to stir a bit of that warmth. "Well?" he
prodded lightly when he finished. Her face looked
flushed, her lips rosy-hued and pouty.

"Maybe there is a chance." Still, she didn't seem
sure.

"What you've told me tonight sets you free, Silver.
You had nothing to do with what happened. No man
is going to blame you—especially not me." He lifted
her chin with his fingers. "Trust me?"

Brown eyes, no longer troubled, fixed firmly on his
face. "More than any man I've ever known."

For reasons Morgan couldn't explain, her words
stirred something inside him, and another decision
was made. Meanwhile, he had set himself a task and
he meant to tackle it as he never had another.

When Morgan Trask made love to Silver Jones,
there'd be no room in her mind for thoughts of another man.

* * *

Morgan left the bed and walked to his desk. Removing the heavy glass stopper from a decanter of brandy, he poured some of the amber liquid into a snifter and returned to where Silver sat on the edge of the bed. She still wore her pantalets, pulled back up to her waist, but only her weighty mass of silver hair covered her beautiful breasts.

"Drink this," Morgan commanded.

Silver blanched as the brandy blazed a path down her throat, but she took several more healthy sips, and some of her tension seemed to ease. Morgan kissed her tenderly, enjoying the taste of the liquor that sweetened her lips. When he reached for the cord to her pantalets, her hand shot up to stop him.

Reluctantly she released her hold on his wrist. "I'm sorry." Apparently she meant to abide by her word and leave the matter of her seduction up to him.

Morgan gently slid the white cotton drawers down her legs, leaving her naked, and eased her back on the bed.

"Do you know how lovely you are?" Silver flushed and glanced away. "You should be proud of your body, Silver. It's one of the most beautiful I've seen."

Silver said nothing, but she seemed to relax a little more. Morgan took that moment to pull off his boots and unbutton and slide off his breeches. Silver watched with quiet fascination as he walked toward her naked, his shaft still rigid with desire.

He stood boldly in front of her. "Touch me, Silver. Feel how much I want you."

For a moment she seemed uncertain, then with trembling fingers, she reached for him, her warm hand sliding around him, tentatively at first, then

with more daring. A slow smile curved her pretty
pink lips.

"That's enough," Morgan said, a bit more harshly
than he had meant to. He touched her cheek.
"There's a good deal left for us to do yet this eve;
we'll need to go slowly. You've just as much power
over me as I do you." *More*, he thought. Already he
ached for her with every heartbeat, and they hadn't
even begun.

Morgan joined her on the bed, settling his long
length beside her. Reaching over, he kissed her,
sweetly at first, bringing a soft response, then with
more urgency. It took only minutes to arouse her,
seconds more to feel her body writhing beneath him,
urging him onward. After what had happened, he
wouldn't have believed she'd respond to him again
so quickly, but this was Silver, not some ordinary
woman. He should have known.

Silver felt his hands on her body, felt the gentle
skill with which he touched her, and the heat he
stirred seemed to sear through her limbs. His mouth
touched everyplace his hands did, tasted, nipped,
and turned her to flame. Only Morgan could make
her feel this mounting tide of passion. Only Morgan.
She saw his face in her mind's eye, saw his warm
green eyes, saw his smile, saw the scar that was so
much a part of him. Morgan lifted a breast into his
hands, bent down, and laved her nipple in such an
achingly sensuous manner Silver moaned.

Her own hands moved restlessly from the muscles
across his shoulders, to the smooth dark skin on his
back, to his tight round buttocks. She kneaded the
sinewy globes just as he had done to her and heard
his low-pitched groan of passion. His hardened shaft
pressed hotly against her thigh.

Morgan eased to his side and continued his patient

exploration, his hands moving to the flat spot below her navel, his hard shaft pressing against her leg. His fingers kneaded and teased, raised gooseflesh across her skin, but strayed no farther.

"You like this, don't you, Silver?"

Silver squirmed beneath his touch, wanting more, yet dreading the consequences. "Yes."

Morgan levered himself up on an elbow and looked down at her. "Take my hand, Silver." His voice sounded rough and husky. "Your body needs soothing. I'm the one who can do it."

This was what she wanted, wasn't it? Both of them knew that it was. No longer uncertain, Silver clasped his fingers and slid them lower, through the pale blond hair at the juncture of her legs. Morgan traced patterns on the insides of her thighs, stroked through the downy thatch, then parted the silky folds of flesh and slid his finger inside.

Silver moaned as a flood of heat rushed over her.

"It's me, Silver, no one else." His fingers slid out and then in, gentle yet determined, and this time Silver knew exactly who it was. "Feel me, Silver. Trust me." Teasing and stroking, stretching her gently, he readied her for what lay ahead. Silver writhed against the growing heat, the building fires of passion. Certain she would die of the pleasure, she strained against his probing touch.

"Please," she whispered.

"Please what, Silver? Please, Morgan, stop?" His hand stilled and with it the fiery sensations.

"Oh, God, no." Morgan's practiced fingers slid in and out, caressing and touching until her skin felt on fire and her body trembled all over. Something was rising inside her, something elusive. But it wasn't dark and loathing, only sweet and inviting, beckoning her to far-off planes.

Just when she thought she might reach it, Morgan stopped.

"Please," Silver begged. "Oh, God, Morgan, please."

"This is what you need, Silver." He pressed her hand against his throbbing arousal. It felt thick and hard and so hot she thought it might scorch her. There was power in that smooth, hard flesh, power and domination. But there was the promise of excitement, too, and reward far sweeter than she had ever dared to dream.

"Yes," she whispered. "Yes."

Morgan positioned himself above her, centering his hardened shaft at the entrance to her soft, damp flesh and easing the tip inside her. When he went no farther, Silver nearly sobbed in frustration.

"Do you want me, Silver?"

"I want you. I need you, Morgan, please."

Morgan kissed her then slid himself inside as far as he could go, stopping only when he had reached her maidenhead.

"There'll be pain, sweet, but only for a moment."

Her loins felt on fire. "Please," she whispered. The pain didn't matter—what she suffered now had to be worse than anything he might do.

And it was; the tearing lasted only a moment. Morgan eased himself full length then stopped, waiting for her body to accept the fullness of his invasion.

"All right?"

"Yes."

"No more nightmares?"

She smiled at him softly. "This dream is nothing like the other." Morgan bent his head and kissed her, his tongue sweeping into her mouth, coaxing hers to do the same, rousing her as it had before. The pain was gone completely. She could feel his hard length as he drew himself out, then slid into her once more. Again and again he drove into her, moving faster and faster, thrusting hard and deep, until Silver gave in to the mindless swirls of passion. She met each of his pounding thrusts, entwined her legs with his, and arched her body against him.

His powerful strokes consumed her, driving against her soft flesh, pounding and pounding, her hips moving beneath him, arching to meet each of his thrusts. Every nerve ending sang with the feel of him, every sinew, every fiber. She clutched his shoulders and cried out his name, and something sweet and hot rolled over her. Her mind swirled; her body tensed; bright bursts of sunlight glittered behind her eyes. It was so incredibly sweet, so deliciously poignant. She felt awed by it, humbled in a way she couldn't explain.

Morgan tensed just moments later. Silver clung to him as he spent his passion and he held on to her. It was a sweet moment, lying there beside him, closer in that moment than she had ever been to another human being. As they spiraled back to earth, Morgan tenderly kissed her, their flesh still firmly joined, the taste of him still heady. Then he settled himself at her side and cradled her in the curve of his arm.

She might have dozed, she couldn't be sure. Sometime later she stirred.

Morgan's hand lifted strands of her tangled blond hair. "All right?"

"You were wonderful." She traced a pattern with her finger in the curly hair on Morgan's chest. "Thank you."

He laughed softly. "Now there's a first. A young woman loses her virginity and thanks the rogue who's accomplished the deed."

"I mean it. If it hadn't been for you . . ."

Morgan turned her face to his. "That's all behind you, Silver. What's happened is past."

Silver smiled softly. "Delia told me it could be this way, but I didn't believe her."

"You care a great deal about them, don't you?"

"They're wonderful people. I've known Quako since I was a child. He taught me a man could be gentle, even a strong man like he is . . . or a tough man like you."

Morgan's eyes, such a vivid shade of green, caressed her face. "He loves his wife very much."

"Delia isn't his wife. Quako wants to marry her, but my father doesn't believe in marriage among the slaves. He thinks they're little more than animals."

Morgan arched a brow. "I never took William for a man of such prejudice."

"Maybe living in England he had no reason to be. Here things are different."

Morgan tucked strands of her tumbled hair behind an ear. "Speaking of your father, I don't suppose you ever told him about the man who attacked you."

This was her chance. Her stomach turned over. What would he think of her if he knew? Lying there naked in his arms, warm with the glow of their lovemaking, she felt so close to him. She couldn't bear the thought of destroying that closeness so soon.

"I didn't think he would understand."

"Silver—"

She pressed her fingers to his lips, stilling his next words. "Not tonight," she whispered softly. "Tonight belongs to you and me."

Morgan smiled. "I'd be a fool to argue with that." Rolling on top of her, he kissed her, slowly, determinedly. His arousal, hot and rigid, pressed once more against her thigh.

They made love slowly this time, getting to know

each other's bodies, taking delight in what they found. Later in the night Morgan awoke, hard with desire. Silver was already awake, enjoying the chance to watch him.

"Not sleepy?" Bold green eyes swept over the curves of her body beneath the thin white sheet.

She shook her head. "No."

"Good." He pressed her into the mattress. "I've got just the sleeping draught you need."

Silver laughed softly. Wrapping her fingers around his thick shaft, she guided him inside her. Their coupling was fiery and joyous, but in the morning when she awoke, Morgan was gone.

Silver dressed quickly, a bit concerned about the day ahead. She felt different this morning, womanly. She prayed to God Colonel Buckland wouldn't be able to see it. Or Jacques, or Riley—or even Morgan, for that matter. She wondered what he would say to her but couldn't for the life of her guess.

He was still her father's friend. He would be worried about William's finding out. And Morgan was a man of conscience. If Silver hadn't practically initiated their lovemaking, she had a feeling it would never have happened.

Reflecting on it, Silver smiled. Morgan had given her a most precious gift: the knowledge of a man and a woman. No matter what happened, she would cherish it always. But how did she feel about Morgan? The answer was easy—she was in love with him.

"So what do I do about it?" she asked herself aloud. Morgan wasn't in love with her; at least she didn't think he was. And she certainly didn't want a man who didn't want her.

Maybe *want* wasn't quite the word. Silver didn't

doubt Morgan's interest in that area. In truth the pleasure they'd shared was exactly what Silver wanted from Morgan and exactly what he wanted from her. She refused to think of the future, of a time when they might part. She would worry about that day when it came.

Bending over the bureau, Silver checked her image in the broken chunk of mirror and straightened the bodice of her soft peach muslin day dress, noting with satisfaction the delicate embroidered flounce around the hem. Since the windows above Morgan's berth had been repaired in Barbados, Silver crossed the cabin to look outside.

"Damn," she whispered, seeing the sun had risen high in the sky. Why hadn't Morgan awakened her? As if in answer, a light rap sounded at the door, and Morgan walked in, carrying a tray laden with food: fluffy scrambled eggs—a concession from the chickens—salt pork, biscuits, and strong black coffee.

He set the tray on his desk, strode over, and kissed her cheek. "None the worse for wear, I see. You look beautiful."

Silver smiled. "Thank you." She walked over to survey the tray. "This looks delicious—I'm starved—but what did you tell the others?"

"That you were still in your cabin when I left—probably a little tired from your late-night stroll with Connie."

Silver laughed, the sound softly tinkling. "I'm sure he puffed up like a peacock."

Morgan laughed, too. "Doesn't he always?"

She sat down at Morgan's desk and took a bite of the eggs, steam rising up from the food on the plate.

Morgan stayed with her until she finished, making idle conversation about the weather, the slight possibility of storm. He seemed a little nervous, she noticed as she continued to sip her coffee.

"There's something we need to discuss, Silver." Morgan came to his feet to stand in front of her. She had to tilt her head back to look at him. "I've done this only once before, so you'll pardon me if I'm not very good at it."

Silver just looked at him, wondering what he was getting at.

"I'm asking you to marry me."

Silver smiled indulgently. She should have expected something like this. "That's very gallant of you, Major, but you told me yourself you weren't a marriage-minded man. This really isn't necessary."

"What do you mean it isn't necessary?" His brows shot up, his expression changing from uncertainty to one of disbelief.

"I mean you don't want to get married and neither do I. I thought we both understood that."

"That was before things . . . changed . . . between us. Now things are different."

"Are you in love with me?" she asked.

"Well, I—I certainly feel something for you."

That was a start, she supposed, but certainly not enough on which to base a marriage—if she was interested, which she wasn't sure she was. "Well, I care a great deal about you, too. But neither of us is ready to take that kind of step."

Morgan's green eyes seemed to glow. "You were a virgin, for God's sake. You can't just sleep with a man and then act as though nothing has happened."

"Why not? That's what you intended to do with Lydia."

Morgan's hands balled at his sides, his expression grim. "Are you turning me down?"

"It isn't anything personal. I'm just not ready for

marriage." *Especially to someone who's proposing out of duty.* "I'm not sure I ever will be."

"You can't be serious."

"Oh, but I am. I've seen the kind of life marriage brings. I'm not convinced that's the way I want to live."

"But surely your mother and father were happy."

"Not as I recall. But that isn't the point. I'm not ready for marriage, and neither are you. I appreciate the gesture, but let's just leave it at that."

Morgan's jaw clamped so hard a muscle bunched in his cheek. *Bloody hell!* Half the women in Savannah would jump at the chance to be his wife. He had wealth, power, social position, a beautiful mansion on Abercorn Street. "If it's money you're worried about or your father's approval, I assure you there's no problem."

Silver actually laughed. "Don't be silly. I know you're a man of means. Even if you weren't, it wouldn't matter to me one way or another. The fact is I don't want to get married. Since you don't either, I don't see that we have a problem."

Morgan ground his teeth. She was right, of course. He was proposing because it seemed the honorable thing to do. He wasn't ready for a wife, wasn't ready to be that tied down. So why the hell did it make him so bloody angry that she wouldn't have him?

"Suit yourself," he said. "You're not exactly what I had in mind anyway."

That stung. "I'm sure I'm not. You'd rather have some sugarcoated woman who simpers at your feet. Someone like Lydia, all sweetness and charm and a mouthful of mush. You couldn't handle a wife with a mind of her own."

"Oh, I could handle her all right." Morgan clamped his hands on his hips and bent over her.

"I'd keep her barefoot and pregnant and take a hand to her backside every now and then just for sport."

"Bastard!" Silver surged to her feet, so furious she accidentally knocked the tray over. The heavy china plates went crashing to the floor, landing with a thud and smashing into bits. The last of her eggs lay in a greasy yellow heap, and drops of coffee splattered across the hem of her peach-hued skirt.

"Same sweet Silver," Morgan goaded. "When you aren't throwing things, you're dropping them."

"Damn you!" Picking up the now-empty coffee mug, Silver hurled it at Morgan's head as he strode to the door. He ducked and it crashed against the wall.

"Have a nice day," he mocked, slamming the door behind him.

Silver sank down on the bed, looking at the destruction at her feet and wondering what had gone wrong. Morgan didn't want to marry her, so why was he so upset? His pride, she thought, his damnable masculine pride.

Maybe she could have handled things better, she conceded, but she hadn't expected him to get so riled up. After all, she'd been doing him a favor. He didn't love her; she wasn't even the kind of wife he wanted. She glanced at the bed, neatly made once more, but the gray woolen blanket on the surface couldn't blot memories of what had happened beneath the sheets.

In three short minutes Silver had destroyed everything she had worked so hard to build. Short of marrying him to ease his pride—which neither of them wanted—there was little she could do. Silver slammed her fist against the mattress. What was it about her that seemed to keep things constantly stirred up? One thing was certain—what she had shared with Morgan the night before was hardly finished.

Even Morgan would have to admit that.

And when he did, things would work out.

Silver knelt on the floor and began picking up the broken dishes and greasy bits of food, careful not to cut her fingers. She had just reached toward the last piece of glass when the ship hit a quartering swell, the sudden lurch reminding her of the voyage that still lay ahead—and the island she had left behind.

Whatever happened between Silver and Morgan, her father's dark presence still loomed like a bitter cloud above them. What would William do when he discovered she had sailed with Morgan? He wouldn't give her up, she knew, not now, not ever.

Maybe she *should* marry Morgan. At least she'd be safe.

Or would she?

William would know where to find her. That her husband was wealthy and powerful would not stop him. There was little the earl would not dare.

Silver sighed. There was no easy answer. No miracle that would end her worries. For the present she was free of William and for that she felt grateful. Until a solution arose, Silver's best course of action was to bide her time, try to mend things with Morgan—and politely try to fend off Connie Buckland.

Chapter 13

"Bring in the darkie." William Hardwick-Jones stood before the black marble mantel in his study. Dressed immaculately in a dark brown frock coat and trousers, cream brocade waistcoat, white shirt and stock, he cut an impressive figure.

"He's waiting in the foyer." Sheridan Knowles opened the heavy wooden door and motioned for the big black slave called Quako to come in. Standing so tall he had to duck his head to step through the opening, once his massive body was inside, Quako seemed to shrink the size of the mahogany-paneled book-lined room.

William arched a disapproving brow at the dirt that stained the big slave's clothes but refrained from making comment. "I hear congratulations are in order," he said with a slightly mocking smile. William was a tall man, taller than Sheridan, thick-chested with large hands and feet. He had a full head of graying black hair, obsidian eyes, olive skin, and a thin-lipped, cruel-looking mouth.

"Yes, suh." Quako twisted the stained felt floppy-brimmed hat he held in his huge pink-palmed hands.

He wore baggy gray linen trousers and a faded homespun shirt that barely buttoned across his massive chest.

"Children are such a delight." William lifted the lid of the humidor that sat on his carved rosewood desk and pulled out a long, fat cigar. Striking a lucifer, he brought it to the tip and puffed until the end began to glow. "I've been told you conversed with Salena on her return . . . you and your lovely lady, Delia. Did Salena mention where she and the major were going?"

"No, suh."

"No? But the three of you are . . . *friends*, are you not?" Sheridan didn't miss William's distaste at the use of the word in context with his daughter.

"Yes, suh."

"Surely she would tell such friends where she was headed."

"She just say she go with da major. He say he bring her bock here when his trip be t'rough."

William blew a wreath of blue smoke into the room. "You'd better hope he does, Quako. Because if he doesn't, I'm going to believe you know where she's gone. That you've been lying to me. Then you and your woman will tell me—one way or another."

Quako said nothing, just raised his massive head and squared his shoulders, his dark eyes fixed on the pair of crossed sabers on the wall behind William's desk. The gleam was there, the unspoken hatred— his unholy wish to wrap his huge hands around the handle of the saber and thrust the blade into his master's heart.

William saw it, too, as he always did. "That will be all," he said coldly, "for now."

Quako stood staring for an instant longer than he should have, then turned and strode from the room.

When the door closed behind him, William turned to Sheridan, who stood just a few feet away. "Give him a taste of the lash. His insolence may be unspoken, but we both know it is there."

Sheridan nodded. "Trask has got to return to Barbados," he said, getting back to the subject at hand. "He's got to bring back the mercenaries he hired." It had been easy to discover the path of the *Savannah* —at least as far as Barbados. Salena had stayed on the island with Lady Grayson while Trask and his men prepared to sail. But when the *Savannah* left port, Salena had disappeared.

"You're certain she's with him?" William pressed. "There can be no mistake?"

"With Salena nothing is ever certain. You should know that far better than I. But I believe she's with him—yes."

"How can you be so sure?"

Sheridan eyed his employer. He knew about William's obsession. There were few on the island who didn't.

Sheridan didn't care. He was the brains behind Katonga, the man who ran the huge plantation, the man who had made it what it was today. And William was smart enough to recognize his talent. The earl paid him a kingly wage, had for the past ten years.

Soon Sheridan Knowles would have enough money to buy a plantation of his own. Let the earl have his sick fascination with his daughter—or whoever she was—Sheridan wasn't really sure. Salena had been a hellion since the day he had met her, always interfering with his orders, always causing trouble among the slaves. He couldn't care less what William did to the willful chit. With luck maybe he would break her rebellious spirit and teach her a woman's place.

"The girl's with Trask," Knowles repeated. "There was something about the way she looked at him. She trusts him, and she thinks he'll help her escape."

William's narrow lips thinned even more. "Then we'll be ready for them. I won't take any chances. I want the best men you can find waiting for them in Bridgetown. Double the reward. I want her back home."

You want her in your bed, Sheridan thought, but didn't say it. "What about the darkie? Shall I make certain he knows nothing that might help us?"

"Give it some time. If Salena is not aboard the *Savannah*, we'll deal with him and his woman. The man will tell us what he knows."

Silver hadn't counted on missing Morgan so much. Now that she had been with him so intimately, just sleeping at night without him beside her seemed a challenge.

Sogger didn't mind Morgan's absence. He had staked out the place at Silver's feet on the narrow berth, arriving well before she closed the tiny cabin door. After his nightly ear scratching, he gathered himself into a scruffy orange-striped ball and settled down to a roaring purr. As Silver lay awake, listening for Morgan on the opposite side of the door, she just wished she could rest as soundly.

Morgan seemed to have no trouble at all. In fact, he rarely looked at her anymore. Oh, he was cordial enough, almost friendly on the surface, but underneath, his disdain for her was clear. It rankled her to think that her refusal of his grudgingly offered proposal made him think her somehow immoral—but not enough to accept, to ruin both their lives. It oc-

curred to her briefly that someday Morgan would
thank her for turning him down, but that thought
was so depressing Silver forced it away.

She did, however, in the days that followed, have a
serious talk with Connie Buckland, carefully explaining that she certainly hadn't meant to lead him
on and that she felt a little more discretion between
them would be in both their best interests. Connie
grudgingly agreed, though she couldn't determine
for just how long.

With more time to herself, Silver had a chance to
renew her friendship with Jordy and even with
Hamilton Riley.

"Jordy tells me your family raises cotton along the
Red River," Silver said to Ham one day as they sat
beneath a makeshift canvas awning, trying to escape
the too-hot Caribbean sun.

"Once my enlistment is up, I plan to return to our
plantation. Evergreen will be mine one day; I hope
to see it prosper." Riley wore his uniform pants but
days ago had shed his jacket. His shirt, now casually
unbuttoned, fluttered softly in the breeze.

"I'm sure you'll be a great deal of help," Silver
said, meaning it. Ham had put on a bit of weight, she
noticed, filling out his slender frame, and his face
was reddened by the sun. All in all, he looked more
of a man.

As the lieutenant entertained her with stories of
his childhood, Silver picked absently at a spot of tar
that had somehow gotten on her rose batiste skirt.
Considering the chaos on deck, the extra men, supplies, and even animals, she felt lucky her clothing
had held up as well as it had. She glanced at the
sailors high in the rigging, at others picking oakum,
mending line, or repairing block and tackle. Up toward the bow, her eyes came to rest on two brawny

seamen, mercenaries Jacques had hired in Barbados, who sat naked to the waist astride a wooden chest.

"What's going on over there?" she asked Ham. Jordy stood grinning beside the bigger of the two, a red-haired, hard-faced, barrel-chested man who always eyed her boldly whenever she saw him on deck.

"They're boxing of a sort—open-handed. Less likely to do any permanent damage, but it smarts like blazes. Mostly it's just to pass the time. Sometimes the men wager on who'll stay atop the box the longest."

"I see." The two men finished sparring, both in high spirits. Then Jordy sat down opposite a slender man who wasn't much bigger but looked nearly twice his age. "Surely Jordy isn't going to try it."

"He'll be all right."

"But he's just a boy."

"He'll be a man soon enough. It's all he talks about. I guess his future worries him some." Jordy slapped and flailed, receiving like treatment, his freckled face turning red from the stinging blows. He was no match for the older man, who had obviously played the game for hours.

"It isn't fair to pit a young boy against someone of so much more experience," Silver said indignantly, intent on stopping the match before Jordy got hurt. Ham caught her arm.

"Let him be, Miss Jones. He'd rather take his lumps than be shamed in front of the men."

Silver glanced from Jordy to Ham and back. Her shoulders sagged. "I suppose you're right, but I still don't like it."

Fortunately the game soon ended, and Silver breathed a sigh of relief. The brawny man who had gone before him settled a beefy arm across Jordy's shoulder, whispered something in his ear, then laughed uproariously. It was obvious from the look on Jordy's face the man had already won the young boy's admiration. From the unkempt appearance of the mean-faced mercenary in his grubby canvas breeches and tattered shirt, Silver was afraid it boded trouble.

She wished she could speak to Morgan about it, but that was hardly possible under the circumstances. Damn it to hell, she'd been sure Morgan would settle down and see reason. Instead he remained distant, determined not to renew their relationship. Lately he'd turned dark and brooding, and more than a little bad-tempered.

As the day wore on, Ham excused himself from her company, and Jacques took his place. It seemed an unspoken rule that Silver was rarely left on deck alone, which, considering the way some of the men looked at her, was probably just as well.

"A fine day, *n'est-ce pas?*" The big Frenchman sat down on the deck box beside her. "The winds 'ave freshened again—we 'ave been lucky so far."

Silver glanced at Morgan who stood near the big teak wheel in the aft of the ship, engrossed in conversation with the helmsman. "I suppose it's all right."

Jacques chuckled softly. "You are lonely? I did not think such a beautiful woman would be lonely with so many admirers."

She forced a smile she didn't feel. "I'm not really lonely."

"It is *le capitaine*—the major," he corrected. "I think 'e is not so 'appy either."

"He looks perfectly happy to me," she said petulantly.

"If you knew 'im better, you would see." Jacques smoothed his mustache, then stroked his heavy black beard. His powerful biceps flexed beneath his home-spun shirt.

"I'm really not his type, you know. He likes his women oozing with sweetness. He expects them to do exactly what he says, whether they like it or not. I'll never be that way."

"Ah, but you *are* sweet, *chérie*, and Morgan knows it. 'E is attracted to you, but 'e is also afraid."

"Afraid! Afraid of what?"

"'E was in love once—five years ago—with a wealthy planter's daughter. She was beautiful. Charlotte Middleton was 'er name." Jacques glanced out to sea, watching the swells, the tiny whitecaps that broke the surface of the water. "They were going to be married. It was only by accident that Morgan found 'er in another man's bed."

"Oh, no," Silver said softly, remembering him with Lydia and knowing exactly how Morgan must have felt. "Why did she do it? If she loved him—"

"Love means different things to different people. I think Charlotte loved Morgan. But she loved 'erself more. She took 'er pleasure in the moment. In the end she may 'ave been sorry, but for Morgan it was too late. 'E does not wish to love another woman as 'e once did Charlotte, so 'e holds 'imself back."

"He asked me to marry him."

Jacques eyed her speculatively as if he could guess what had happened between them. Silver felt the heat creep into her cheeks.

"Why did you not say yes?"

"How do you know I didn't?"

Jacques grinned at that. "Because you would be 'appy, not sad."

"He didn't really want to marry me."

"Maybe 'e did; maybe 'e did not. *Le capitaine* is a man of great conscience. 'E will do what 'e thinks is right. But 'e would never marry a woman unless 'e wanted to."

"I don't want to marry a man who doesn't love me. In fact, I'm not sure I want to marry a man at all."

Jacques chuckled and patted her hand. "Morgan —'e was right about one thing—you are quite a 'andful, Silver Jones. Whether 'e knows it or not, I believe you may be exactly the woman for 'im."

As the day wore on, the wind began to blow, and the huge puffy clouds overhead grew dense and gray. Whitecaps breaking against the bow tossed salty sea spray into the air and dampened the unwary. Morgan only seemed pleased.

"If the seas don't get no—any—rougher, we'll make some real good time," Jordy told her. "Cap'n's real worried about his brother . . . guess that's why he's been so bad-tempered lately."

"I hadn't noticed," Silver said.

"Perty hard to miss," Jordy said with a grin.

Silver didn't answer.

"You like him, don't you?"

"Sometimes."

"I think he likes you, too."

"Don't be so sure—" She noticed Jordy's eyes were fixed on the two rough-looking men he had been talking to earlier. "Those men you're looking at, Jordy, they seem a bit disreputable. . . . Are you sure about them? I mean—"

"Big one's Farley Weathers—they call him Stormy 'cause he's so mean-tempered. Other one is Dickey Green."

"Just be careful," Silver warned. "Men like that sometimes bring trouble."

"They're okay, Silver. They're just tougher'n most is all."

Silver nodded, hoping Jordy was right and her instincts were wrong. "I think I'll go below for a while," she said. "Thanks for the company."

At supper that night, Morgan didn't appear. He had work to do in his quarters—or so he told Ham, who made his excuses for him. Disgruntled at his abandonment and beginning to get bored, Silver accepted Connie Buckland's invitation for an after-supper stroll. It was the first time she had walked with him in the evening since she had been in Morgan's bed.

"You seem pensive tonight, my dear," Buckland said. "I hope nothing is wrong." Dressed immaculately as always, his dark blue uniform spotlessly pressed, Constantine Buckland presented a picture of masculinity. He was charming and gracious—and pompous and patronizing.

"Of course not, Connie." Silver pulled her black woolen shawl a little closer around her shoulders. The breeze had remained brisk all afternoon, the ship cutting through the water with record speed, but it felt only the least bit chilly. "I guess I'm just getting eager to reach our destination. That seems to be a common ailment among those at sea."

Connie patted her hand where it rested in the crook of his arm. "Another week should do it. But never forget there is grave danger in Mexico. You must stay aboard the ship at all times."

"I will," she promised, but only halfheartedly. It would feel good just to walk on solid land again, even for an hour or two.

They strolled the pine deck, talking about Texas, the republic's ongoing skirmishes with the Mexicans, their fervent wish to end the conflict once and for all, but Silver found it hard to keep her mind on the conversation. Instead her eyes searched for Morgan. She cursed herself soundly, calling herself a fool. She shouldn't give a fiddler's damn about a man like Morgan. A man who would abandon her at the slightest provocation. Still, she did care, and she missed him.

As the ship sliced through the water beneath a waning moon, the hour grew late, but Silver felt reluctant to go below. She hadn't slept well for the past three nights; tonight would be no different. Instead she let Connie guide her toward the bow of the boat, her thoughts disjointed, her mind someplace else. She didn't notice until too late that he had led her behind the small white deckhouse that held the cooperage.

"Silver," he whispered, just before he lowered his head and kissed her. Though she tried to turn away, his wide mouth covered her lips and his tongue slid forcefully between her teeth.

Silver broke away. "Stop it, Connie, this is hardly the place." She pressed her hands against his chest and tried to wedge some space between them, but the colonel only tightened his hold.

"If you would only give me a chance." He pressed her back to the rough wooden wall and kissed her, his lips hard against hers, his tongue possessive and not the least bit thrilling.

When he wouldn't let go, Silver's hands balled into fists against his chest in angry protest, but before she had a chance to break free and deliver her assault, she heard footfalls ringing behind them, then the sound of Morgan's voice sliced bitterly through the still night air.

"So, Her Ladyship has snared fresh game," he taunted, his voice cold and mocking.

Silver tore away from Buckland's grasp and whirled to face him, her breasts rising and falling with her rapidly speeding heart. "What's that supposed to mean?"

"It means as soon as I stop chasing after you, you set your sights on something bigger. I should have guessed a colonel would be more to your liking than a major."

"See here, Trask—" Buckland cut in.

"Are you saying this is my idea?" Silver raged, as if the colonel hadn't spoken.

"You're a woman, aren't you?"

"Damn you!"

"Watch out, Salena, you wouldn't want the colonel to see that nasty temper of yours."

"Why, you—" Silver swung at him and missed. Her petticoats caught between the colonel's long legs, and only his arm around her waist kept her from falling.

Morgan just laughed. Turning on his heel, he started walking away. "Enjoy your evening, Colonel," he called back over one wide shoulder.

Silver wanted to kill him. Instead she turned the force of her fury on Constantine Buckland, bringing her palm across his cheek in a stinging blow that nearly flattened him. Hoisting her rose batiste skirts, she stormed away, leaving him staring after her.

Silver marched across the deck, descended the ladder into the main salon, and pulled open the door to Morgan's cabin. Knowing he wouldn't be there, she entered her tiny steward's quarters and began to unfasten her clothes. As mad as she was, she nearly tore off the dainty cloth-covered buttons in her furious effort to loose them. Though her hands still shook, eventually she accomplished the task, shed her petticoats, pantalets, and chemise, and pulled on her nightgown. At the sound of Sogger's familiar mewing outside her door, she opened it and let the mangy cat inside to join her.

"He's a real bastard," she pronounced, scooping the furry feline into her arms and stroking his pitiful orange-striped fur. "How could I possibly care about a man like that?"

When Sogger didn't answer, Silver sighed and sank down on the berth. *Why does he always think the worst of me?* she asked herself, not for the first time. Then she thought of her own opinion of the opposite sex, which, except for Quako, and until she'd met Morgan, hadn't been one whit better.

Determined to get some sleep and knowing the odds were against it, Silver slid beneath the covers and punched her pillow, trying to get comfortable. But she didn't fall asleep until she heard Morgan's heavy footfalls on the other side of the door.

"Hey, Jordy!" Farley Weathers's harsh whisper rasped across the quiet deck. Though the hour was late, he and Dickey Green were still awake. They had spotted Jordy making a trip to the rail to relieve himself in the darkness. Along with the marines and mercenaries who crowded the ship, Jordy had slept on deck every night since the *Savannah* had sailed from Barbados.

Jordy finished his task and sauntered over to join them. "What's up, Stormy?"

In the moonlight overhead, the brawny man's eyes gleamed dark and forbidding below his thatch of bright red hair. "Me and Dickey was just thinkin' . . . we seen that gal—that friend o' yours—on a poster back in Bridgetown. Her daddy's offering a big reward to fetch her home. We figured maybe, when this trip is done, we oughta do the fetchin' and claim the reward. You bein' her friend and all, she'd go wherever you took her. It'd be real easy."

Jordy shifted uncomfortably and squatted down on the deck beside the men. "Ain't no reward left to claim. Cap'n's already been to Katonga. Picked up the gold for Ferdinand Pinkard—he's the fella that found her."

Stormy Weathers grunted. "Knew it sounded too good to be true."

"Wait a minute, Stormy," Dickey Green put in. He was a skinny little Englishman with frazzled mouse brown hair that didn't quite cover his egg-shaped head. "If Trask has the money, that just makes things easier. We'll pocket the coin and leave off the ship as soon as we reach Campeche."

Jordy felt the blood drain from his face. "You're not meanin' to steal it from the cap'n?"

Stormy chuckled. "No, we ain't. You're gonna do it for us."

Jordy shook his head and started to stand up. Weathers caught his arm, his grip so hard Jordy winced.

"You been tellin' us how you had no place to go when this trip was ended," Weathers reminded him. "You said you'd be left on your own. Well, this here money'll give you a way to fend fer yourself."

"I won't do it," Jordy said, vehemently shaking his head.

Weathers's voice turned hard. "You will do it, you little bilge rat, or you won't live till the end of this voyage." His free hand disappeared inside the pocket of his canvas trousers. Jordy caught the flash of silver as the blade of his knife gleamed in the light of the moon. "Do I make myself clear?"

Jordy swallowed hard. "Yes."

"Good." He folded the knife and stuffed it back in his pants. "Now where's the major keep it?"

"How should I know?"

Weathers's hand snaked out once more, grasped Jordy's shirt near his throat, and jerked him to within inches of the thick-lipped mercenary's face. With his weather-roughened skin and cold, dark, heavy-lidded eyes, his expression looked demonic.

"You know 'cause you're his cabin boy. You do all the cleanin' and straightenin'."

Jordy felt the heat of the man's massive fist beneath his chin. One powerful blow, and he'd be a dead man. "He keeps it in his sea chest," Jordy croaked to appease him, looking for a chance to escape. Weathers slowly released him, brushing imaginary wrinkles from the front of Jordy's shirt.

He waited until Weathers removed his hand. "But I ain't stealin' it, no matter what you do to me!" With that he sprang to his feet and darted away, scurrying across the deck as if the hounds of hell dogged his heels.

Weathers just chuckled. "Don't make a damn. Now that we know where it's hid, we'll do it ourselves. Kid would prob'ly just get caught anyhow."

"Ye don't think he'll talk, do ye?"

"Nah. Kid's hung up on bein' a man. He wouldn't sell out a shipmate if they cut his heart out."

Dickey Green smiled, his narrow face nearly splitting in two. "Always wanted a trip to ol' Me-hi-co," he said, imitating the Spanish pronunciation. "Hear tell a bloke can live like a king for just a few shillings."

"Gonna git me one o' them luscious senoritas." Weathers lay back on his bedroll and shoved his hands beneath his head. "Gonna keep her flat on her back until I use her up."

"Too bad we couldn't take that little silver-haired mort along—bet she could warm a man's bed with the best o' 'em."

"Too risky," Weathers said. "Major's got the hots for that little piece of fluff. He'll be riled enough we take off with his money. We take his woman, he'll track us to the ends of the earth."

Dickey Green just laughed. "A dark-haired wench suits me fine. When do we steal the gold?"

Two days passed, Silver and Morgan coolly civil at best. Every time he looked in her direction, she could have sworn he mocked her. *Fine*, she thought, *if he wants to think the worst, then let him.*

Still, his hard looks bothered her, and she found it difficult to sleep. Already there were smudges beneath her eyes, and her loss of appetite was beginning to take its toll. She would get some rest tonight, she vowed, Morgan or no.

To ensure the fact, Silver downed several snifters of brandy after supper, enjoying the relaxing warmth and the sleepiness it invoked. She refused to think of Morgan Trask for a single moment more. She would sleep the sleep of the innocent, which, as far as Silver was concerned, was exactly what she was.

As she hoped, the liquor numbed her senses, dulling her thoughts and making her drowsy. She fell asleep soon after she reached her cabin, just minutes after she undressed and lay down on her berth. Tonight she didn't toss and turn, just enjoyed the deep, drugging sleep that held her captive, giving her body a long-needed rest.

It wasn't until the hours just before dawn that she stirred. She was dreaming, some distant part of her knew, an ugly nightmare that had plagued her several times before. She wanted to pull her eyes open, end the terrible visions that haunted from the edges of her mind, but she was just too groggy.

Instead she fell deeper under the spell, swept up in a cross between memory and fiction until the terror in the nightmare seemed as real as any she had known.

She heard the rending of her nightgown, felt the warm, moist fingers skimming over her flesh. A hand surrounded her throat, cutting off her air supply, silencing her scream, and pinning her to the bed. Though her vision dimmed and blackness hovered near the edge of her consciousness, she could see his harsh features, the heated look in his cold black eyes.

It was her father—but it couldn't be! She didn't know this man who acted like a stranger. This horrible man whose moist hands stroked her flesh, bringing the bile to her throat. Silver jerked her arm free and clawed at his face, her nails scraping skin and drawing blood. If only she could loosen his hold on her throat, if only she could—

She didn't realize she was screaming until Morgan burst into the room, the small door slamming against the bulkhead as he rushed in. He stood beside her in an instant, knelt, and drew her into his arms.

"It's all right, Silver," he soothed, "it's all right. You're only having a nightmare." Brushing damp tendrils of hair from her face, he cradled her head against his chest.

Silver clawed her way to the surface of consciousness, blinking frantically and trying to clear her muddled thoughts. She noticed Morgan's jaw was set, and tiny lines of worry creased his brow. They eased when she looked up at him.

"I'm sorry," she whispered, awake at last and feeling just as foolish as the major surely believed. She noticed he wore only his breeches; his bare chest felt hard where it pressed against her cheek, and his dark blond, sleep-tousled hair curled softly at the nape of his neck. Silver felt the urge to slide her fingers through the glistening strands.

Morgan was looking at her as if his thoughts were much the same. He started to speak when a determined rap at his door drew their attention. Morgan set her away with a determined gesture and went to assure the men who had heard her screams that she was all right.

Shivering against the chill she'd begun to feel, Silver heard him close his cabin door and wondered if he would return to her tiny steward's room. Not that she wanted him to, she assured herself. After the way he had treated her, she wanted nothing more to do with him. Still, she couldn't forget the gentle way he had held her.

"Are you all right?" Morgan asked from the open doorway between their two cabins.

"I didn't mean to do that," she said. "I'm sorry for making such a commotion."

His eyes raked her, assessing the curves of her body beneath the thin white cotton nightgown. His tender expression had faded, and a hard look gathered in his eyes.

"There seem to be an endless number of things you don't mean to do, Silver. You didn't mean to get kidnapped at the White Horse Inn; you didn't mean to stow aboard my ship; you didn't mean to make love to me; you didn't mean to kiss Colonel Buckland—"

"You're wrong, Major," Silver said with a defiant tilt of her chin. "I meant to make love to you. And I'm not one bit sorry!" With that she slammed the door.

Bloody hell! As he swore in frustration, Morgan's hands balled into fists. The woman was driving him crazy. He knew what she'd been dreaming—he had seen the anguish on her face, the way her hands clawed the air, doing battle with her imaginary attacker.

He couldn't help feeling sorry for her though he damned well shouldn't. Why did she have to look so alone, so afraid? Why did he have to see her in her nightgown, her hair tumbled loose around her shoulders?

Why did she have to look so damned beautiful?

For days after they had made love, he'd done nothing but think about her. At night it had been nearly impossible for him to fall asleep. But he wasn't about to bed her again—not after the way she had scorned him.

The willful little baggage had all but thrown his offer of marriage back in his face. Any other woman would have been flattered, would have done handstands to snare a catch like him. Any woman but Silver. On top of that there was William to consider. What the hell would William say if he returned Silver to Katonga and three months later she wound up carrying his child?

Morgan moved to his carved oak desk and poured himself a brandy. Without bothering to warm it between his palms, he brought it to his lips and tossed it back. The fiery liquid jolted his insides but soon began to relax him. A second shot eased some of the tension from his shoulders. He wished it could ease the heavy ache he was feeling lower down.

Morgan cursed Silver for the tenth time that day. He had to admit he'd been surprised to find her kissing Buckland. Only days ago she'd been an innocent —curious yet frightened by the passions of a man.

But then Silver had always been a quick study.

Try as he might to fight it, the image of her high, round breasts and slender hips rose before him. He could almost feel the silky texture of her skin beneath his palms. The thought of Silver with Buckland, of the colonel's thick hands moving over her body, made Morgan's stomach churn.

To hell with women, he silently swore, vowing he would never get involved with another. He should have learned his lesson the first time, should have known Salena was no different from the rest.

At least he'd found out the truth—before he had fallen in love.

Chapter 14

"All right, where the hell is it?"

Silver paused just outside her cabin door. "Where the hell is what, Major?"

"Pinkard's reward money—the two thousand dollars in gold. It was in the bottom of my sea chest."

Silver's chin came up. "You think I stole your money?" Morgan didn't miss the flicker of hurt that crossed her face, the wounded look in her dark brown eyes. "Your opinion of me must be even lower than I thought."

Morgan released a weary breath and forced himself not to glance away. "You and Jordy are the only ones who have access to this room."

"If you're so sure I took it, why don't you just clamp me in irons and be done with it?"

Morgan fought a smile, sure by now that his instincts had been correct and Silver wasn't involved. He was also thinking, if she weren't such a vixen, he wouldn't mind clamping her in irons—and chaining her to his bed.

Silver turned to leave. "If you're through with your little inquisition, Major, I'm going up on deck.

If you care to hear the truth, I didn't take Pinkard's damnable blood money."

She tried to brush past, but Morgan caught her arm. "I know."

"You know?"

Morgan smiled at her look of astonishment. "I never really thought you did, but in truth I almost wished it had been you."

Silver's hand tightened on his forearm, her fingers biting into the muscles beneath his skin. "Surely you're not thinking Jordy took it."

"I'm afraid I am."

"But he wouldn't do a thing like that, and even if he did, he's just a boy."

When Morgan said nothing more, Silver released her hold and backed away.

"I apologize, Silver," Morgan said. "I shouldn't have accused you that way. But I—"

"It's all right, Major. Jordy means a great deal to me, too."

Morgan watched her a moment more, reading the concern that darkened her pretty face. Turning, he walked to his desk, where his ship's log lay open and a quill pen rested in the inkwell nearby.

"Be careful, Morgan," Silver said softly from the open cabin door. "If you accuse Jordy unjustly, he won't be as forgiving as I."

Morgan watched her leave, regretting the way he had handled things. In fact, he regretted having accepted the damnable money in the first place. But in his haste to get Silver off Katonga, he'd forgotten all about it. When it came to Salena, it seemed he had a hard time thinking clearly, had since the moment she'd come spitting and fighting into his life.

He smiled at that, thinking what a little hellcat she could be. She was different from other women. Bold, fiery, determined—more full of life and passion than any woman he had ever met.

Morgan's smile faded. Silver was different—and yet she was not. He'd found her with Buckland, hadn't he? Just as he should have expected. At least she hadn't taken the money—which meant most likely Jordy had.

With that disquieting thought, Morgan sat down at his carved oak desk, picked up his white plumed pen, and dipped it into the inkwell. Glancing down at the unfinished entry he had made, he scrolled in a few more words about the weather and the ship's position, his projected arrival in Campeche near the end of the week, then jammed the pen back into its holder.

Putting off the problem of the theft wouldn't make it go away.

Morgan shoved back his oak chair and came to his feet. He'd have Jacques and Riley search the men's gear. There was always the chance someone had slipped into his quarters unseen. But nothing was out of place except the missing reward money. How the devil would one of the men know where it was?

It didn't look good for Jordy, yet Morgan prayed the boy had not done the deed. The others thought of Jordan Little as a man; they'd expect his punishment to be equal to that of any other man in the crew.

The first round of searching—the bunks and lockers, the gear stowed in the hammocks of the men in the forecastle—turned up nothing. By now every man aboard knew about the stolen money; they were edgy and grumbling, and speculating among themselves about who might be the guilty man.

Morgan figured the thief hadn't counted on the missing gold's being discovered so quickly. They'd be in Mexico soon. Whoever had taken it must have meant to leave the ship when they reached Campeche.

Unless Jordy took it, hoping the loss wouldn't be discovered until they returned to Savannah. Then the blame could be laid on one of the mercenaries or one of the Texas Marines.

Jacques searched the men on the quarterdeck while Hamilton Riley searched men and equipment near the aft, where Jordy's bedroll was stored. With a growing amount of dread, Morgan watched Riley at his task, saw the grim, disgruntled faces of the men gathered on the deck around him. When Ham reached Jordy's gear, he stopped, his hand deep in the folds of Jordy's bedroll. When he brought his hand back out, his fingers clutched the leather pouch that had once housed the gold—only the pouch was empty.

Damn! Morgan set his jaw and moved forward with grim resolve. From the corner of his vision he saw Silver, her eyes dark with worry, her hand poised nervously near the base of her throat.

Jordy stood beside his bedroll, staring at Ham as if he couldn't believe his eyes. Morgan took the pouch from the lieutenant's outstretched hand.

"How do you explain this, Master Little?" Morgan asked, holding aloft the condemning bit of leather.

Jordy's eyes looked like two hazel moons. "I didn't do it, Cap'n. I swear it." By now the men who milled the deck were beginning to whisper and point in Jordy's direction.

"Then how did this get in your bedroll?"

Jordy glanced up at Morgan, his look beseeching. His eyes slid toward the men in the crew, men he worked with, men he respected. Until this moment they had respected him, too.

Something shifted in Jordy's expression, a subtle closing up. "I ain't—I'm not sure."

"You're not sure?" Morgan repeated. "But you *are* sure you didn't steal the money."

"I didn't take it," Jordy repeated.

Morgan watched his changing expression, the uncertainty mixed with fear. "But you know who did."

Jordy's jaw clamped. He glanced to Cookie, standing a few feet away, his bushy gray brows drawn together in a worried frown. Jordy said nothing.

"Would you excuse us a moment, Lieutenant?"

"Of course, Major." Ham stepped away, toward the line of men who watched with grim fascination. Some of them looked relieved; others looked disapproving; still others betrayed concern for their friend.

Morgan spoke to Jordy so the men couldn't hear. "Listen to me, son. I know you think you're doing what's expected of you, that not telling who else is involved in this is the manly thing to do, but—"

"I didn't take your gold, Cap'n."

"Damn it, Jordy, it isn't just the money. If you know who did it, that makes you as guilty as they are. Tell me the man's name."

Jordy said nothing.

Morgan took in the set of the young man's jaw, the resignation, and knew no amount of coercion could change the boy's mind. In a way he admired him. Under the same circumstances, Morgan would probably have done the same.

"You know what I have to do," Morgan said.

Jordy stepped back, his shoulders squared. "Aye, Cap'n."

"You men, gather round!" Morgan called out, and the cluster of men on deck closed in. "You all know what's going on here. There is two thousand dollars

in gold missing from my cabin. The money has not
been found, but apparently Master Little is somehow
involved. Since he has refused to cooperate by giving
up the name of the man we seek, he will receive the
punishment instead."

The men murmured among themselves, and the
blood seemed to drain from Jordy's face.

"The punishment for thievery is set. The man shall
hug the cannon. Two dozen lashes, no more no less."
Jordy seemed to sway on his feet; his hand gripped
the mast to steady himself. Morgan started to continue but stopped when he caught the blur of yellow
skirts racing in his direction.

Bloody hell!

"Morgan, you can't!" Silver pushed her way to his
side, her dark eyes wide with fear. She insinuated
herself between him and Jordy, as if her presence
could somehow protect him.

"Damn it, Silver, stay out of this."

"He's only a boy, Major. Two dozen lashes. It's—
it's barbaric! Surely even you can't be that cruel."

Morgan worked a muscle in his jaw, her barb
smarting more than it should have. With a firm grip
on her arm, he led her some distance away. "Listen
to me, Silver. Jordy has to pay for what he's done.
He's got to be punished."

"I'll pay it back for him. I'll find a way—just give
me a little time."

Morgan arched a brow. "You would work off two
thousand dollars in gold for a cabin boy you hardly
know?"

"Jordy is my friend. What few I have mean a great
deal to me."

"Where would you get that kind of money?" Morgan pressed, knowing he shouldn't but unable to
stop himself.

Silver lifted her chin. "I'll think of something. I can do it, Major. I know I can."

Morgan surveyed her look of sincerity, and one corner of his mouth curved up. "I don't doubt it for a moment. But I don't think that will be necessary."

"Please, just—"

"Let me handle this, Silver."

"But he's only thirteen!"

"You said once before that you trusted me."

Some of her tension seemed to ease. "I used to."

Morgan bristled a bit but let the words pass. "Stay here," he commanded, and for once she obeyed.

Morgan returned to Jordy and the crew. "Master Little has stated his innocence, and I believe him. But he refuses to name the perpetrator. Though he is doing what he feels he must, that doesn't change things."

Morgan heard Silver's intake of breath and prayed she wouldn't interfere. Flashing her a hard warning glance, he noticed her hands trembled so badly she had to hide them in the folds of her skirt, and her eyes had grown nearly as big as Jordy's.

"To most of you, Jordan Little is a man," he continued. "On board a ship there's only a fine line between boyhood and manhood, but it's a line just the same." He fixed his gaze on Jordy, who seemed rooted to the spot. "Jordan Little, you will work double shifts for the balance of this voyage. You'll do every dirty job Cookie or Jacques can dream up, and you'll do it with a smile and a thank-you."

Jordy's look of relief was so poignant something moved in Morgan's chest.

"Aye, Cap'n," Jordy said softly.

"Do you men have any problem with this?" Morgan asked the members of the crew.

"No, sir," came the muttered response, also with a

sense of relief. The men liked Jordan Little, and they believed him. They'd be looking for the man or men who had caused Jordy trouble. The real culprit might just turn up yet.

"That's all, gentlemen." Sailors, mercenaries, and marines all walked quietly away.

Jordy said something to Silver, who hugged him before he could stop her, and he flashed her a grateful smile. Jacques pointed toward Cookie, who pointed toward the galley, and Jordy moved off in that direction.

"Thank you, Major." Silver approached with a wide, soft smile.

"Surprised?"

"A little."

"I guess we've both received our share of surprises."

"Meaning?"

"Meaning your concern for Jordy was also a surprise."

"If you took the time, Major, you might discover a few more."

"Such as?"

"For starters, you might find out I'm not really the hardhearted creature you believe me to be."

Morgan glanced from Silver to Constantine Buckland, who appeared to be waiting for her at the rail. "Now that would be a surprise." With that he turned and stalked away.

Silver felt a hard lump swell in her throat. The man was a heartless monster, yet he held a power over her she could not explain. Determined to ignore the tears so close to the surface, Silver set her jaw. For days she had hoped he would search inside himself and see the truth—or at least let her explain. Instead he remained determined to believe the worst. Nothing she could do or say would change things. Summoning her anger to force out the hurt, Silver cursed Morgan roundly, calling him every vile name she could dream up. He wasn't worth the trouble he caused her, wasn't worth a moment of concern.

He certainly wasn't worth loving.

There and then Silver made up her mind. She would forget Morgan Trask. Once she had loved her father; now she knew better. Trask was no different after all. Trask was only a man.

That night Silver dressed for supper with care. She would show Morgan Trask he meant nothing. She was tired of being nice to him, tired of hoping he would see reason or seek her out for comfort, if only in his bed.

After arranging her hair in shiny silver swirls behind her ears, she put on the beautiful turquoise gown she had worn to the cockfights, one of the two elegant dresses she had brought along. She would flirt with Connie, flirt with Jacques, and with Ham. She would prove to Trask he was right about her—then she would laugh in his face.

"Good evening, gentlemen." She flashed a radiant smile from the door to the plush salon. The men shoved back their chairs and came to their feet—all except Morgan. His smile was mocking as he slowly stood up.

Hamilton Riley seated her. "You look lovely, Miss Jones."

"Thank you, Ham."

"Your presence in the room is like a beacon of light, my dear," said Connie.

"*Belle extraordinaire*," Jacques said.

"Surely this must be an occasion." Morgan goaded, "Pray, tell us, Miss Jones, what is it?"

Silver just smiled. "It's the occasion of my liberation from the yoke of society."

"Ah, now that sounds intriguing."

"I'm afraid the rest is my secret. You gentlemen need only know that from now on convention holds no place in my life. I shall do exactly as I please."

Morgan arched a brow. "Since when haven't you?"

Silver ignored him. For the rest of the evening she flirted outrageously, laughed uproariously, got a little bit drunk, and in general had a smashing good time. The others seemed enthralled—all except Morgan, whose mood grew blacker by the hour.

Finally he excused himself and returned to his quarters. Silver enjoyed her triumph. That she had ruined his evening she had no doubt. With a pointed look at Connie that warned him not to ask, she accepted Ham's gracious offer of a stroll on deck and finally returned belowdecks a little after midnight.

Morgan opened the door even before she knocked. "Well, if it isn't Lady Salena. Home from her evening at the ball."

Silver bristled. "Get out of my way." With more effort than she needed, she shoved open the door, pushing Morgan aside. She could tell he'd been drinking by the subtle scent of brandy and the slightly glazed look in his eyes. His hair was mussed and his shirt unbuttoned to the waist and hanging open. Silver fought not to notice how dark his skin looked, the way the muscles rippled across his chest.

She moved toward the door to her cabin, but Morgan caught her arm.

"How about a brandy?" he asked. "Surely milady isn't ready to retire."

"Lonesome?" she taunted. "Surely a man of such high moral standards wouldn't lower himself to the company of an unprincipled woman like me."

His eyes moved down her body, raking her, his gaze so hot it made the heat curl in her belly. "He might."

"You're a bastard, Morgan Trask."

"And you're a flirt and a tease." Morgan hauled her against him. "I showed you once before what would happen if you acted that way. Apparently that's exactly what you're after." Morgan pressed her back against the wall. His hands captured her wrists, pinning them effortlessly on each side of her face.

"Let me go!"

"Is this what you want, Silver?" Morgan ground his hips against her, his arousal hot and hard.

"No."

"Say it. Tell me you want it, and I'll give it to you."

"I just want you to let me go."

"I don't believe you." Morgan's mouth came down hard, covering her soft pink lips, his tongue plunging inside. Silver fought to resist the sweep of passion, the hunger that sent hot blood through her veins. Morgan's body pressed against her; she could feel his shaft growing harder, thicker, hotter. God, how she wanted him.

Morgan pulled away, his breath warm and male beside her ear. "Say it, Silver, tell me what you want."

"I hate you," she whispered.

"Show me. Show me how much you hate me."

A sob caught in Silver's throat. Morgan trailed hot kisses along her neck and shoulders, then lowered his mouth to the pale flesh swelling about her dress. When he released her wrists, Silver whispered his name. Her arms slid around his neck, and she twisted her fingers in his hair. *Morgan,* she thought, wanting him more each moment, hating herself for it, despising her building need. With a groan of surrender, she kissed him with all the savagery she felt, all the hurt, all the anger. Molding her lips to his, she thrust her tongue inside his mouth and demanded a response that matched her own.

Morgan gave it to her. His tongue fenced with hers, furious, then teasing, bold, then relentless. He kissed her eyes, her cheeks, and returned to her mouth, nibbling, tasting, sampling, driving her mad.

"Tell me," he demanded, his fingers pulling the pins from her hair, letting the heavy mass cascade around her shoulders. "Tell me what you want."

When Silver only moaned, Morgan slid her gown off one shoulder and bared a breast, his hand cupping it, lifting it, his mouth lowering, then fastening on the crest of her nipple. Silver swayed against him, his arm around her waist the only thing holding her up.

As Morgan's tongue laved and tasted, circled the stiff peak, hot sensation washed over her. Silver's palms ran over his chest, feeling the stiff, tantalizing strands of his chest hair, making his muscles bunch.

Morgan's mouth moved back to hers, exploring, arousing. Then he pulled away. "Say it, Silver. Tell me what you want."

Silver wet her lips, praying he would continue, wishing she didn't care. "I need you," she whispered.

"Not good enough." Kissing her again, he set to work on the buttons down her back, freeing her bodice, sliding down her chemise until she stood naked to the waist. His eyes raked her, burning into her flesh. His hands followed his eyes, gliding along her skin, cupping and kneading her breasts, working a nipple between his thumb and forefinger, making it tighten rock hard. His mouth moved lower, suckling fiercely, working its magic until both breasts felt full and achy, and the place between her legs throbbed and burned.

"Tell me," he demanded, his voice husky.

She wouldn't say it, she vowed; she wouldn't give him the satisfaction.

Morgan lifted her skirt, his hand moving up her thigh, the heat of it scorching her flesh. He cupped her bottom, kneaded it, then found his way through the slit in her cotton pantalets. Long brown fingers parted the folds of her sex, and he slid them inside her.

"Say it, damn you!"

Silver licked her lips. Morgan's finger slid farther inside, out and then in, the rhythm sending white-hot fire through her body. Silver stifled a sob in her throat.

"Say it, Silver."

"I want you," she whispered, "please." She hated herself for begging but couldn't seem to stop the words. "I need to feel you inside me."

Morgan smiled with grim satisfaction. As he pressed her harder against the wall, his hands worked the buttons up the front of his breeches, and his hardened shaft sprang free. He lifted her up, settled her legs around his waist, kissed her hard, and drove himself inside.

Silver gasped at the white-hot heat that careened through her body. Morgan made a husky sound in his throat, and Silver felt the pounding of his heart beneath her hand. Her own heart thundered wildly.

"Tell me you want me," Morgan commanded. "Tell me you like the way this feels."

She wet her lips. "I want you."

One of Morgan's hands cupped her buttocks, holding her in place; the other caressed the peak of a breast. She felt shaky all over, hot and damp and tense with unspent passion. Morgan moved inside her, his hard shaft throbbing, filling her, plundering the sweetness within her. Both his hands gripped her now, holding her buttocks as he plunged himself inside. Silver moved against him, on fire with the burning sensations. Thrusting her hips up and down, she worked his hardness inside her, kneading him with her body until he groaned.

"Silver," he whispered, his fingers laced in the long, thick masses of her hair.

His body grew taut, his muscles contracting, his urgency matching her own. He thrust harder, deeper, faster, impaling her again and again. Silver felt consumed by her passion, the tension so great she was certain she would unravel into a thousand glistening threads.

"Come with me," he beckoned, and with a hot surge of fire, Silver's taut cord of passion came undone. Brilliant spirals of sweetness washed over her, a sea of forbidden delights promising to drown her in pleasure. As the joyous sensations reached their crest, Silver cried out Morgan's name. She wasn't sure when he lifted her into his arms, only felt the softness of the bed beneath her, saw his hard body poised above her, knew that her pleasure had not ceased and that Morgan still plunged into her.

With a last great spasm, his head fell back, and he stilled, his body sagging against her, the sheen of his exertion mingling with her own. Morgan kissed her gently, tenderly, his hands cupping her face as he looked into her eyes. Afterward they lay quiet, sweetly entwined, their anger and passion spent, replaced by a glowing warmth. As her heartbeat slowed, he moved to her side and eased her into the circle of his arms.

For the first time in days Silver knew a rightness, a wholeness that she had been missing, a peacefulness she had never known before. As she slipped into a restful, dreamless sleep, Morgan loomed in her final thoughts—and the hazy notion that she was right where she belonged.

Chapter 15

They made love two more times that night, not in anger but with a tenderness neither could explain—or deny.

Though she feared the consequences, Silver felt her love for Morgan grow with every passing hour. Lying there beside him, she sensed a rightness, a feeling of unity with herself and the world around her. Though Morgan didn't understand her, and certainly didn't approve, she believed he felt something, too.

Hearing his movements in the cabin, Silver roused herself sometime near dawn. Propping herself up against the head of his berth, she shoved sleep-tangled hair from her face and hooked it behind an ear.

"Good morning," Morgan said. He stood in front of the broken shard that served as mirror, his shaving mug in hand.

Silver watched with fascination as he whipped the short-bristled shaving brush over the cake of soap in the bottom of the mug, then spread the thick white lather over his jaw and down his throat. Picking up his straight-edge razor, he began the long, clean strokes that swept the night's growth of beard from his face. There was something intimate about watching him, something sensual that made her want to slide her fingers down those same hard planes and valleys, to touch the scar that marked his cheek.

As he stood there naked to the waist, his breeches snug over a pair of hard-muscled hips, Morgan's broad back and narrow waist stirred memories of the night before, and soft heat curled in her stomach.

"How did you get the scar?" Silver impulsively asked.

Morgan's smooth, sure strokes didn't slow. "I was fifteen . . . living with my uncle. We didn't get along." He sloshed the razor through the water in the basin on the bureau and started shaving the other side of his face. "I was trying to prove myself, I guess—something like what happened to Jordy."

"Go on," she prompted when he didn't continue.

"I got in a brawl at a tavern in London. Ended up in a saber duel with a viscount. I got the scar—he wound up dead." He washed the balance of the soap from his face, then dried with a white linen towel. "It isn't something I'm proud of, but I was pretty hotheaded back then."

Silver smiled. "And now you're a man of gentle disposition."

Morgan grinned at that. "Let's just say I've mellowed a little." He shrugged into his shirt and began to do up the buttons. "Your father got me out of England on a ship bound for America. I've never been back."

"My father did that?" It seemed incredible. "Why?"

"Because he and my father were friends. Edward Trask was a minister to the king."

"How much did you pay him?"

"It was a gesture of friendship, Silver. No money

was expected. In fact he gave me enough funds to get
Brendan and me started in the States."

"So that's why you owe him."

"Yes."

"He must have been different then," she mused,
more to herself than to him.

Morgan walked to the berth and sat down beside
her, his heavy weight creaking the slats beneath the
mattress. Leaning over, he brushed her lips with his.
"We need to talk about last night, Silver."

She had known this was coming, just as she was
beginning to know him so well. "You're worried
about making love to me." Her voice held a hint of
trepidation. She had known he would want to discuss it—she just didn't know what he would say.

Morgan smiled. "I guess you could say that." His
hand cupped her cheek. "I know I should apologize,
but I find the task difficult, if not impossible. Maybe
if I hadn't been drinking, things might not have gotten out of hand. As it is—"

"Are you telling me you're sorry it happened?"

"No," he said firmly. "Not unless you are."

Silver smiled at that. "Not in the least."

Morgan looked relieved. "I want you, Silver. Just
looking at you lying there makes me desire you all
over again."

Silver lifted her arms to him, beckoning his em-
brace.

"Not until we get things settled between us."

Always the practical one.

"You've already turned down my offer of marriage," he continued. "After what happened with the
colonel—" Morgan broke off at the look on Silver's
face. *Surely he didn't still believe she was carrying on
with the colonel behind his back?* "Let's just say, I'm
convinced you aren't ready for that sort of commit-

ment. Since marriage isn't something you seem to
want either—"

"I won't marry a man who doesn't love me," Silver said flatly. "Not for any reason."

"What if I get you with child?"

"That will be my problem."

Morgan looked incredulous. He couldn't seem to
believe she was offering herself to him with no
strings attached.

"We'll discuss that course of events when and if
it's necessary," he said, a bit disgruntled. "In the
meantime, if you're happy with this . . . arrange-
ment . . . so am I."

"I want you, too, Morgan." *And I'm going to win
your love.* It was a decision that had come to her in
the wee hours of the morning. Then again, maybe
the notion had been there all along.

"There's just one last thing." The warmth in his
expression fled. "I won't share you, Silver. Not with
Buckland or any other man. I need to know if you've
been in his bed. Once I know the truth, I can put it
behind me, but I have to know."

Silver gasped. *How could he?* She sat up in bed,
gripping the sheet in front of her. "After what we
shared last night, how can you ask me something
like that?"

"I have to know."

"Why?"

*Because I have to protect myself. Because of Char-
lotte. Because I'm afraid to believe in you.* "Because I
need to know how things stand. If you've made love
to Buckland—"

"Go to hell!" Silver snapped. She had tried to
make him see, hoped against hope he would finally
understand. "You wouldn't know the truth, Morgan
Trask, if it hit you over the head! I must have been

crazy to let you make love to me. Crazy—and naïve! I won't make the same mistake again."

Silver stormed off the bed, grabbing up her clothes on the way to her cabin, stumbling in her haste to be away and nearly falling, her hair flying wildly around her shoulders.

"I have to know, Silver," Morgan called after her, stopping her just as she reached her cabin door.

Silver whirled to face him, her body tense with anger. "You can bet on it, Major. And I'll be back there anytime I feel like it!"

Morgan's hands balled into fists. He stood with his feet apart, his jaws clenched tight.

"As for you," Silver finished, "if you ever come near me again, I'll tell Buckland you raped me. He'll bring you up on charges, and I'll testify against you. I'm the daughter of an earl, as you so constantly remind me. They'll lock you up and throw away the key!"

The door slammed so hard Morgan feared it might fall off the hinges. Bloody hell! The deceitful little baggage would probably do it. But it wasn't her threats that bothered him; it was knowing the truth about Buckland. He had suspected, of course, from the moment he had found them together. She was a woman, wasn't she? One who did exactly what she wanted. But God, he had hoped to hear her deny it. Had prayed that he had been wrong.

He should have taken what she offered, bedded her as hard and as often as he liked. Instead he had goaded her into anger and ended any chance of her willing submission. What the hell was wrong with him? Why had he pressed her? Why did he give a damn if she'd been with Buckland or not? With Lydia it wouldn't have mattered.

He thought about the night he'd spent with Silver.

No woman had ever affected him so profoundly. He wanted her with a passion that seemed endless, and he knew she wanted him, too. He wondered how long she would stay away this time, wondered how long *he* would—threats or no threats—or if in her anger she would seek out the colonel again. Just thinking about Silver with Buckland made his chest feel leaden.

Morgan alternately cursed himself, then praised himself for being smart enough to end the affair before it ever really got started. He had enough on his mind already: the men, the war, most of all, the safety of his brother. As far as Morgan was concerned, Silver Jones could go straight to hell.

She had certainly sent him there.

"You done good, *Master Little*." Stormy Weathers leaned his thick frame insolently against the rail, Dickey Green beside him.

"You stay away from me," Jordy said, his head snapping up at the sound of Weathers's deep voice.

"Hold on now, Jordy lad." Dickey Green caught his arm as he tried to walk away. "Me and Stormy was right proud a ye. Ye took ye punishment like a man; not a bloke aboard can say different."

"It weren't—wasn't—my punishment. It was yours. You two stole the money, not me."

"It was you what told us where it was," Stormy reminded him.

Jordy eyed them warily. "What do you want this time?"

"We just wanted to give you a little something for your trouble is all." Stormy glanced around to be sure no one was watching, then opened his wide palm to reveal three shiny gold coins. "Take 'em," he said. "You deserve 'em."

Jordy backed away. "I don't want nothin' from you. You just stay away from me." Jordy took a few steps backward, then turned and hurried off toward the forward ladder that led to the galley.

Stormy Weathers chuckled, watching him go.

"I told ye he wouldn't take the money," Green said. "Why was ye so all-fired determined to give it to him?"

Scratching his bright red beard, Stormy watched the waves on the distant horizon where seabirds dived for fish. "Getting that gold was a whole lot easier'n I thought. Got me to thinkin' . . . we got the money without a hitch, why not take the girl, too? She's about the pertiest piece I've ever seen. Hardens a man's loins just to watch her stroll the deck."

"But ye said Trask would come after us, we took his woman."

"He's been with her, that's for damn sure, but scuttlebutt is he ain't beddin' her regular. Maybe she don't mean as much to him as I thought. Besides, we got plenty of money. Be easy to get away whenever we've a mind to. Takin' the girl would just be a bonus."

"So what's Little got to do with it?"

"Be easier to take the girl with his help. You seen the way she defended him. She's real protective, that one. If she thought the boy needed her, she'd come after him. It'd be real easy with Little's help."

"Well, the lad made it clear he ain't gonna help us."

"Maybe he is; maybe he ain't."

Dickey Green released a raspy chuckle. "Ye know, Stormy, ye always was the bright one. Ye tell me what to do, I'll do it. We'll give that uppity little mort something she won't soon forget."

"We'll be reachin' Mexico in the next day or two. We'll play things as they come. Till then all we got to do is bide our time."

Silver stayed in her cabin for most of the day. Just thinking about Morgan and his terrible accusations made her feel like crying—or raging—or both. But she didn't. It happened to her that way. When the hurt was too great, she retreated into a world of numbness. It tempered the way she looked at life, stole a little of the joy, but also protected her when nothing else could.

Hiding within her protective shell, Silver avoided the others, even Jordy and Jacques. She needed time to sort through her thoughts and deal with her wayward emotions. She shouldn't have lied to Morgan, yet under the same set of circumstances, she would surely do it again. He had to learn to trust her, had to care for the woman she was, not some creature he designed, someone who would pretend to be whatever it was he thought he wanted.

He had to believe in her.

If he didn't, she didn't want him.

Of course she'd gone a little further than she intended with her threats about the colonel. Buckland was the last person she would go to—no matter what Morgan did. Those words she'd call back if she could. Damn her bloody temper!

Her thoughts still in turmoil, Silver stood on the deck of the *Savannah*, alone and more than a little bit lonely, watching the distant approaching shoreline.

"We're a few miles north of Campeche." Hamilton Riley walked up beside her, and for the first time in days Silver smiled.

"You've been here before?"

"Once. The marines have been on maneuvers on the Yucatán off and on for several years. The major is quite familiar with the place. He's traded here often."

She glanced to the shore, which looked low and swampy and endless. As they sailed farther south, the landscape elevated a little, and Silver spotted what appeared to be a fortress.

"There are eight of them in all," Ham told her, following the line of her gaze. The redness had left his face, which now looked tanned, and his sandy hair was streaked by the brilliance of the sun. "Fort Soledad is near Puerta del Mar, the entranceway. Can you see the wall?"

Silver searched the distance and discovered the entire city was surrounded by a massive hexagonal stone wall. The town itself stood on a plain, bordered on three sides by a small amphitheater of hills. "Good Lord, it must have taken years to build."

"Eighteen, so I'm told. It was started in the 1680s to protect the city from pirates. They say Fort San Carlos has secret underground passageways linked to many of the houses. They were used to hide the women and children whenever Campeche fell under siege."

"Sounds dreadful to me." Silver could just imagine hiding in the dank, murky passageways that must have been crawling with rats.

"There's one on the outskirts called San Miguel that has a moat filled with crocodiles."

Silver shivered. "They certainly sound hospitable." She wondered if it was the kind of place Morgan's brother and the rest of the Texians were being held but didn't ask.

"The Federalists—those are the rebel forces we came here to aid—took control of the city about a year ago and set up a sovereign government. So far they've been able to maintain their position, but the Centralists are pressing them hard."

"Why have we come to Campeche? Are the prisoners being held near here?"

Riley assessed her a moment. "I gather you know just about everything else that's going on. Since you're involved, I suppose you have a right to know the rest." Ham glanced at the heavily fortressed walled city, fast approaching off the larboard bow. "Major Trask has a meeting with General Canales. Canales should be able to update the situation with the Centralists, tell us the location of the remaining Texas forces, and the location of the prisoners."

"Isn't Colonel Buckland in charge? He outranks the major."

"Technically, yes. But Buckland's never been to Mexico, and he doesn't speak Spanish. Since Trask was ship's captain, he has pretty much run the show so far. Things will be somewhat different from here on out."

"I see."

As the ship sailed through Puerta del Mar into the harbor, Ham excused himself and went below. It seemed everyone had a job to do, except Silver.

"Stay out of the way," Morgan said to her as he passed. He'd been brusque all morning, but his mood seemed more an effort to concentrate on the task at hand than a result of their argument. In fact, absorbed in his duties, Morgan appeared to have forgotten their quarrel altogether. Though it galled her to be dismissed so easily, Silver really couldn't blame him. His brother's life was at stake—she knew what it felt like to lose someone you loved.

Once they reached the wharf and the ship was secured, Morgan and the colonel and a party of marines left the boat, accompanied by a squad of Mexican soldiers. Their uniforms were a bit bedraggled, not nearly so smart as those worn by the Texians, but they marched erectly, a hint of Spanish pride forged with Indian courage and strength.

When they returned late that afternoon, Morgan surprised her by seeking her out in her tiny steward's cabin. Since her door stood open, she heard his voice instead of his knock.

"What are you doing down here?" he asked. "Ham wasn't enough of a distraction?"

"What do you want?" she grumbled, glancing up from the book she'd been reading—ironically, Richard Henry Dana's *Two Years Before the Mast.*

Morgan's mouth curved up in a smile that really wasn't. "The governor of Campeche has requested the honor of Her Ladyship's presence. You'll be attending a ball tonight being held in his honor."

Silver tossed the book down on the bed and came to her feet. "We're going to a ball? What about your brother and the men in the prison?"

"Apparently they've been taken some distance from here. General Canales is gathering as many men as he can spare, the necessary horses and provisions, and of course the weapons we've brought along. We'll be leaving day after tomorrow. In the meantime, I can hardly refuse to attend a ball in the general's honor."

Silver tried to read his expression. "And you're asking me to go with you?"

Morgan scoffed. "Hardly. General Canales invited you. It seems his men saw you standing at the rail. When he asked who you were, I told him about your father and the reward money that had been *mistakenly* offered. Since you are here under my protection, he insisted I bring you along."

"I should have known," Silver said, feeling the heat in her cheeks. "You'd scarcely be concerned about my entertainment."

"The colonel will also be attending. I'd appreciate your being somewhat discreet."

Silver's arm snaked out to slap him, but he caught her wrist before her palm connected with his cheek. "Behave yourself, Silver. I've enough on my mind without worrying about you."

Silver set her jaw.

"We'll be the general's guests until we leave, so pack what you need and be ready to go by eight."

"Without fail, Major Trask."

Silver wore her elegant turquoise gown. It would be far simpler than those worn by most of the Spanish ladies, but it was the best she had with her. To enhance the effect, she twisted strands of her hair into ringlets atop her head but left the rest in a shiny cascade down her back. Her shoulders were bare, and the deep V neckline of the gown accented the pale half-moons of her breast.

At eight o'clock sharp she answered Morgan's rap on the door. Immaculately dressed in his navy blue uniform, brass buttons polished and gleaming in the lamplight, he stood erect, appraising her with intense green eyes, his plumed hat tucked beneath his arm.

"I'm ready," she said stiffly.

"So I see." Morgan's eyes moved over her. God, she was lovely. Though he'd seen the gown several times before, he hadn't really appreciated how beautiful she looked in it. Or maybe she looked different to him now that he knew her womanly secrets. As he watched the rise and fall of her soft full breasts, he knew the perfect pink shade of the nipples hidden just beneath the low-cut bodice. He knew exactly how luscious they tasted, how to bring them to a peak, then how to satisfy the ache in them he had created.

He knew that even without the whalebone corset she wore he could span her waist with his hands. He knew the roundness of her bottom, the shapely curves of her hips and thighs. He knew the feel of being inside her. . . .

Morgan's body stirred, his shaft beginning to harden, and silently he cursed the evening ahead. He had to remain aloof, he thought, ignoring the heavy ache of wanting that would accompany him all evening. It wouldn't be easy.

Silver watched the play of emotions that crossed Morgan's face, the softness that had crept into his expression, then the hunger. He looked so handsome standing there it made her heart turn over. When he reached for her arm, she stopped him. "Before we go, there's something I want you to know."

Morgan arched a fine dark blond brow.

"The other morning . . . when we were arguing . . . I didn't mean those threats I made. I'd never do a thing like that. I was just angry. *And I wanted to hurt you the way you'd hurt me.* Sometimes my temper gets the best of me."

"Sometimes?"

"I just wanted you to know." She knew she should tell him the truth about the colonel, but he probably wouldn't believe it, and one confession for the evening was all her pride could bear. She started for the door.

"Wait a minute." Turning away, Morgan strode to the trunk at the foot of his bed, dug through the blankets and clothes he had stored there, and pulled out the pearls he had intended to give to Lydia. He had traded them off a sailor in Spain, just for the hell of it, figuring one of his lady friends would enjoy them. Once he got to Barbados, he had changed his mind and kept them, though he wasn't quite sure why.

"That dress needs a little something more," he said, draping the pearls around Silver's throat. "These ought to do nicely." He fastened the small gold catch and handed her two delicate matching pearl earbobs.

"They're lovely." Silver toyed with the strand, her fingers running over the smooth round beads. She put the earrings in her ears and turned in his direction, awaiting his assessment. "Whose are they?"

Morgan looked at the way they rested at the hollow of her throat, at the creaminess of her skin, almost the same satiny texture and shade as the pearls. "Yours," he said. "No one else could do them justice."

'But I couldn't possibly—''

"We'd better be going," he said, cutting off her refusal. "We wouldn't want to be late." It seemed right that she should have them, though he couldn't say why. Lacing her arm through his, he picked up her satchel, hefted his own, and guided her out the door. On deck Hamilton Riley and Constantine Buckland stood at the taffrail.

"My dear, you look lovely," the colonel said.

Silver smiled. "Thank you, Colonel."

"I hope you'll save a dance for me," Ham said.

Morgan fought the urge to tell them her dance card was full. Damn, the woman had a way of getting under a man's skin. Vixen or not, Buckland or not, he wanted her. It was useless to deny it. Still, he would not take her.

He was afraid he would only want more.

* * *

Silver spotted the carriage that awaited them at the dock, a fine black barouche pulled by two glistening black horses. The top was down, and a red-liveried servant sat in the driver's seat. Morgan helped her alight, then climbed in beside her and leaned back against the tufted leather seat. Riley and Buckland followed suit.

The carriage rumbled off down the dirt street past a pier where fishing boats bobbed at their anchors. "Shrimpers . . . *camaroneros,*" Morgan said. "It's a big industry here." The strong odor of fish mingled with the dust in the air. It was the dry season in the Yucatán, though any day now that respite from the heat and humidity would be coming to an end. "Mostly they grow henequen; that's the plant they use to make hemp. You'll see plenty of it before we leave."

They rode along the streets, bypassing numbers of Campechanos, as the usually easygoing residents were called. Parks and open spaces made the city look like paintings of Europe she had seen.

"That's the oldest convent church on the Yucatán," Morgan told her, pointing to a huge stone building. "The Franciscan Cathedral, built in 1540."

"Very impressive," Ham put in.

"Looks a bit musty to me," said the colonel.

The streets were not crowded, just a few peons returning to their families after work, a few drunken paisanos in front of the cantinas. *Soldados* prowled the streets, as did well-dressed ladies and gentlemen, *gente de razón,* on their way to dine in one of the finer Campeche restaurants.

"Shrimp and fish are specialties here," Morgan said, "but they also eat cochinita pibil, pork baked in banana leaves flavored with achiote—that's a sort of paste ground from red seeds."

"Where did you learn to speak Spanish?" Silver asked, remembering Ham's words and appreciating Morgan's fluent accent. She was determined to be just as cordial as he, no matter what their differences.

"I spent some time in Spain."

"And of course you've been here."

"I've been to most of the Mexican trade centers." Morgan's glance moved over her face. Though he worked at being friendly, there was a tightness around his mouth every time he looked at her. That he wasn't with her by choice was more than apparent.

Still, she was glad for the conversation. As forced as it was, it helped ease her nerves.

"I rather like the Mexicans," Morgan said, "though I'm sure Lieutenant Riley and Colonel Buckland have mixed emotions about them."

"Why shouldn't we?" Buckland said defensively. "They butchered a hundred and eight-seven of our men at the Alamo, to say nothing of the three hundred fifty poor unlucky bastards—pardon me, my dear—at Goliad. God knows what they've done to the fifty marines they're holding at this very moment —including your brother—or have you forgotten?"

A muscle bunched in Morgan's cheek. "Hardly, Colonel. General Santa Anna is not on my list of favorite people, but General Canales is a good man. Need I remind you, we're his guests this evening— and we need his help."

"I assure you, Major, I'm well aware of our situation."

Morgan said nothing more until they arrived at the governor's residence—a three-story pale pink structure with black wrought-iron balconies and massive carved double doors. The house faced inward, centering on an interior courtyard, as did most of the other dwellings.

Silver leaned through the carriage window. "What a lovely home."

"There are lots of beautiful houses in the city," Morgan said casually.

"If you like this damnable place so much," Buckland snapped, "maybe you should join up with the Federalists."

Morgan clenched his jaw but didn't answer. While the servants took their bags, the driver pulled open the carriage door. Morgan stepped down and helped Silver alight. She took his arm and smiled sweetly, though the smile felt as forced as Morgan's words. He'd brought her only because he had to, still believed she was dallying with Buckland, and in general had far more on his mind than her.

"General Canales." Morgan greeted the man in the elegant foyer who stood beneath a crystal chandelier. Papered in rose brocade, the walls reflected the soft lighting, and so did the black-and-white marble floors. Silver crystal sconces flickered beside the arched entryway that led into the main salon. "May I present Lady Salena Hardwick-Jones, daughter of the earl of Kent."

"Senorita." The general bowed over her hand. "It is a pleasure to meet the beautiful woman my troops call *Dama de Luz*."

Morgan arched a brow. "Lady of Light," he translated with a trace of amusement, and something else she couldn't quite name.

"The *soldados* watched you depart your ship," the general told her. "They said you had hair as pale as moonlight and eyes the soft brown velvet of the doe." He bowed over her hand. "They have not lied."

"It's an honor to meet you, General Canales." He was an imposing man, not as tall as Morgan, but with flashing eyes and an intelligent smile. Across his chest, his uniform glittered with row upon row of medals and bright-colored ribbons, and a gleaming satin sash ran from his shoulder to his waist.

"This is Lieutenant Riley," Morgan said, "and you know Colonel Buckland."

"Lieutenant Riley, Colonel Buckland." The men shook hands all around. Strains of guitar and fiddle played softly in the background. "The dancing began some time ago, senors," the general said to the men. "I hope Senorita Jones will grant me *un baile*."

"I'd be pleased if you would—" *Call me Silver*, she intended to say, but Morgan's grip on her arm tightened in warning. Apparently he didn't want the general on too-familiar terms. For once she didn't argue. She was in a foreign country; she didn't know the customs here. "I'd be pleased to dance with you, General Canales," she said instead, correctly guessing the Spanish word.

"I look forward to it, senorita."

After a last warm smile from the general, Morgan swept her beneath the archway and into the main salon, a huge, beautifully appointed room where most of the furniture had been removed to allow space for dancing. Some of the men wore the uniform of officers in the Federalist Army; others were dressed in clothes that were far more European: black evening clothes with wide white stocks and ruffle-fronted shirts.

The women wore silks and satins cut in the latest vogue or colorful lace dresses, tortoiseshell combs, and lace headdresses Morgan called mantillas. Six men, dressed in short-jacketed black suits unlike any she had seen before, played violins and guitars at one end of the room. Except for an occasional waltz, the tunes were lively, the dancing far different from that she had seen on St. Vincent with Michael Browning.

"What do they call those pants with the flared bottoms and the silver circles down the leg?" Silver asked Morgan just as the orchestra began another buoyant tune. Around them couples moved in sensuous rhythm, their backs arched, their feet moving first one way and then another.

"They're called *calzoneras*." His words were clipped; his tone was a little bit harsh. Taking her hand, he started toward the dance floor, but Silver pulled away.

"I can't dance like that."

Morgan looked annoyed. "It isn't difficult. I'll lead, you follow, just like any other dance." The longer they were together, the more distant he became. A growing tension simmered beneath his surface calm. Silver glanced around at the beautifully dressed men and women, at the luxurious surroundings of the general's sumptuous residence and wished he would let her enjoy this rare and wonderful evening. She felt the pressure of his hand leading her toward the dance floor but stopped him again before they reached it.

"I've danced only once in my life," she admitted. "It was a long time ago. I don't even remember how to start."

Morgan turned her to face him, surprise in the eyes that held hers, so green, so probing. The hardness in his expression eased. "You've danced only once? Surely your father held parties, soirees there on Katonga."

She only shook her head. "My father is a very private man."

Morgan watched her a moment more, as if pondering some grave decision. Then his hand touched her cheek. "All right, Silver, just for tonight, we'll pretend things are different between us. That you're Lady Salena and I'm Morgan Trask, your devoted suitor. We'll dance as if we haven't a care in the world. How does that sound?"

Silver grinned so wide the dimple in her chin disappeared. "It sounds wonderful."

Morgan tucked her gloved hand in the crook of his arm, covered it with his, and they moved out onto the dance floor. The lively music ended, and the lead musician announced a *vals*, the Spanish word for waltz.

"Thank God," Silver whispered, though even that simple dance seemed suddenly foreign. Morgan turned her to face him, placed one of her hands on his shoulder, gently gripped the other, and settled his palm at her waist. The heat seemed to burn through her clothes. When his feet began gliding to the rhythm, Silver stepped on his shiny black boots two times before she picked up the proper motion, the dance lessons she'd been forced to suffer and her single experience with Michael finally returning to mind.

"I've never been to anything so elegant," Silver told him. "Father took me to a ball on St. Vincent once, but—"

"But what?" Morgan asked lightly.

"It didn't work out too well."

"Why not?"

If she told him the truth, he'd think even worse of her than he did already.

"It couldn't be that bad," Morgan said with a smile when she didn't answer. "How old were you?"

"Fifteen."

"So you went to a ball on St. Vincent when you were fifteen and?"

Silver lifted her chin. "I let a boy kiss me, and my father saw him. He called me a harlot and a whore. It was the worst night of my life." Tears welled in her eyes, and she had to look away.

Morgan's grip on her waist grew tighter, but he didn't miss a step, just whirled her around the room as if no one else were there. "He shouldn't have done that, Salena," he said softly. "You were only a child."

He's done far worse, she thought. She looked at Morgan, surprisingly saw no rebuke, and managed a smile. "I probably wouldn't have done it, except I wanted to see what it felt like."

"How did it feel?"

"Nothing at all the way your kisses do," she admitted, and Morgan laughed. He looked so handsome with the tension gone from his face.

"You never fail to amaze me, Salena."

This time Silver's smile came easily. "I always hated my name until I heard you say it. It sounds different somehow."

"It's a lovely name," he said.

"Truly?"

"Yes . . . a beautiful name for a beautiful woman."

Silver felt the heat creep into her cheeks. The dance ended, and another, more vigorous version began. Both Riley and Buckland stood eagerly waiting on the sidelines, but Morgan didn't return her.

"This is called 'El Capotín,' the rain song. A *capotín* is an ancient rain cape, a thatch of leaves that is draped around one's shoulders."

Silver looked at Morgan, seeing a charming side of

him she had only suspected, then at the men and women already engrossed in the tune.

"Shall we try it?" he asked.

"I hope I don't step on your feet." In seconds she had picked up the energetic beat and was laughing and twirling, dancing just as they were. She would never have guessed the *baile* could be so much fun.

From beneath her dark lashes, she watched Morgan's graceful yet masculine movements. His smile remained warm, and so did his expression. Was he really enjoying himself as he seemed? Or was he just pretending? If only she knew what he was thinking.

Chapter 16

"*Bailecitos caseros*," Morgan said, "a house party with dancing."

Silver laughed. "I'd say it's a bit more than that." In their elegant silks and satins, whirling beneath crystal chandeliers, the revelers danced and sometimes sang in accompaniment to the orchestra. A few times they shouted, "*¡Bamba!*"

The waltz was popular, as well as the polka and mazurka. There were spirited folk dances and the beautiful fandago, in which just one man and woman held the attention of the crowd with their sensual, graceful movements.

Silver couldn't remember a better night. She danced with Ham, danced with the general, and finally danced with Buckland. Morgan scowled when he saw them and began dancing with an elegant black-haired woman with fiery eyes and creamy skin. Just seeing Morgan's hand on the woman's narrow waist made Silver's stomach turn over. God, how could one man affect her so?

"Why don't we take a walk on the terrace?" the colonel suggested. Silver glanced at Morgan, saw the way the dark-haired woman smiled at him and fluttered her red lace fan, the same bright shade as her dress. She started to agree, but she didn't really want to go, and she didn't want to ruin her enchanted evening, as undoubtedly would happen if Morgan saw them leaving together.

"Would you mind fetching me a cup of punch?" Silver asked Buckland instead, hoping to distract him.

"But I thought—of course, my dear." Connie left her alone, and Morgan rejoined her a few moments later.

"Having a good time?"

"Yes. Thank you, Major."

"What for?"

"Playing Prince Charming."

Morgan's eyes swept over her. "The pleasure has been mine, milady." Taking her arm, he led her out onto the terrace. The tropical night engulfed them, the fragrance of hibiscus and frangipani filling the air with a sweet scent that mingled with an occasional whiff of ladies' perfume. Overhead, bright stars shone beside a milk-white fragment of moon. Beyond the terrace, a high-walled garden, infinitely manicured, beckoned to lovers who wished to stroll its hedgerow paths.

"What happened to the colonel?" Morgan asked, drawing her uncertain attention, but the smile remained in his eyes. "The last time I saw him, he was carrying two cups of punch, one of which I presume was yours."

At the teasing note in his voice, Silver smiled up at him. "I'm afraid I must confess to a bit of duplicity. You see, it wasn't the colonel's attentions I wanted."

"Oh? And just whom, pray tell, has captured your fancy?"

"Well"—she flashed an impish grin—"the man I had in mind is of far lower rank—merely a major—but a man I find infinitely more to my liking."

Morgan's hand touched her cheek, his fingers warm and firm against her jaw. "If only I could believe that."

Silver's look turned serious. "I hope one day you will."

His hands cupped her face, tilting it toward his. Lowering his head, he brushed her lips with a feather-soft touch that left her breathless. It was a gentle kiss, almost achingly tender.

"There you are—" Connie Buckland interrupted from the open terrace doors. With a guilty start, Silver turned away. Casting Morgan a look of suspicion, Buckland walked across the patio and handed Silver a cup of punch.

"Thank you, Connie, that was very thoughtful." But after several small sips, she set the crystal punch glass aside. She noticed Morgan's scowl had returned. Inside the house, the orchestra struck up a fresh tune, the strains a lilting melody on the warm evening air.

"I believe this is the dance the major has promised to teach me." That was a bald-faced lie. She glanced up at Morgan, whose dark look faded, and his mouth curved up in a smile.

"So it is. If you'll excuse us, Colonel?"

"Of course," the colonel said, but he looked none too pleased.

Inside the salon, Silver moved into Morgan's arms, quickly catching the steps, dancing with graceful abandon.

Morgan's eyes, bright green and hungry, bored into her. While at first he'd been careful to hide his interest, now his look seemed hotly possessive, his desire no longer concealed. The feel of his eyes on her breasts made them grow taut and achy. The hand at her waist burned her flesh. When his gaze came to rest on her mouth, it was all Silver could do to stifle a moan.

Unconsciously her tongue ran over her lips, and Morgan's fingers, entwined with hers, increased their hold.

"Do you know how much I want you?" To demonstrate, he pulled her closer. Silver's eyes went wide at the feel of his hardened arousal, pressing against her through the fabric of her skirt.

Oh, God, I want you, too, she thought, but she wasn't about to say it. Not now. Not when so much still lay between them. There was a time when she would have given in to her physical desire for him, let him make love to her without a thought for tomorrow. Not anymore.

Now she wanted his love. Wanted him to know the person she was inside. Wanted him to believe in her. When the dance ended, Morgan walked her to the edge of the floor, and General Canales approached.

"Major Trask," he said with a little too much force. The worry on his face stole Morgan's attention completely. "I must speak with you. Might I have *un momento, por favor*?"

"*Ciertamente.* Shall I find Colonel Buckland?"

"One of my men will bring him and Lieutenant Riley." The general turned to Silver. "I must beg your indulgence, Senorita Jones."

"I understand completely."

"If we have not returned by the time you are ready to retire, the servant at the foot of the stairs will show you to your room."

"Thank you, General."

Morgan and Canales left her in the care of one of

the general's aides, a middle-aged man of medium
height and build who spoke little English. Silver
danced with him and several other men, including a
dashing black-haired man named Don Raúl de la
Guerra. De la Guerra was charming and one of the
most darkly handsome men she had ever seen. But
his attentions were fastened on the fiery-eyed
woman Morgan had been dancing with earlier, and
Silver didn't blame him. She wondered what their
story was, why the woman flirted so outrageously
with everyone except the handsome don, but Silver
had enough problems of her own.

As the evening wore on and Morgan didn't return,
some of Silver's excitement began to wane. Though
dozens of handsome men surrounded her, lavishly
praising her beauty in their beautiful, mellifluous
Spanish, without Morgan to witness their attentions,
it didn't seem to matter. As politely as possible, she
excused herself and made her way to the small dark-
skinned servant standing at the foot of the sweeping
staircase.

The little man smiled and led her upstairs along a
wide, lengthy corridor. Small candles shimmered in
gleaming silver sconces, and the tartan carpets beneath their feet muffled their footfalls as they walked
along. The house, a great U-shaped structure, appeared formal and impressive. Silver's room lay at
the very end of one long wing.

The servant opened the door, and Silver stepped in
to find a large high-ceilinged room dominated by a
huge canopied bed draped with mosquito netting,
which had been tied up out of the way. The shuttered
windows stood opened to the gentle breeze, and the
room felt balmy and pleasant.

She wondered who had chosen the lavish appoint-
ments—gold and pale blue silk. Whoever it was had

elegant taste. Silver appreciated the delicate work-
manship of the gold-brocaded, white-painted sofas
and matching white and gilt furniture. The feeling
was very European, not at all what she had expected.

Spotting her empty leather satchel, Silver opened
a huge gilded white wardrobe and found her clothes
hung carefully inside. Her silver-backed hairbrush
had been laid out on the dresser, where she sat to
brush her hair. But her thoughts remained on Morgan, on the handsome, charming escort he had been.

There was something in the way he had looked at
her, a longing that gave her fresh hope for their future. If he could put aside his mistrust and come to
know the woman she was inside, there might be a
chance for them yet. What did she want from him?
she asked herself, and the answer came swift and
hard.

She wanted him to love her as much as she loved
him.

Tonight, for the very first time, the depth of her
feelings had surfaced. It had happened the moment
of their separation, when the general's urgency had
taken Morgan away. In two days' time he would be
leaving. Going off to fight for the Texians imprisoned, to fight for his brother's life.

For the first time it occurred to her he might not
return.

And that was when she had known.

Silver's fingers trembled on the handle of the hairbrush. The thought of Morgan's death made her
stomach churn, and a wave of nausea swept over
her. She hadn't meant to love him, didn't want to
love any man. How had she let herself become so
deeply involved?

Silver cursed herself, called herself a fool, but still
could not deny it. She loved Morgan Trask whether

she wanted to or not. Then she remembered the look in Morgan's eyes—the passion, the gentleness, the yearning—and a soft smile curved her lips. She had much to offer a man—a man wise enough to see it.

And Morgan Trask was just such a man.

Time was on her side—and a physical attraction even Morgan could not deny. A few more evenings as pleasant as this one, and Morgan might begin to see the woman beneath her tough facade. Silver's smile grew wider. Handling a man was fairly new to her, but she had her instincts to rely on.

Her instincts and her newly discovered passion.

Together they might just render one Morgan Trask on a Silver platter.

Beginning to feel sleepy, Silver pushed thoughts of Morgan away, fought the buttons at her back, then heard a knock at the door. When she opened it, she found a young Mexican girl no more than twelve or thirteen standing outside in the hall.

"*Yo soy aquí ayudarle,*" the girl said. It meant nothing to Silver until the girl mimed unbuttoning Silver's dress.

"Thank you. Please come in."

Dressed in a peasant blouse and simple black cotton skirt, the girl smiled warmly. She wore leather sandals on her small feet, had glistening black hair, and interested, eager eyes.

"*Me llamo Cecilia.*" She pointed to herself.

"My name is Silver."

"*Dama de Luz,*" she said, and Silver recognized the name the soldiers had given her. Cecilia touched her pale hair, freshly brushed and hanging well below her shoulders. Then she motioned for Silver to turn around, and started on the small covered buttons that closed up the back of her gown. Cecilia had unfastened only half of them when a second knock sounded at the door.

"Excuse me," Silver said, hoping the girl would understand her attempt at politeness.

"Sí, senorita."

Silver opened the door to find Connie Buckland standing in the hallway, plumed hat in hand.

"Might I have a word, Salena?" Spotting the small, dark Mexican girl, he added, "Alone?"

"Of course." Thinking of the meeting Connie and Morgan had attended with General Canales and worried about what might have happened, Silver let him in and dismissed the girl, who yawned discreetly behind her hand and flashed a grateful smile.

"What is it, Colonel?" Silver stepped away as Connie closed the door. "Has something happened?"

"I was worried about you, my dear. I wanted to be sure you were all right."

"I'm fine, Colonel. I appreciate your concern, but—"

Connie moved farther into the room, backing Silver several paces toward the bed. "There are things I wish to say to you, Salena. Things of some importance. You know the way I feel about you. Surely you return those feelings at least a little."

"I thought you came here because of what's happening."

"I came here because of you."

"I told you before, Colonel, I'm not interested in becoming involved with you. I thought I made that clear the night Major Trask confronted us up on deck."

Buckland's arms encircled her waist, and he pulled her close. "I won't deny you have a bit of a temper. I'll not soon forget the resounding blow you dealt me, nor do I wish to incur another."

"Let go of me, Colonel." Silver tried to pull away, but Buckland only tightened his hold.

"What I want from you, Salena, is your affection, not your scorn. I'm willing to risk your fury again if you will but give me a chance to express my feelings for you."

Buckland forced her back against the bed, then down on the gold brocade counterpane.

"I'm not interested," Silver warned, her temper growing hotter by the moment. "I wasn't then; I'm not now. Stop this—"

Smothering her protests with his mouth, Buckland thrust his tongue between her teeth. Silver's fury swelled until she could barely remember where she was. The colonel's heavy weight held her down on the soft feather mattress. She could feel his stiff arousal pressing against her thigh.

His hands gripped her wrists, and when she struggled, he held her surprisingly immobile. Shifting her wrists above her head with an ease she wouldn't have guessed, he grasped them both in one hand, then slid his fingers over her bodice to cup a breast. Only Silver's fury tempered her growing sense of alarm.

Buckland was bigger and stronger than she had realized. Without a weapon of some sort, she might not be able to stop him. Silver twisted, trying to break free. Buckland's grip tightened, and Silver struggled harder. His mouth stifled her protests while his body held her fast. Silver arched beneath him, twisting and fighting to dislodge his heavy weight. She heard the rending fabric, the sound of buttons bursting free, and the front of her gown popped open, exposing her corset and the soft pale flesh that rose above it. Buckland's fingers settled over the rounded swell.

That was the way Morgan found them.

"Let her go," he commanded, and Connie Buckland froze. Morgan's voice had never sounded more deadly; hard, cold anger bit into every word.

Silver saw him standing in front of the door he had softly closed behind him, feet splayed, hands balled into fists, and felt a bitter despair well up inside her. *Dear God, this can't be happening.* But it was. One glance at Morgan's taut features, the muscle that bunched in his cheek, and Silver read the truth.

Whatever hopes she had nurtured were gone. Her last chance to right things had flickered and died like the embers of a once-bright fire.

There was nothing she could do or say, no way to convince him. He would think the worst, just as he always did, treat her with the cold, hard scorn she had never once deserved. The lump in her throat threatened to choke her. Tears burned her eyes, but she refused to let them fall.

"Get away from her, Buckland." The warning was so harsh they cut through Silver's grief and turned her misery to anger.

To hell with Morgan Trask! she vowed. He would win the game, but in winning, he would lose. When the colonel's grip on her wrists grew slack, Silver slid her arms around his neck.

"Don't go, Connie," she coaxed. "This is none of his business." Silver pulled his mouth down to hers, and Connie stiffened in protest. She ground her hips against him and made passionate whimpers in her throat. Connie strained away from her, though she held him fast, then his body jerked upright like a puppet on a string.

"It's all I can do to keep from beating you sense-less," Morgan told him, releasing his hold on Con-

nie's uniform coat and shoving him toward the door.
Silver pulled her gown back in place with trembling
fingers and stood up, her eyes fastened on Morgan.

"I'm the senior officer here," Buckland warned,
straightening his jacket with a dignified air. "You
don't order me to do anything. And unless you're
willing to risk court-martial, I suggest you keep your
hands off me."

"Court-martial?" Morgan repeated. The scar
across his cheek looked taut and strained. "I doubt
you'd want this little . . . indiscretion . . . ban-
died about. Besides, you need me, Colonel—and we
both know it."

Buckland looked at Silver, who swallowed hard,
torn between fury and tears. Mumbling an oath beneath his breath, he turned and stormed from the
room, slamming the door behind him. Morgan
swung his gaze to Silver, pinning her with an impen-
etrable green-eyed stare.

"You can get out, too!" Silver stiffened her spine
and turned to face him.

One corner of his mouth curved upward. "Surely
you'll be lonesome now that the colonel has gone."

"Thanks to you." She tilted her chin in a show of
defiance, but her bottom lip trembled.

"Yes . . ." he said, "thanks to me." There was
something in his voice, an inscrutable note that
shouldn't have been there. With arrogant nonchalance, he pulled off his jacket and tossed it onto the
gold brocade chair in the corner.

"I told you to get out."

"I'm staying."

Silver watched in utter disbelief as Morgan untied
his stock, unfastened the cuffs on his ruffle-fronted
white shirt, the buttons down the front, then tugged
it from the waistband of his breeches. Bare-chested,

he moved to the chair, sat down, and pulled off his boots. When the second boot hit the floor with an echoing thud, Silver snapped out of her daze.

"Fine," she said, her fury barely contained. "You may stay if you like—I will leave." Holding her dress together as best she could, she stormed across the room toward the door. Morgan surged to his feet and caught her arm, spinning her to face him and pulling her hard against his chest.

"You're staying, too."

She could feel the heat of his body, but the fires he ignited were of anger, not passion. The lump in her throat threatened to choke her. He had witnessed Buckland's assault and believed she'd enjoyed it, encouraged it. "The hell you say! Let go of me and get out of my room."

"You'd rather have Buckland?" he asked, but she heard no trace of anger in his voice. Instead a smile softened the lines of his mouth, and his bright green eyes were warm on her face.

Silver eyed him warily. "Wasn't that obvious?"

"I'll admit that's what it might have looked like to some."

"But not to you, I suppose." She strained against his chest, trying to pull away.

"To me it looked like a beautiful young woman being set upon by a pompous, overstuffed ass."

"What?" Silver stopped struggling. "You're taking my side? I don't believe it. You—you're just saying that because you want to take Buckland's place. You think you can sweet-talk your way into my bed." Silver arched away from him, but Morgan's hold only tightened.

"I'm saying it because I was standing outside your door. I heard every word you said to him."

"But—"

"Every word," he repeated. "I've been a fool, Silver. A crazy, jealous fool who ought to be taken out and horsewhipped for the things he has said."

"You heard him? You know the truth about what happened?"

"From the colonel's own mouth."

For a moment Silver just stared at him. Then tears touched her eyes, and she had to glance away.

Morgan turned her face with his hand, forcing her to look at him. "I was a fool," he repeated, "I'm sorry."

Silver slid her arms around his neck and leaned into his chest.

"Forgive me, Silver," he whispered into her ear. When she straightened, Morgan brushed the tears from her cheeks with the pad of his thumb.

"I'm not like Charlotte," she said softly. "I never will be."

Morgan kissed her then, with all the passion he had withheld. *God, he wanted her.* Silver kissed him back with equal abandon, her fingers clutching his shoulders, then sliding once more around his neck. Morgan laced his hands in her hair, feeling the silky strands beneath his fingers. Tilting her head back, he kissed her eyes, her cheeks, the line of her jaw, then the graceful arch of her throat. His loins swelled and hardened, his shaft growing thick and heavy and pressing against the front of his breeches.

Through the open back of her dress, Morgan's fingers skimmed over her flesh; he eased the gown off her shoulders, lowered the strap of her chemise, and bared her breasts. He could feel her trembling as he cupped and lifted the heavy weight, then used his thumb and forefinger to tease her nipple to a hard, taut, dusty rose peak.

"Morgan," Silver whispered into his ear. Her lips

felt warm against his throat, then they returned to his mouth. Her tongue found its way inside, the honey-sweet taste of her causing an ache close to pain. With a groan of surrender, Morgan lifted her into his arms and carried her over to the bed.

As his fingers freed her garments, his eyes moved over her face. The tears had dried, no glistening trail marked their path, but Morgan had not forgotten. What if he hadn't heard the truth? What if he had found them together and believed the worst, accused her unjustly, just as Silver expected? The joys she offered would have been lost to him. But something told him he would have lost a gift far more precious.

Morgan removed the last of her clothes, brushing her lips with a kiss, but when she reached for him, he pulled away.

"Don't lie to me again, Silver," he warned softly. "I know I deserved it, but I'm asking you now— please—don't ever do it again."

Silver brought his hand to her lips and gently kissed the palm. "Only tiny white lies," she promised. "I'm afraid they're part of my nature."

He didn't press her. She was Silver. She would do as she pleased. Still, he hoped his words would give her pause. He wanted to trust her, and he was beginning to. It was dangerous, he knew. He'd been hurt before. He would never forget the awful pain of Charlotte's betrayal, the agonizing months of trying to block the image of her, naked and writhing beneath another man.

Trusting Silver meant opening himself up to her, allowing long-buried feelings to surface. There was grave risk involved.

Morgan inwardly smiled. Silver Jones was worth the risk.

Chapter 17

Silver watched with quiet fascination as Morgan stripped off his breeches. Lamplight played over the hard planes and valleys of his chest, the subtle indentations of his ribs, the muscles across his arms and shoulders.

His waist was narrow, his stomach flat. Her fingers itched to touch the round, hard curves of his buttocks. The memory of them flexing beneath her palms as Morgan drove into her sent a jolt of heat through her body. Standing beside the bed, naked and aroused, Morgan untied the mosquito netting to keep out the small flying creatures of the night and joined her on the soft feather mattress.

"I've never desired a woman the way I do you," he said softly, lowering his mouth to take her lips. His kiss seemed less urgent, but there was a leashed quality in the taut way he held her.

Silver recognized the power he withheld, his determination to give as much pleasure as he took. His mouth moved over hers, his tongue sweeping in, urging hers to fence and parry. The warm moist cavern felt smooth, his breath tasted of brandy, a hint of tobacco she hadn't noticed before, and the coppery taste she had come to know as desire.

It was a taste that inflamed her. Morgan's mouth moved down her body, kissing and nibbling, making her writhe beneath him. When he cradled a breast and drew her nipple into his mouth, Silver moaned. He was taking his time, moving with slow, agonizing purpose. The sweet torture felt almost painful.

"Please, Morgan," she whispered, the words she'd once held back now slipping with ease from her tongue. "I want to feel you inside me."

"Soon, sweet vixen." His mouth trailed a burning path from her throat to her shoulder.

Not soon enough, Silver thought. When Morgan moved lower, his tongue darting into her navel, Silver almost begged him for the pleasure she knew he could give. How much longer would he make her wait?

As if in answer, Morgan nudged her legs apart and settled himself gently between her thighs. His hands laced through the soft blond hair that protected her sex, then he separated the delicate folds and lowered his mouth to the rigid bud at the entrance. Too late Silver realized his intentions. Not until his mouth and his tongue lapped at her with such determination that waves of pleasure rushed over her and passion roared in her ears. She fisted her hands in the bed sheets and bit her bottom lip to keep from crying out.

With a burst of white-hot fire, a profound sweetness washed over her and tiny stars burst inside her head. Her body went rigid, the spasm of pleasure hurling her higher and higher.

That was when she felt him, probing the entrance to her core, his shaft thick and pulsing. With fierce possession, he drove himself inside her, the heat of his arousal firing her passion anew. He slid out and then in, hot and hard and wanting, urging a mindless pleasure like nothing she'd known.

"Morgan!" she cried, arching her body to receive each powerful thrust. He was driving against her, lifting her buttocks, pounding, pounding, and still she wanted more.

Morgan gave it to her, his long, powerful strokes thrusting home again and again. When she was sure she could stand the sweet fury no more, fresh waves of pleasure broke over her. Morgan must have felt the grip of her body tightening around him, for his hot seed spilled deep inside her, flooding her with its welcome warmth.

Silver clutched Morgan's neck, and he held her trembling body. *Love me*, she thought, but didn't say it. He had come this far. For now it was enough.

They lay quiet for a while, Morgan's breath slowing until his chest rose and fell with an even, steady beat. Through lowered lashes, she turned to see if he slept but found his eyes open and watching her.

Silver drew a pattern on his chest with her finger. "I was worried about you and the others," she said. "I wouldn't have let Buckland in if it weren't for your meeting with General Canales. I thought something might have happened."

Releasing a weary sigh, Morgan shoved his hands behind his head. "It looks as though it soon will. Centralist forces are building up outside the city. Attack seems imminent. General Canales will be able to spare only a very few men."

Silver's finger stilled. "What about your brother, the men in the prison? Are you still going after them?"

"We leave in the morning. The rest of the Texas forces are moving in to converge with us a little northwest of the prison. You'll be returning to the ship. Jeremy Flagg will be in charge, along with a skeleton crew. The rest will go with me."

"And the *Savannah* . . . will she be leaving Campeche?"

"If the Centralists overrun the city, I don't want the ship trapped in the harbor. She'll move south along the coast, anchor at a set rendezvous point as near the prison as she can get. As soon as the Texians are freed, we'll join back up with you there."

He made it sound simple, though she knew it wasn't. "I wish you didn't have to go."

"So do I."

Silver leaned down and kissed him. When Morgan's arms went around her, the kiss turned hot and fiery. They made love with abandon then once more with great tenderness. Finally they slept.

Morgan gently shook her awake before dawn. "You had better pack your things. We'll be leaving soon."

Shoving sleep-tangled hair from her face, Silver nodded. Morgan kissed the tip of her nose, then strode back to the bureau and finished getting dressed.

"I'll see you at breakfast." He flashed her a last warm smile, his mind already on the task ahead. Lifting the black wrought-iron latch, he pulled open the heavy wooden door and disappeared into the hallway.

With Cecilia's help, Silver dressed hurriedly in her yellow muslin day dress and headed downstairs. Her bags were brought down and taken outside to the carriage that would return them to the ship. In the dining room, a long narrow affair with molded ceilings and a huge rosewood table seating twenty, Morgan sat to the right of General Canales. Colonel

Buckland sat to his left, and Hamilton Riley sat beside Buckland. All four men came to their feet when Silver appeared in the doorway.

"*Buenos dias*, Senorita Jones," said the general, who looked nearly as regal as he had the night before. Only the tiny lines of fatigue at the corners of his eyes gave away his worry.

"Good morning, General. Gentlemen."

"I hope you slept well," Canales said.

Silver searched his face for a knowing expression but found none. "Yes, General. The room was quite lovely. Thank you."

Morgan pulled out her chair and seated her beside him, a warm smile playing on his lips. A breakfast of crisp fried potatoes, eggs, which the Mexicans called huevos, and chorizo, a pork sausage made with red chiles, was served with hot corn tortillas and thick black coffee.

The men ate heartily while Silver only picked at the spicy food. She was worried about the fighting that would soon take place, the danger the men would be facing.

"Not hungry, my dear?" Buckland asked with false concern, and it was all Silver could do to force a smile in his direction.

"It's delicious," she said, aiming her comments instead to their host. "I'm just a little worried, I guess."

"We are all a little worried, senorita."

The meal ended quickly; there was much left to do in readiness for the journey. Everyone said goodbye, Morgan led her out to the waiting carriage, and Hamilton helped her aboard.

"What about your men?" Silver asked Morgan once they had settled inside and were rolling along the dusty streets. "I thought they were given leave until tomorrow."

"Leave was canceled last night," Ham answered for him. "With most of the cantinas near the wharf, they shouldn't have been difficult to find. I'm sure they've all been rounded up by now."

"My men will be ready," Buckland vowed. "I hope that scurvy lot from the Indies is set to fight."

"Jacques will have them ready," Morgan said. And they were.

All but Farley Weathers, Dickey Green, and Jordan Little.

By the time they reached the ship and discovered the news, they found Jacques looking haggard from his night of searching, his black hair mussed, his clothes wrinkled and dusty. "I 'ave looked for them everywhere. I cannot believe Jordy 'as run away, but—" He shrugged his shoulders in a gesture of despair.

"I'd like a chance to look for them, Colonel," Morgan said. "Something might have happened."

The colonel started to say no, then saw Morgan's determined expression. The major's request was a mere formality. He was staying, one way or the other.

"I'll take the men ashore," the colonel grudgingly conceded with a note of hostility. "We'll pick up the horses, munitions, and equipment, then head out the eastern entrance to the city."

"I'll catch up to you before nightfall," Morgan promised. "Jacques, you come with me."

"*Oui, Capitaine.*"

"Mr. Flagg," Morgan said to the second mate, "is she ready to sail?"

"Aye, sir."

"Be prepared to make way just as soon as I return."

"Jordy didn't run away," Silver said to Morgan as the others left to complete their assignments. "Let me help you find him."

"No. Jacques and I will split up, and I'll hire a few men along the docks to help with the search. We can move faster if we don't have to worry about you, too."

"Please, Morgan. There must be something I can do."

Morgan smiled and touched her cheek. "When you say 'please, Morgan,' I think of far different things than searching for a wayward boy." He gave her a swift, hard kiss. "Stay here till I get back."

She meant to. She really and truly meant to. But the scruffy little urchin who raced up the gangway changed her mind. He spotted her standing near the rail and rushed up to clutch her skirts. Speaking rapidly in Spanish, he pointed toward the quay. One small dirty hand pressed a folded piece of paper into her palm. Silver opened it quickly.

Dear Silver,
I am in some trouble and need your help. The boy will show you where to find me.

Your friend,
Jordy

P.S. Please don't tell Captain Trask.

Damn it to hell! Morgan would be furious. But what other choice did she have? Jordy was in trouble. She'd been afraid of that since the moment they had discovered he was gone. And if he were, Morgan wouldn't be as forgiving this time.

Two dozen lashes.

That was what Jordy would receive. And Silver couldn't bear the thought. "Where is he?" She pointed to the note and then to the quay.

"Está in la cantina," the boy said. *"¡Vamos!"* He tugged at her yellow muslin dress and pointed toward the city.

Silver glanced around. There were only a few men on deck, and Jeremy Flagg had gone below. If Jordy wasn't far, she could find him and return before anyone noticed she was gone. Jordy could say he hadn't heard about the canceled leave. No one could fault him for that.

Silver hurried down the gangway, reached the dock, and raced along behind the scruffy little Mexican boy. His clothes were full of holes and so black with dirt it was difficult to tell what color they were. Still, he had a wide, bright smile, and he led her with unerring ease through the crowded streets of the city.

Around them, merchants hawked woven straw hats called *jipijapa*, hammocks made from henequen, and small carved wooden statuettes. The smell of rotting fish, seaweed, and animals—chickens, pigs, and donkeys—filled the air. Silver prayed the cantina would not be far, but as she hurried through the narrow dirt streets, the dock fell away in the distance, and still the boy raced on.

"How much farther?" she asked, knowing full well he didn't understand but needing a moment to catch her breath.

"¡Andale! Andale!" he said, tugging at her hand.

His urgency pressed her on, and she hurried after him. It wasn't long before they crossed into an even

shabbier section of town, and the boy held open a
hide-covered doorway to a small adobe structure
that sat off a bit by itself. She could hear the strum of
guitars and the boisterous sounds of laughter.

Looking at the run-down condition of the building,
at the drunken man passed out beside the door with
an open jug of *aguardiente* in his hand, Silver felt a
prickle of fear. It was crazy to have come to a place
like this alone. Still, if she could help Jordy, the risk
would be worth it.

Squaring her shoulders, she let the small boy lead
her inside. Instantly the music ceased, and the men
in the tavern stopped to stare. Several plump serving
women openly gawked, but the boy paid no heed,
just led Silver toward a faded red curtain at the back
of the room. The floors were earthen, and rafters
supported the thatched roof above her head.

Silver stepped behind the curtain. The room was
dimly lit by an opening that served as a window high
up on the wall. A cornhusk mattress lay in one corner beside a burned-out candle in a battered tin cup.
In the opposite corner Jordy, bound and gagged, his
eyes wide with fear, huddled on the earthen floor.

"Jordy!" Silver cried, racing to his side. Jordy
madly shook his head and strained wildly against his
bonds, grunting something behind the gag. Silver's
fingers fumbled with the knot that held the dirty rag
in place, trying to work it free. "Damn." Tearing a
nail in her efforts, she continuing to dig at the tight
scrap of cloth.

"Well, if it ain't the major's woman come to call."
Farley Weathers chuckled softly. Strong fingers bit
into Silver's shoulders, forcing her to stand and spinning her to face him. "Told you she'd come runnin',"
he said to Dickey Green over one beefy shoulder.

"Mi dinero, senor," the small boy urged, holding out a tiny brown hand.

"And a little bit extra for hurryin', just like I promised." Stormy dropped several coins into the child's outstretched palm. He raced away without a backward glance.

"What have you done to Jordy?" Silver faced him squarely.

"He's just restin'. He'll be fine."

"Ye said she'd come, and ye was right as rain." Dickey Green stepped closer, and Silver felt his bony hand cup her bottom, giving it a not too gentle squeeze. "Ye always was the bright one, Stormy."

Jerking away from Weathers, Silver whirled toward the little Englishman and slapped him hard across the face.

Farley Weathers laughed aloud. "She's got spirit, ain't she? I mean to ride her hard and fast."

Dickey Green rubbed his cheek, pink with the imprint of her hand. "Ye break her in real good, Stormy. Then I'll teach the mort a trick er two."

"Untie Jordy, and get out of our way," Silver warned, wishing she'd had the good sense to bring a weapon along.

"Ye think we went to all this trouble just to let ye go?" Green asked.

Weathers rubbed his crotch, the back of his calloused hand sprinkled with curly red hairs. "I'm wantin' this piece, Dickey. I ain't about to wait till we git outa here. I been watchin' her sashay around that ship for nigh on three weeks. I'm just achin' for a little relief, and I mean to take it."

Silver bolted for the curtained door, but Weathers's heavy arm whipped around her waist, jerking her up short. "Get away from me," she warned, feeling a jolt of anger that gave her a shot of strength. She knew where this was leading, and it wasn't going to happen!

Silver trounced hard on one of Stormy's big feet and then the other, scratching and fighting like a woman gone mad. She bit his hand, kicked him in the shins, and punched him as hard as she could. Stormy Weathers cursed her, grimaced at the nails she raked down his cheek, tried to protect his eyes from her slashing clawlike fingers, and finally slapped her so hard she gasped and went crashing down to the floor.

He fell on her in an instant, shoving her down on her stomach, wrenching her arm up behind her back.

"You bloody bastard, let me go!" Silver called him every vile name she could think of, which were too numerous to count.

"I say, Stormy, this un's no lady." Dickey Green's eyes looked bigger than Farley's. "She deserves whatever she gets, wouldn't ye say?"

"She's a salty bitch, that's for sure. But I mean to tame her."

Silver struggled anew, but Weathers's knee in the middle of her back, the heavy weight of his body, and the pressure on her arm stilled her efforts. Pain shot into her shoulder, and Silver fought not to cry out. Tiny pebbles cut her cheek where it pressed against the hard earth floor, and the metallic taste of blood filled her mouth. Outside the strains of guitars continued along with the sound of men's laughter. *Surely someone out there would help her!* But Weathers's hold on her arm kept her from calling out.

His hand moved over her body, along her back, and over her hips. He squeezed her buttocks, and the bile crept into her throat. Then his hand moved lower, caught the hem of her dress, and jerked it up to her waist.

"There's a way to treat a woman like you," Stormy said. "Let's 'em know who's boss right from the start." Up went her petticoats. She heard Dickey Green's gleeful laughter and Jordy's thrashing movements. *Oh, God, don't let Jordy see this.*

Silver tried to scream for help, but Weathers wrenched her arm even higher. The driving pain silenced her and brought a sweep of nausea.

"They ain't gonna help you. Never seen a more cowardly lot of curs." He sat on his knees astraddle her, his big hand skimming over the curve of her hips. With a grunt of satisfaction, he pinched her bottom through the soft white fabric of her lacy cotton drawers. Silver squirmed and cursed him again.

"I say, Stormy, couldn't you hurry a mite? I'm itchin' to see that fine-lookin' bum o' hers." Green laughed again, the sound a little tighter.

Stormy ignored him, enjoying her discomfort as he stroked each rounded globe. "You learn your place," he told her, "I'll pleasure ya proper. Not this time—I mean to see to that real good. Next time you'll do as you're told."

With that he worked the buttons at the front of his breeches. Even with her face pressed into the dirt, Silver could see the bulge that strained against the front of them, and the thought of it inside her made her sick.

"God in heaven," she whispered aloud, but Stormy only grunted. One hand reached beneath her stomach to loosen the cord of her pantalets; then he started tugging them down.

"You will let the lady go." Jacques's deep voice cut through the air like a knife. Never had his soft French accent been so welcome.

"This here's no lady, mate." Green stepped closer to Stormy. "This un's a real she-bitch, she is. Ye got here just in time for a piece o' her."

"Release 'er." Jacques's blade appeared in his hand almost from nowhere. "Do it now, and back away."

Weathers let go of her arm and adjusted his breeches, buttoning himself back up. When he came to his feet, Silver sat up and discreetly rearranged her clothing. Her face flamed scarlet at what had almost happened, but her worry was for Jacques and Jordy.

"You are all right, *chérie*?" Jacques asked, still holding the blade in front of him. It was ten inches long and wickedly curved.

"We've got to free Jordy."

Jacques glanced to the corner, where Jordy thrashed against his tightly bound arms and legs.

"You ain't takin' her," Weathers warned. "There's two of us against you." Weathers pulled his own knife, which was even bigger than Jacques's, and Green pulled a long, thin dagger with a stag horn handle.

"Oh, God," Silver moaned.

Both Green and Weathers lunged for Jacques at nearly the same moment, their blades slicing the air just inches from Jacques's wide chest. Jacques darted away, slashing with his own blade. It landed with the clank of steel on steel. Weathers spun away; Green danced closer. Jacques stepped away, whirled and lashed out, slicing into flesh, and Dickey Green yelped in pain. A streak of crimson trailed down his arm, but he looked no less determined.

"Ye shouldn'a done that, mate."

Silver glanced from Jacques to Weathers, who smiled grimly, awaiting his chance to administer death. Determined to help, she frantically surveyed the near-empty room, searching for some kind of weapon. Beside the curtained doorway, a broken pottery ale mug rested. Silver crouched down and picked it up, the jagged edges surrounding the handle making it easy to grip. Jacques caught her movement from the corner of his deep blue eyes.

"Stay out of this, *chérie*. You will only make things 'arder."

Maybe she would, and maybe she wouldn't. She'd do her best to let him handle the situation, but she wasn't about to stand by and watch him get killed.

Dickey Green feinted right and lunged left, bringing his knife in low and slashing Jacques's right thigh. Silver stifled the scream in her throat. Jacques ignored the pain and the red stain spreading down his leg. Spinning away from Weather's blade, he brought his own knife down in a sweeping arc that laid open Green's shoulder. The smaller man's shirt turned red in an instant, and his face contorted in pain.

"I'm gonna kill ye, Frenchy," Green vowed.

Again the three men dodged the gleaming death each held in front of him, steel ringing against steel, the task more difficult in the confines of the narrow room. Then Green did the unexpected. He dodged Jacques's blade and lunged for Silver instead. In the instant it took for the threat to register and Jacques to parry the move, Jacques stood open to Weathers's attack.

"No!" Silver screamed, barely dodging the knife Green thrust toward her breast. With a twisting motion, she stepped in to protect Jacques's defenseless side and shoved the jagged edge of the mug into Weathers's broad, thick-lipped face.

His agonized shriek of pain echoed against the

walls of the room, and his hands shot up to the
bleeding gouges. It was the moment Jacques needed.
His blade surged home, slicing between Stormy's
ribs, then thrusting upward. As quickly as it went in,
he pulled it out, whirled, and slid it against the Englishman's throat, one muscular arm going around
the man's skinny neck in the same quick motion.

"Drop your blade or die, *anglais.*"

Green held his knife for an instant; then it clattered to the floor. "'Twas Stormy's idea," Green
pleaded, "Stormy what wanted to take her—he
never were too bright."

"I should kill you for the dog you are."

"No, Jacques." Silver's trembling fingers touched
his arm. "Please don't kill him."

Jacques's blue eyes ran over her. "The decision is
yours, *chérie.* But know that the Mexicans 'ave even
less use for a man who defiles their women. 'Is treatment will be 'arsh indeed."

"That is for them to decide."

"*What* is for them to decide?" Morgan stood in the
doorway, his bright green eyes fixed on the blade
Jacques held beneath Green's chin. He glanced from
Jacques to Weathers, dead and bleeding on the floor,
then to where Jordy lay bound and gagged. When at
last he turned to Silver, he saw that her dress was
torn and wrinkled and covered with dirt and twigs.
The pins had come loose from her hair, spilling it
around her shoulders.

Ignoring him, the embarrassing explanation sure
to come, and the heat that burned her cheeks, Silver
moved toward Jordy. She picked up the knife Green
had dropped and began to cut his bindings.

"Would one of you care to explain what's going
on?"

Silver just kept working.

It was Jacques who finally answered. "These two pigs kidnapped Jordy and 'eld him captive. Silver came to 'is rescue—and to mine."

"She doesn't look like she fared too well herself."

"She will be all right," Jacques assured him, noting the tight lines of Morgan's face, the emotions he fought to control. "I am just grateful for the man on the quay who saw Jordy being taken. I see 'e carried 'is message to you, as I instructed."

"Yes."

Steeling herself to the harshness in Morgan's tone, Silver sliced through the last of Jordy's bonds, reached down, and hugged him.

"I'm sorry, Silver. They made me write the note."

"It wasn't your fault." She gave him another brief hug.

"But what they tried to do to you. . . ."

Silver glanced from Jordy to Morgan, found his hard look fixed on her, and flushed all over again.

"You all right, son?" Morgan asked.

"Yes, sir."

"We'll talk about this when we get back to the ship. Right now you go with Jacques. See that this scum is taken care of, will you?"

"Aye, sir, you kin—can—count on that."

"Get Cookie to see to that leg," he said to Jacques. The brawny Frenchman wrestled Dickey Green out the door, and Jordy followed him out. Silver glanced down at her feet, at the rough adobe wall above Morgan's shoulder, everywhere but at his face.

Reaching out, he captured her chin with his hand, his grip unrelenting. "I told you to stay on the ship."

Silver tried to turn away, but he wouldn't let go. "Jordy was in trouble. I had no choice."

Morgan turned her cheek to assess the purple

bruise beside her eye, the cut at the corner of her mouth. "I want to know what happened to you. I want to know what those men did."

Silver watched him a moment, reading the anger mixed with concern. She thought of the rough way Stormy had intended to use her, and embarrassment rose in her cheeks.

Morgan released his hold, and his voice turned gentle. "There is nothing you can't tell me, Silver. You don't have to be ashamed."

She wet her lips, which suddenly felt dry. She didn't want him to know, but there were enough secrets between them. "I fought with Stormy. He knocked me down and . . . he would have forced himself on me if Jacques hadn't arrived when he did."

Morgan pulled her into his arms and cradled her head against his chest with the palm of his hand. "You've got to start listening to me, Silver. You're going to get hurt. I can't promise you someone will always be there to save you."

"I wish I could say I was sorry, but I'm not. I was able to help, so the danger was worth it."

Morgan's hand skimmed over her hair. "You're sure you're all right?"

She nodded against his chest.

"Green's just lucky I wasn't holding the knife," he muttered, and Silver softly smiled.

Chapter 18

It was well past noon when they returned to the ship. Jacques met them at the top of the gangway.

"You 'ave a visitor," he said to Morgan. "She waits for you in the salon."

Silver eyed Morgan warily, wondering which of his women this one was, but he only urged her toward the ladder with a firm hand at her waist.

Belowdecks a woman leaned against the smooth oak paneling, facing away from them. She turned at their approach. Standing no taller than Silver, she had glistening black hair pulled into a tight knot at the nape of her neck. Around her shoulders she clutched her worn fringed shawl. She had luminous black eyes and smooth dark skin. A white cotton peasant blouse and orange skirt brightly embroidered near the hem showed a full-busted figure with well-rounded hips.

"You must be Senor Trask," she said in passable English.

"I'm Trask."

She smiled at Silver. "And you are Dama de Luz. There is much talk of your beauty."

"My friends call me Silver." Silver smiled, too, responding to the woman's warmth.

"I am Teresa Méndez. I have come to seek your aid."

Morgan moved farther into the room and pulled out one of the carved oak chairs around the table "Why don't we sit down?" Teresa took a seat. Morgan seated Silver, then pulled out a chair for himself "How may we be of service, Senorita Méndez?"

"I have spoken to your friend Senor Hypolyte Bouillard He was very understanding " She smiled softly, and something flickered in the darkness of her eyes "He has agreed to speak to you on my behalf should you refuse my request."

Morgan's posture stiffened. She was working the two men against each other, trying to sway one by showing the other's support. It wouldn't work on Morgan. Still, Silver admired the woman's ploy

"And just what exactly is it you wish me to do?" Morgan asked, his tone a little less friendly.

"Many know of your journey to Rancho de los Cocodrilos—the land of the crocodiles. It is a French henequen plantation, or was before the Centralists turned it into a fortress "

"Go on," Morgan urged

"You seek the Texas soldiers there, held in the ruins that lie to the east of the great hacienda. But there are other men there of no less importance Political prisoners captured in the fighting for Campeche My father, Alejandro Méndez, is among them."

"I'm sorry to hear that "

"You must free him, Senor Trask, along with the others He is a poor man, but a man of great learning Alejandro Méndez is revered among his people He has helped them often in these troubled times."

"We will free all we can, whoever they may be."

"That is not enough. You must take me with you. Word has come back from the prison that he has been taken ill. My father is old and frail. Even if you help him escape, he cannot survive the journey back to Campeche without me."

"That's impossible, senorita. There will be dozens of soldiers on this mission. There'll be fighting. It's not the place for a woman."

"Our army is not like yours, senor. The *soldados* often take their women when they leave for battle. The women care for them, cook and mend their clothing, warm their beds."

"I'm sorry, but it just isn't possible."

"I will take 'er." Jacques's heavily accented French rang from the open hatch as he descended the ladder. "If you will but say the word, I will see to 'er safety."

Morgan looked hard at his friend. It wasn't like the big Frenchman to go against his wishes, yet the woman had convinced him, had somehow won his support. Jacques was no fool, not even when it came to a pretty face. Morgan surveyed Teresa Méndez, saw the hope—and the desperation.

"You believe your father's life depends on you?"

"*Sí*, senor. I alone know how to care for him."

"I don't mean to be cruel, senorita, but you realize he may already be dead."

"*Sí*, senor, but if there is any chance at all, I must take it."

"We'll be leaving within the hour. Can you be ready?"

"I am ready now, senor."

Morgan released a weary breath. The last thing he needed was a woman tagging along, but he wouldn't be responsible for a good man's death if he could help it

"We'll be riding hard to catch up with the rest of the troops. Once we reach them, the pace will slow a little. We should reach Rancho de los Cocodrilos late day after tomorrow "

"*Sí*, senor I was raised near there. I know the place well I may even be able to save you some time."

Morgan's mouth curved upward "Then I shall find it less difficult to forgive my big French friend for his unseemly interference "

Jacques just chuckled.

"We'll meet on deck in fifteen minutes "

Teresa and Jacques said their farewells to Silver and climbed the ladder to the deck

"I don't suppose you'd let me go, too," Silver asked Morgan once the others had gone.

Morgan pinned her with an icy green-eyed glare "Don't even think about it."

"I just thought I might keep Teresa company "

"No "

"I'd stay out of the way and—"

Morgan gripped her arms and hauled her against him "Damn it, Silver, for once I want you safe "

"But I might be able to help "

"Just how much help do you think you'd be? With my mind on you instead of the fighting, there's a damned good chance I'd wind up getting killed "

Silver's chest tightened "You'd be that worried?"

"Damned right I would."

She reached a hand to his cheek, traced her finger along his scar "Promise me you'll be careful "

He smiled at that. "There's a lot left unfinished between us. . . . I'll be careful."

Morgan bent his head and kissed her, so thoroughly her knees went weak. She followed him into his cabin, watched him check his cap-and-ball pistol, the knife in the sheath at his waist, and the saber that hung at his side. He picked up his satchel and started for the door.

"I'll miss you," she said softly, drawing his attention.

Setting his bag aside, Morgan strode across the room and swept her into his arms. "I'll be back, milady vixen. You just stay out of trouble until I get here."

With a last hard kiss, he headed out the door. Silver followed him up on deck, fighting back tears, then stood at the rail to watch their departing figures while Jeremy Flagg gave the orders that would move the ship from the harbor.

In minutes the lines were cast off, a brisk wind snapped the canvas taut above her head, and the *Savannah* began to make way.

The terrain was even worse than Morgan imagined, just a thin layer of earth over the jagged rocky limestone beneath. The forest was scrub—thorny, dense, and hostile—the ground flat and so thickly overgrown it was impossible to see anywhere but along the rutted wagon road they followed. A harsh sun parched the landscape.

Morgan glanced at his two companions. So far the woman had held up well, though the going was tough and he had been pushing her hard, but she'd known the going would be hard from the start. He hoped to hell they'd catch Buckland and the troops by nightfall. The danger of crossing this primitive terrain in the dark would be multiplied tenfold.

"How much farther till we reach the others, Senor Trask?" Teresa Méndez rode her scrawny bay mare

up beside him. She was obviously stiff and sore, and
the inside of her leg, exposed below the hem of her
skirt, looked red and chafed from the big Spanish
saddle. Still, she did not complain.

"Another hour, maybe two Buckland is pushing
them hard."

Jacques nudged his bony white gelding in their direction "We would rest if we dared, *chérie*, but it
will soon be dark."

"*Gracias*, Senor Bouillard, for your concern, but
do not worry for me I am fine." She flashed him a
grateful smile and an appraising look that Morgan
suspected was one of approval. With his thick black
hair, well-kept beard and mustache, Jacques Bouillard was a handsome man. The warmth in Teresa's
dark eyes seemed to agree.

Morgan smiled inwardly. Something was happening between the two, for Jacques looked at Teresa
with the same gentle approval—and something
more.

They rode without stopping for most of an hour,
but when the troops had still not been spotted, Morgan reined up his sorrel stallion, a fine vaquero's
steed provided by General Canales, and indicated
they should rest and water their mounts.

"You are all right, *chérie*?" Jacques asked Teresa
as she sat down on a rock in the shade to work the
kinks from her back and shoulders. Parrots
screeched in the trees above them. Lizards and small
tree toads scampered away in fear.

"There are more important things than comfort."

Jacques moved her fingers away, replacing her
strained efforts with a pair of beefy hands that
kneaded her stiff and aching muscles. Teresa's expression said she knew a man should not be touch-

ing her in such an intimate fashion, but relief from
her pain was worth the slight indiscretion.

"You will stay close to me when we reach the others," Jacques told her. "As you say, your *soldados*
will be used to the presence of a woman. Some of the
others may not be so understanding."

"But surely your soldiers will obey their com-
mander?"

"There are others among them, not so used to following orders. Stay by me, and you will be safe."

Teresa nodded, accepting without question the
truth of Jacques's words.

"We'll be leaving the road soon," Morgan said,
though the path so far had been little more than a
trail in the ever-increasing denseness of the landscape. Though it was the end of the dry season, the
ground hot and dusty, he was grateful it hadn't begun to rain "There could be Centralist troops
nearby."

"*Sí*, senor."

After collecting the horses, Jacques swung the
small dark woman up into her saddle, his eyes fixed
on the smooth olive skin exposed where her skirt
bunched up on her thighs. She was just the kind of
woman Jacques liked. Stouthearted. The kind of
woman who could bear a man strong sons. Unlike
Morgan, Jacques had always enjoyed the comforts of
a home and family. Morgan wondered if his friend
might take the woman to wife.

Mounted again, they rode for two more hours. Off
to the west the hot sun turned orange and pink, then,
as Morgan had promised, faded into darkness just
minutes before they reached Buckland and the men.
The soldiers they passed looked weary but strong.
With a good night's rest they'd be ready for the second day's march.

"It's about time you got here." Buckland rode up on a big black horse also provided by the general. With the grazing so scarce here in the Yucatán, the other mounts were thin and scrawny. The mercenaries and marines were making the march on foot; the only other mounted soldiers were Hamilton Riley and the two Mexican officers the Federalists had sent as guides.

"I've chosen a campsite down near that small stream we've been following," Buckland said. "I assume that meets with approval, Major." His tone implied Morgan had been running the show so far, but that had come to an end.

"It looks fine to me," Morgan said, ignoring the man's hostility. "Any sign of Centralist forces?"

"None so far. Canales believes they'll move north along the coast and head straight for Campeche."

"The city's in a better position to defend than we are. I hope he's right."

Buckland glanced to Jacques and for the first time spotted Teresa. "What in the name of God is she doing here? Surely even you can't be so brazen as to drag your doxy along."

Morgan bristled, and noticed Jacques did the same, sitting a little straighter in his saddle. "Senorita Méndez is not a camp follower, Colonel. She's the daughter of one of the prisoners from Campeche."

"See that she's escorted back there immediately. This is certainly no place for a woman."

"I agree completely, Colonel," Morgan said, surprising Buckland and hearing Teresa's intake of breath. "In fact, I said those same words to the lady myself. Unfortunately she accompanies M'sieur Bouillard, and he is not under your command."

Buckland's mouth thinned, and his hands grew taut on the reins.

Jacques chuckled softly "I will see to the woman, Colonel You need not worry "

The colonel muttered something beneath his breath. "Keep her away from my troops, Bouillard, I'm warning you " Whirling his mount, he dug his heels into the animal's sides a little harder than necessary, and the stallion leaped away.

"I believe you 'ave made an enemy," Jacques said

"Long before now," Morgan agreed

Morgan checked on Hamilton Riley and the rest of the soldiers who had traveled with him aboard the *Savannah*. Then Morgan, Jacques, and the Mendez woman found places near the edge of the camp. Tomorrow they would make the second leg of the journey On Tuesday, barring any problems, they would reach the prison.

For the first time in days, Morgan allowed himself to think of Brendan. *Hold on, little brother It won't be long now.*

He refused to consider that something might have happened to him. In a few days, four at most, Brendan would be free, and the rest of the prisoners would be safe The two navy vessels that had brought the men to the peninsula would be sailing up from Ciudad del Carmen for the rendezvous off Champotón and the return trip to Texas. Morgan would be returning to the *Savannah*—and to Silver.

He shook his head. Damned if he hadn't started missing her already—and he'd been gone only one day. How the hell would he feel when he left her with William in Katonga?

Grudgingly Morgan admitted he was falling in love with the feisty bit of baggage. She wasn't what he'd thought he wanted, wasn't the prim and proper, obedient kind of woman he had in mind. She wasn't conventional; she wasn't predictable.

She was just Silver.

Just the most courageous, most giving, caring woman he had ever known.

She was fire and ice, desire and beauty. She was passion and sweetness rolled into one. She was a treasure far greater than any he had ever possessed and he wasn't about to let her go.

Morgan listened to the sounds of the forest-jungle. Small fires, carefully tended, dotted the greenery where men heated coffee or sat in quiet conversation.

Jacques sat talking to Teresa, smiling warmly while she smiled back. Jacques had been married twice, loved both his wives, mourned their deaths, and would probably marry again. Morgan had tried that kind of involvement once and failed miserably.

"I'm not like Charlotte," Silver had said. "I never will be." He wondered how she had known about the woman in his past, but then Silver had a way of finding out whatever she wanted. Even Morgan had found himself close to revealing things he rarely divulged. He hadn't because he had to be sure he could trust her.

But did he?

He wanted to say yes. That he knew without doubt the things he'd been thinking were true—that Silver Jones was everything she professed to be and more. Then he thought of the things she had said about William, the hatred for her father she had never really explained, her reasons for running away. What was the rest of her story? How much of what she'd told him was the truth? *Take your time*, a cautious voice inside him said. *Find out for sure.*

And so he would. He would miss her; when he

returned, he would take her to his bed. But he wouldn't let himself love her—not all the way—not until he was sure.

Silver slept fitfully, worried about Morgan, praying he would find his brother alive and be able to free him and the other Texian men. At dawn she wearily climbed to the deck then went forward to the galley for a hot cup of coffee. With the few men left aboard, she certainly didn't want anyone going to extra trouble for her.

For the first time since she'd come aboard the *Savannah*, Cookie sat at the huge wooden table looking pensive instead of standing at the cookstove stirring boiling kettles or frying meats They hadn't talked much during their weeks at sea, but now his worry for Morgan and Jacques had brought them together

"How about a cup of coffee, Cookie?"

His brooding expression faded, and he smiled "Sure." He was friendlier toward her since the talk they'd shared last night after supper while Silver helped him scrub the big black pots Jordy had joined them for a while, but with the men away, he carried a full seaman's duties. He had too much work to stay for long At least the boy had straightened things out with Morgan, explained he'd had no part in what had happened with Dickey Green and Stormy Weathers.

"I saved you some salt pork and biscuits." Cookie moved toward the stove as Silver took a place on the long wooden bench across from him.

"It smells delicious, she said, sniffing the familiar aromas, "but I'm not very hungry Just the coffee will be fine."

Cookie nodded, understanding her lack of appetite Grandison Aimes was a sensitive man, Silver had discovered, though he often hid his feelings beneath a gruff facade.

He poured her a mug of the steaming coffee, which he set down in front of her on the table. Silver smiled, but it came out a bit forlorn. "Thanks." She wrapped both hands around the mug but didn't bring it to her lips.

"He'll be all right," Cookie told her, reading the train of her thoughts. "We been through rougher seas than this."

Silver's head came up. "I remember you saying the two of you have fought together. Where did it happen?"

Cookie laughed, the sound hoarse and rough. "We been in many a tavern brawl, but those don't count for much. We came close to our end once in '34. In Aragón—that's a place in Spain. We just happened to be in the wrong place at the wrong time. The damned Carlist War broke out over who should sit on the throne. Got real bloody before we got outa there."

"What were you doing in Spain?"

"Same as we were doin' on the Niagara in '37, when the Canadians sank the *Caroline*. Trading mostly—with folks who got problems. Pays a whole lot better than most. That time the U.S. was aiding the insurgents, though it didn't do 'em a parcel of good and managed to cost 'em a damn fine ship."

"So he's done this kind of thing before."

"Ever since he bought his first vessel—a schooner some smaller than this one. Cap'n's a man who knows his talents—and how best to use them. It's made him a wealthy man. Weren't for his brother, he'd be brokering cotton, livin' the life of luxury in that fine mansion o' his."

"I think he likes this kind of life."

"Some," Cookie agreed, "but I believe he's ready to settle down."

She wondered at his pointed expression. "Do you really think he'll be all right?"

"Cap'n's a damned fine hand with rifle and saber. I just wish he'd a let me go along."

"Why didn't he?"

Cookie looked at her hard. "Cap'n's real taken with you, missy. He left me to see you come to no harm. He knows I won't let him down."

"But surely the ship is in no danger."

"Prob'ly not . . ." He reached for the huge blue tin coffeepot that sat at the back of the stove and topped off her cup. He started to say something more when Jordy rushed in.

"Benson's spotted troop movements." He was the man on duty in the crow's nest. "They ain't—aren't —headin' north; they're headed inland. Looks like they may be trying to intercept the major."

"Oh, my God." Silver came to her feet.

"Mr. Flagg wants to see you," Jordy finished.

"How many?" Cookie asked, forcing Jordy to calm down.

"Two, maybe three hundred men. They're ridin' with lance and long arm and draggin' cannon and caisson. Cap'n don't stand a chance."

"He will if we get word to him," Cookie said

"But how?" Silver asked.

"I'll ride after him." Cookie seemed suddenly taller. There was no mistaking the fierce resolve in his eyes. "Cap'n's marked his trail on the map he left behind. It shows the location of the prison, the direction he and the men are taking to get there, and the place we're supposed to meet him on his return."

"But you'll need horses," Silver pressed, "and someone who knows the country."

"There's Mexicans and Indians all along the coast. Enough money'll buy all the help I need."

"I'm going with you," Silver said

"No, miss. Cap'n wouldn't want that."

"Listen to me, Cookie. Something might happen to you out there. We can't take any chances. This message has got to get through, and there isn't anyone aboard who can be spared besides you and me. I can ride as well as a man and shoot if I have to. Something happens, one of us will make it."

Cookie seemed to ponder her words.

"Let me go instead," Jordy said to him. "Cap'n will skin you alive, you take Silver."

"You got a job to do here," Cookie told him. "She can't handle sail and line."

"But—"

"Cap'n's in a heap of trouble, son." He looked at Silver, who stood with her shoulders squared, her jaw set with determination "This woman loves him. She'll get through when nobody else can."

Silver felt a hard lump swell in her throat. Were her feelings so transparent? "He's right," she said softly. "I've got to help him."

"It's gonna take the devil's own luck to reach him before those troops do."

"Mr. Flagg said something about sailin' upriver," Jordy said. "Goin' inland as far as we could get."

"The Champotón. Damned good idea," Cookie agreed. "That's about the only way we can get ahead of those bastards." He'd no more than said the words when Silver felt the ship shudder and begin to come about. In minutes the *Savannah* heeled the opposite way, cutting across the water toward the shore.

"Won't take long to reach the Champotón. I hope

she's deep enough. Won't do the cap'n much good, we run aground."

"I'll change clothes and meet you on deck." Silver turned and dashed toward the ladder.

"I'll fetch what supplies we'll be needin'," Cookie said to Jordy, "then speak to Flagg."

"Aye."

"Flagg'll take the ship back out to sea, soon as we're ashore. We gotta set a rendezvous point. We don't want those soldiers findin' out the ship's location."

"No, sir," Jordy said. Cookie hurried for the ladder. "Look out for Silver," Jordy called from behind him "She ain't—isn't—as tough as she lets on."

Cookie smiled. "I know that, son. I'll watch out for her. She's the cap'n's lady, ain't she?"

"Isn't she," Jordy corrected.

Cookie grunted, but inside he smiled

Chapter 19

The harrowing trip upriver set all their nerves on edge Determined to get as far inland as they could, the men poled the depths from shore boats when the river narrowed, and the ship kept on sailing. The sun rested low on the horizon when they finally gave up and readied a boat to row Silver and Cookie ashore.

"Take care o' yourselves," Jordy said stoically, and Silver gave him a hug

Flagg shook their hands "We'll be waiting for you," the lanky second mate assured them "You just warn the cap'n and get yourselves back to the ship."

"Aye, Mr. Flagg," Cookie said

Once they reached the shore, just as Cookie had predicted, it was easy to buy the needed horses—crowbait that they were—and even a short, hook-nosed, broad-faced Mayan man to guide them inland.

They had come upon the small native village a few miles farther upriver, just a cluster of oblong thatched houses called *huotoches* made of saplings plastered with mud The village circled a cenote, a deep limestone well, shaded by a grove of chicle trees.

Wearing Jordy's breeches and shirt, Silver caused quite a stir among the Mayans, who gathered around just to look at her pale blond hair. Although the people welcomed them, the task of explaining their needs seemed impossible, since the Indians spoke only their native tongue. Then the wife of one of them, a wide-girthed Mexican woman, appeared, and Cookie, who spoke a goodly amount of Spanish, was able to convey his wishes and the urgency of their request. Apparently the Centralists held no popularity with the woman, and the lure of the gold *real* Cookie held up to glint in the sunlight sealed the bargain.

Mounted on a scrawny, swaybacked horse, Cookie followed the Mayan, who wore the skin of a jaguar and carried only a water gourd, a food bag made of henequen, and a billhook machete. Silver followed Cookie, moving northeast across a terrain that was far more tropical than any they had seen so far.

Overgrown ferns covered the ground beneath towering trees, and the dense vegetation had to be teeming with spiders and snakes. Bright-plumed birds screeched above them, hibiscus bloomed, and monkeys shrilled in the tops of the tallest trees. The badly overgrown trail they followed forced them to ride single file.

Though Silver had ridden often back on Katonga —astride much of the time—she hadn't been in the saddle since she'd left there some months ago. The ache in her thighs and calves convinced her that she was badly out of condition, but the breeches she wore eased the friction of her legs against the woven wool blanket, which was all that covered the horse's bony back. In time she knew her body would limber and begin to move in the familiar jogging rhythm.

"We gotta keep ahead of the main body of soldiers," Cookie told her. "Hope to God I made that clear to the heathen."

Silver hoped so, too. Morgan's life was at stake, along with dozens of others. Her own and Cookie's as well.

They rode for the better part of the day, resting only briefly, pushing the animals as hard as they dared, pushing themselves even harder. The Mayan seemed tireless, and the horses far tougher than at first they had appeared. Though the trail they followed led them in the right direction, discovering the exact location of Morgan and his men seemed a Herculean task at best.

Still, they rode on. Never had two more determined people set off to accomplish a task.

"Lieutenant Riley!" Buckland shouted, and the sandy-haired man rode up beside him. "Give the men fifteen minutes' rest." They had been marching for hours, the sun hot overhead through the dense canopy of trees. The farther southeast they moved, the thicker and greener the foliage, the hotter and more humid the weather.

Morgan reined up his big sorrel stallion and dismounted along with the others. He might have pressed on a little farther, but then he had a personal stake in driving the men. Besides, for once Buckland was right. They still had a day's march ahead of them; staying fit and able to fight was of utmost importance.

Morgan sat down on a rock and took a drink from his tin canteen. Jacques sat down beside him. "Where's Teresa?" Morgan asked.

"She needed à moment alone," Jacques said, explaining the lady's need for privacy. "She is some woman, *n'est-ce pas*?"

A corner of Morgan's mouth curved upward. "So what do you plan to do about it?"

Jacques looked perturbed. "What do you ask, *mon ami*? You think I should marry again?" He scoffed at the notion. "I 'ave 'ad two lusty wives, two grown sons any man would be proud of. What more could I ask?"

Only Jacques knew the answer to that. "What did she say to get you to bring her along?"

The Frenchman chuckled softly. "She was bound and determined to 'elp 'er father. 'If you will not take me,' she said, 'I will follow in your path. I will be there when you break into the prison—with or without your 'elp!' " He chuckled again. "She would 'ave done it. I saw it then; I see it now."

Jacques watched the woman who stepped from behind a cluster of low thorny bushes and walked toward them, her hips swaying with unconscious seductiveness. "You, *mon ami*, 'ave your hands full with Silver. Hypolyte Jacques Bouillard 'as a problem of 'is own."

"Riders coming in!"

At the sound of the lookout's words, both Jacques and Morgan came to their feet. They strode the rocky path toward the colonel, who awaited the two approaching men. One was dressed in the uniform of a Texas Marine, though the clothes had seen better days; the other was a thick-chested, brawny-looking man with a clean-shaven head and a long, thin, drooping black mustache. With his smooth, slitted eyes, he appeared to be Asian, maybe a Mongol or a Turk. Morgan figured him for one of the mercenaries who were part of the original Texian forces.

It was the younger man, the marine, who spoke.
"Corporal Nathan Gibbons, sir." He forced a weary
salute. "This man is Bayram Sit. We bring greetings
from Archibald Spray, our commanding officer."
The young corporal grinned. "And if you'll pardon
my sayin' so, Colonel, we're mighty glad to see you."

The colonel swelled a little, Morgan thought. With
warm words of welcome, Buckland led the corporal
beneath a tree and offered him a drink of water. The
Asian approached the major.

"You are Morgan Trask?"

Morgan nodded. "How did you know?"

"I bring word of your brother. You look a good
deal like him."

Brendan's hair was brown instead of blond, his
eyes light blue instead of green. But the brothers
were built much the same, with the same shaped
brow, hard jaw, and straight nose. Brendan had always smiled a lot more. Morgan wondered if his
brother was smiling now.

"How is he?"

"Alive. How well he fares I cannot say. Word
comes to us only now and then."

"How is it you bring this message?"

"He and I are friends of a sort. We met on board
ship. It seems we had a mutual acquaintance. My
good friend Alexandre du Villier is also a friend to
you and your brother."

Alex du Villier was a wealthy Creole sugar planter
from New Orleans. Morgan had known him for
years. "Bayram Sit." Morgan rolled the name across
his tongue, stirring distant memories. "Yes. I know
of you. The Ram." A Turk, as he recalled.

The big man chuckled softly. "I am called Ram by
my friends . . . and maybe those who have not
fared so well at my hand."

"Alex has spoken of you often. We met over shipping contracts, many years ago. He's a good man."

"As he says of you."

Morgan acknowledged the compliment with a nod. "What else have you heard?"

"The rest is even more unpleasant. It seems two weeks ago news reached the prison of your journey to Campeche. General Hernández—he is in charge of the prison—wanted information about your ship and your men. They began torturing the prisoners. Still, the men would not speak. Each day for the last ten, they have forced the prisoners to draw straws. The man who holds the short straw dies by the firing squad."

Morgan's stomach clenched along with his jaw, and a muscle jumped in his cheek.

"There is little more I can tell you," Ram finished. "Our last report was that your brother still lives. But you can see the urgency of freeing him and the others. Each day that passes, another good man dies."

Morgan raked a hand through his thick dark blond hair. "Will we reach your men by tomorrow?"

"Yes. The prison is another day's ride southeast."

"What are our chances?"

"With the guns you bring, there is a chance. As long as the Centralists get no more reinforcements."

Morgan extended a hand. "Thank you, my friend, for coming so far."

"Do not worry. Soon your brother will be free."

Unless he draws the shortest straw.

"¡Alto!" came the gruff Spanish command.

The Mayan looked surprised. Cookie and Silver hesitated only an instant, whirled their horses, dug their heels in, and charged off in different directions. They'd gone only a few great leaps when a group of mounted *soldados*, lances in hand, blocked their path.

They spun again, trying to rein away, but more men rode up until they were completely surrounded. At least twenty men encircled them, silently halting their movements.

"What do we do now?" Silver said softly, tightly gripping the reins.

"Not much we can do." Cookie moved his little bay horse closer. "Leastwise not yet You just stay calm. Either one of us gets a chance, he makes a break for it"

"I would not try that, senor," said a pleasant voice in English from behind them. They reined their horses around to face him.

"Who the devil are you?" Silver demanded, noting the man with brown hair, hazel eyes, and European features who was dressed in the uniform of an officer in the Mexican Army.

"I am Capitán Paulo Carrillo, at your service, Senorita Jones."

Silver hid her surprise at the use of her name. "What right do you have to accost three innocent people? Why are you blocking our way?"

"I am sorry for the inconvenience, senorita. But you must all come with me."

"Where to?" Cookie's hand tightened on the reins, and the little horse danced nervously beneath him.

"You will be taken to my commanding officer at Rancho de los Cocodrilos, where a portion of my troops are headed."

So they wouldn't all be attacking Morgan, Silver thought. "What have we done to deserve this treatment?"

"Is it not enough that you are foreigners in my country? That your ship brings weapons to the rebels? We know all about you, Dama de Luz I am sure General Hernández will enjoy meeting you When you sailed from Campeche aboard the *Savannah*, I had despaired of the pleasure. Fortunately your journey inland has remedied that."

"Your spies are very efficient. But how did you get so far ahead of your troops?"

"I lead an advance party. We watched your journey upstream with great fascination Even now a portion of our troops are blocking the mouth of the river, ending any chance of your ship's escape."

Silver's heart sank. Were all of them doomed to capture?

"Why don't you let the lady go?" Cookie put in "She's just a woman. She'll do you no harm."

"Who are you?" the captain demanded.

"You mean your spies don't already know?" Silver snapped

"I'm Grandison Aimes, ship's cook and damned proud of it."

Captain Carrillo just smiled "Senor Aimes, do not take me for a fool The woman rides with you to warn your major of our attack. She is no less a threat than you are "

He turned to one of his men and said something in Spanish. The small dark man removed a length of braided rope from his saddle horn, walked to Cookie's side, and securely tied his hands behind his back Silver's wrists were bound in front of her

"*¡Vamanos!*" the captain shouted as soon as the man had finished. One of the soldiers took their horses' reins and led the animals behind the others into the forest-jungle Silver wondered how far back the rest of the troops were—and when they would catch up with Morgan.

* * *

"Mexican troops, Colonel!" Hamilton Riley galloped up beside Buckland. Morgan rode a few feet away. "Centralist troops to be sure."

"Good God!" Buckland gasped.

"How many?" Morgan asked. "Which way are they coming?"

"Looks to be more than two hundred. They're coming from the southwest, most of them mounted They'll be on us in no time at all."

"We've got to pull back." Buckland glanced nervously toward the rear.

"Pull back to where?" Morgan snapped. "What we've got to do is get these munitions through. Ham, you take Jacques and Senorita Méndez and the rest of the mounted men. Pick men to ride my horse and the colonel's, then take that wagon and get the hell out of here."

"Are you mad?" Buckland's eyes looked huge beneath the brim of his plumed felt hat. "We can't hold off two hundred men with this handful of troops."

"We've got no choice. Those weapons have got to reach the rest of the Texians and the balance of the Federalist forces. They're our only hope of getting those men out of prison. Besides, most of our men are afoot. We can't outrun them "

"But—but—"

"Colonel?" Ham pressed, urging his superior's approval.

"We'll take cover near that rocky promontory," Morgan continued when Buckland didn't answer. The hill was little more than a granite rise among tangled weeds and thorny yucca. "We've got plenty of ammunition. We can keep them pinned down for hours, give Lieutenant Riley a chance to get clear."

Buckland still looked uncertain.

"There isn't much time, Colonel." Ham's horse shifted nervously beneath him.

"Maybe you should go with them, Colonel," Morgan said—anything to get the damnable man to agree.

Buckland stiffened. "You heard the major. Carry on, Lieutenant."

"Yes, sir." With a smart salute, Ham spun his mount and thundered away. In minutes the men and munitions wagon were readied and rolling down the rocky overgrown trail. They would pull back a little, skirt the area, then make their way to the rendezvous point.

Jacques rode up with Teresa. "You are certain that this is the only way?" he asked Morgan.

"Just get Brendan out of that hellhole."

"If it can be done, I will do it."

Morgan extended a hand. "I know you will."

Jacques grasped it firmly. "Take care, *mon ami*."

"*Vaya con Dios*." Teresa forced a smile, but her face looked drawn and pale.

"Go with God, my friends." Morgan turned and strode toward the men who were busy building fortifications near the top of the hill. The dense cover would help them, but there wasn't a man among them who wasn't aware that sooner or later their position would be overrun.

"What the hell?" Morgan stopped at the sight of Ram's broad back, bent over as he dug a small depression in which to settle himself for the assault. He had tossed his shirt aside, exposing smooth dark skin that rippled with muscle and glistened with perspiration.

"I thought you could use the help." Ram emptied a shovelful of dirt.

"You had a horse. You should have ridden with the others."

He shrugged his brawny shoulders. "Another man rides in my place. Besides, I was tired of those old faces."

Morgan smiled tiredly. "Thanks."

Uncrating long wooden boxes that held Hawken muzzle-loading rifles, another that held powder, shot, and wad, Morgan and the men readied themselves to do battle. Within the hour the Mexican forces arrived, and the shooting began.

As Morgan had hoped, their position made it hard to tell how many Texians were fighting, and the slight rise in terrain provided another small advantage. For hours shots rang out, men reloaded their rifles, and more shots pierced the air. Morgan's shirt, damp with sweat and stained with dirt, clung to his back and shoulders. Bare to the waist, Ram fought doggedly in only his breeches and boots.

"How much longer do you think they will wait?" Ram asked.

"Not much. Eventually they'll discover there's fewer of us than they thought. As soon as they're sure, they'll come."

And so they did.

Wearing their fancy red and white uniforms, tall plumed hats, and shiny black knee-high boots, they screamed for blood, firing their rifles at anything that moved, their long bayonets gleaming wickedly in front of them, thrusting death into those who fell to their bullets.

"Good God!" Buckland shouted, "there are hundreds of them. We haven't got a chance!"

Closer to 150, Morgan guessed, still far too many for his roughly three dozen men. In minutes the

Mexicans would overrun the hill. Of all the deaths he had envisioned, this wasn't one of them.

Morgan fired his rifle, the blast echoing among the others. As he swung the long-barreled weapon up to reload, the muzzle flashed silver in the sunlight.

Silver. He pictured her face and for the first time in his thirty years of living considered his mortality. He didn't want to die. Not now. Not when he had something so precious to live for.

He tipped up the powder horn that hung over one wide shoulder. So much woman, he thought. More than he deserved. Pouring a small amount of powder down the barrel, he dropped in the ball, rammed the wad home, and set the cap. Why had he waited until now to realize what he'd been given? Taking careful aim, he fired, bringing a scream of pain from a Mexican soldier, followed by a bright red blossom of blood on the man's broad chest.

Morgan reloaded. He would die here today—it was almost certain now. He wondered if Silver would miss him. If she had come to care for him as much as he cared for her.

He wondered if she loved him.

Morgan thrust the butt of the rifle against his shoulder and took deadly aim. She was so damned beautiful, he thought as he squeezed the trigger, bringing another Mexican down. So damned caring and good. Beside him, a young marine aimed and fired, and another enemy fell.

Morgan reloaded and aimed his smoking rifle. *Silver!* his mind screamed just before he pulled the trigger. He could see her face in the eye of his mind, smiling down at him as they lay together in his wide bed, her pale hair teasing his shoulder, making him want her again.

He remembered her laughter, the soft, sweet

sound of her voice. He remembered the feel of her skin against his hand, the full, lush curve of her breast. He remembered the way her eyes grew dark with passion, then gentle and loving when they had finished.

At least in death the pain of missing her would end.

Reloading, Morgan snapped the rifle to his shoulder and eased back the trigger, feeling the heavy recoil of the gun slamming backward with the explosion. He ached to see her again, to touch her. He ached to make love to her one last time. Maybe he would say the things he'd been holding back, tell her the way he felt.

Maybe he would take the risk.

It occurred to him then that Silver might also be in danger. If the Centralists had known of the plan to attack the prison, they might also know about the *Savannah*. Maybe they would find a way to board her. They'd take Silver and . . . Morgan swallowed hard, unable to finish the thought Imagining Silver at the hands of the Mexicans was unbearable. He could not die in peace if he believed there was even the slightest chance.

"God in heaven," he prayed, "don't let them hurt her." It was crazy, he knew. Praying for Silver, safe aboard ship, when he should have been praying for himself. Still, she was all he could think of, her safety more important than his own. *Don't let her mourn,* he thought. *Let her find someone who will love and protect her.*

A lead ball slammed into the man on his right. The boy slumped forward with a groan, his shirtfront covered with blood. Ram fired with deadly accuracy on his left, one arm bleeding from a bayonet thrust. Another good man who would die here today.

Silver would have liked the Ram. And Morgan didn't doubt the big Turk would have approved her spirited nature—something he himself had only begun to appreciate.

Ram would have liked Silver Jones.

It was Morgan who loved her.

It took dying for him to admit it.

Half a dozen Centralists broke through the lower defenses, firing, killing, their bayonets glistening with blood. Shouting their triumph, they rushed up the hill; three men raced toward Morgan while the other three stormed the Turk. Morgan fired, killing one, used the butt of his rifle as a bludgeon on another, jerked the third man's gun from his hands, and thrust the bayonet into his chest. A few feet below him, a dozen more followed in their wake.

No time for regrets, but still Morgan felt them. Sadness for the things he had left unsaid, the joys of Silver's passion he hadn't yet unveiled, the children they would never share.

God be with you, Silver, he thought, recognizing these next few seconds as the last precious moments of his life. *I love you.*

Blue steel flashed in the enemy's hands. No chance to reload. Morgan leveled the razor-sharp point of his bayonet toward the onrushers They'd be on him in an instant—time had run out. His last thought fixed on the woman he loved.

"Cease fire!" The words, spoken first in Spanish, then in heavily accented English, echoed across the forest-jungle.

Stunned, Morgan crouched down in his trench. Beside three dead Mexican soldiers, Ram did the same The volley of bullets trickled to a few scattered bursts. From a few feet above him, he heard Buckland's shaky command.

"Cease fire!" he ordered in response to the enemy's words, and the last remaining men stopped shooting. More than a dozen lay dead or wounded on the ground, shrieking in agony or whimpering softly. The rest waited tensely to see what the Centralists would do.

"You are no match for us!" the Mexican officer shouted. "Surrender or you will die."

Buckland crawled along the ground until he reached Morgan's trench, then recoiled at the bloody corpse that sprawled in the dust beside him. "What do you think?" he whispered. "We can't hold them off any longer."

Morgan released a weary breath. "God only knows what they'll do to us. But we've done all we can for Riley and the others; they've got a damned good chance of making it. As for us . . . we'll die here for certain if we don't surrender." *And I want to live.* "At least we might buy some time."

"Quite right, Major," Buckland said with relief.

In truth Morgan had been surprised by the offer. The Texians were soundly defeated, just minutes from total annihilation. And the Centralists were known for their bloodthirsty battles. Most likely the Mexicans would take their weapons, line them up, and shoot them. Unless there was something they wanted.

"As long as we're breathing," Morgan said, "there's always the chance of escape."

Buckland grabbed Ram's discarded white shirt, stuck it on the end of Morgan's empty rifle, hoisted it into the air, and waved it madly.

"Throw down your weapons!" ordered the Centralist. "Come out with your hands in the air."

"Shall we?" Morgan said with a sardonic twist of his lip. Tossing down his weapon, he climbed to his feet, thoroughly expecting to feel the bite of a lead ball ripping through his flesh at any moment. He glanced across at Ram, who stood beside him grinning.

"So far, so good," Ram said.

The rest of the men followed suit, and the Mexicans cautiously approached. Their leader, a grimfaced man with graying hair, ordered them bound, and they were marched away without so much as a word.

Where they were headed and what would be their fate once they got there, Morgan couldn't say. For the moment he didn't care. He knew only that he still lived. That he had someone that he loved to return to. And that somehow he had to survive.

Chapter 20

"What have you done to Cookie!" Silver stood in the doorway of the elegant dining room in the great hacienda—Rancho del los Cocodrilos—land of the crocodiles.

Seated at the head of the long wooden table, Capitán Paulo Carrillo came to his feet and flashed a welcoming smile "Your friend has joined the others in the prison. I assure you he is unharmed."

They had been separated the moment they had reached the hacienda, Cookie marched away at gunpoint, Silver brought inside and locked in one of the spacious bedchambers. She'd been given food and clean clothing—a bright yellow skirt and an embroidered white peasant blouse that left her shoulders bare, and a pair of flat leather sandals. She'd been allowed to bathe and wash her hair and generally treated like a guest instead of a prisoner.

It only made her feel worse

Carrillo pulled out a carved wooden chair, one of twelve that hugged the long wooden table beneath the heavy wrought-iron chandelier. "Please, Senorita Jones." He indicated she should have a seat.

"What do you want with me? Why have I been kept locked up for two days without a single word?"

Carrillo arched a light brown eyebrow. "You have been mistreated?"

"You know I have not."

"Please . . ." Again he indicated her chair. "Our food is growing cold." The table gleamed with sparkling cut crystal and expensive porcelain. Heavy carved silverware glittered beside each plate, and pink hibiscus arranged in a lovely crystal bowl formed a fragrant centerpiece.

"What do you want with me?" Silver repeated, still not moving from the doorway.

"I?" he asked pleasantly. "I want nothing but your company. It is General Hernández who commands your presence."

"Where is he?"

"Not here as of yet, I'm afraid. He will arrive sometime tomorrow. In the meantime, I suggest you enjoy his generous hospitality."

Silver studied the table, the steaming platters of chicken and beef, the hot tortillas and mounds of squash, and thought of those in the prison not far away. The smell of the food made the bile rise up in her throat.

"I wish only to join my friends." With that she turned and walked away, returning to the sparsely furnished bedchamber she occupied down the hall.

She sank down on the low wooden bed, her fingers moving absently across the bright red woolen blanket. Cookie suffered in prison, along with Morgan's brother and half the Texas troops. Had Jordy and the crew of the *Savannah* also been taken prisoner? Were they on their way here to join the others? And what about Morgan? By now he could be lying dead

in the jungle, his body left to rot among the steaming
vegetation.

No! Silver refused to believe it. Couldn't believe it.
She needed her strength; she wouldn't let her courage be destroyed by her worry for Morgan. He'd be
all right, she told herself firmly. He had to be. And
until she knew differently, she would be strong.

Strong for herself. Strong for Morgan.

The grueling march to Rancho del los Cocodrilos
nearly broke them. Two days of heat and bugs, little
food and less water, and a pace few strong men
could endure. Both Morgan and Ram pulled litters
that carried injured soldiers, as did a few of the others. The Centralist leader never approached them.
But his men did.

One long-legged soldier carried a leather romal, a
short braided quirt that was used to discipline the
horses. With great enthusiasm, the slicing leather
thongs came down on the backs of the tardy, shred-
ding the fabric of their shirts, biting into flesh, and
leaving a trail of blood in its wake. Morgan felt the
lash no less than the others, his pace beginning to
slow as his burden grew heavier. Time and again he
suffered the heavy blow of a fist or boot, wielded by a
name-calling *soldado*. Still, they trudged on.

By the afternoon of the second day their goal lay in
sight—Rancho de los Cocodrilos. It was a harsh, flat
piece of land, dotted with the dark green spikes of
the sisal plant. In the distance to the south the land
grew more humid, more dense, and even less hospitable.

"¡Vamanos!" one of the soldiers called out, bringing his romal down with heavy force against the lead
prisoner, sending the small man sprawling into the

dirt. The Texian soldier beside him helped him back on his feet, and the men marched on.

As they neared the great hacienda, Morgan saw a two-story adobe structure with an arched portico out front. Through the arches he could just make out the massive carved wooden doors, the fountain that bubbled pleasantly, ignorant of the death and destruction around it.

"Leave the injured to the others," the long-legged soldier told him, then repeated the words to Ram. One of the men shoved Colonel Buckland forward, and another bound their arms behind them. The three of them were marched toward the hacienda. The rest of the troops changed direction, skirted the house, and marched farther east.

"Why do you think they have separated us from the others?" Ram asked.

"¡Silencio!" one of the guards warned. "You will have your chance to talk soon enough." He roughly shoved them forward. They bypassed the main house and marched toward the stable some distance to the rear. Made of adobe, cool and dark inside, the structure smelled of horses and grain. Half a dozen soldiers milled around the interior, some standing, others squatting on their haunches. The tallest moved forward at their entrance.

He grinned, exposing slightly pointed, wolfish-looking teeth, visible even in the dimness of the barn. "I am Sergeant Renaldo Ruiz," he said in Spanish. "I am in charge of your interrogation."

"What did he say?" Buckland asked.

"¡Silencio!" Ruiz demanded. "From now on you will speak only when spoken to. Then I expect you to answer the questions we ask. If you do not . . ." He pointed upward, where ropes hung suspended from the rafters. Morgan's stomach turned over. "Take the others outside. We will start with this one."

Morgan watched Ram and the colonel depart. They both looked as haggard as he. Buckland's shoulders sagged, and his usually spotless uniform, torn and crusted with dirt, hung on his weary frame. Ram's bare back carried the mark of the lash. Morgan glanced to the soldier called Ruiz, who motioned toward two of his soldiers. With his hands bound behind him, there was little he could do but let them drag him into a waiting chair. His arms were lashed to the back, and Ruiz began his questioning:

"Where is your ship? Where are the rest of your troops? Why have you come here? Where are the guns? When will the troops move against us?"

The barrage seemed unending—each punctuated with a reeling blow more powerful than the last. They knew more about the Texians' movements than he ever would have guessed. Still, he said nothing. By the end of the session, his lips were split and bloody, his face a mass of bruises, and blood ran freely from a gash on his jaw. The blows to his ribs had surely cracked some of them, and the pain made it difficult to breathe.

"That is enough for now," the sergeant said. "Bring in the Turk."

And so it had gone, through an agonizing day and night that had progressed to the point of unconsciousness. Screams were coming from the barn now—Morgan was surprised to discover that they were his own. He hadn't seen Ram or Buckland, but he knew their torture was the same—unless they had answered the sergeant's questions.

Time dragged interminably, until every agonizing hour meshed into the next. Morgan blinked awake with the rising of the sun. He'd been sleeping—no he'd been unconscious. Where was he now? The ache in his arms and shoulders, the agony that sliced the skin from his wrists drew his gaze upward. It was difficult to focus, difficult even to keep his head from lolling against his shoulder, but eventually he saw the peak of the roof, the tiny nests of straw built there by the birds.

His eyes moved lower, to the rope that looped the beam above his head, trailing down to capture his bleeding wrists. Naked to the waist, he swung more than a foot off the ground, his weight supported only by his aching, bloody arms, which were slowly being wrenched from their sockets. His head slumped forward. Never in his life had he prayed for blessed unconsciousness.

Morgan prayed for it now.

"Bring him down."

They were the last words he remembered, all that registered through the blinding haze of pain until he opened his eyes in the cool interior of the main hacienda. Soldiers supported him, one on each side, the sound of their footsteps echoing down the long many-doored hallway. Oil paintings lined the walls beside flickering candle sconces. He noticed the floors were earthen but swept to a hard-packed sheen. The furniture, massive and dark, appeared to have come from Europe.

The Frenchman who had built the great plantation had expensive taste, Morgan thought fleetingly. General Hernández had chosen well.

At the end of the hall, one of several, it seemed, someone opened the door to a large book-lined study. Seeing Morgan with the soldiers, the man behind the desk shoved back his chair and came to his feet. When the men let go of Morgan's arms, he propped himself against the doorframe for support. The edges of his vision dimmed, and he fought to bring the room back in focus.

"*Buenos dias*, Major Trask," said the man behind the desk. He was a short man, Morgan saw, with dark eyes and a narrow, heavily waxed mustache. When he motioned for Morgan to take a seat in the chair across from him, Morgan noticed the man's powerful chest and arms. Fighting to make one foot move in front of the other, he reached the high-backed chair and sank down heavily.

"Who are you?" Morgan asked.

"General Alberto Hernández. And you are Morgan Trask."

"Where have the others been taken? Bayram Sit and Colonel Buckland?"

"For the present they remain in the *establo*, though they will soon be removed to the prison. Like you, their torture has ended."

"Why?"

The general shrugged muscular shoulders. "There is little the Turk could tell us that we do not already know, even if he were willing. The colonel was . . . shall we say, a bit more cooperative."

"That bastard," Morgan hissed through his cracked and bloodied lips.

"Some men are cut out for this sort of life; others are not."

Morgan didn't answer. His head was throbbing again, and his lack of food and water was making him feel light-headed. "Why have you brought me here?"

"You intrigue me, Major. We have known from the start it was you and not Buckland who truly commanded this effort. His presence was merely a facade—you alone would succeed or fail. You have failed, Major, but even in failing, you have brought about the deaths of many of my soldiers."

"That's what happens in battle," Morgan said sarcastically, and got a vicious blow to the ribs for his words. His stomach reeled, the bile rose, and grayness swirled around him.

"You are not afraid of dying, Major. That is why I have brought you here." He motioned to one of his men, who strode across the room to a small door near the corner. "I have a different kind of torture in mind for you." He turned to the man at the door. "Bring her in."

Morgan watched the door slowly open. It was hard to concentrate, hard to focus his thoughts. Darkness swirled just inches from his mind, wooing him with its promise of freedom from pain. It was then he saw her, a vision of loveliness, silver-haired and dark-eyed. He knew he had begun to hallucinate, yet he did not want the dream to end.

"Morgan!"

The scream that rent the air forced his eyes to open wider. Unconsciousness receded, and his vision began to clear. Still, he could see her, fighting against the soldier whose arm gripped her waist, her hair tumbled wildly about her shoulders.

"Morgan!" There was agony in the sound of her voice—Silver's voice—there could be no other.

"Silver," Morgan whispered as the terrible truth struck home. He prayed to God he was wrong. Silver couldn't be here. Not now. Not in this hellhole! He tried to gain his feet, but a man's rough hand pressed him back in the chair. *Stay calm*, he told himself, fighting to gather his strength, pushing back the darkness. He had to help Silver. Panic would gain him nothing.

"What have you done to him?" She demanded,

her voice shaking with outrage. Tears blurred her eyes, but she refused to let them fall. "How could you do such a thing?"

"This is war, Senorita Jones. The major was well aware of the consequences when he accepted his assignment."

Stay calm, she told herself. *You've got to stay in control.* Morgan was hurt—badly, but at least he was alive. It was up to her to help him. "I demand you release him." It broke her heart to look at him, to see the cruelty he had suffered.

"This man has invaded my country. Brought arms to the worthless rebels who fight us."

"You have rendered him helpless. Surely his troops have all been captured—he is no further threat."

"The guns he has brought have not been found. That in itself is enough to earn him the firing squad. I have been generous in my treatment of you foreigners."

Generous! Torturing a man, beating him senseless was generous? She forced herself not to say the words. "In a way I suppose you're right. You could have killed him and the men you hold in your prison. Since this man is my friend, I thank you for that."

"The girl has no part in this," Morgan said, his parched voice raspy. "Surely as a man of honor you will let her go."

Beneath his waxed mustache, the general's mouth curved upward. "I think not."

Silver watched his eyes, glittering with satisfaction, the hungry look that swept down her body. She glanced to Morgan, saw his pain, his battered and beaten condition—and made her decision.

"The man is no use to you, General. But he is my

friend, and his life holds great value to me. I would bargain with you for his release."

Arching a sleek black brow, the general moved to face her more squarely. "What is it you bargain with, Dama de Luz?"

Silver came closer, her hips swaying seductively, a soft smile curving her lips. "The only thing of value I have left, General Hernández—my body."

"Silver, no!" Morgan surged to his feet and started toward her. Three *soldados* captured his arms and dragged him back to his chair.

"Silence, *Anglo!*" one warned harshly.

Silver cast him a look that pleaded the same.

The general chuckled softly. "I already own your body, senorita. I shall take you this night, whether you wish it or not."

Morgan strained against the men who held him. "She's done nothing. You've got to let her go!"

"Silence him," Hernández commanded.

Silver watched helplessly as Morgan's arms were wrenched cruelly behind his back and he sagged against the pain. Ignoring the anguish she saw in his eyes, she continued to the general's side and slid her arms around his neck.

"You can take me by force," she said softly, "but I assure you, General, that which you can take cannot begin to match that which I can give." With a warm look of seduction, she leaned down and kissed him.

Hernández slid his arms around her, pulled her down on his lap, and kissed her back, pressing her body against his until she felt his arousal stir. Morgan fought and cursed until the men bound and gagged him into silence.

When Hernández finally released her, Silver ran a finger along his cheek and smiled in silent invitation.

"Do this for me, and you will not be sorry, I promise you."

The general smiled in return, but his mouth looked more wolfish than pleasant. "Take the major to the edge of the woods and release him."

"You must let someone go with him," Silver insisted, sliding off his lap. "He's too weak to survive on his own."

"No."

"His brother is here. Let him go."

"No! I will release this one. That is all. Do not tempt your good fortune, senorita."

"I must see him freed," Silver said. "I must know for certain he is safe. Do that, General Hernández, and you will have a fiery temptress in your bed this eve."

With only a moment's hesitation, the general nodded and ordered Morgan removed from the room. Though he kicked and thrashed and cursed them from behind his gag, the soldiers finally managed to haul him out.

"They will take him to the edge of the encampment and release him. You can watch from the upstairs balcony. I will join you there."

Silver nodded and hurried toward the stairway she had seen in the foyer. She closed the door behind her.

Hernández turned to the *soldado* on his left. "Have him watched from a distance. As soon as the woman goes back inside, you will capture him and return him to the prison. If that becomes a problem —shoot him."

With an aching heart, Silver watched Morgan loaded aboard a *carreta*, a small two-wheeled cart, and driven away. The lumbering brown and white oxen moved slowly, though the man at the reins cracked a long, thin whip above the animals' heads. The cart rumbled up the road until she could barely see it. Then the oxen stopped, and the soldiers pulled Morgan from the back.

When one of the men drew his saber, Silver thought her heart might stop. But he only sliced through Morgan's bonds, and his arms swung free. The cart turned clumsily around in the road and along with the soldiers started back to the hacienda. Morgan stood in the lane for only an instant, then disappeared into the dense cover of his surroundings.

Silver fought the sting of tears. *Dear God, please help him.* If she knew for certain he was safe, she would somehow survive the loathsome task she had set for herself.

"Shall we go, senorita?" The general took her arm to lead her inside.

Silver pulled away. "Just a little longer. Then I'll go in."

The general looked disgruntled. "You need not fear. Your evening's performance will be just that. I have business to attend until later."

"I assure you, General, that is the least of my concerns." Inwardly she lauded her performance. God, how she loathed the very thought of the man's too-eager touch.

Silver pulled her gaze from the general's hungry smile and fixed her eyes on the rutted, overgrown road. Hearing no shots or any other signs of disturbance, she felt a little better. Still, she couldn't trust these men, and every passing second meant a greater chance for Morgan's escape.

God be with you, my love, she prayed, hoping against hope that he would succeed.

* * *

Morgan slipped silently through the tangle of leaves and vines. He could hear footsteps behind him—soldiers. They had no intention of letting him go.

Crazy little fool. Silver actually believed they would release him. Stupid, idiotic, wonderful little fool.

Morgan crouched low in a ravine. The fury that still pumped through his veins had given him a shot of strength. His vision had cleared, and though his ribs ached like holy bejesus, he was sure now that none of them were broken. Water and food would revive him faster than anything—if he could just elude the men who followed.

A branch snapped not more than ten feet away. Bloody hell! They were closer than he thought. Morgan glanced around and spotted a rotting fallen log. He carefully dug away some of the dead leaves and bark, crawled into the dark, bug-filled interior, then layered dirt and leaves over the part of him left exposed. Waiting for the sound of their dreaded footfalls or the pressure of a cold steel muzzle against his ribs made his heart thunder, and a fine sheen of perspiration broke out on his forehead.

"¿Donde está?" came harshly from a man standing only inches from his shoulder. Where is he?

"Yo no sé. No está aqui." I don't know. He isn't here.

"¡Buscale!" Find him!

Morgan held his breath, listening as the men moved off through the forest-jungle. They were spreading out, searching farther and wider. They would expect him to run—and so he would not. Morgan's head throbbed, his ribs ached, he was hungry and thirsty—but for the time being he was free.

Come hell or high water, he intended to stay that way.

Silver had sacrificed herself for him. He wasn't about to let her down.

Resigned to his discomfort, Morgan ignored the crawling, biting creatures that moved across his flesh, the moist heat that dampened his clothes. Instead he closed his eyes and forced himself to sleep. He'd been awake most of the night; sleep would help him garner his strength. When he felt it was safe, he would leave.

Though it seemed only minutes, Morgan stirred. Something long and slithering moved across his arm, paused, then silently slipped away. Morgan breathed a sigh of relief. Through the cracks in the log, he noticed the sun had changed position; he'd had at least three hours of rest. He felt stiff and sore, but his head was clearer, and his dizziness had fled.

He listened for the sound of men but heard only the screech of birds and the chatter of monkeys. Shoving the leaves aside, he climbed from the log on unsteady legs. Still, he felt stronger. He would find a weapon, food, and water. Then he'd head in the direction he believed he might find the Texas forces. In a way he hoped they weren't there. If Buckland had divulged the rendezvous point, as the general had implied, the troops would be easy prey for Hernández's men.

In fact, even now they might be under siege. He didn't think so. There were too many Centralist troops still in camp.

Morgan pressed on, moving through the ravines and gulleys, the dense foliage, and thorny scrub brush. His hands were cut and bleeding by the time he came into a clearing hours later and crept be-

neath a granite outcrop. He leaned against the huge
gray stone to take a moment's rest.

"At last, *mon ami,* you move with the steps of a
man not those of an injured panther." Jacques's
huge arms enveloped him, and Morgan clung to his
friend in relief.

"Thank God," he whispered, finally breaking
away.

"I had given you up for dead."

"How did you find me?"

"I and some others 'ave been watching the prison.
We caught glimpses of a few of our men, so we knew
your position 'ad been taken, but no one saw you or
the colonel until today."

"They've been holding us in the barn—for *interrogation.* Apparently Buckland has given them the location of the rendezvous point. You did get through
with the guns?"

"*Oui.* And we anticipated there might be problems, so we moved to a new position. It is well 'idden
and not far from 'ere." His eyes ran over Morgan's
battered and bloodied face. "We saw them take you
from the camp. We watched your escape, but we
could not find you. I 'oped you would move toward
the rendezvous point."

"There are men following me. They're liable to
spot the others."

"I sent them back. If I could not find you, I did not
think they could."

Morgan nodded, glad to have Jacques for a friend.
"Teresa?" he asked.

"She is safe in camp. We should get started. I will
carry you if you cannot make it."

"I'll make it," Morgan said, "but I could use a
little water."

"Of course." Jacques handed Morgan his canteen. "Drink slowly."

Morgan nodded and tipped up the flask, letting the reviving liquid trickle down his throat. Jacques handed him a piece of beef jerky when he finished. It tasted like prime roast beef. He ate while they moved cautiously through the scrub brush. As Jacques had promised, it took only a few hours to reach camp. Since they'd moved closer to the prison, Morgan figured plans had been made to go ahead with the attack.

"When do you plan to move?" he asked a lanky, rawboned lieutenant named Archy Spray, the only officer left to the original Texas forces who had not been captured.

"Tomorrow, unless you've learned something that could change things." Along with Jacques and Ham, they crouched around a makeshift map drawn into the dirt.

"I'm afraid I learned nothing of the prison," Morgan said. "I wasn't even able to verify where it was."

"Fortunately we know a great deal about it," Ham put in. "Several Federalist sympathizers have joined our forces. One of them, a Mexican man named Paco, worked the henequen farm. He knows the place like the back of his hand."

"Good."

"Better than good," Ham said. "There's a tunnel. Paco discovered it years ago near the base of the central pyramid."

"Pyramid?" Morgan repeated.

Ham grinned. "Apparently the men are being kept in the ruins of a Mayan city. It's damned logical really. The walls are several feet thick, and none of the rooms have windows. It's pretty overgrown, I gather."

"Like everything else around here," Morgan said dryly.

"Yes, but that should make things easier," Archy said, drawing approach lines on the map with the end of a broken twig.

"You figure to go in through the tunnels?" Morgan asked.

"Yes," Ham answered. "Attack from inside instead of out."

Morgan pondered Ham's words as the four men came to their feet. "Are your men ready?" Morgan asked Spray, referring to the original Texas forces that so far had escaped capture.

"More than ready, sir. Eager would be closer."

"Then what do you say to a small change of plans?"

"Such as?" Spray asked.

"Such as going in tonight."

"We'd have to fight this damnable terrain in the dark," Ham pointed out.

"You wish to go back there so soon?" Jacques asked, a frown of concern on his face. "You need to rest and recover."

Morgan's face turned grim. "They've got Silver." He hadn't been able to tell them, couldn't bear to say the words until he'd come up with a plan.

"*Sacrebleu.*" Jacques ran a hand over his face, unconsciously smoothing his beard.

"I intend to get her out before . . . I'm going in there tonight."

Reading Morgan's look of determination, one Jacques knew only too well, he nodded. "I will 'ave the men ready."

"One more thing," Morgan said. "We'll use the majority of our troops as a diversion—attack them head-on. There're too many of them to defeat—inside or out. Our only chance is for four or five men to go in and free the prisoners, get everyone outside through the tunnel, then pull back to cover. We can hold them off from right here. Once our position is secure, we'll move south, as we originally planned. We'll tie up with the ships and get the hell out of this godforsaken place."

Ham grinned and so did Jacques. "Sounds damned good to me," Ham said.

Still, it would take time to ready the men and equipment and make the arduous trip to the prison in the darkness. They couldn't risk leaving until sundown, couldn't risk being spotted. There would be no second chance—not for Brendan—not for Silver.

Morgan refused to consider the hours she would spend with the general until then.

Chapter 21

"I must go with you." Teresa looked pleadingly at Morgan and Jacques. After three grueling hours of traveling through root-bound ravines and vine-clogged trails in the ever-increasing darkness, they had finally reached the entrance to the tunnel outside the prison.

"I am sorry, *ma chère*," Jacques said, *"le capitaine* 'as been generous in bringing you this far."

"But my father—"

"You can wait near the entrance," Morgan told her. "If your father's alive, we'll see that he gets to you."

Her dark eyes flicked from Morgan to Jacques for reassurance.

"You 'ave my word, *chérie*. If 'e is there, I will bring 'im out myself."

"Let's go." Morgan turned abruptly, knowing every second was crucial to their success. Morgan, Jacques, and three Texas Marines would move inside through the tunnel, following Paco, the Mexican man who would guide them. The rest of the troops would take up positions outside the perimeter and lay siege to the prison. Since there were too many prisoners to escape unnoticed, their best chance was to run for the tunnel during the confusion of the attack.

Grabbing one of the long pitch-soaked wooden torches they had fashioned for use in the passage, Jacques turned to follow Morgan. Teresa's hand on his shoulder stopped him. When he turned to face her, Teresa stepped into his arms, and she hugged him to her. Jacques's powerful arms slid around her waist, pressing her closer. His mouth came down over hers, and he kissed her long and hard. Then he set her away.

"*Vaya con Dios,*" she whispered, but Jacques was striding off behind Morgan, already out of sight in the tunnel. Teresa crossed herself and said a silent prayer for their safety—and the safe return of her father.

Inside the tunnel, Morgan lit a torch and waited for Jacques and the others to catch up. In was damp and musty, the air heavy and the odor unpleasant.

"Let Paco lead and stay close together. There may be other tunnels branching off the main one. We don't want anyone getting lost."

They moved into the darkness, the other men's torches following Morgan's, glowing eerily, casting ominous shadows against the walls. Spider webs clung to their clothes, and water dripped down from the ceiling. Their footsteps echoed hollowly; then one man stumbled and went down in a thundering heap.

"Keep quiet!" Morgan hissed. "Damn it, we don't know who else is in here."

"Sorry." The young blond soldier flushed with embarrassment.

As they walked along, rats scurried out of their

way, squeaking in protest to the men's invasion. In the dark recesses off the main corridor, bat guano marked the sleeping places of the ugly black creatures who had flown off into the night in search of food. Wings fluttered above their heads as the last few darted away. Morgan hoped they wouldn't return until the mission was complete and the men were back outside the tunnel.

Pulling his watch fob from the pocket of his breeches, he flipped open the lid. Twenty more minutes before the troops would begin their attack. The soldiers would keep up the siege for as long as they dared, then they'd be forced to pull back to safety. There was little margin for error.

Morgan ignored the throbbing in his head, the slashes on his back, the ache in his ribs, and the exhaustion that seeped into his very bones. All that mattered was getting inside and saving the people he loved.

He just hoped the man named Paco, who nervously led the way, knew as much about the ruined Mayan city as he claimed.

Silver glanced through the wrought-iron bars on her window, much like those in her room back home. One way or another, it seemed her freedom was always denied her. Tonight she would lose even more.

Earlier in the day she'd been moved upstairs to a bedchamber on the second floor, nearer, she presumed, to the suite of rooms occupied by General Hernández. This chamber was larger than the one downstairs and far more extravagantly furnished. Floor-to-ceiling draperies of expensive ruby brocade covered the windows, and a large carved bed rested against one wall.

There were few personal objects in the room. Just a silver-backed brush, comb, and mirror set on the carved wooden dresser beside a tiny heart-shaped silver jewelry box. When she lifted the lid, it played a bittersweet tune, but there was nothing inside.

An hour ago a bath had been brought up, along with fresh clothing similar to that she had worn before, only the skirt was bright red and not at all faded. She stood bathed and ready and awaiting the man who had bought her—like a harlot of the lowest order. Still, if she had it all to do over, she would do it again.

Silver stared out her window. She could see, lit by a sliver of moon, the abandoned drying racks where long strands of henequen, once meant for market, now shriveled up and blew away. Though she couldn't see that far in the darkness, earlier she had noticed the spiny fields of sisal, stretching endlessly into the horizon on the north until at last it meshed with the flat thorny plateau of Yucatán scrub. With the fighting and the abandonment, the land looked bleak and desolate, just like the days that lay ahead.

How long would the general use her as his plaything? How much would she suffer before she found the chance to escape? She didn't doubt that she would—sooner or later. She'd find a way, or the rebellion would end, or Hernández would be called to duty somewhere else. It wasn't the future that frightened her—it was the present.

Silver looked back outside. It had been dark for some time, and still the general had not summoned her. What could have happened to detain him? Dear God, how she wished he would not come.

A hard knock sounded at the door. Silver's heart started pounding with the same heavy rhythm. Moving woodenly, she crossed the room and waited for the locked door to open. When it swung wide, she saw the broad-hipped Mexican woman she knew only as María, the woman who had seen to her needs since her arrival. Stone-faced and unsympathetic, María was obviously a loyal Centralist supporter.

"General Hernández awaits you in his quarters," the woman said in her heavily accented English, almost with relish.

In the hallway two *soldados* stood not more than three feet away. They were watching her, as she had known they would be.

"Come." The woman started past her down the corridor and opened the first door on the right.

Summoning her courage, Silver stepped into the room. The hollow thud of the closing door sent a ripple of fear down her spine.

The room was even larger and more splendid than the one she now occupied, with massive carved wooden furniture, paintings on the walls, and tapestry-upholstered overstuffed chairs. A huge four-poster bed, draped with mosquito netting, sat on an angle in one corner. Fat white candles glimmered softly from tall brass holders.

Near the foot of the bed, General Hernández stood replete in a floor-length burgundy dressing gown, his slippered feet sticking out from beneath. He held a brandy snifter in one short-fingered hand and a long cigar in the other.

"*Buenas noches*, Senorita Jones."

Silver started to reply, but her lips felt so dry she could barely move them, and the words lodged somewhere in her throat.

"Surely you did not believe I had forgotten our assignation?"

I couldn't be that lucky. "I assumed you had been delayed," she told him, finding her voice at last.

"And so I was." *Chasing that* bastardo *you convinced me to set free.* "But I am here now . . . as are you." He poured her a glass of brandy from a decanter on the heavy wooden table beside the fireplace and crossed the room to place it in her hand.

The brush of his fingers sent a shiver of dread across her skin. Silver took one sip of the burning liquid, needing it for courage, then another.

"I would prefer you change into something a bit more . . . comfortable," the general said. Silver followed his gaze to a length of black silk that was draped across the back of an overstuffed chair. "It is French," he said proudly. "A gift I bought for a lady friend. You may have it instead."

She couldn't say thank-you. Could not possibly. She picked up the skimpy black garment.

"Come here, *querida*, and I shall help you put it on."

God in heaven, help me find a way to endure this. She couldn't fight him—at least not yet. He would only call his men into the room to hold her down. He might even share her with them. It was her first impulse—to snarl and claw and scratch—but not this time. For once she would play the game with cunning instead of rage.

"Why don't you sit down, General? Wouldn't you enjoy watching me?"

His smile turned wolfish. Taking a seat in a tapestry-covered chair, he took a long draw on his cigar, then a healthy sip of his brandy. "By all means."

She wouldn't fight him, but neither would she grovel or beg for his mercy, which she knew he would not give.

With a breath of resignation she hoped he didn't hear, Silver bent down, unfastened her sandals, and slid them off her feet. Facing him squarely, she pulled the peasant blouse over her head and tossed it away. When her hands started to tremble, she forced them to be still. Next went her skirt and its one thin petticoat, until she stood before him in her simple chemise and soft cotton drawers.

With a smile and a nod, Hernández urged her to continue.

You mustn't let him break you, Silver vowed. *You're made of stronger stuff than that.* Fighting a sweep of nausea, she reached beneath her chemise and untied the cord of her pantalets. This time the trembling of her fingers would not cease. Steeling herself, she slid the soft white cotton down her thighs and stepped out of them, facing him in just her chemise, the hem riding just below her bottom.

When she reached for the black silk nightgown, meaning to pull it over her head, then remove the last of her clothes, the general's husky voice stopped her.

"I should like to see your body, *querida*. It appears to be exquisite."

She would not cry, she wouldn't. She glanced to the narrow doors leading onto a small wrought-iron balcony. The curtains fluttered softly in the evening breeze, and no bars blocked her exit. There was nothing to stop her—nothing but the stocky man in front of her, several hundred soldiers, and endless miles of murderous terrain. Still, if she thought she could escape, she would try it.

"Hasten, *querida*, I grow impatient."

Lifting her chin, Silver forced a smile in his direction. She wouldn't let him see her anguish, would not give him the satisfaction. In a single graceful motion, she reached for the hem of her chemise and pulled it over her head. Chin held high, she stood before him, a few pale strands of her unbound hair the only thing hiding his view of her flesh.

The general's eyes, looking darker than before, fastened on her upturned breasts. Beneath his waxed mustache, a satisfied smile curved the thin, cruel lines of his mouth.

Silver reached for the black silk nightgown, careful not to show her revulsion, eased it over her head, and down her shoulders. Though the deep V in front displayed all but the tips of her breasts, she felt a little better within its soft folds—until she saw the general coming toward her.

"This afternoon, when your major made good his escape, I cursed you and the bargain we had made. Now I am grateful—for it is I who has struck the better deal."

The general's mouth covered hers in a rough, brutal kiss, his tongue thrusting past her teeth and down her throat, but all Silver thought of were his words. *When your major made good his escape.* Morgan had made it! The general had tried to stop him, just as she had feared, but Morgan had gotten away!

She felt one blunt hand on her breast while the other squeezed her bottom, kneading it roughly. His mouth bruised her lips, and his breath tasted sour with liquor and tobacco. None of it mattered. Morgan was safely away.

"We've got to hurry," Morgan whispered. "Time's running short." They had reached the inner opening of the old abandoned tunnel, well hidden inside the prison, and extinguished their torches, leaving them for their return through the damp dark passage. With little light from the moon, it was nearly as dark outside.

"You each know your assignment. Jacques will

lead you into the chambers. You'll free the men and
help them back to the passage. Corporal Saxon,
you'll come with me." Saxon was the young marine
who had fallen down in the tunnel.

"Remember the layout as Paco has drawn it."
Morgan checked his pocket watch. "We want the
guards out of the way and the men ready to run for
the tunnels the minute the shooting starts."

"Do not worry for your brother," Jacques said. "I
will get 'im out."

"I know you will. There's no one else I would
trust."

Jacques took his hand in a bone-crushing grip,
and Morgan clamped the big Frenchman's shoulder.
"Take care, my friend." With a last brief nod,
Jacques and his men hurried off to their task. Morgan prayed they'd be ready to flee when the fighting
began.

In the meantime, he had to find Silver. Most likely
she'd be with General Hernández, had been for quite
some time. Morgan's stomach knotted. Fighting
down an image of Silver being brutalized by the
short but muscular man, he hurried along the rough
stone wall of the pyramid where the tunnel had
emerged. He stopped near the corner.

"According to Paco," he said to Saxon, "the
owner's suite of rooms is upstairs in the north wing
of the hacienda. Since the general seems to fancy the
good life, chances are that's where he'll be."

Corporal Saxon nodded.

"Follow me, stay quiet, and stay low." They had
blackened their faces and clothing with soot so
they'd be less easy to spot. Now, as they crept farther
into the ruins, Morgan glanced up at the sheer rock
walls of the pyramid that towered above them, at the
crumbling corridors overgrown with thorny weeds

and vines, at the trenches that had once been part of the entrance to a temple, and thanked God for another small advantage.

The ruins provided the best cover they could have asked for. They were eerie, yes. Pervading and humbling and ghostly. But they also supplied doorways to endless vacant chambers a man could duck into, empty defensive moats, tall stone figures, and huge granite arches—dozens of places to hide.

Jacques had a better than average chance of reaching the prisoners, if Paco was right about where they were. Morgan's job would be tougher. He and the gangly young corporal would have to make their way across the open fields between the house and the ruins. Midway, a tall guard tower, once a water tower built to protect the fields from fire, surveyed the area from above.

Still, there were sisal plants and drying racks, even a few old bales of fibers that would help disguise their movements.

Crouching, ignoring what that bent position did to the pain in his ribs and the pounding in his head, Morgan darted from one location to the other. With Saxon close behind, he headed straight for the tower, meaning to disarm the men inside and then angle over to the house. As they ran then crawled, crouched, then ran again, Morgan prayed for Silver's safety.

She was clever, he told himself firmly. She would think of a way to hold the general at bay until he could get there.

Surely she knew he would come.

Just a little bit longer, he thought. *You can do it. I know that damnable determination of yours.* Morgan cursed the lateness of the hour, changed position once more, and moved closer. He hoped to hell that for once Silver would keep her temper in check, keep her fury aimed at the general—and not try to battle the entire Mexican Army.

"Come," the general said, extending his hand, his voice rough with desire.

Lifting her chin, Silver forced a smile in his direction, but her eyes surveyed the room, looking for something—anything—that might help save her. Then she saw it: a massive brass candle holder resting beside the big four-poster bed, its candle burned down to just a few inches and threatening to sputter out. If she could distract him, keep his attention until she could grasp it, she could use it as a weapon.

Silver accepted his hand, hiding her revulsion at how damp it felt, and let him lead her to the bed. The general tossed back the covers, exposing the smooth white sheets, sat on the edge, and removed his slippers. Silver climbed up on the mattress, trying to work her way toward the candle holder on the opposite side, but Hernández caught her ankle and dragged her back, rumpling the sheets. She hadn't even gotten near.

"Do you not wish to see my body? I assure you, I am quite a virile man."

That was the last thing she wanted. "Of course, General Hernández." *I can hardly wait.*

"It would please me to hear you call me Alberto—at least while we are alone."

"Alberto," Silver repeated softly as the general untied the sash of his dressing gown. Her eyes went wide when she discovered he was naked underneath. Naked and aroused.

Oh, God. Silver felt the heat in her cheeks and glanced away. Hernández merely chuckled.

"I am pleased to see, *querida*, that you are not so

well schooled as you pretend. It will give me great pleasure to assist your education in the art of making love."

Though he wasn't very tall, Alberto Hernández had not lied about his masculinity. His thick chest glistened with curly black hair. His waist and hips were stout, but corded and hardened with muscle. His shaft, blunt and thick, rose in arrogance. Silver fought down the bile in her throat.

He came to her slowly, kissing her, pressing her down in the soft feather mattress. Silver inched backward, forcing him to follow, determined to reach the candlestick that now seemed her only salvation. Her legs thrashed wildly, and she moaned, but with each feigned moment of passion, she inched her body closer to the opposite side of the bed. The general's hand squeezed her breast, bared it, and began to massage her nipple. His other hand shoved up the black silk nightgown and began to knead her bottom.

Silver silently cursed him, but she thrashed and arched and gained nearly a foot toward her weapon. The general threw a thick leg over her slender one. Silver strained and moved. His tongue thrust down her throat, disgusting her. A few more inches, and she could reach it. She let him kiss her, ignoring the bitter taste of him, desperate her attempt would not fail.

"Let her go." The deadly tone of the words were punctuated by the murderous click of a hammer being cocked. Hernández whirled toward the sound. "Make one wrong move, Hernández, and you're a dead man."

For an instant Silver just gaped at the men who stood near the back of the room. Behind them, the curtains billowed softly, the doors open wider than

before. Morgan had never looked more grim. The
general reached for his dressing gown.

"Leave it," Morgan warned.

"But surely you do not wish me to—"

"I said leave it!" Reluctantly the general let it
drop.

Still, Silver did not move. Not until the young
blond man beside Morgan swept her with a look that
reminded her of her partial nudity. Only then did she
swallow the lump that had risen in her throat and
adjust her skimpy black garment in an effort to cover
herself.

"Are you all right?" The words were clipped and
brittle, Morgan's eyes running over her black silk
nightgown, taking in the tangled mass of her hair,
then glancing to the rumpled sheets. The candle beside the bed cast a seductive glow, and the pillows
looked crumpled and used.

"Yes," she whispered, but her throat had closed
up, and the ache felt so painful she could barely say
the word. She knew what he was thinking. Dear God
in heaven, she knew!

He picked up the general's dressing gown and
tossed it to her. "We've got to hurry. There isn't
much time."

Silver pulled it on quickly and tied the sash. Tears
stung her eyes and blurred her vision as she moved
blindly across the room. She needed Morgan's com-
forting arms around her. Needed to tell him what
had happened, make him understand, yet she knew
without doubt he would not.

"You will fail, Major Trask," Hernández warned
while the blond marine bound his wrists. "Just as
you did before."

"Not this time, General." The young soldier finished tying the general's feet, bound him to a chair, and stuffed a gag into his mouth.

"Let's go," Morgan ordered. "Corporal Saxon, you cover the rear."

Silver paused only long enough to gather her clothes and roll them into a bundle. The three of them silently hurried to the balcony and climbed the trellis to the ground. When Silver stumbled over the too-long robe, Morgan caught her arm and pulled her up against the adobe wall of the building. Brusquely he leaned down and tore a length off the robe and then off the nightgown.

"Put your sandals on." Every word sounded clipped and cold. Not a trace of warmth touched his voice. With shaking fingers, Silver put on the flat leather shoes, and they started back across the fields toward the prison.

"What about the tower? Won't the guards up there see us?"

"They've been dealt with," was all he said.

They had just reached the tower when the shooting started. Morgan cursed roundly. "Move, damn it! We've got to reach the tunnel!"

Mexican soldiers poured out of tents and sheds that served as makeshift barracks. Pandemonium broke out as each man darted for cover or tried to find the direction in which to return fire. A tall Mexican soldier, shouting words in Spanish, grunted as a lead ball slammed into his chest and he fell at Morgan's feet.

Gripping Silver's hand, Morgan sidestepped the body and dragged her relentlessly through the melee of half-dressed men, horses, wagons, and cannon being readied to fire. Where to aim did not seem quite certain.

"This way." Morgan pulled her into the dark interior of a crumbled stone building. Saxon flattened himself against the wall on the opposite side of the doorway.

"What is this place?" Silver whispered, noting the hieroglyphic inscriptions carved on the walls, the serpents, and evil-looking creatures that watched their every movement with hostile granite eyes.

"Some sort of Mayan temple. The place has been abandoned for centuries." It was the most he had said, but he sounded so detached it made her feel worse than ever.

"Morgan, I want you to know—"

"Not now." With that he grabbed her arm and guided her out of the roofless building. They moved through rock-walled corridors thick with scrub, vines, and bushes and finally reached the side of a pyramid.

"Take her into the tunnel and wait for me there," Morgan instructed the corporal. "I'm going after the others."

Saxon nodded. Silver glanced around but saw nothing until the corporal indicated a low dark bush. Pulling it out of the way, Silver saw an opening about four feet high. She shivered at the thought of going in, got a last quick glimpse of Morgan's broad shoulders as he rounded the corner out of sight, then ducked and stepped inside. The shooting seemed to go on forever; then she heard the sound of running feet.

In minutes men began pouring into the tunnel, some on their own, others being assisted, a few being carried. By now Saxon had lit a torch and some of the others did the same, quickly moving off down the passageway. Silver didn't budge. She wasn't leaving until Morgan arrived.

She heard him before she saw him, and there was

relief in his voice. Three men ducked into the tunnel ahead of him. One she recognized as Jacques, the other, a tall dark-haired man who had to be Morgan's brother, and Cookie, grinning from ear to ear.

"Knew the cap'n would find ya," Cookie said to her with a touch of pride.

"It is good you are safe, *chérie*."

"Let's go," Morgan urged before she could respond to either of her friends. He gripped her hand and pulled her along the tunnel, slowing only when she threatened to fall. She heard the sound of rats nearby, felt one touch her foot, and stifled an urge to scream.

"It isn't far now," Morgan assured her with the same reserved detachment as before. Silver forced one foot in front of the other, driving away thoughts of spiders and snakes and the bugs that grew in profusion in the dank tunnel's depths.

Then she smelled it—a whiff of clean air. In moments they stood outside the opening but lingered only an instant. Morgan yanked her forward, off into the woods, and swung her up on the back of his big sorrel stallion, waiting where he had left it. His brother stepped on a rock and settled himself behind her.

"Get her back to camp," Morgan said to Brendan.

"Not to worry, big brother." But the lightness sounded forced in Brendan's voice.

"What about you?" Silver asked. "Aren't you coming with us?"

"I'll be right behind you."

Brendan whirled the stallion, and that was when she noticed his left arm hanging limply by his side. For the first time she realized the man in back of her could barely hold on. He was injured, and thin to the point of starvation.

"Give me the reins," she commanded. "Just put your arms around my waist and hold on." For a moment he seemed uncertain. "Trust me, Brendan. I'll get us both out of here. Just show me which way to go."

"Morgan says the camp is that way." Wearily he lifted his good arm and pointed toward a trail that led northwest. "Morgan's helping some of the others. He'll meet us at the midway point." Exhausted from his efforts so far, Brendan slid his arms around her waist and his head slumped onto her shoulder.

Silver ignored the rifle fire, the sound of Mexican soldiers searching through the undergrowth, and the cries of the wounded whimpering into the darkness. Instead she urged the big horse along the overgrown path, giving him his head, letting him choose his footing. As Morgan promised, he joined them an hour or so along the trail, silently slipping in behind them to protect the rear. They reached the camp— and safety—sometime later.

Jacques helped Brendan down and then helped Silver. Morgan was nowhere to be seen.

Chapter 22

Against all odds they had done it. Successfully freed the Texian prisoners and gotten away with a minimum of casualties.

All except Buckland. Constantine Buckland was missing. He had not been among the men in the prison. The man called Ram, who along with Morgan and Buckland had been tortured, believed that Buckland had been given a room in the hacienda for his "much-appreciated cooperation."

"The colonel will suffer for our escape," Ram told Silver. "I will not mourn his passing." Silver liked the big Turk who was a friend of Morgan's brother. And it was obvious Ram liked her.

"You remind me of someone, a lady I met in New Orleans," he said. "In a different way, Nicole St. Claire has the same strength of will as you." Ram chuckled. "Only her hair shines the color of copper, not silver, like yours."

Two days passed before they began their journey back to the coast, long enough to tend the men's wounds, give them a chance to regain some strength, and make preparations for the arduous trip. They were traveling south, back the opposite way Cookie and Silver had journeyed with their small Mayan guide, though that one had fled the moment he'd escaped the prison.

Cookie had come by to see her, finding her outside the tent that had been provided for her and Teresa. But most of the time caring for the men had kept him busy. Teresa had remained distant, buried in the grief of her father's death.

"I am sorry, *ma chère*," Jacques had told her. "Your papa did not survive." Teresa wept bitterly into his arms, and he seemed to share some of her pain. "Do not cry," he soothed. "Alejandro Méndez died a 'ero. 'E had grown ill. 'E knew 'e would not live to gain 'is freedom. When another, younger man who 'ad befriended 'im drew the shortest straw, your father faced death in 'is place. It is said 'e spit in the face of 'is executioners."

Teresa clutched him tighter, but pride shone in the youthful lines of her face. Silver left the beautiful Mexican girl to her grief.

Silver carried a grief of her own.

Since the night of their escape, when they had safely reached camp, it was Jacques, not Morgan, who watched after her, taking her to Teresa's tent, fetching her blankets, and helping her make up her bedroll. In his own strong way, Jacques tried to reassure her without interfering.

"Where's Morgan?" Silver had asked, knowing full well he was avoiding her.

"'E needs a little time to 'imself," he said. "This 'as been 'ard on you both." That something had happened between Silver and Morgan he knew, yet he said nothing more. Neither did Silver.

In the days that followed, Morgan had spoken to her only briefly, inquiring of her health, listening to the tale of her capture by Paulo Carrillo and his men, and the proposed attack against the *Savannah* and her crew. Though his face still looked bruised and battered, and he winced with the pain in his back and ribs, he would not let her attend him. Never once did his vacant look soften, or the sound of his voice grow warm.

Nor was any mention made of Hernández or the scene he had witnessed in the general's suite of rooms.

"I appreciate what you did for me," was as close as he came, spoken brusquely, his eyes fixed somewhere on the gray-green horizon.

"I wanted to help you. What happened with the general wasn't—"

"If you'll excuse me, Silver, it's time I saw to the men."

And so it had gone. Whenever she tried to raise the subject, Morgan simply excused himself and walked away. He wasn't unfriendly, wasn't impolite—he just wasn't there.

And the gap that yawned between them broke Silver's heart.

The five-day journey to the coast seemed like weeks. An agony of walking and riding, of making camp and breaking it, of tending the wounded, feeding them, and helping them recover. The terrain to the south of the prison was damp and tropical, humid, and increasingly hot and buggy. It all seemed a haze of discomfort and despair.

Missing Morgan terribly, Silver found herself seeking out his brother. Brendan was usually off somewhere alone, quiet and withdrawn, not at all the wildly impulsive fun-loving man Morgan had described. Still, when Silver was with him, she felt a little closer to the man she loved.

"How are you feeling?" she asked, approaching

where he sat beside a granite outcrop that overlooked a ravine. He was a tall man with light blue
eyes and coffee brown hair. Though his face looked
gaunt and hollow, he was still a handsome man.

"Better." *Outside at least.* Inside, Brendan wondered if he would ever be the same. "I'm beginning
to put on some weight. Cookie always was a better
than passable cook."

"I take it you're getting preferential treatment."

"Definitely. And I don't mind a bit." Actually he
would mind, if all the men weren't being coddled
just a little. They deserved it—after what they had
suffered, they damned well deserved it.

"Your brother's been worried about you. He loves
you very much."

*I think he loves you, too. Though the blasted fool
probably wouldn't admit it.* "We've always been
close. When we were younger, Morgan sacrificed everything for me. He worked twenty hours a day just
to give me the 'advantages' he thought I deserved.
Most of the time I paid him back with a healthy dose
of mischief, but I guess he didn't mind."

"He's a fine man," Silver said.

Shifting on the rock, Brendan winced at the pain
that shot up his arm. He'd taken a lead ball right
before he'd been captured, but one of the men had
dug it out. His arm still hung limp and useless, but
there was a good chance it would recover.

Silver must have noticed his grimace. She leaned
over to check the bandage, seemed satisfied, and
smiled. "It looks to be healing well."

"At least I didn't lose it, like some of those other
unlucky devils." Brendan studied her closely. There
was a sadness in her dark-fringed eyes that had been
there since the first time he had seen her, standing
inside the tunnel, looking at Morgan with such a

mixture of love and despair Brendan had felt a tightening in his chest. Morgan's green eyes had reflected regret—and something else he couldn't quite name.

Brendan wondered what his own eyes looked like. Bleak, he imagined, no longer shining with boyish anticipation. No longer bright with the dream of worlds he thought to conquer. He'd lost the last of his youth in the confines of a Mexican prison. Seen and done things he hadn't known he could. Endured when he should have died, wept for the loss of his friends, and carried the burden of his survival like a weighty stone across his shoulders.

"Did he—has Morgan spoken to you about me?" Silver asked.

Brendan shook his head. "The subject of you seems to be closed at the moment." Brendan had tried to approach him, tried to discover what had happened between the two. That Morgan felt more than a simple attraction for the woman was obvious. But his brother wouldn't discuss it, and Brendan's own heart felt so heavy he hadn't the will to press him any further. "I'm sorry."

Silver nodded, feeling an ache in her throat. When Brendan looked at her with pity and concern, it was all she could do to keep the tears behind her eyes from sliding down her cheeks. She knew why Morgan had abandoned her. It was more than just what he wrongly imagined had happened between General Hernández and her. It was the fact she had sold herself to him. Bartered her body like a high-grade whore. That was how it must have seemed—and Morgan would never forgive her.

"I think I hear someone calling me." It was a lie, and they both knew it, but Brendan just nodded. He was a man who had learned the value of privacy. "I'd better be going."

The day before they reached the coast, the atmosphere in the camp began to change. The soldiers' worry turned away from their fear of being attacked by Centralist soldiers to the possibility that the ships waiting to carry them home had been taken or destroyed. Silver was especially worried about Jordy.

"They'll be there," Morgan told her with more determination than conviction. "Jordy and the others will be fine." It broke her heart to look at him, so far removed from her now that she barely recognized him as the man who had held her in his arms and passionately made love to her. That had been another lifetime.

Some other man.

Some other woman.

This woman was so in desperately in love she could think of nothing but memories of the person she knew to be locked inside this other—this soldier to whom she meant nothing. Thoughts of him clouded her world so thoroughly she plodded along in silence most of the time, placing one foot wearily in front of the other, barely noticing the towering trees overhead, the miserable humidity, the rain that had started to fall, or the dense tropical foliage that enshrouded them like a wet green coffin.

Then one morning the exhausted caravan climbed the final incline and looked down on the coastline near the mouth of the Champotón River. A huge cheer went up. Anchored just a short distance offshore, three tall-masted ships bobbed at anchor. At last they were going home.

"Take care, little brother." Morgan clasped Brendan in a great bear hug.

"Take care, big brother—and thanks." Brendan

turned to Silver, who carefully avoided his injured arm and gently kissed his cheek.

"Don't stop fighting for what you want," he whispered against her ear, and they both knew what he meant. She nodded and wiped away her tears—the ones she shed for the loss of her newfound friend, and the ones she shed for Morgan.

"I'll take care of him," Ram said with a grin, and Silver hugged him, too.

"Good-bye, Ram. I'm glad I met you."

Ram touched her cheek. "You are quite a woman, Silver Jones."

The Texians, all but Hamilton Riley and the four marines who had sailed with Morgan from Georgia, straggled down the beach toward the waiting shore boats. Only Morgan and his crew, the lieutenant and his marines, and the mercenaries Jacques had hired in Barbados would be returning aboard the *Savannah*.

"As soon as we reach the Georgia shore," Morgan told her, with his now-customary reserve, "Riley and the marines will be leaving my command. My commission will expire, and I'll be a civilian again."

She wondered if he'd be glad to get home but couldn't tell from his vague expression. Immediately he excused himself and continued making ready for their departure.

"What about Teresa?" Silver asked Jacques, who had not yet said his good-byes to the woman standing some distance away, next to the small group of Federalist soldiers ready to return her to Campeche.

"She is just a child," Jacques said, but his face looked grim. "I have grown sons nearly her age."

"She is a woman," Silver said.

Jacques didn't answer. His eyes remained fixed on the small dark woman whose skirts whipped her brown-skinned legs in the stiff ocean breeze. She brushed something from her eye and turned away. Still, Jacques did not move.

"Do you love her?" Silver asked softly.

"It does not matter. We do not suit."

"I haven't known you long, Jacques Bouillard, but I never thought you were a fool." Sweeping strands of pale hair back from her face, Silver lifted her skirts and walked off down the beach. Jacques stared after her only a moment. Then with grim resignation, he started walking toward Teresa. When he reached her side, he turned her toward him and found her face wet with tears.

"Why do you cry, *chérie*? What 'as made you so sad?"

"I did not think you would say good-bye."

Jacques's chest tightened. "Does it matter so much?"

Teresa watched him sadly, searching his face for something, looking deeply into his eyes. When Jacques said nothing more, Teresa straightened her shoulders. "You have been very kind, senor. I only wished to thank you for your efforts to save my father."

One of Jacques's big hands lifted to cradle her cheek. "That is all? Just thank you. No good-bye kiss?" When Teresa didn't move, Jacques lowered his mouth to hers, fitting it to the softness of her lips, molding them, tasting them until he heard himself groan. When at last he pulled away, Teresa was trembling, her eyes glistening with a mist of fresh tears.

"*Adios, mi amor*," she whispered just before she turned to leave.

Jacques's hand on her shoulder stopped her. He watched her a moment, taking in the stout yet feminine width of her hips and shoulders, her smooth dark skin and big dark eyes. Something moved inside him. "You 'ave no one in Campeche to return to," he said softly. "No man there to look after you. What will you do?"

"I will get by."

"You need a man."

Teresa said nothing.

Jacques cleared his throat. "I would be that man if you would let me."

"Why?" Teresa asked. "You have already done more than enough."

"You are a strong woman. The kind a man wants by 'is side."

She only shook her head. "I do not want your pity."

Jacques cursed roundly. When Teresa turned to leave, he grabbed her wrist and pulled her against him. "It is not my pity I offer you—it is my love. Please, *mon coeur*, say you will be my wife."

Teresa stared at him as if she hadn't heard his words. Then her hands cupped his face against his heavy black beard, and Jacques's powerful arms crushed her to him.

"Te adoro, mi amor," she said past her tears. "You are the finest man I have ever known. I would be honored to be your wife."

Jacques smiled into the shiny black hair that grazed his cheek. "I am only a seaman, *chérie*. I will sometimes be gone. But I 'ave put away some money, and Morgan has 'elped me invest it. I will provide for you well, and the sea does not beckon so strong as it once did."

"I love you. I care for nothing except being by your side."

"If Morgan no longer needs me, we will return to

Campeche and be married." Jacques smiled with
such happiness it overwhelmed him. "You can
gather your things and say your good-byes. Afterward we will sail for Barbados. I own land there and
'ave often thought of making it my 'ome. The island
is beautiful, and there are no wars."

Teresa just smiled and hugged his neck. "Wherever you are is beautiful to me."

When the first shore boat from the *Savannah* arrived, Jordy and Jeremy Flagg jumped over the gunwales and onto the sand.

"Silver!" Jordy raced up the beach in her direction. When he reached her side, he hugged her
openly, as he hadn't done before. "We was—were—
so worried."

"Thank God you're safe." She clasped his hand.
"How did you escape them? They said their men
would be waiting to block your way."

"They were waitin' all right," Jeremy Flagg put in
as he approached. "Trouble was we were waitin',
too." Laughing, he pointed to the ship. "See those
big five-pound cannon amidship?" Silver nodded.
"Blew 'em clean outa the water, we did. Sailin'
downstream's a whole lot easier than goin' the other
way." He laughed again. "Ship plowed through 'em
like corn through a goose—pardon me, ma'am."

Jordy grinned, and Silver smiled for the first time
in days. "It's all right, Mr. Flagg."

"It isn't all right," Morgan snapped, striding up
just moments after Jacques and Teresa. "There are
ladies in your presence, Mr. Flagg. From now on
you'll do well to remember that."

"With your permission, *mon capitaine*," Jacques
said with a grin that ignored Morgan's biting retort,
"Teresa and I will be staying—at least for a while.
She 'as agreed to become my wife."

Morgan's eyes flashed some unreadable emotion. He smiled, but the lines of his face seemed taut. "Congratulations." His expression said he meant it. "You're a very lucky man."

"Oh, Jacques, that's wonderful." Silver hugged the big Frenchman, then turned and hugged Teresa. "We haven't known each other long, but I know Jacques loves you. If you love him half as much as I think you do, you'll both be very happy."

"*Gracias.*" Teresa smiled warmly. "For you I wish this, too."

"Thank you," Silver said softly, feeling an ache in her heart.

"You're stayin' here?" Jordy said to Jacques with such a forlorn expression Silver's despair changed to concern. "You ain't—aren't—comin' back with us?"

"I am sorry, my young friend, but this is as far as I go—at least for now." Jordy seemed stricken. "Do not be sad. It will not be forever."

"But I thought maybe I could sail with you aboard the brigantine."

"It's all right, Jordy," Silver soothed. "Jacques will be back one day and you still have me."

"You'll be leaving, too. Soon as we get to Katonga."

"No, I won't, Jordy. I'm not going back there." But when she looked up at Morgan and saw his grim expression, she wasn't so sure. *Dear God, not that, too.*

"I'll have one of the men bring your sea chest ashore," Morgan said to Jacques. "Take care of yourselves." They said their final farewells, and the couple walked arm in arm toward the waiting Federalist troops.

"Well, Mr. Flagg," Morgan snapped, turning away

from them, "what are you waiting for? I'm sure Miss Jones would like to get back aboard ship."

And that was the way he had been for the past three days. Gruff and unreachable, standing at the helm for hours, rarely going belowdecks, pushing the men as if some demon rode his back. He looked beaten and exhausted and older than his years. Silver stayed away from him, finding it unbearable to see him, knowing the way he felt about her, sure he looked at her with eyes that recalled her half-naked body writhing beneath Alberto Hernández in what he must have believed was passion.

If only she had been fighting—and she would have been in just a moment more. Instead he had found her wedged beneath the man's big body, her arms entwined around his neck.

He had found her that way once before, but then he had heard the words that made him believe in her. Buckland himself had declared her innocence. This time Morgan had seen exactly what he'd witnessed when he burst in on Charlotte Middleton—a woman betraying him in the arms of another man.

And even if Silver could convince him that nothing had happened—as she knew she couldn't—she had bartered her body for his freedom, sold herself like a well-paid whore. Morgan wanted the delicate kind of woman who would kill herself rather than let a man use her body—no matter what the reason.

Silver glanced out the portholes that stretched above Morgan's wide berth, remembering the times they had made love there, sometimes with fiery anger, sometimes with gentleness, always with a burning passion neither could deny. Now he was living in the tiny steward's cabin, had insisted Silver take the bigger room, wouldn't have it any other way. He was doing everything in his power to see to her comfort, yet she felt him pulling farther and farther away. Soon she'd be nothing but a woman who traveled aboard his ship, someone to receive the usual shipboard courtesies—nothing more.

Maybe that would work for Morgan. Maybe he could set her away from him and never look back. But Silver couldn't. Every night she lay awake listening for his footfalls, wishing with every ounce of her will that he would come to her with understanding, at least give her the chance to explain. Sometimes she tossed and turned for hours, waiting, listening, but his steps came only in the wee hours just before dawn. When their paths chanced to meet, Morgan remained polite but withdrawn, and he never approached her unless he had to.

Through the porthole, lightning flashed in the distance. A norther, Morgan had called it on their inbound journey, when they had sailed into one of the small spring squalls that tossed the Caribbean this time of year. This one was still some distance away, but the seas were beginning to stir, and dark clouds covered the moon. It looked black and forbidding, grim and depressing.

Silver watched the storm, and desperate sobs welled up in her throat. For days she had maintained control. Held her terrible fears in check, kept her powerful emotions of love and loss from overwhelming her. But like the winds of the storm, they hovered not far away.

For the first time it occurred to Silver that she felt worse now than she had in those moments when she'd faced Alberto Hernández. Then she'd had Morgan's love—or at least some part of it. She had known he was free and the thought made her heart soar. It had given her the strength she needed. Believing he still cared for her, she could endure anything—even the general's brutal advances. Now that she was safe on board Morgan's ship, her strength deserted her as it never had before.

Silver got up from the bed and walked absently toward the bureau, her eyes fixed on Morgan's razor, resting beside the basin. A sad smile curved her lips as she remembered with fondness the morning she had watched him shave. He'd looked so achingly handsome standing there bare-chested, so masculine, and even a little domestic. What a wonderful husband he would make. Caring and kind and considerate. Obstinate, to be sure, but proud and honorable and strong.

Knowing some other, more genteel lady would one day share his life, Silver felt a hard ache close her throat. How would she make it without him? How could she go on as she had before? He had changed her, she suddenly realized, touched and gentled her in some way she couldn't explain. It made her feel vulnerable and more than a little afraid.

I won't let it happen, she vowed. *I've faced worse than this and survived. He's just one man among many, just a man like all the rest.*

It was a lie, and she knew it. Morgan was like no other man she had known. He was power and passion, strength and gentleness. Morgan was her light in the darkness. He was her heart and her love. Without him, life stretched ahead of her, bleak and empty. For her there could be no other.

Dear God, I love him so.

Silver glanced toward Morgan's desk, where his feathered pen rested in the inkwell. His log lay open, but no entries had been written since the day of their departure from Mexico. She wondered what he was thinking, wondered if he might be as lonely as she. It seemed impossible. Morgan had only to reach for her and Silver would be there. She would go into his arms without a moment's hesitation, as certain of her love as she was that she still breathed.

She thought of Jacques and Teresa, of the happiness the two of them shared. They could speak to each other with just a word or a touch. But she and Morgan weren't that way. They were private people who shared little of themselves with others. Was that what each of them wanted? To live separate and apart, afraid to share, afraid to love? It wasn't what Silver wanted.

With a burst of clarity, Silver made the painful decision she had known she would make from the start. Tonight she would go to him, admit her feelings, the love she held in her heart. It would take all the courage she possessed, all the strength of will she could muster. Still, she would go.

Though the hour was late, Morgan would be up on deck, as he had been each night since their return. Now was the time to approach him—before she could change her mind. Even the next few moments seemed crucial. Her tenuous thread of courage might desert her at any time.

Squaring her shoulders, Silver started for the door, but her hand stilled on the latch. The broken shard of mirror reflected her wan appearance, the hair that hung loosely around her shoulders, always a little bit tumbled. Absently she picked up her brush and began to smooth it. Anything to postpone the task ahead. Half of her wanted to hurry, to say the words and end her torture one way or the other. But the other half cautioned, *You know he won't listen. He's never believed in you, he won't believe you now, and even if he does, it won't matter*. He thought of her differently now, not worthy of his attentions. Certainly not worthy of his love.

What kind of woman are you? he had said. The kind who would use her body to buy his freedom. She would never be the gently reared lady Morgan wanted; she had proved that beyond all doubt. She refused to consider that he might return her to her father. Even that for now seemed unimportant. All that mattered was that she somehow reach him, regain the passion they had shared.

With trembling fingers Silver picked up the black wool shawl she had been given when she'd first come aboard and draped it across her bare shoulders. It wasn't really cold outside, just chilly and windy.

Inside was where she was cold.

Outside the cabin, the wind whipped her skirts as she walked along the deck, determined to seek him out. As she had hoped, most of the men lay sleeping, sprawled on the deck near the center of the ship. Up toward the bow, she saw a man's broad shoulders silhouetted in the intermittent moonlight that shone between the clouds and instantly recognized Morgan's perfect V-shaped frame. A rush of warmth swept over her, so poignant it nearly made her weep.

Dear God, let him listen.

He turned at her approach but didn't move, just stood watching from the shadows of the darkness, his sun-browned fingers tightening on the rail.

"You're out late," he finally said in that guarded way of his.

"Yes," Silver whispered, forcing the word past the tightness in her throat. "I needed to speak to you."

"Oh?" He arched a dark blond brow. "What about?"

She couldn't do it. She couldn't. She had to. Her

breath seemed lodged in her throat. "I know what you think of me. I know what you must feel."

"Silver—"

"If I told you nothing happened, would you still think me a whore?"

Morgan's head came up. "What? What did you say?"

"In the general's chamber"—she rushed on—"it wasn't at all what it seemed. I was trying to reach the candlestick to use as a weapon. In another minute or two I would have had it. I know what it must have looked like—"

"Stop it."

"I know what you must think, but I—"

"Stop it!"

At the harsh tone of his words, tears stung Silver's eyes and slipped down her cheeks. "I know you think the worst of me, that I acted like a whore—"

"Whore?" Morgan repeated. "Whore!" He took a step in her direction, his face a mask of pain. "Surely you can't believe that I . . ." But his words trailed off as he read her tortured expression. "God in heaven, Silver—" It was almost a plea. "How could I think you less than a saint for putting yourself in such danger? You put your life before mine. How could I fault you when you sacrificed yourself for me?"

Silver was crying now, soft, broken sobs that seemed to come endlessly from somewhere inside her. She willed him to reach for her, wanted him to hold her so badly she thought she would die of it. *Touch me!* her heart cried. *Love me!*

"It is I who failed you, Silver," Morgan said, his voice rough with emotion. "I can't bear to face you. I can't forgive myself for what I let happen. I keep seeing you lying there beneath him, struggling against his thick body, fighting Hernández, when it should have been me."

Silver tried to grasp his words. She couldn't accept the regret on his face or the torment she read in his eyes. "You came for me," she said, feeling a tiny glimmer of hope. "You were tortured, and you were beaten, and still you came back for me."

"I should have come sooner. I should have protected you. If I'd taken you back to Barbados when you stowed aboard the ship, none of this would have happened. Hernández never would have hurt you."

"Hernández failed; you came before he could finish. But even if he hadn't, it wouldn't matter. I love you," she said softly, "and I would do it again."

Morgan just looked at her, his eyes moving over her tear-stained face, the trembling fingers that clutched the folds of her apricot skirt. She was so much woman. So passionate and strong. *God, how I love you.* Powerful strides, long overdue, carried him to her side, and he swept her into his arms. "Forgive me, darling Silver. Forgive me."

He kissed her eyes, her nose, her lips, the sweet taste of her giving him nourishment, bringing sustenance to his parched and empty soul. "If I had known what you were thinking, if I had believed for an instant that you blamed yourself, I would have come to you and begged your forgiveness. I beg for it now."

"I need you," Silver whispered, kissing him with such fierce desperation Morgan groaned. "And I love you so."

I love you more, he thought, but he didn't say the words. Couldn't. Not now. Not after what he had done to her. Regret welled up in his heart, regret that he had not gone to her—and a relief so profound it overwhelmed him. He felt like a dead man who had just been resurrected. There was life in his veins, not bleak, stark emptiness. There was joy in the world, and all of it was Silver.

"You're mine, Silver Jones. You belong to me, and I'll never let you go." With that he swung her up in his arms and carried her off toward his cabin.

There was a time he would have worried about his men, worried about appearances and the propriety of his actions. Now all he thought of was Silver. He should have known she would blame herself, take responsibility for what had happened even though it was he who should carry the burden. He should have gone to her that first night, knew he should, but felt such bitter remorse he could not face her.

Tonight he would make amends. He would worship her body, earn her forgiveness in the only way he knew how. Tomorrow he would speak the words in his heart.

Chapter 23

Silver slid her arms around Morgan's neck and rested her head on his shoulder as he carried her down to his cabin.

She felt as if she'd come home.

Morgan lifted the latch on his door, shoved it wide with a booted foot, then closed it behind them. "Every night, when I finally gave up and tried to sleep, I'd come in here and see you lying in my bed. I wanted you so badly that most of the time I wound up leaving again."

"If you had come in a little earlier, you would have found me waiting for you."

Morgan smiled at that. "I was a fool to put you through this, but I intend to make it up to you." He bent his head and brushed her lips then settled his mouth over hers, fitting their lips perfectly together.

Morgan let go of her legs, and she slid gently down his body, feeling the muscular contours, the ridges in his thighs, and finally his hardened arousal. Her fingers laced into the silky strands of his hair.

"I want you," Silver whispered, feeling Morgan's hands on her breast, cupping and caressing, then moving to the buttons at the back of her dress.

"Not nearly as much as I want you." In minutes he had freed the confining bodice and peeled it away. Long brown fingers dipped below her chemise to her breasts. Then he bared one, lowered his head, and gently took her nipple into his mouth. Silver gasped for breath as she felt him suckling gently, teasing and nipping until the peak grew taut and achy. Shivers of heat raced through her body, erasing the last of her despair.

Morgan stripped away her garments, leaving her naked, his eyes bold and hungry. Then with hands a little unsteady, he lifted her up on the bed. She was certain he would remove his own clothes before he joined her, but instead he kissed her hard and began to place small, moist kisses down her body, trailing a path of fire.

"Morgan?" she whispered, unsure of his intentions as he settled himself between her legs.

"Let me love you," Morgan whispered. "Let me make amends for the hurt I've caused." Before she could form a protest, his mouth nipped teasingly along her thigh and his fingers slipped into the wetness at the juncture of her legs, easing out and then in in a sensuous rhythm.

When his tongue followed his hand, Silver instinctively arched against him, urging him onward, spiraling higher and higher. Morgan licked and soothed and sampled. The feel of his mouth stirred white-hot fires that shimmered across her skin, the sensations so delicious she could almost taste them. As if she could, her tongue wet the corners of her mouth and she moaned. Surely she should stop him, give him back some of the pleasure he gave her. She wanted to, she meant to, but Morgan fought any attempt to move away, and his skillful ministrations finally whirled her over the edge.

Trembling all over, Silver cried out his name, begging to feel him inside her.

He left her for only a moment, then his heavy weight settled at her side and he kissed her, his tongue thrusting deep into her mouth in an age-old possession Silver gladly accepted. When she felt him part her thighs with his knee and guide himself to the warm wet opening at her core, she arched against him. Morgan drove home in one powerful surging stroke.

"I'll never let you go," he whispered against her ear.

Silver clutched him tighter. "I never want to leave."

Morgan shifted on the bed, drawing her up on top of him. She rode him like a fiery wild stallion, her head falling back, her hair hanging down to tease his groin.

They made love for hours, Morgan teaching her joys she hadn't imagined, delighting her, and allowing her to please him in return. Once in the middle of the night she felt warm tingling sensations and opened her eyes to find Morgan fitted against her, spoon fashion. He grinned and nipped her shoulder just as he slid himself inside. Silver gasped at the heated sensations, the feel of his rock-hard body, and the fullness of his shaft. Closing her eyes, she gave herself up to the long, deep strokes that aroused her to frenzy and let him continue his magic.

She wished he would say that he loved her, but for now the words didn't matter. Morgan was back in her arms, and Silver was the happiest woman on earth.

Morgan awoke before dawn. For the first time in days he felt rested. He felt alive and whole, and he owed it all to Silver. She stirred on the mattress beside him.

"Good morning." He nibbled the side of her neck, and soft strands of hair tickled his nose.

Silver smiled. "Yes, it is. In fact, it's a fabulous morning."

He propped himself up on an elbow to study her face, saw the enchanting glow of her happiness, and felt a surge of leftover guilt. "These past few days have been a nightmare for both of us. It was my fault. I should have come to you, tried to explain the way I felt."

"It isn't easy for you," Silver said. "It's never been easy for me either."

Morgan brushed a stray lock of hair from her cheek. "We'll just have to learn."

She kissed him softly on the lips. "Where do we start?"

"We started last night. You came to me and now there are no more secrets between us, no dark mysteries, no worries."

Silver glanced away.

"Are there, Silver?"

She forced a smile in his direction. "Of course not." She knew she should tell him about her father; it was a secret that would always lie between them. Then she thought of what he might say, how he might feel . . . In the end she might have to tell him, but she couldn't do it now. Going to him last night had been the hardest thing she'd ever done. She didn't have the strength to deal with that kind of emotion again so soon. "Besides, we've got time to learn more about each other. We've got at least two weeks till we reach Barbados." She wasn't about to mention Katonga. That could come later.

"Yes," Morgan agreed, his gaze moving over her,

"we have plenty of time." But his jaw tightened at the lie he saw in her eyes—the lie he had seen there before. Bloody hell, when would they learn to trust each other? Yet how could he blame her after what he had done? If Silver hadn't come to him, would he have gone to her, trusted her with his feelings? As soon as they'd returned from the prison, he had started to distance himself, to shield himself from his emotions.

After Charlotte, he had taught himself well.

"Neither of us is much good at trusting," Morgan said. "But we care for each other—a great deal, it seems. In time trust will come." He couldn't say the word *love*. He just couldn't. Not after the lie. Not until he knew the truth she had hidden for so long.

"About Hernández . . ." Silver said softly. "He was delayed while he searched for you. He wasn't with me long before you arrived."

Morgan sat up beside her. "I'm glad he didn't hurt you, but even if he had taken you, it wouldn't change the way I feel. Nothing he could have done would have made me stop wanting you."

Silver lifted his hand to her lips and kissed the calloused palm. "Enough to move your clothes back in here?"

"That, milady, will be a pleasure."

"You're looking lovely, Delia." William Hardwick-Jones stood in front of the tall window behind his desk, his large hands clasped behind his back. "Fertility seems to agree with you."

Delia's hand lifted protectively to the rounded swell of her stomach.

"You know why I've brought you here." William's hard black eyes fixed on her face.

"I don' know where Miss Silver go. She don' say. Mon jus' say he bring her bock."

"So you have no idea where he might have taken her."

"No, suh."

"I don't believe you." William rounded the desk and strode toward the willowy woman in her faded blue shift who stepped back at his approach.

"It's de truth, I swear it."

William gripped her chin. "One more week. That's what I'll give you and that black demon you call your man. If you don't know where they've gone, find someone who does. There are boats in and out of here with supplies; someone somewhere must have seen them." When he reached toward her, Delia tried to back away, but William caught her arm and dragged her up close.

His cold hand closed over her stomach. "That little bundle you carry belongs to me, just like you do. Find out where she is, or I'll see it's disposed of, one way or another."

Delia stared at him in horror. A sob rose in her throat, and her fingers flew to her lips to stifle the sound. When William released her, she backed away.

"Remember what I've said," he told her. Delia turned and fled the room.

"I don't think she knows anything." Sheridan Knowles got up from the tufted leather chair where he'd been sitting.

"Maybe not, but you can bet if any of the darkies know, she'll find out."

"I tell you she's with Trask. Rumor has it they're due back any day. The Frenchman who hired Trask's mercenaries promised a two-month hitch. Time's almost up."

"Good." William smiled thinly. "Double the welcoming party. I want no slipups. I want her home, and I want her home now.''

In the days that followed, Morgan and Silver spent every spare moment together. They walked the decks for hours, talking about the future, discussing private dreams and goals, though it wasn't easy for either of them.

"What do you want, Silver?" Morgan asked as they stood at the rail on a bright, windswept morn. The sky appeared blue, the sea frothy, and the sun felt warm overhead. "What would make you happy?"

She smiled up at him, admiring his handsome features, the strong line of his jaw. "I never asked myself that until I met you. All I could think of was getting away from Katonga. Trying to find some small bit of happiness that I could call my own. I liked being independent, even if it meant working in that god-awful tavern."

"Is being independent so important?" He looked as imposing as he had the first day she'd seen him. The tan was back in his face, the bleakness gone from his eyes.

"In a way it is. But now that I've met you, I understand that two people can be independent and still be together. You make me feel that way, Morgan, as if I'm finally complete. Can you understand that?"

Morgan nodded. He wanted to tell her he knew exactly what she meant, that he couldn't imagine life without her. But he didn't. Damn, it was hard to tell her how much he cared. "Unlike you, I've always been on my own," he said instead. "I was twelve when my father died; my mother died soon after. At fifteen I left England for good. My brother was five years younger, a big responsibility, but I didn't

mind. He made me feel needed. After I got older, I
didn't think I cared about that anymore. Now I know
differently."

"I need you, Morgan."

Morgan bent his head and kissed her, a gentle, re-
assuring kiss that made her feel safe and warm. "No
more than I need you."

They spoke about Jacques and Teresa, how happy
they had seemed. "I think he fell in love with her the
first time he saw her," Morgan said. "She was a
sassy little thing, just the kind of woman Jacques
needs." He cast Silver a hungry glance, and a corner
of his mouth curved up. "Jacques taught me to appreciate a woman with fire."

Silver smiled, but too soon she glanced away.

Morgan cupped her cheek with his hand, forcing
her to look at him. "What is it? Tell me."

"I know what you want in a woman," she said
softly. "I hardly fit the description."

"You're wrong, Silver. You know what I thought I
wanted. I was a fool. It's clear to me now, just as
Jacques said, I could never be happy with a woman
like Lydia Chambers or any of the others I've spent
time with. I need a woman who isn't afraid to stand
up to me. A woman of strength and passion. I need
you, Salena."

Silver slid her arms around his neck and kissed
him with all the love in her heart.

Reluctantly Morgan pulled away. "Keep that up
and I'll haul you back to my bed." He smiled roguishly. "Which brings us to another subject: How do
you feel about children?"

Silver smiled, too. "I love children. Delia and I
used to sit with the newborn babies on Katonga
whenever we could sneak away. They were so tiny

and helpless. I'd love a little boy who looks just like you."

"A little girl like you wouldn't be bad either. As I recall, you were the apple of your father's eye."

Silver's smile faded. "You won't take me back there. I mean, you'll take me to Georgia, won't you?"

Morgan took her hand. "I've got to see William. I'd like his approval if he'll grant it. I want him to know that you're well and safe and that you'll be cared for properly. As my wife you'll—"

"Wife? But we haven't talked about marriage. You haven't even asked me."

Morgan grinned. "My darling Salena, what do you think we've been talking about? I've been waiting for the proper moment. I wanted to do it right this time."

Silver didn't know whether to laugh or cry. She'd thought about it, of course; she couldn't deny it. But was marriage really what she wanted? He'd asked her once before, though that had been different—or had it? Morgan had always been concerned with propriety. Love had not yet been mentioned. And there were other considerations—like the problems she still faced with her father.

"I don't want to go back to Katonga," she said, avoiding the subject. "If I go back, my father will never let me leave again."

"Your father and I are friends, Silver. This isn't going to be nearly as difficult as you believe."

You're wrong, she thought, *so terribly, painfully wrong.* "You don't know him like I do. He won't let me go."

Morgan took both of her hands, which had started to tremble. "Surely you can't believe that."

"He'll find a way. He's no longer the man you once knew—he couldn't be."

"Listen to me, Silver." He gently squeezed her hands. "Besides myself, there are five marines, four-teen crewmen, and nearly a dozen mercenaries aboard this ship. If it takes all of them to get you off Katonga, then that's what they'll do. Now will you trust me?"

It isn't a matter of trust. "I know you don't agree with me, but it seems this ought to be my decision. If you care for me enough to marry me, surely you can respect my wishes."

Morgan's look turned hard. Eyes a sparkling green just moments before now looked dark and unreach-able, and tiny lines creased his suntanned brow. "Damn it, Silver, don't put me in this position. I owe this to your father."

She wanted to argue, to shout and rail and plead with him not to make her go. But she didn't. "All right," she finally conceded though it galled her to do so. "We'll do it your way." Didn't they always?

They spent much of their time alone; even Sogger was banned from their quarters, much to his furry chagrin. But at supper Hamilton Riley joined them, and sometimes Jeremy Flagg, whose swift action in battle had earned him a promotion to first mate. Mr. Flagg was generally cheerful, and Ham was good-natured as always.

"I really liked your brother," Ham said to Morgan one night as they supped on the last of the chicken and some fresh squash and fruit Mr. Flagg had req-uisitioned from a small Mayan village. "As far as I'm concerned, Brendan's a damned fine soldier."

During the weeks since they'd left Georgia, Ham had really matured. He was a man now. In combat he had distinguished himself, led his men bravely, and remained clearheaded. Morgan planned to rec-ommend him for promotion.

"To tell you the truth," Morgan said, setting his fork aside and lifting his wineglass, "I'm worried about him. He was always so brash and impetuous. Now he just seems brooding and withdrawn. It isn't like him."

"He's suffered a great deal," Silver said.

"It must have been terrible in there," Ham added. "He lost some very good friends, to say nothing of the physical abuse he endured."

"I got a small taste of what went on in there." Morgan took another long drink of his wine. "I can imagine what Brendan went through. Damn, I wish there'd been something I could have said or done to help him."

"When will Brendan be back in Savannah?" Silver asked.

"He isn't coming back. That's another thing that bothers me. Brendan plans to stay in Texas. Before all this happened, I would have thought he was staying for the challenge, the chance to spread his wings in such wide-open country, but now . . ." Morgan sighed wearily. "There was a time I would have believed him capable of anything. Now I'm not so sure."

"He'll be all right," Silver said. "Underneath it all, Brendan's a very strong man—just like his brother."

"If you want to worry," Jeremy Flagg put in with a look of concern, "you best be worryin' about Master Little."

"Jordy?" Morgan said. "What's the matter with Jordy?"

"Beats me, but the lad's not himself lately. He's been real blue since Mr. Bouillard done left the ship."

"I've tried to talk to him," Silver said. "I think he's worried about what will happen to him once we get back to Savannah. Jordy's got no family, no one to look after him. Morgan's all but quit the sea, Jacques is gone, and Cookie has a lady friend he seems quite serious about. Where does that leave Jordy?"

"I hadn't thought of it that way. I knew he loved the sea. I thought he'd want to stay on with the ship."

"He's awfully young, Morgan. As long as the others were with him, Jordy felt he had family. Once we reach Georgia, he'll have no one."

Morgan covered her hand with his. "He's got me," he said, "and he's got you. We just haven't told him so lately."

Silver smiled and felt another burden lifted from her heart.

As soon as supper ended, they went up on deck to look for him. "Have you seen Jordy?" Morgan asked Cookie, who stood busily hanging pots above the table in the galley.

"He finished up here and took off by himself. He's been doing that a lot lately." Cookie smiled at Silver. "You get enough to eat? Wouldn't want you gettin' skinny."

"It was delicious, Cookie. I couldn't hold another bite."

Morgan searched the fo'c'sle but turned up nothing.

"I bet he's gone below," Silver said.

"Down in the hold? Surely he isn't down there."

"I've found him there before. It may be damp and musty, but it's quiet, and there's nobody around to bother you."

"You ought to know." His mouth curved up in amusement. "I should have taken you to task for stowing away like that, but in truth I was damned glad you did. God knows where you'd be right now if you'd stayed in Barbados."

"I'm sure dear Lydia was glad to see me gone."

Morgan chuckled. "I can't say I blame her. She knew the moment she saw you that she didn't stand a chance."

As Silver predicted, when they descended the ladder to the hold, a yellow light glowed in one corner. With a yowl, Sogger came racing toward them and brushed against Silver's legs as she walked along.

"You never could keep a secret," she scolded him, but he just purred and yawned.

"Come on." Morgan took her hand and led her over the ship's ribs to the corner. Jordy set his seaman's manual aside and came to his feet. Considering how hard he'd been working, his striped shirt and pants looked clean, though the toes of his flat-heel boots were scuffed and worn.

"Somethin' wrong, Cap'n?"

"Yes, son, there is. But it's nothing you've done. It's something I've done—or more correctly, haven't done."

Jordy looked confused.

"Why don't we sit down?" Silver said, indicating several empty crates Jordy had arranged to sit on. The lantern flickered, casting long dark shadows on the walls.

"Kind of lonely down here, isn't it, son?" Every time Morgan called him that, something flickered in Jordy's eyes.

"I like it 'cause it's private."

"Private can sometimes be lonesome."

Jordy swallowed hard. "Figure I might as well get used to it, what with you all goin' away when we git —get—back home."

Morgan's jaw tightened. He cleared his throat. "I

know you've worked hard, Jordy, I know you have plans for a ship of your own one day, but I—we—that is, Silver and I—we thought maybe you might consider waiting awhile before you shipped out again.''

Jordy's head came up. Strands of auburn hair fell over his forehead, but he shoved them back with the palm of his hand. "What—what do you mean? You ain't—aren't—gonna give me a berth? But I thought, I mean, I know you was—were—mad about the reward money, but I didn't take it. I thought you believed me. I thought—"

"That's not what I meant, Jordy."

Jordy swallowed hard, looking close to tears. "Please don't ask me to leave the ship, Cap'n Trask. I got no place else to go."

"Oh, Jordy," Silver whispered, wanting to go to him but knowing this wasn't the time."

"I want you to come home with us, son. To my house in Savannah. You could go to school there for a few more years, catch up on your education. When you're ready, you could go back to sea."

For a moment Jordy just stared at him. "You want me to live with you?"

Morgan smiled. "If you want to. I know it's kind of an imposition, you being a seaman and all, but well, we could sure use the help and—"

"Oh, yes," Jordy said. "I won't be no trouble—any trouble—and I'll earn my keep and"—he glanced up at Morgan with such longing Silver's heart turned over—"and when you call me son, you'll be proud to say it."

Morgan blinked hard and had to glance away. Stepping forward, he clasped Jordy's shoulders, then gripped him in a warm bear hug. "I've always been proud, son. I just never told you."

* * *

Silver pulled out the long wooden bench in the galley and sat down. Steam billowed up from the roiling kettles of broth on the stove. "He's doing it again, Cookie." The stout old sailor handed her a steaming mug of coffee. "He's making decisions for me without even asking, and I don't like it."

"I wondered how long you'd let him keep the upper hand." He chuckled softly.

"What's that supposed to mean?"

"Just means lovin' someone doesn't mean you can't disagree with them. What's he done now?"

"He's told me I'm going to marry him. He's even told Jordy, in a manner of speaking."

"I thought every woman wanted to get married. I know my Mildred does. That's pret' near all she can talk about."

"Not this woman. At least I never wanted to before. I wanted to live my life on my own. I don't want to live under some man's domineering rules—even Morgan's."

"You love him, don't you?"

"The question is, Does he love me?"

"Why don't you ask him?"

"Maybe I will."

"And maybe you won't."

How did he know that? "If he loved me, surely he'd say so."

"It's hard for him."

It was hard for me. "There are things I haven't told him, Cookie. I suppose I should have. I hoped I wouldn't have to."

"Do you think it will make any difference?"

"I don't know."

"We'll be in Barbados in a day, two at most. If I

was you, I'd get it off my chest while you've still got him all to yourself."

Silver didn't answer, just took a sip of her coffee, cradling the mug between her hands.

"While you're about it, missy, you damn well better make up your mind about gettin' married."

Silver scoffed. "My father bullied my mother. He was dominating and overbearing, cruel and malicious. Sheridan Knowles—that's our manager— treats his wife just the same."

"Cap'n's a man; he's bound to be a bit high-handed at times. He's as stubborn as they come, he's bossy and sometimes downright cantankerous, but you ain't some sweet-mouthed little schoolgirl neither. Takes a powerful strong man to handle you, missy. Never you believe no different. Most likely you two got some pretty hard-fought battles ahead of you, but if you care enough, you'll make things work out."

"How do you know so much about marriage?"

"My ma and pa were the happiest two people you ever coulda known. It can happen, Silver. Believe it, and it can happen to you."

Silver watched him a moment, mulling over his words, thinking about Morgan and how much she loved him. "Thank you, Cookie."

Never had she meant the words more. Damn it to hell, now she knew what was the matter. She loved Morgan—desperately—and she had almost lost him. She was letting him run over her because she didn't want to lose him again. But Cookie was right. Her opinions were just as important as Morgan's—and if he didn't care enough about her to listen, she didn't want him.

Chapter 24

Morgan watched the set of Silver's shoulders, the stiff way she carried herself. She'd been edgy all through supper, relieved, it seemed, when the meal had ended and they'd gone up on deck for their late-evening stroll.

Watching the tension in her profile, Morgan stopped at the rail and turned to face her. "Why do I get the distinct impression you have something you're dying to say to me?" The moon, full and glistening on the water, lit the small empty space where they stood near the bow of the ship. Beneath them the frothy seas parted and slid away against the hull.

Silver lifted her chin as if readying herself to do battle. "Will we reach Barbados tomorrow?"

"Yes. Probably sometime early in the morning."

"Then it seems now would be a good time for you to ask me."

"Ask you what?"

Silver bristled even more. "Why, to marry you, of course—if you still want to."

"Of course I want to. I thought we had all this settled."

"*You* had it settled. I have yet to have a say in the matter."

"You have yet . . . ?" Morgan raked a hand through his thick dark blond hair. "Damn it, Silver, you know how hard this is for me."

"You've had little trouble ordering me around these past few months, but then *asking* instead of commanding is always more difficult."

Morgan might have smiled if she hadn't looked so damned serious. "You little vixen, you're enjoying this."

Silver's firm look softened. "Just pretend I'm not here."

Morgan laughed at that. "I suppose you want me down on my knees."

"Considering the circumstances"—she glanced to the men who worked in the rigging—"I don't think that will be necessary."

Morgan took her hands, warm and soft in his dark, calloused ones. "Will you marry me, Silver?"

A ripple of tenderness crossed her features, then it was gone. "I will if you'll agree to meet my terms."

"Terms! What terms? I had hoped that vowing to honor and cherish till death do us part would be enough."

"I'm serious, Morgan. We've never talked about this and it's very important to me."

"All right, lady vixen, tell me your terms."

"First, I want you to promise you won't make decisions about my life without asking my opinion. Second, I want equal say in this marriage. And finally, I want you to find something for me to do. Sitting around your musty old mansion while you're off working is hardly my idea of a happy life."

Morgan's mouth twitched. "It's hardly a musty old

mansion. As a matter of fact, it's quite a lovely old mansion.''

Silver didn't comment, just waited for him to go on.

"In regard to your first and second terms, it hardly seems unfair for you to have a say in things. However, should we come to an impasse, my word will be final.''

She mulled that over. "Agreed.''

"As to finding you something to do, how would you like to learn the cotton trade?''

Silver's eyes went wide. "Do you mean it?''

"You've a sharp mind, Silver. I think you would be quite an asset—at least until the children come. After that we'll just have to see.''

Silver eyed him a bit warily. "You're being awfully reasonable about this.''

"Am I?'' Morgan's warm look faded. "That's because I have a condition of my own. I want to know the real reason you fled Katonga. I want to know what secret you've been hiding from me.''

A moment of surprise, then one of desolation. Silver turned away from him and her hands gripped the rail. "I hoped you would never have to know. I hoped we could just—'' She swallowed hard and glanced out at the frothy dark water. "But I guess it wouldn't be fair to keep something like that from you since it might change the way you feel about me.''

"Nothing is going to change the way I feel. I want you to understand that.'' She didn't really believe him; he could see it in her eyes.

"Remember the first time we made love?'' she asked.

He smiled softly. "How could I forget?''

Silver let the comment pass. "I told you about my

childhood . . . about the man who had . . . attacked me."

"Yes." His smile faded.

"That man still lives on the island. Every day since I was thirteen he has watched me; every night I feared he would try it again. The night before the immigrant ship set sail, he had been drinking. I was afraid of what he might do, so I stole a butcher knife from the kitchen and took it up to my room. Just after midnight he came in." She started to tremble, and Morgan drew her against him.

"Go on," he gently urged.

"I threatened to kill him. I meant it, Morgan, and he knew it. He left me alone, but he was furious. I knew he would beat me in the morning, as he had many times before. If he tried—" Her voice broke, and Morgan tightened his hold, one wide palm cradling her head against his chest, his hand stroking her hair, soothing, encouraging.

"It's all right, Silver, he can't hurt you now."

"That man was my father, Morgan. William Hardwick-Jones."

Morgan froze. *It couldn't be.* He wanted to deny it. Wanted to say she was wrong, make her admit it. No man—especially not William—would do such a thing. He felt her shaking, heard the gentle sobs that shook her slender frame. It was the truth; he knew that beyond all doubt. God in heaven, what she must have suffered. Might still be suffering if he had left her there.

With the force of a saber the vicious blow struck him. He remembered the way she had acted when she'd first come aboard the *Savannah*, her wild attempts to escape, risking her life, not caring for the danger she put herself in. She'd been fighting for survival, for her very existence. *If only she had told me*. Another truth hit him: *You wouldn't have believed her!* She could have said those very same words, and he would have scoffed. He would have treated her worse for the lie he would have been sure it was.

He pressed his cheek against hers, felt the wetness of her tears, the terrible sadness that gripped and held her body. Morgan clung to her, wanting to take away the pain, wishing he could somehow make it up to her. He rocked her gently back and forth, his heart aching for what she'd been through.

Silver eased away to look at him, her fingers warm against his cheek. "You're crying," she whispered.

He hadn't realized it until she said the words. "For all that you've suffered. For the things I've done—or should have done. For the things that might have happened. I love you, Silver. I've loved you from the moment I saw you, and I'll love you till the day I die."

Silver wrapped her arms around his neck. "I love you," she said softly, "more than you'll ever know."

Morgan held her close, soothing her, speaking the words of love he hadn't been able to say before. But all the while his mind screamed at the wrong that had been done, and his heart hardened with a cold, dark purpose.

When he reached Katonga, he would kill William Hardwick-Jones.

As Morgan predicted, they arrived in Barbados the following morning. Silver went ashore with Jordy, obeying Morgan's strict instructions to buy whatever she needed for their upcoming wedding. One of the crew went to Lady Grayson's to pick up the clothes she had left there, while Morgan completed his duties and made arrangements for the ceremony.

Tomorrow they would travel the six miles southeast to Christ Church and be married. To Silver's delight, she discovered she could hardly wait.

"You should wear this, Silver." Jordy stood beside her in the tiny millinery shop on Tudor Street, pointing to a lovely cream lace veil encrusted with seed pearls and small satin flowers.

Silver touched the delicate netting with reverence. "It's beautiful."

"What color is your gown?" asked the graying, very British-looking, pointed-nosed clerk behind the counter. The shop overflowed with bonnets of every shape and size, some flowered, some feathered, some lace. There were tasseled parasols and handpainted fans and ribbons of every size and color.

"The dress is pale blue, but the trim is cream lace, about the same shade as the veil."

"Then you must have it, my dear," the shopkeeper said.

"Jordy?"

"You'll be the prettiest bride ever."

"All right, I'll take it."

They finished their purchases and had just started back to the ship when a tall, rawboned man in baggy canvas duck pants stepped in front of them.

"Afternoon, Miss Jones." He had short-cropped hair and long-lobed ears—criminal ears, someone once told her.

Silver stopped short, wondering how the man could possibly know her name. "Good afternoon." She started walking again, but the man didn't move. "If you'll excuse us . . ."

"Sorry, ma'am, afraid I can't do that." The man glanced down at the paper he held in his hand, a paper Silver knew only too well—the reward poster with the etching of her face. She turned to flee, but the tall man grabbed her, his long arms constricting as he dragged a heavy sack over her head and hauled her into the alley. Silver tried to kick him, tried to break free, but he held her fast.

"Let her go!" Jordy screamed, flailing at the man's broad back, punching him, then trying to pry his big hands off Silver. A second man, almost as tall as the first, rounded on him, throwing a solid punch that knocked Jordy hard against the wall of a narrow wooden building lining the alley.

"Jordy!" Hearing the commotion, Silver lashed out, fighting to free her arms from those that imprisoned her, desperately working to dislodge the restricting rough sack that fell well below her hips. She was frightened for Jordy, sure her father was responsible, and terrified he would succeed.

She screamed inside the bag, hoping someone would hear her, but the man's hands and the heavy cloth muffled her cries. She fought to twist free, tried to scream again; then something solid slammed against her head, and her knees buckled beneath her. As her vision dimmed and faded to darkness, she thought of Morgan and the wedding she would miss: *Dear God, let him find me before it's too late.*

"They took her, Cap'n!" Jordy started yelling before he stumbled to the top of the gangway, blood flowing from a cut in his forehead. "They jumped us! They're takin' her to Katonga!"

Morgan dropped the papers he'd been reading and ran across the deck in Jordy's direction. He caught the boy by the shoulders, noting the blood on his clothes, the ugly purple bruise beside his eye, his torn shirt and dirt-covered clothes.

"Take it easy, son." He was working hard to stay

calm himself. "Just take your time and tell me what happened."

"Two men—big men—seamen by the look of 'em. They took her. They must have wanted the reward money."

"Bloody hell! I thought by now word would have been out that the money had already been claimed."

"Musta been the reward, Cap'n. They was carryin' one of them posters, and they was waitin' for us."

For once Morgan didn't correct Jordy's grammar. "How long ago did this happen?"

Jordy looked even more upset. "Three, maybe four hours. They hit me real hard, sir. I'd still be out if some sailor hadn't found me."

Morgan checked Jordy's battered face. "You'd better go below and have Cookie take a look at you."

"What about Silver?"

Morgan clamped the boy's slender shoulder. "We know where they're taking her." His hands balled into fists. "We'll just be going to Katonga a little sooner than we planned."

For the first time he noticed the small paper sack Jordy clutched in his fingers. Dried blood darkened his knuckles, and Morgan thought with a grim smile the boy was more like his own than he knew. "What's that?" he asked.

Jordy opened the sack and pulled out the cream lace veil. "She bought it for your weddin'."

Morgan's jaw tightened. He took the veil with a shaky hand, turned, and started aft to make preparations to sail.

Jordy caught up with him. "She'll be all right, won't she? I mean, once she gets home, no one's gonna hurt her or nothin'?"

"No, son," Morgan vowed, praying it was the

truth. "We'll get there before anyone has the chance."

"I trust you enjoyed your little . . . adventure?" William Hardwick-Jones pulled out the carved high-backed chair at the end of the elegant mahogany table in the dining room. Above them, long white tapers in the crystal chandelier flickered and cast dark shadows along the gold-flocked walls.

"As a matter of fact, I did," Silver replied. "So much so, I'm looking forward to another in the very near future." She shouldn't antagonize him—it was dangerous, she knew—but she couldn't seem to stop herself.

Her father's hand tightened on the back of her chair. "I believe, my dear, your travels are over for quite some time."

Silver didn't answer, just let him seat her at the end of the table, then seat himself at the opposite end. William looked just as dark and sinister as she remembered, but immaculate as always; his formal black evening clothes, burgundy brocade waistcoat, and wide white stock glinted in the candlelight.

Silver wore a gown of ruched gold peau de soie, which had been chosen for her and laid out carefully across the foot of her canopy bed.

She had arrived at the dock in Katonga early in the afternoon the day following her abduction, with a splitting headache, a lump at the back of her neck, and wearing her very wrinkled rose silk day dress. She had regained consciousness not long after the small ketch she'd been taken aboard left Carlisle Bay but was too far at sea to do more than watch the tiny dot of an island recede in the distance.

Once she reached home, she was led straight up to her room, locked in, and ordered to rest, which was

hardly possible. When Millie, the upstairs maid—
hand-chosen by her father—arrived with a tray of
food, Silver stood at the window, staring through the
wrought-iron bars toward the sea. She dreaded the
ordeal ahead but clung to the hope that by now Morgan had found her missing and had figured out
where she'd been taken. She prayed Jordy had not
been hurt.

Silver glanced to the end of the table, set with
gleaming crystal, heavy carved silverware, and gold-
rimmed porcelain plates. She found her father
watching her, his eyes dark and cold.

"Care to tell me about it?"

"About what?" Silver asked with feigned nonchalance and a steadying sip of her wine. "My trip to
Georgia or my voyage to Mexico? The first was most
unpleasant, I assure you. The second, however, was
. . . intriguing . . . to say the least."

"And Major Trask?"

Don't say it. Don't! "We're going to be married."

William laughed aloud, a harsh, grating sound. "Is
that what he told you? That he intended marriage? I
didn't expect him to stoop to deceit to win your fa-
vors."

"You may believe what you wish. Morgan will
come for me."

William eyed her sharply, then shrugged his thick-
muscled shoulders. "Let him come," he said, his
tone cool, though he pulled his napkin from its silver
ring with more effort than he needed. He smoothed
it across his powerful long-boned thighs. "I'm your
legal guardian. You're merely a woman; you've no
more rights than those darkies out in the fields. I
shall refuse his suit—if he really intends to pursue it.
I'll forbid the marriage and send him away."

"You can't do that."

His mouth thinned in warning. "Can't I? How quickly you forget. I am the law on Katonga. You will remain here with me."

An icy dread swept over her. Her hand shook as she lifted her wineglass for another steadying sip. "Why? Why do you wish to keep me here against my will?"

William smiled, his black eyes hard. "We both know why, Salena. After your . . . involvement . . . with the major, you should understand far better than you did before. In a way I should thank him."

"For what?"

His eyes moved over her face, down her body in sweeping appraisal, then returned to settle on her breasts. "It is only too clear that you are no longer a virgin. Though that is hardly what I had planned, at least your sensibilities on the subject no longer stand in our way."

Silver stared at him in horror. "Do you know what you're saying?" Her voice rose higher with every word. "It's—it's unholy. Unnatural. What kind of man would lust for his own flesh and blood?"

William merely looked pensive, as though he weighed some unpleasant decision. "If it will set your conscience to rest, you and I are not blood-related."

"What? We're not . . . are—are you telling me you're not my father?"

"Not in the physical sense. Though we shall both continue the pretense."

"I don't believe you."

"Believe it, my dear. The details are unimportant. What matters is that you belong to me, you always have, and you always will. You're mine, Salena. No

Morgan Trask or any other man is going to change that."

"You're mad." But part of her believed his words. Relief swept over her, so powerful it almost made her dizzy. William wasn't her father! Or was this just another attempt to seduce her, this time with words?

"I assure you I'm quite sane. Once you accept your position as my mistress, you'll find your lot in life will be much improved. I'll see that you have everything you've ever wanted—clothes, jewels. We'll travel, if that is what you wish. Europe is out of the question, but we can go to America or maybe visit the East."

The room spun crazily. This couldn't be happening. There was too much to grasp, too much she didn't understand.

"What about my real father?"

"Your supper is getting cold," William said, pointedly ignoring her question. "This goose is delicious." He sawed off another juicy morsel and brought it to his lips.

Silver couldn't eat a mouthful. It would lodge in her throat and choke her to death. "I'm afraid I'm not very hungry."

William laid his knife aside. "You'll eat, Salena, or I shall have to discipline you for your disobedience. Since I have more than sufficient in store for you already, I suggest you do as I say."

Silver gripped the table to steady herself. This was the man she knew, coldly detached, achingly cruel. At the end of the table, his eyes glittered with anticipation. He enjoyed cruelty. Fear was an aphrodisiac. She lifted her fork, took a bite of the steaming buttered corn on her plate, nearly gagged, but washed it down with a sip of her wine.

"That's better," William said, looking triumphant

as he always did whenever she gave in. She would rather face that look than the one of satisfaction he wore whenever she fought him.

"Your . . . *friends* . . . send their greeting," he said.

Silver wet her lips, which suddenly felt dry. "Quako and Delia? Are they—are they all right?"

"Quako has tasted the lash, thanks to you. Your timely return has saved the woman a similar fate."

"But Delia's with child." Silver twisted the napkin she clutched in her lap. "Surely you wouldn't do anything to harm her."

William eyed her coldly. "I believe I'll leave that up to you."

"Me?"

"Your . . . cooperation, Salena, will ensure Delia's welfare. You, of course, may decide but either way in the end I shall win. It's up to you."

Silver just stared at him. If she remembered him as cruel, she had been kind. "My God, you're a monster."

"And you, my dear, are the most enchanting creature I've ever seen. I have wanted you since the very first budding of your womanhood. I've been patient to a fault. Had I taken this step sooner, none of this unpleasantness would have occurred. You would have accepted your lot in life as a woman long before now. Resign yourself, Salena, and let us get on with it."

Silver sat frozen in her chair. Who was this man who pretended to be her father? Where was her real father? Where was Morgan?

"Finish your supper, Salena. The hour draws late, and there is much I have in store for you this eve."

His eyes ran over her breasts, rising and falling above her gown with each of her too-rapid breaths.

Unconsciously her fingers closed around the hilt of the butter knife that lay beside her plate. If only it were the razor-sharp butcher knife she had wielded against him once before.

For years he had tortured her with his evilness, lied to her about who he was, and treated her brutally. Now that she knew the truth, she could kill him without a twinge of conscience.

A noise in the entry drew her attention. She heard men's voices arguing loudly, the sound of shattering glass and scuffling feet. Then Morgan's tall figure strode into the room. His jaw was set, his mouth a hard, grim line. Candlelight shadowed the scar on his cheek, making him look tough and forbidding, and his green eyes glinted his fury.

"Morgan," Silver whispered, sliding back her chair and coming to her feet.

"Silver!" Morgan strode toward her, his eyes assessing, worried. Silver watched his approach through a mist of unshed tears. "Are you all right?" he asked, noticing the sheen of wetness.

"Now that you're here."

His arm went protectively around her waist, and he drew her against him. "Everything's going to be fine."

Silver just nodded; the lump in her throat ached too much for her to speak.

"Where is he?" Searching for the earl, Morgan surveyed the end of the table, looking past the black-clad figure who watched them with arrogant menace.

William pushed back his chair and slowly came to his feet. "So your intentions were honorable after all," he said. "I can't say I blame you."

"Who the hell are *you*?"

"I had hoped Sheridan could persuade you to leave—in Silver's best interests of course."

"Knowles is nursing a broken jaw. As for you, I'm not interested in your money. I want to know who you are and where I can find the earl."

Silver started to speak, but Morgan's warning look silenced her.

Without answering his questions, William turned to the short black servant who stood near the door. "Bolen, you will fetch the twin sabers above my desk."

"Yes, massuh." The servant left, and William fixed his gaze on Morgan. "You, Major Trask, have sullied my daughter. I demand satisfaction."

"Your daughter?" Morgan repeated before Silver had a chance to speak. "She's William's daughter. I demand to know where he is."

"That information, I'm happy to say, died some years ago. Tonight it is your turn."

Silver clutched his arm. "Don't do it, Morgan."

"Is this the man you believed was your father?"

"Yes. But now I know he isn't."

"Your father was a decent man, Silver. This man—whoever he is—deserves to die."

The servant appeared, carrying two long curved blades with gleaming silver handguards. Bolen extended them both to William, who drew one out of its scabbard, then motioned for the black man to give the other one to Morgan.

Silver gripped him harder. "You don't understand. Fencing is my father's—this man's passion. He's a master of the blade."

"Good," Morgan said, drawing out the second saber and testing its feel in his palm. "Then I'll enjoy killing him all the more."

William removed his evening jacket and hung it

across the back of a chair. Morgan wore only his loose-sleeved white linen shirt, snug brown breeches, and knee-high boots. William untied and removed his stock, and the two men strode past Silver into the spacious marble-floored entry.

William flexed his saber, tested his stance, and rounded on Morgan.

"En garde."

Chapter 25

With the clang of steel against steel, Morgan's blade clashed against William's. Only weeks had passed since Morgan had been fighting in the Yucatán. His saber arm felt strong, and he had always possessed a natural skill with the blade.

Today he was damned glad of it. The man who posed as the earl of Kent was a master, just as Silver had said.

As they battled back and forth, their long, sharp weapons connected time and again. They fought across the entry, down the narrow hall, and back into the foyer, vicious blows ringing shrilly, the sound chilling against the walls of the high-ceilinged room.

"Getting tired, Major Trask?" William taunted, slashing downward, forcing Morgan to parry, and hitting with such power the handle of the blade sent vibrations into Morgan's shoulder.

"On the contrary. I'm just beginning to enjoy myself." Morgan thrust and lunged. William stepped back, parried, and arched a cutting blow to Morgan's left. Morgan parried and danced away. Again they clashed, blade against blade. Advance, advance, advance, parry, retreat, advance.

Silver watched them in awe, terrified for Morgan yet mesmerized by his daring, the deadly elegance of his movements. Though each man fought with cunning and skill, there was a power and beauty in Morgan's form that surpassed even William's. Still, William was a master, and his years of experience gave him an edge.

Unconsciously Silver's fingers crept to her throat when William's blade sliced just inches from Morgan's head, embedding itself in the doorjamb with a hollow, resounding thud. William jerked it free just as Morgan's blade arced toward him, blocking a blow that would have been fatal.

"A worthy opponent, Major," William said. "Something difficult to find out here on the island."

"Your *last* opponent," Morgan told him, bringing the saber down with a hammering force that rang through the halls.

William parried the blow and lunged. Silver screamed as Morgan's shirtsleeve blossomed red with blood.

"Tired of playing yet?" William goaded. "Why don't you make this easy on both of us?" He smiled, his mouth thinning cruelly.

But when he lifted his blade, Morgan lunged, finding the opening he had been seeking. The blade thrust home, entering William's body just below the rib cage. For a moment William's saber hung suspended in the air. Then it tumbled, end over end, and clattered to the floor. William fell hard against the wall, sliding down on the cold marble floor and leaving a slick trail of blood.

The tip of Morgan's blade settled against William's throat. "Who are you?" he demanded.

William tried to laugh but winced instead at a sharp jolt of pain. "You still don't remember me? But then you were merely a youth."

Morgan assessed him coldly, trying to imagine him younger, lean and hard, without the gray in his hair. "Ballantine."

William nodded almost imperceptibly. "Geoffrey Ballantine. I haven't spoken that name in fifteen years." He coughed, and a trickle of blood ran from his lips.

"You were William's estate manager. His most trusted employee. You and your wife left with William and Mary for Katonga."

"Correct, Major Trask. Except William and Mary never reached the ship. They had an unfortunate . . . *accident* along the way. My wife, Althea, had come to love the child, Salena, so we took her to raise as our own. We came to Katonga as William and Mary."

"You murdered them?" Silver said, finally finding her voice. "You killed my parents?"

"It was the chance of a lifetime." He coughed again. "The chance for riches beyond my wildest dreams. I hadn't really planned it. Things just fell into place. The servants left us alone at the docks the day before the ship arrived. I knew once it came and we set sail, Althea and I would be safe—as long as we stayed on Katonga. William and Mary were unsuspecting. A simple blow to the head, muffled gunshots in an alley, and they were disposed of. I weighted their bodies down with stones and dumped them into the river."

"God in heaven," Silver whispered, her eyes bright with tears.

Tossing his saber away with a clatter, Morgan came to her side, and she leaned against him.

Slumped on the floor near her feet, the man she had hated for so many years coughed up more blood, closed his eyes, and quietly slipped away.

"He—he killed them." Silver turned into Morgan's arms and sobbed against his shoulder.

"Your parents loved you, Silver," Morgan said softly. "Mary was kind and gentle. William was courageous and determined. I think you inherited the best of both of them."

"My father loved me," Silver repeated, still unable to grasp the truth. "He loved me."

"They both did. I hope wherever they are they know that you're safe now and that I'm going to take care of you. Maybe they'll be able to rest in peace."

"Oh, Morgan"—Silver clutched him tighter—"if only I could have known them."

"I knew them. When you're ready, I'll tell you all about them. We'll tell our children what fine grandparents they had."

"Yes," she whispered, "surely they would like that." She felt the pressure of his cheek against her hair.

"I'm certain they would. But more than anything, they would have wanted you to be happy."

Silver turned to face him. "I'm going to sell this place, Morgan. I want the workers set free; I want them to have a choice: They can stay and work for the new owner or leave, live wherever they wish. The decision must be theirs."

He nodded. "All right."

"I want them to have a portion of the proceeds, enough to get them started somewhere else. And Quako and Delia—I want them to have money for a place of their own."

"I'll take care of it as soon as we reach Savannah.

In the meantime, I'll speak to Knowles. . . . I believe he'll see reason.''

"Thank you," Silver said softly, blinking against a fresh round of tears.

Morgan wiped them away with a dark-tanned finger. "I love you, Lady Salena," he said gently. "And I know, wherever they are, your mother and father are proud of you."

Epilogue

Sea and sun glinted blue-green in the distance, where the *Savannah* bobbed peacefully at anchor. Above their heads, gulls wheeled and turned, gaily spiraled upward, then soared back toward earth.

Timeless words, spoken with quiet reassurance, asked the Lord's blessing over those gathered together for such a joyous occasion. There was a chorus of "Amen."

The preacher said a few more words, getting on with the ceremony, then asked, "Who giveth this woman to be married to this man?"

The gray-haired man stepped forward. "I do, Grandison Aimes." With a warm smile and a bit of a mist in his hard old eyes, Cookie placed Silver's hand in Morgan's. They stood on a windswept knoll in back of a tiny parish church in Kingstown on St. Vincent, the closest island to Katonga.

The small fair-skinned minister in his frayed black frock coat looked up from the pages of his marriage book. He smiled at both of them but fixed his gaze on the tall blond major.

"Wilt thou, Morgan, take this woman, Salena, to

thy wedded wife? Wilt thou love her, comfort her, honor and keep her, for richer, for poorer, in sickness and in health, forsaking all others, for as long as you both shall live?''

"I will," he answered clearly, looking at Silver with such love she felt an ache well up in her throat.

"Wilt thou, Salena, take this man, Morgan, for thy wedded husband? Wilt thou love him, comfort him, honor and keep him, for richer, for poorer, in sickness and in health, forsaking all others, for as long as you both shall live?''

"I will," she said softly, clutching her beautiful white bouquet a little tighter. Beside her, in Silver's hastily altered rose silk gown, Delia reached over and squeezed her hand. Massive, black, and proud, Quako smiled at both of them, his shoulders and thighs straining against the fabric of a frock coat and breeches far too small for him. He gave Silver a wink and a grin.

"Do you have the ring?"

Standing tall at Morgan's side, Jordy handed Morgan the glittering diamond and ruby ring Morgan had purchased three days ago in Barbados. One of Jordy's eyes still looked purple and swollen, his lip a little puffy, but he smiled at them with love.

"Dost thou, Morgan, giveth this ring in token that thou wilt keep this covenant and perform these vows?''

"I do." Morgan's voice sounded husky.

"You will repeat after me." The preacher said the age-old words.

"With this ring I thee wed," Morgan repeated with a possessive note few could have missed. He looked dashingly handsome in his dark blue major's uniform, gold buttons gleaming, and more pleased than Silver had ever seen him.

"You may place the ring on Salena's finger."

When Morgan lifted her trembling hand and slid on the glittering stones, a soft mist gathered in her eyes.

"As you, Salena, and you, Morgan, have pledged your troth in the sight of God and in the presence of this company, in the name of the Father and the Son and the Holy Spirit, I now pronounce you man and wife. Whom God hath joined together, let no man put asunder. You may kiss your bride."

But Morgan hadn't waited for permission. He had already lifted his lovely wife's cream lace veil and pulled her into his arms.

"I love you, Mrs. Trask," he said just before his mouth claimed hers.

Silver felt the heat of it and, for a moment, forgot the minister, forgot Delia and Quako—whose turn would come next—forgot Hamilton Riley and his marines, and the entire *Savannah* crew surrounding them.

She felt breathless when they finally broke apart. "I love you, my darling husband—and I always will."

Morgan kissed her again, this time more thoroughly, matching her vow with a fiery promise of his own.

Silver could hardly wait.

Author's Note

Though no record surfaced of Texas Marine activity on the Yucatán Peninsula itself, ships of the Texas Navy, carrying sailors and marines, blockaded coastal waters for several years during the young republic's struggle to maintain independence from Mexico.

Texas aided Federalist forces, and though the rebellion failed, naval efforts contributed to British recognition of the Republic of Texas as a sovereign nation, which many believe helped the vast new territory finally achieve statehood.

I also took liberties with the color of Texas Marine uniforms. Alas, I found no record of what they actually wore. Aside from these things, I hope that you enjoyed reading Silver and Morgan's exploits as much as I enjoyed writing them and that you'll want to read Brendan's story in *Natchez Flame*.

And look for NATCHEZ FLAME, the next historical romance from Kat Martin. Journey with Brendan Trask and Priscilla Wills as they cross the hostile Texas landscape, fighting outlaws and Indians to reach Priscilla's fiancé, powerful landowner Stuart Egan. What is there about Egan that Trask disapproves? What is it about Trask that makes Priscilla wish it were the handsome gunman she was about to marry, instead of the wealthiest man in the country?

From the barren landscape of Texas to the glittering ballrooms of Natchez, Brendan and Priscilla learn the dangers of passion—and the boundless joys of love.

The following is an excerpt from the first chapter of Kat's next book.

CHAPTER ONE

Galveston, Texas
July 20, 1846

Lord in heaven, what had she gotten herself into this time? Priscilla Mae Wills stood at the rail of the steamship *Orleans*, surveying the weathered buildings and unkempt, seedy-looking men who lined the dock of the strand.

In the distance, the dirt streets of Galveston bustled with activity, wagons heavy with bales of cotton rumbling toward the wharf, men and animals clattering along in confusion. The rest of the passengers had already departed, but Priscilla still stood at the rail, searching the long wooden dock, hoping against hope that Barker Hennessey, the man sent to meet her, had discovered the *Orleans*'s early arrival and might yet appear.

You're a grown woman, Priscilla, you can do this on your own. But in all her twenty-four years she had never traveled by herself and even with her aunt Madeline had never gone this far from home. And she'd certainly never expected the newly formed state of Texas to be this untamed.

With a sigh of resignation, Priscilla walked down the

gangway and along the pier, dodging stevedores unloading cargo, barking dogs, braying mules, and even a few drunken sailors.

A hot, muggy breeze whipped the dark brown skirts of her serviceable cotton day dress, and with each of her weary steps the stiff white ruffle around the neck scratched the delicate skin beneath her chin. Strands of dark brown hair had come loose from the tight chignon hidden at the back of her coal scuttle bonnet, and the strands whipped tauntingly in the wind.

Up ahead, the sign for the Galveston Hotel and Saloon gleamed red and white in the hot July sun beside another large painted sign advertising Samuel Levinson's Bath House. Barker Hennessey, the man her fiancé, Stuart Egan, had sent to escort her on the final leg of her journey, would look for her at the hotel once he discovered her ship had come in.

Ignoring the heat and the tightly laced stays of her steel-ribbed corset, Priscilla walked the bustling dirt street toward the hotel, by far the best-looking building in town. At least the paint wasn't peeling and the walk in front had been swept clean. Just the thought of being inside, out of the blistering sunshine, urged her to quicken her pace.

That's when she noticed the commotion out front. A crowd had gathered, grumbling among itself, then seemed to be backing away.

"Look, Jacob—ain't that Barker Hennessey?" a slender man in a red-checked shirt asked the smaller man beside him. The name registered immediately, and Priscilla glanced toward the big-boned man at the opposite end of the porch.

"That's him, all right. Barker's madder'n a wet hen 'cause he lost his poke to some gambler."

Gambling, Priscilla thought, feeling sorry for the big, strapping man in the black felt hat who stood in front of the swinging double doors to the saloon, *the devil's own sport.* She also felt a wave of relief that she had found him so quickly.

"Excuse me. Could you possibly let me pass?" Nudging her way through the crowd, she headed for the porch. With her mind on the coming introduction, it took a moment for her to realize he was speaking.

"I said, you're a cheat and a liar!" Hennessey called out as she stepped on the boardwalk. "I want my money back, Trask, and I aim to get it!"

At the angry tone of his words, Priscilla turned her head toward the object of his wrath, the tall, broad-shouldered man standing right beside her.

"I won that money fair, and you know it," Trask said.

"Mr. Hennessey!" Priscilla called out, waving a white-gloved hand and starting in his direction.

"Goddammit!" The tall man gripped Priscilla's arm so hard it made her flinch. His free hand slapped the leather holster tied to a long, muscular leg, she saw the bluish flash of metal, and heard the deafening roar of gunfire. Whipping her head toward Barker, Priscilla breathed the smell of burnt powder and stared in horror at the opposite end of the porch.

Barker Hennessey's eyes remained open, his mouth gaping wide in an expression of astonishment, his sausage-size fingers still clutching the pistol in his hand. Only a trickle of blood ran from the small, round circle that marked the entrance of the tall man's bullet—right between his eyes.

Watching Hennessey crumple to the porch, Priscilla's knees went weak. She tried to make a sound but her mouth had gone dry, and the words seemed to lodge in her throat. Feeling the grip of Trask's hand on her arm, Priscilla swayed against him. Angry blue eyes locked on her face just seconds before her lids flickered closed, the world tumbled sideways, and Priscilla sank into darkness.

"Holy Christ, what next?" Brendan Trask swung the slender young woman up in his arms and stepped off the boardwalk onto the street.

"Nice shootin'," Jacob Barnes said to him as he strode toward the shade of an oak tree beside the watering trough half a block away.

"You'd better get the sheriff," Brendan answered without breaking his long-legged stride.

"She all right?" The little man caught up with him, then hurried to keep from running.

"Just fainted. She's lucky she didn't stop a bullet." Brendan recalled only too well the moment she had started to step in front of him. He glanced down at the small, round hole in the full white sleeve of his shirt, and the little man followed his gaze.

"Boy, you surely got that right."

"Get the sheriff," Trask reminded him.

"Sheriff got hisself kilt last week. I'll see if'n his deputy's down at Gilroy's Saloon." The man scurried off to find the law, though Brendan figured what little there was in town had probably already been summoned. Galveston might be the wildest port on the Gulf, but a shooting was a shooting, and Barker Hennessey worked for one of the most powerful men in the country.

"Damn." Brendan wished he could have avoided the killing, but Hennessey had left him no choice. He just hoped to hell there wouldn't be trouble.

He'd had enough of that already.

Brendan knelt and propped the lady against the trunk of the oak tree, noting her somber brown dress, high-necked and long-sleeved, and the tiny waist pulled tight by her corset. Clothes like that in this heat —no wonder she'd fainted. Sometimes women didn't have the sense God gave a mule.

He crossed to the watering trough, dipped his handkerchief into the water, wrung out the excess, and returned to the base of the tree. He untied the woman's bonnet strings and pressed the wet cloth against her lips. They were full, he noticed, and a delicate shade of pink. Her features held a trace of that same fragility: slim, straight nose, fine chestnut eyebrows, thick dark lashes. She wasn't really a beauty, but she was definitely attractive.

He thought of Patsy Jackson, the woman he'd spent the night with, of her full, ripe curves, red-painted mouth, and fun-loving warmth in bed. There was nothing frail about Patsy, nothing prim or proper. She was the kind of woman who could pleasure a man, have a frolicking good time in bed but didn't give you trouble in the morning.

Not like this one. This little miss would probably pass out again just thinking about what he had done to Patsy. Pretty as she was, Brendan liked his women lusty. This one held little appeal, though in a town where men outnumbered women a dozen to one, she'd undoubtedly be considered quite a catch. He wondered which man she belonged to—and why that man hadn't the good sense to keep her out of trouble.

She moaned a second time, and her lids fluttered open. Warm brown, gold-flecked eyes looked up at him in confusion. Brendan shoved his broad-brimmed hat back on his head and assessed her pale, oval face. If he hadn't spotted her from the corner of his eye, she'd probably be dead right now.

The thought sent a shudder down his spine.

"Lady, you are some piece of work." The words came out a little harsher than he had intended. "What the hell did you think you were doing? Don't you know any better than to stroll into the middle of a gunfight?"

"Gunfight?" she repeated. Then her pretty face paled even more. "What—what about Mr. Hennessey?" She sat up a little straighter. "Is he—is he—"

"Barker picked that fight, not me. I won his money fair and square, and I shot him in self-defense."

"Oh, dear." She looked ready to faint again. "I don't feel very well. I think I'm going to be sick."

"Oh, no, you don't." Brendan pressed the cool, wet cloth against her brow. "Just lean your head back, and try not to think about it."

The woman swallowed hard and closed her eyes, her thick black lashes making dark half-moons against her cheek. Eventually the color returned to her face, and he noticed again how pretty she was.

"Thank you," she said softly, "I'm feeling a little better now."

Brendan felt a wave of relief, then an unpleasant thought occurred. "Barker wasn't your husband, was he?" Until that moment it hadn't crossed his mind that a man like Hennessey could have a wife. Especially such a young and tender one.

She shook her head. "No. He's the man my fiancé sent to escort me on to his ranch." Her bottom lip trembled. "I never met him before, but he looked like a nice enough man."

Brendan's face grew taut. "There wasn't a nice bone in Barker Hennessey's body. He'd have killed me without a second thought if I hadn't shot him first."

Priscilla chewed on that for a while and took a long, assessing look at the man who squatted with menacing grace on the stiff salt grass beside her. His hair was as dark as hers, but a richer, warmer shade of brown, and he wore it longer than he should have. Several days' growth of beard roughened his jaw, but his mouth curved nicely, and his eyes, a light shade of blue, watched her with a look of concern that melted away the fear she should have felt.

How could that be? she wondered. He had just killed a man—a man whose help she desperately needed. He was a gambler and a gunman, yet there was something about him. Something that told her the words he had spoken were the truth.

"Does that mean the sheriff won't arrest you?"

"Not as long as he knows I only did what I had to."

Priscilla had a knack for judging people. She could size them up in a heartbeat. Even her aunt Maddie would ask her opinion, though she never admitted Priscilla's assessment actually mattered.

And this man *had* saved her life—probably at considerable risk to his own.

When he took her hand and helped her to her feet, Priscilla gripped his arm to steady herself, and solid muscle flexed beneath his shirt. Though she stood taller than the average woman, Trask towered above her, his wide shoulders blocking the sun. Hard-edged, unkempt, and rugged though he appeared, even in his worn homespun shirt and frayed blue twill breeches he looked handsome.

When he discovered her watching him, Priscilla flushed and glanced away. "I—I can't believe Stuart would have sent the kind of man you describe here to meet me. I don't think—"

"This is rough country, Miss . . . ?"

She swung her gaze to his. "Wills. Priscilla Mae Wills, and I believe your name is Trask."

He nodded. "Where did you say you were headed?"

"Rancho Reina del Robles—the Triple R. Stuart Egan is my fiancé."

Trask's hard features closed up. There was an edge to his voice that hadn't been there before. "That explains Hennessey; he's Egan's right-hand man."

"Then you know Stuart?"

He shook his head. "No, but I've heard of him. Most folks 'round these parts know who he is. Why didn't Egan come for you?"

"Apparently he was shorthanded. The ranch is quite large, you know."

"So I've heard." Something flickered in his light blue eyes. "I'll have someone get word to him, and he can fetch you home."

Priscilla's dark brows shot up. "But that would take weeks. I can't stay here—" She felt his hand on her arm, halting her protest and urging her back toward the hotel.

Priscilla let him lead her down the street, trying to gather her thoughts. As she had said, it would take weeks for a letter to reach Stuart and just as much time for him to come or send someone to get her. In the meantime, she'd be alone in this wild Texas town— a place where people got shot in the streets! She had only enough money for a few days' lodging and food. What would she do after that?

Trask tugged her the last few paces up onto the boardwalk, his grip a little harder than it should have been. "Where you from, Miss Wills?" He shoved open the door to the lobby, ringing the bell, then held it so she could walk in.

"I was born in Natchez, but I was raised in Cincinnati. As I told you, I was on my way to join my fiancé, which, thanks to you, has just become an exceedingly difficult task." Priscilla felt like crying. *Difficult* was hardly the word.

"I suppose you'd prefer I let him shoot me."

"Maybe. Maybe I would at that." Shoulders thrown back, Priscilla marched up to the desk, where a green-visored clerk leaned over a huge leather-bound guest book.

"I'd like a room, please, and I need someone to obtain my trunks from aboard the steamship *Orleans*."

The gray-haired clerk eyed her from top to bottom. "You ain't by yourself?"

"Well, yes . . . I . . ." Priscilla lifted her chin. "My traveling companion fell ill some ways back. I was forced to continue alone." She glanced at Trask, daring him to contradict, and found his mouth curved up in amusement.

"This is a respectable hotel, miss. You look proper enough, but . . . well, if you got somethin' else in mind, you'd best be lookin' for a room somewheres else."

Priscilla flushed crimson. "Surely you aren't implying—" *Dear God, what kind of people are these?*

"Get the lady a room," Trask ordered, resting his gun hand casually on the desk, "and be quick about it."

The little man swallowed and shoved the guest book in her direction. "Yes, sir, Mr. Trask. Sign here, ma'am." He dipped the quill pen in the inkwell near her elbow, handed it to Priscilla, and she scrawled her name in graceful blue letters.

"How long will you be stayin'?" the clerk asked.

She studied the sign on the wall behind him. Even at the modest rate posted, she couldn't stay more than four days.

"I—I'm not really sure." She'd expected Barker Hennessey to see to her needs until she reached the Egan ranch. She clutched her reticule tighter, wondering what in heaven she would do when her money ran out.

"She'll be here at least three weeks," Trask told the desk clerk. "It'll take that long to get word to her people and for them to come get her."

Priscilla swallowed hard. She couldn't afford that much time, but she certainly wouldn't tell him that. If only she could find someone to take Mr. Hennessey's place. Someone who knew the country, a man who could protect her along the way. Priscilla glanced at Trask—hard, capable, determined—and felt a jolt of inspiration that seemed almost divine.

Trask could do it! He was obviously well suited for the arduous journey. And he owed her. He had shot

Hennessey—it was only fitting Trask should be the one to take his place.

She flashed him the brightest smile she could muster, which under the circumstances wasn't all that much. "Do you think Mr. Hennessey booked passage in advance for our journey to Corpus Christi?"

"Probably. But I'm sure the steamship company will be happy to refund the money."

"How far is it from there to the Triple R?"

"From what I know of it—and I've never been there —I'd say a good four-day ride over some very rough country. Why?" he asked warily.

"Surely, Mr. Trask, it is obvious I cannot remain unprotected in a town like this for the length of time it would take for Stuart to arrive." She smiled again. "The most practical solution is for you to escort me in Mr. Hennessey's place."

"No," he said simply.

"Why not? Since you're the man who—who—posed this particular problem, you are obviously the man who should solve it."

Trask shook his head. "Not a chance, Miss Wills. You're Egan's problem, not mine. Besides, I'll be leaving Galveston at dawn. I've got a job waiting for me on the Brazos."

Priscilla clutched the folds of her skirt, determined he would not see her cry. "What kind of job, Mr. Trask? Some sort of hired gun—or do you plan to make your money gambling, foxing weaker people out of theirs?"

Trask's look turned hard, his full lips nothing but a thin, grim line. "As a matter of fact, I plan to do a little bit of both."

"You owe me, Mr. Trask. Barker Hennessey was here to protect me. Who's going to protect me now?"

Good question, Brendan thought, for she had just voiced the problem that had been running through his mind. Who the hell would look after her? Egan had chosen well with Hennessey. For all his faults, Barker was loyal to Egan and tougher than a cob. Now, thanks to Hennessey's too-quick temper, the woman was left with no one.

He glanced in her direction, saw the worry she tried to conceal—and a surprising amount of determination. "Goddammit! This isn't my problem."

Priscilla spun on him in outrage. "Don't you dare blaspheme! If you hadn't been gambling in the first place, none of this would have happened. Mr. Hennessey would still be alive, and I'd be safely on the way to my fiancé."

"There's not a damn thing safe about the country you'll be crossing on your way to the Triple R. And I'll damn well swear if I want to."

"I believe you have an appointment with the law, Mr. Trask," she said with a haughty little tilt of her chin. "Surely the sheriff will have something to say about what happened to poor Mr. Hennessey. Thank you for your assistance, and good day." She whirled toward the man behind the counter, but Brendan caught her arm.

"I told you I shot him in self-defense."

"You shouldn't have been gambling. It's a sin, just like swearing. Now Mr. Hennessey is dead, and I'm stranded in the middle of nowhere with no money and no way to get to my fiancé."

"No money? What do you mean *no money*? Surely Egan gave you the money to get here."

She looked as if she wanted to cut out her tongue. "Mr. Egan offered; I refused. I've never even met the man, I wasn't about to accept his money."

"You've never met him?"

"We've been corresponding, of course, and my aunt Maddie had met him."

Brendan turned toward the man at the counter, dug

into his pocket, and tossed the man a coin. "Have someone fetch the lady's trunks up to her room." He turned back to Priscilla. "I'll pay for your stay. Egan will come for you, and everything will work out fine."

"Not on your life. I wouldn't accept Stuart's money; I certainly won't take yours."

"It was Hennessey's money. He would have used it to get you to Egan, so in a way it belongs to you."

She chewed her bottom lip, and Brendan thought how soft and pink it looked, how delicate she looked all over.

"If I do take the money, I'll simply use it to hire someone else."

"The hell you will. You're staying here. I'll pay for the room in advance if I have to."

"I'm not your prisoner, Mr. Trask. Somehow I'll find a way to get to Stuart—with or without your help."

Brendan eyed her from top to bottom. She was a fiery little thing when she got riled up. She just might try it. "You'd better take a long, hard look at the men in this town. Where you gonna find somebody you can trust?"

"There's got to be someone. If Stuart's as well known as you say, there's bound to be someone who will take me to him. Stuart can pay him when we get there."

"You're bluffing. You'd probably faint again if one of those men came near you." *But what if she wasn't?* What if she was crazy enough to try it? A lot of those men were hardened gunmen; they'd chew her up in little bitty pieces—after they pleasured themselves with her soft little body.

Damn her! "This is blackmail, Miss Wills, and I don't like it one damned bit." Grabbing her arm, he tugged her toward the door.

Priscilla let him lead her. "Where are you taking me?"

"I've got an appointment with the law, remember? You happen to be a witness. You can tell the deputy what happened—how I shot Hennessey in self-defense —and on the way we can discuss our trip."

"I didn't see that much." Priscilla stopped short. "Does this mean you're taking me?"

"It's beginning to look like I've got no choice."

She still didn't budge. "Why?" she asked, suddenly wary.

Brendan almost smiled. "Probably because I'm crazy. But you're right about one thing. Hennessey's dead, and I'm the man who killed him. In a way that makes me responsible for you. Egan might not get your letter for weeks. In the meantime anything could happen." *And probably would.*

"I'm sure Stuart will reimburse you for your trouble."

"Word reaches him about Hennessey's death before we get there, he'll probably shoot me on sight." Brendan tipped her chin up. "You realize you'll be traveling with a stranger—a man who just killed another man right in front of you."

Priscilla searched his face. "I trust you, Mr. Trask."

"You don't even know me. Why the hell would you trust me?"

"I have my reasons."

"Such as?"

Priscilla flushed but didn't glance away. "You've got kind eyes."

"Kind eyes?" he repeated, incredulous. "You trust me because of my eyes?"

"That's right."

Brendan shoved his hat back on his head and looked at her with a mixture of amazement and frustration. "Then, Miss Wills, I guess I'd better take you. Any woman who's that big a fool hasn't got a chance in a town like this."